Praise for author
Carla Cassidy

"Carla Cassidy has deftly created these broken
characters and reels readers into *Last Seen...*,
a moving, exciting read from start to finish."
—*RT Book Reviews*

"The talented Carla Cassidy has written a story
that will pull you along for this magnificent ride
of true love and adventure."
—*RT Book Reviews* on *Once Forbidden...*

"With flawed but heartwarming characters, and
a flair for storytelling, Carla Cassidy shines."
—*RT Book Reviews* on *To Wed and Protect*

CARLA CASSIDY

is an award-winning author who has written more than fifty books for Silhouette Books. In 1995, she won the Best Silhouette Romance award from *RT Book Reviews*.

Carla believes the only thing better than curling up with a good book to read is sitting down at the computer with a good story to write. She's looking forward to writing many more books and bringing hours of pleasure to readers.

Carla Cassidy
Shattered Trust

Harlequin®

TORONTO NEW YORK LONDON
AMSTERDAM PARIS SYDNEY HAMBURG
STOCKHOLM ATHENS TOKYO MILAN MADRID
PRAGUE WARSAW BUDAPEST AUCKLAND

Recycling programs
for this product may
not exist in your area.

ISBN-13: 978-0-373-68834-0

SHATTERED TRUST

Copyright © 2011 by Harlequin Books S.A.

The publisher acknowledges the copyright holder
of the individual works as follows:

LAST SEEN...
Copyright © 2003 by Carla Bracale

DEAD CERTAIN
Copyright © 2003 by Carla Bracale

This edition published by arrangement with Harlequin Books S.A.

For questions and comments about the quality of this book
please contact us at Customer_eCare@Harlequin.ca.

® and TM are trademarks of the publisher. Trademarks indicated with ® are registered in the United States Patent and Trademark Office, the Canadian Trade Marks Office and in other countries.

www.Harlequin.com

Printed in U.S.A.

CONTENTS

LAST SEEN...

CHAPTER ONE

"I always did have a thing for Pocahontas." The middle-aged man with the paunchy waistline grinned, exposing two missing teeth on the upper right side of his mouth.

Breanna James stifled a groan and instead toyed with the end of her braid and smiled coyly. "Then I guess this is your lucky night, cowboy," she replied. She'd be teased unmercifully by her fellow vice cops over the Pocahontas reference but she couldn't worry about that now.

"So…what are you doing out here in the middle of the night?" she asked the man.

"Looking for a party, sweet thing," he replied.

"What kind of a party?"

He grinned eagerly. "I was thinking maybe I could give you twenty-five bucks."

"Sounds like my kind of party," she replied and released her hold on her long braid. "And what would I have to do for that twenty-five dollars?"

He named a specific sex act and Breanna nodded. "You've got a deal, cowboy," she replied. "How about we go back here in the alley." She pointed to the dark alleyway between two storefronts where she knew two fellow officers were waiting to make the arrest.

He started into the alley, but stopped when he realized she wasn't following him. He slapped his forehead in a comical gesture of absentmindedness, then dug a twenty and five ones from his pocket and handed them to her.

"Now we're ready to party," she said as she tucked the bills into the purse she carried.

Eagerly, he walked into the alley, Breanna just behind him. "Hey, cowboy, you said you've always had a thing for Pocahontas. You ever had a fantasy about a woman cop?"

He stopped walking and frowned thoughtfully. "No, but now that you mention it, it might be kind of fun with handcuffs and all."

The man shouldn't be arrested for solicitation, Breanna thought. He should be arrested for stupidity. It wasn't until the two male officers stepped out of the shadows that he realized he was busted.

His smile fell and he cursed soundly, but didn't fight the officers as they handcuffed him and led him to an unmarked car along the curb.

"That's it for tonight." Abe Solomon, Breanna's partner, grinned. "You did good, Pocahontas. Looks like John, one Mr. Craig Bullock, won't be looking for a date again anytime soon."

She smiled at the gray-haired Abe. "All I know is I can't wait to get out of this outfit and into a baggy T-shirt and I hope I never see a pair of spike heels again in my life."

Abe chuckled. "Ah, but you wear them so well."

"Thank goodness I won't have to put them on for at least

another week." Saturday nights Breanna often worked as an undercover prostitute, a detail she abhorred.

She and Abe got into their car to head back to the Cherokee Corners police station. "So, you have big plans for your days off?"

"Tomorrow my mother has planned one of her family gatherings. You know she's only happy when she has all of us under one roof." Breanna sighed tiredly. "It will be the usual madness and mayhem."

"Count your blessings. Some of us without families would give anything for a little bit of that madness and mayhem."

Breanna's heart instantly went out to her partner. Abe had lost his wife two years ago and they'd never had children. At fifty-five years old, his parents were gone and he'd been an only child.

She placed a hand on his forearm. "Come over to Mom and Dad's tomorrow. You know they'd love to have you join us."

Abe smiled. "Thanks, honey, but I've got a date with a basement that needs cleaning."

Breanna wrinkled her nose. "You know dinner at my parents' house would be far more entertaining than cleaning your basement."

"True, but it would also be far less productive. Besides, I promised myself if I plowed through the basement I'd take off and do a little fishing." He pulled into the parking lot in front of the brick building that housed the police department.

"Well, if you change your mind, the offer stands," Breanna replied. She and Abe had been partners for the past five years and Breanna thought of Abe as a favorite uncle.

Every time he spoke of retirement, Breanna got a sick feeling in the pit of her stomach.

Thirty minutes later she walked out of the building, eager to get home, to kiss her sweet little girl and get some much needed sleep.

More than anything she couldn't wait to get out of the tiny leather skirt and midriff blouse, the black lace hose and the dangerously high spiked heels. She looked like a floozy, which, of course, had been the idea. But, after standing out on a street corner for the past four hours being propositioned, she felt dusty and dirty and wanted a long, hot shower.

As always, a sense of homecoming engulfed her as the rambling Victorian two-story house came into view. The rest of the houses on the street were dark. It was after two and most people were asleep, but as usual Rachel had left the front porch light on for Breanna. Thank goodness for Rachel.

She barely gave the tiny cottage on the side of her property a glance as she pulled into the driveway. The place had been empty for months, much to Breanna's landlord's chagrin.

She shut off her car and climbed out. She had only taken a couple of steps toward the house when she froze, an uneasy tickling sensation at the back of her neck. As a cop, she never ignored this nebulous feeling.

She opened her purse and placed her hand on the butt of the gun resting inside as she looked around. Nothing seemed amiss at the front of the house. There was nobody lurking in the shadows, no reason for her to feel what she felt.

Then she heard it...the almost imperceptible slap of a bare foot against the grass. She shifted her gaze sideways and that's when she saw him…coming toward her from out of the shadows in front of the cottage.

Without hesitation, she pulled the gun from her purse and fell into an official stance, legs apart, gun held steadily before her with both hands.

"Whoa!" The deep voice broke the silence of the night and he instantly raised his hands out from his sides. "I hope you don't intend to shoot first and ask questions later."

Shadows still clung to him, making it impossible for her to discern his facial features, but she could see the broad width of his shoulders, his slim hips and long legs. "Who are you and what are you doing out here?" she asked as she kept the gun focused on the center of his body.

"Can I lower my arms without getting shot?" he asked.

"Not until you answer my questions."

"My name is Adam Spencer. I moved into the cottage this evening and I was just sitting on the porch relaxing before going to bed."

"Awfully late to be relaxing on a porch. Who did you rent the place from?"

"His name is Herman DeMoser. He looks like a young Jerry Lewis with Jimmy Durante's nose."

Breanna had never thought about it before, but the description perfectly fit her landlord, Herman. She eyed the stranger for another long moment. "You can put your arms down," she said, but didn't lower her gun.

"I had visions of a welcome wagon greeting me to the neighborhood," he said wryly. "None of my visions involved a beautiful woman holding me at gunpoint."

Suddenly Breanna felt a little silly, aware that she might have overreacted because of her police training. She finally lowered the gun, although she didn't put it back in her purse. "I apologize. All I saw was a man coming toward me from the shadows and…well…a woman can't be too careful."

"No, I apologize. I should have realized how it would look coming at you in the dark at this time of night." The shadows that had hidden his features fell away as he stepped closer, into the faint illumination of her porch light.

Her breath caught in her chest at the sight of his handsome features. Intense blue eyes gazed at her with obvious interest. His dark brown hair had just enough curl to fall impishly over his broad forehead. He had a classic nose over nicely shaped, sensual lips. A small cleft in his chin only added to his attractiveness.

As she watched, his gaze slid down the length of her, lingering on her bare midriff, then moved slowly down her lace-covered legs. She felt that gaze deep in the pit of her stomach, like a heated caress over her skin.

It had been a very long time since the sight of a handsome man had caused her heart to beat just a little bit faster, her hands to feel slightly clammy and shaky. She was obviously overtired and her reaction to him made her more than a little bit irritable.

"It was nice meeting you, but it's late and I've had a long night. I would highly recommend in the future you don't sneak up on a woman alone in the middle of the night."

He nodded. "Point taken. Good night." He stepped back into the shadows, then turned and walked toward the cottage. A moment later she heard the front door of the small house open, then close.

Only then did she tuck her gun back into her purse and head for her own front door. As she stepped into the hallway, she kicked off her high-heeled shoes and allowed her toes to splay in the throw rug that covered the gleaming hardwood floor.

When she'd first viewed the house for the possibility of renting, it had been a mess. Abused by former tenants, neglected over the course of time, the Victorian beauty seemed destined to remain abandoned for the rest of its days.

Breanna had seen the potential and had come to an agreement with Herman. For the next three years she would pay a minimal rental fee a month and she would do all the repair work at her own expense.

Since she had moved in, the house had slowly transformed itself thanks to the labor of her family. Her elder brother, Clay, had helped sand and refinish the floors. Her older sister, Savannah, and her mother had wallpapered and painted and Breanna's father had rebuilt the front porch and seen to the painting of the outside of the house.

Even though she'd only been in the house two years, the place had quickly become home and she now couldn't imagine living any place else.

As she walked through the living room, she was surprised to see the kitchen light on and hear the faint sound of a television playing.

Rachel Davies, Breanna's live-in nanny, sat at the kitchen table, staring at the small portable television on the counter.

"Can't sleep?"

Rachel jumped in surprise and whirled around to face Breanna. "You scared me," she exclaimed.

Breanna smiled apologetically. "I just assumed you heard me come in." She sat in the chair opposite Rachel. "Nervous about tomorrow?"

Rachel smiled and tucked a strand of her long blond hair behind her ear. "More than I thought," she admitted.

The next day Rachel was going on her first date in almost two years. "It's just a picnic, Rachel, and David is a very nice man."

"I know...but I can't help but remember that I thought Michael was a nice man."

Breanna reached across the table and covered her friend's hand with her own. "That's in your past, and now it's time for you to look forward to a great future filled with love and respect."

Rachel squeezed her hand. "I don't know what I would have done without you."

Breanna pulled her hand back and laughed. "You seem to have it backward. I can't imagine what I would do without you! And speaking of that, how was my little munchkin today?"

Rachel smiled. "Wonderful, as usual. I swear, Breanna, Maggie is the brightest, sweetest child I've ever known."

Pride swelled up inside Breanna. "And you are obviously a woman of enormous judgment, which is why I hired you to take care of her in the first place."

"By the way, we have a new neighbor in the cottage. I watched him unloading this evening and he's a definite hunk!"

"I know. I met him."

Rachel frowned. "You did? When?"

"Just a few minutes ago when I pulled my gun on him." Breanna tried not to think about that swirl of heat that had swept over her as Adam Spencer had looked at her.

"You pulled your gun on him?" Rachel asked in surprise.

"He came out of the darkness at me without warning. I didn't know who he was or what he wanted."

"And what did he want?"

Breanna shrugged. "I guess just to introduce himself to me."

Rachel smiled wickedly. "I'd like to hold him at gunpoint and have my way with him."

Breanna laughed. "This from a woman who is too nervous to sleep because she has a date with a preacher tomorrow."

"You know what they say about the preacher's kids... they're the wildest ones in town."

Breanna smiled. "Not in this case. David Mandell is a nice guy." She stood, suddenly exhausted and more than a little eager to kiss her sweet sleeping daughter on her cheek. "I'm off to bed and if you're wise, you'll do the same. You don't want to scare David tomorrow with huge black bags under your eyes."

Rachel nodded. "I'll be up in just a few minutes."

The two said their good-nights, then Breanna climbed the wide staircase. She peeked into her daughter's bedroom just to assure herself that all was well, then went directly into her own bedroom and the private bath.

She never kissed her daughter when she had the stink of the streets on her, when her skin crawled from all the men who had whispered dirty things to her, leered at her with hungry eyes.

Minutes later she stepped out of the hot shower, dried off, then pulled on her comfortable cotton nightshirt. It took several minutes to brush and dry her long, thick dark hair, then she quietly crept into Maggie's room.

A cartoon character night-light illuminated the area

around the twin bed, and Maggie's little face peeked out from beneath the covers.

Breanna sat in the chair at the edge of the bed and breathed in the scent of the room...the sweet mixture of peach bubble bath and childhood.

She loved to watch her daughter as she slept, loved the way Maggie's little cupid bow lips puffed out with each breath, the way her curly brown hair decorated the pillow.

Kurt Randolf had been a bad choice for a boyfriend, a worse choice for a husband, but his genes and Breanna's had combined to create the miracle Breanna had named Maggie.

When she was awake, she was a bundle of energy and curiosity, a delight that made all the heartache of Kurt worthwhile.

Breanna stood, leaned over and kissed Maggie's sweet cheek, then left the bedroom and headed for her own room across the hall. She turned out her light and used the illumination of the moonlight streaking in through the window to guide her into bed.

She had just pulled the sheet up and snuggled in when the phone rang. She quickly snatched up the receiver on her nightstand, dread coursing through her. Good news rarely came at this hour of the night.

"Hello?"

Silence.

"Hello?" she repeated, then a soft click greeted her. The line filled with a woman's voice singing the standard lullaby of "Rock-A-Bye Baby."

Breanna knew instantly it was some sort of a recording and so she remained silent, listening to the soft melodic voice.

When the last note faded away she heard a second click.

The line remained open and she knew somebody was there because she could hear breathing.

"Who is this?" She sat up in bed. "What do you want? You must have a wrong number."

A noise answered her. She wasn't sure but it sounded like a male sob, then the line went dead.

She held the receiver for a long moment, fighting the sense of unease that crept through her. Just a wrong number, she told herself as she finally hung up the phone.

Rather than settling back in her bed, she got up and padded across the hall. Standing in the doorway, she peered in to see Maggie still sleeping peacefully.

There was absolutely no reason for Breanna to feel such a strong sense of disquiet, but she did. She returned to her bedroom and once again slid beneath the sheet. A wrong number…or somebody's idea of a prank, she told herself again.

Still, it was a very long time before she finally drifted off to sleep.

Adam Spencer sat on the shabby sofa that was part of the furnishings in the small cottage right next to Breanna James's residence. Finding this place for rent so close to his quarry had been a godsend. Although the ramshackle cottage wouldn't have been his first choice of a temporary residence, it would do for now.

"Damn you, Kurt," he said aloud as he popped the top off a bottle of beer. He was tired…exhausted in fact. He'd driven from Kansas City, Missouri, to the town of Cherokee Corners, Oklahoma, that day and had spent most of the evening unloading the personal items he'd brought with him. He should be in bed, but he knew sleep would be elusive.

He needed to process his initial impression of Breanna James. That she was strikingly beautiful didn't surprise him. Kurt had always dated beautiful women.

He frowned and took a sip of the cold beer as he thought of his cousin. Kurt had been an adventurer, both in his relationships and with the way he lived his life. As the only son of wealthy parents he'd enjoyed too much money and not enough goals.

He'd been buried a week ago after a tragic motorcycle accident. He'd been riding too fast without a helmet on a rain-drenched highway. The accident had pretty well summed up Kurt's life...flying too fast with too little sense.

Kurt had clung to life for six long hours in the hospital...long enough to confess to Adam that six years before he'd briefly been married to a woman in Cherokee Corners named Breanna James.

He'd further astonished Adam with the news that there had been a child...a daughter. With his dying breath he'd begged Adam to find them and make sure they were doing okay. Caught up in the emotional turmoil of losing the man who had been like a brother to him, Adam had agreed.

So here he sat in a rental shack next to the woman who had briefly been Kurt's wife. He had yet to see the child, didn't even know her name. But she was the real reason he was here.

Adam had seen his aunt and uncle's utter grief over losing their only son. Kurt's death had devastated them. A grandchild would be a gift, a legacy of the son they had lost.

But Adam didn't intend to tell them of the child's existence until he'd assessed the whole situation. He loved his aunt and uncle, who had raised him since the age of eleven when his own parents had died in a freak small plane accident. He would not invite more pain into the lives of the couple who had raised him.

Kurt's women had always been beautiful, but they'd also always been extremely dysfunctional. Some of them, aware of Kurt's family money, had been nothing more than gold diggers, others had been mentally unbalanced, or on drugs, or just plain needy.

Adam sighed and took another sip of beer, his thoughts returning to Breanna. It had instantly been obvious she was of Native American descent. High cheekbones gave her face a proud strength, but her long-lashed, liquid brown eyes had hinted at vulnerability.

Her long black hair had been tightly confined in a braid and he'd found himself wondering what she'd look like with those rich, thick strands loose and flowing around her shoulders.

Her skimpy clothing had done little to hide a lean, sweet, killer of a body. He frowned and downed the last of his beer.

"Damn you, Kurt," he repeated. He'd spent most of his life cleaning up Kurt's messes and he had a feeling that this was going to be the monster of messes.

He intended to hang around here for a week or two and see exactly what kind of a woman Breanna James was before he told his uncle Edward and aunt Anita that they had a grandchild.

His biggest fear at the moment was that somehow, someway he was going to have to figure out a way to tell them that the mother of their grandchild was a prostitute.

CHAPTER TWO

It was just after ten when Breanna heard a car door slam shut and her mother's voice drifting in through the open living-room window. She went to the window and moved aside the gauzy curtain to see her mother talking to Adam Spencer.

Rita Birdsong James was a short, petite woman who had never met a stranger in her life. Breanna groaned inwardly as she wondered what sort of personal information Rita was giving to her new neighbor.

When Breanna had gotten out of bed at eight, Adam Spencer had already been up and weeding the pathetically neglected flower bed in his front yard.

Breanna had spent far too long standing at her bedroom window watching him. She told herself she was observing him as a cop would any person who invaded her personal space. But it was a woman's gaze that admired the play of his arm and back muscles as he worked. It was a woman's gaze that noted how the bright sunshine teased hints of impish red into his dark brown hair.

She had whirled away from the window, irritated with herself and the stir of heat her observations had created in the pit of her stomach.

She now returned to the kitchen table and the cup of coffee she'd been enjoying, knowing her mother would come inside when she was finished chatting up Adam.

Ten minutes later, Rita flew into the kitchen, dark eyes snapping and a satisfied smile on her face. At fifty-eight years old, Rita was still a stunningly beautiful woman. Her face was smooth, unlined…as if life hadn't touched it with heartache or strife.

Her short hair was just as black as it had ever been, the cut emphasizing her defined cheekbones and generous smile. She was like a china doll in a collector's case, always perfectly made-up and elegantly dressed.

"So did you spill all the James's deep, dark family secrets?" Breanna asked.

Rita laughed and walked to the cabinet to grab a coffee cup. "I wish we had some deep, dark family secrets to spill. It would keep life interesting." She poured herself a cup of coffee, then joined Breanna at the table. "And where's my baby girl this beautiful morning?"

"With Rachel. They went to the grocery store. Rachel decided she needed a few more things for her picnic lunch this afternoon."

"It's nice to see her opening up to the idea of dating again." She raised a dark, perfectly formed brow and peered at Breanna over the rim of her coffee cup. "That's something you might consider. He's very handsome and he's not married."

"Don't even start," Breanna warned.

"He's a painter, studying Native American art. I told him all about the Cherokee Cultural Center and invited him to dinner this afternoon."

Breanna wanted to protest. She'd been looking forward to their first barbecue of the year, to a relaxing time with family and close friends. But she knew it did no good to protest. As her father, Thomas, often said, the Birdsongs were the most stubborn people in the Cherokee nation.

The sound of the front door opening halted any further conversation. "Grandma!" Maggie exclaimed as she burst into the kitchen.

"Hello, my little doe. Come give me my kiss." Rita opened her arms and Maggie climbed up on her lap.

"Look what Rachel got for me." Maggie held out a pink cord necklace; dangling from it was a plastic charm in the shape of a horse.

"She's named him Thunder and swears she's never taking him off," Rachel said as she entered the kitchen carrying a sack of groceries.

"Never taking him off?" Breanna smiled indulgently at her daughter.

"Not even to take a bath," Maggie replied. She wiggled down from Rita's lap, unable to remain confined for another moment. "I've got to show him to Mr. Bear. Mr. Bear always wanted a horse friend." With these words Maggie tore out of the kitchen, her footsteps resounding as she raced up the stairs to her bedroom.

"Ah, to have her energy," Rita exclaimed.

"Mother, you have more energy than ten Maggies put together," Breanna replied dryly.

"Your father says there are times it's quite irritating. Did I tell you I was mad at him?"

As Rita began to catalog her most recent complaints

against her husband, Breanna thought of her parents' marriage.

For thirty-eight years they had shared a spirited relationship. They fought as loud and passionately as they loved... and it was obvious to anyone who spent any time in their company that they were true soul mates.

That's what Breanna had once wished for herself. The kind of love that strengthened rather than diminished with time, the kind of commitment that didn't have to be spoken aloud but was just there...in the heart...in the soul.

Her brief, disastrous marriage to Kurt had destroyed those dreams and broken her heart. Despite her mother's wish to the contrary, she had no desire to date, no desire to involve a man in her life. She and Maggie were just fine alone.

"Well, I'd better get out of here," Rita said. She stood and finished the last of her coffee. "We're having everyone's favorite food today," she said as Breanna walked her to the front door. "I'm putting beef ribs on the grill for your father and Clay. I'm making bean bread for Savannah and grape dumplings for you."

"Sounds wonderful. What can I bring?" Breanna asked as they stepped out on her front porch.

"Your new neighbor. I told him you'd pick him up at three."

"Mother!" Breanna protested.

Rita reached up and kissed her youngest daughter on the cheek. "He's a stranger in a strange town and the Cherokee are known for their hospitality. I expect you to honor your heritage and be a gracious hostess. And I know you will."

After the two had said their goodbyes, Breanna watched her mother get into her car, then she went back into the kitchen where Rachel was putting together her picnic lunch.

She grinned at Breanna. "So, it sounds like I'm not the only one who has a date this afternoon."

"This is definitely not a date," Breanna protested and poured herself a fresh cup of coffee. "I'm merely transporting a person to my parents' home for a barbecue."

"I think your mother hopes it will be something quite different," Rachel observed as she slathered bread with mustard.

Breanna sat back down at the table and sighed. "I'm afraid my sister and brother and I have disappointed Mother when it comes to our love lives."

"I'm surprised Clay has never married," Rachel said.

Breanna shook her head as she thought of her older brother. "Clay has never had a lasting relationship with anyone. He spends all his time either at a crime scene or cooped up in his lab."

"A terrible waste of hunk-hood," Rachel exclaimed.

Breanna grinned. She knew her brother was considered a hunk by most of the women in Cherokee Corners, but he was positively possessed by his work as a crime scene technician.

"It's so sad that Savannah and her husband seemed to have such a wonderful marriage and then he got killed in that car accident last year." Rachel grabbed the sliced ham from the refrigerator and continued. "And it isn't your fault that Kurt turned out to be a selfish little boy who wasn't prepared to take on the role of husband and father."

"Sometimes it feels like my fault," Breanna replied. "I should have seen the signs, I shouldn't have married him so soon after meeting him."

"And I should have seen the signs that Michael was a

possessive, obsessive, brutal man, but I didn't until it was too late." Rachel touched her cheek, where a small scar puckered the skin. "I had no idea what he was capable of."

"At least he's behind bars where he belongs," Breanna said. "Unfortunately they don't put immature men in jail."

Rachel grinned. "If they did, they'd definitely need to build more jails."

"Isn't that the truth," Breanna agreed.

Later that afternoon, as Breanna dressed for the family barbecue, she thought about her brother and sister and how sad it was that none of the James siblings had been successful in their quest for happy marriages.

Savannah had come the closest, having been married to Jimmy Tallfeather for just a little over a year before tragedy had ended their marriage. The entire family had been worried about her because she still clung to her grief as jealously, as deeply as she had on the day she'd learned her husband had been stolen from her.

Maybe Adam Spencer was the man to bring Savannah back to life. Maybe that had been her mother's ultimate hope. This thought made Breanna less tense about spending any time at all in the handsome newcomer's company.

She would suffer the short drive from her own home to her parents', then introduce him to Savannah and hope for an instant love connection between the two.

At exactly quarter to three, Adam stepped out on his front porch and looked at the house next door. She was a cop, not a prostitute and the knowledge filled Adam with relief. When he'd met Breanna's mother that morning, one of the first things she'd shared with him was the fact that her family was comprised of law enforcement officials.

It would certainly be easier to tell Uncle Edward and

Aunt Anita that the mother of their grandchild was a vice cop rather than a prostitute.

He was interested in learning more about the James family, who would forever be bound to him by the existence of a little girl. He wanted to see that Breanna and her daughter were okay, set up a trust fund for Kurt's daughter, then go on with his own life knowing he had cleaned up Kurt's final mess.

He sat down on the porch stoop, wondering if she would be one of those women who were perpetually late for everything. He looked down the street, breathing in the sweet scent of spring that filled the air.

Cherokee Corners had been a surprise. He'd expected a dusty little town and instead had discovered a bustling metropolis. The downtown area was built on a square, with the city buildings in the center, and unique shops and familiar chain stores surrounding them.

He'd found Breanna's home on the west side of town, only a few miles from the Cherokee Cultural Center that included a replica of a village and Cherokee life a hundred years before.

Rita Birdsong James had indicated that she spent a lot of time at the center and was actively involved in the running of the educational tourist attraction.

And he'd told her he was an artist…a painter, for crying out loud. He swiped a hand through his curly hair and sighed. He'd regretted the words the minute they had left his lips, but she'd surprised him by asking what had brought him to Cherokee Corners and what he did for a living.

Painting had sprung into his head because he'd found a half-completed paint-by-number of a Native American on horseback in the kitchen when he'd moved in. Telling

Rita Birdsong James that he was an artist leaped to his lips
before he'd had an opportunity to think it through.

Of course, an artist was certainly more exciting, more
exotic than his real job as the owner of a small, but successful accounting firm. And he had a feeling that telling Rita that he was interested in Cherokee culture had
granted him instant access to their family gathering that
afternoon.

At that moment Breanna's front door opened and a little
girl danced outside, followed by Breanna. Adam stood and
his heart jumped into his throat as his gaze was captured
by the child.

Kurt. Her long, curly brown hair was all Kurt's, as was
the slender oval of her facial structure. As she smiled up
at her mother, another arrow pierced through Adam as he
saw the dimple that danced in one cheek…just like the
dimple that had made Kurt's smile so infectious.

Breanna saw him and waved him over as she opened
the driver door to her car. "Good afternoon," she said as he
approached. "This is my daughter, Maggie. Maggie, this
is Mr. Spencer. He's going with us to Grandma's house."

"Hi, Maggie." Adam fought the impulse to lean down
and grab the child to his chest. He hadn't expected the
emotions that now rolled around inside him as he continued to gaze at Kurt's child. "Mr. Spencer is kind of a
mouthful. You can call me Adam."

"Okay," Maggie agreed with a bright smile. Even her
eyes were all Kurt's…dark gray and sparking with life.
"You want to see my horse?" She held out a necklace,
where a plastic charm in the shape of a horse dangled.
"His name is Thunder."

"That's a fine name for a horse," Adam replied.

"Maggie, get inside and buckle up. We need to hit the road."

As Adam got into the passenger seat, Breanna watched as her daughter buckled into the backseat, then she got in behind the steering wheel.

The shock of seeing Maggie wore off somewhat and he became conscious of Breanna's scent...a mixture of wildflowers and patchouli, slightly exotic and definitely appealing.

Her appearance was just as appealing. Her coral-colored T-shirt was a perfect foil for the darkness of her hair and her white shorts set off the rich, bronze tones of long, shapely legs.

Last night her features had been almost garish with heavy makeup. Today her face had a freshly scrubbed kind of beauty.

"Tell the truth, Adam." Kurt's voice filled his head. "You've always been jealous of my life and you've always wanted my women." Adam frowned and consciously shoved his cousin's voice out of his head.

"Thank you for letting me ride with you," he said, trying not to dwell on the fact that today her hair was down, loose and flowing and more beautiful than he'd imagined. "It was so nice of your mother to invite me."

She flashed him a quick smile as she backed out of the driveway. "If my mother had her way, all of Cherokee Corners would come to their barbecues. She loves people."

"That was obvious in the brief time I spoke with her."

"She tells me you're a painter. Would I have seen any of your work anywhere?"

Again Adam regretted his impulsive claim. "Only if you rummage through trash cans on a regular basis," he replied dryly. She laughed and a wave of pleasant heat swept through him at the sound of her melodic amusement.

"If that's the case, I hope you don't paint for a living," she replied.

"No. Actually I'm an accountant by trade. That's how I make my living." It felt good, to be able to give her this much truth.

"So what brings you to Cherokee Corners? This isn't exactly a financial center. Unfortunately this town has far too high a quota of people living in poverty."

"My office is in Kansas City. I'm not here in Cherokee Corners permanently. With tax time behind us for the year, I decided to give myself a little vacation and with my interest in Cherokee culture and art, this seemed like the place to spend a month or two."

"Do you have any little girls or boys?" Maggie asked him from the backseat.

Adam turned and again felt that jarring burst of emotion as he looked at her. He tried to steel himself against it. The last thing he wanted was to become emotionally involved with this child and her beautiful mother. "No, honey. I'm afraid I don't. I don't have a wife or children."

"How come?" Maggie asked, her gray eyes gazing at him with open curiosity.

"That's a personal question, Maggie." Her mother replied before Adam got a chance to answer. "It isn't nice to ask personal questions."

"Oh. Is it personal to ask if he could get some kids so I'd have somebody to play with?" Maggie asked.

Breanna flashed Adam an apologetic look. "There aren't any children Maggie's age in the neighborhood and so she's always hoping somebody will move in with kids her age."

"I'm afraid I can't help you, honey," Adam said. "I don't

see any kids in my life now or in the future." He turned around to look at Breanna once again. "Your mother mentioned that you all work in law enforcement."

She nodded and made a left turn at an intersection. "My father retired from the police force a year ago. He was chief of police for a number of years. My brother, Clay, works in crime scene investigations, my sister, Savannah, is a homicide cop and I work vice."

"Rather unusual, isn't it, that all of you chose that line of work?"

She shrugged. "I guess. For me, it was just a natural choice. Dad loved his work and listening to him talk about it as I was growing up, I knew very early that I was going to be a cop, too."

"Why vice?"

"Why not?" she countered. "It's a job somebody needs to do and it's where my superiors feel I'm most needed."

"You had just gotten off work last night when I met you?" he asked. She nodded and he grinned. "You make a very convincing lady of the night."

She cast him a glance that was distinctly cool. "And you almost got yourself shot as a prowler." She returned her focus out the front window.

Prickly, Adam thought. Or maybe it wasn't the best thing to tell a woman she made a perfect streetwalker. Maybe his people skills were rustier than he thought.

He decided the best thing to do was to keep quiet and turned his head to look out the window. They had left the outskirts of Cherokee Corners proper and were passing the Cultural Center and village.

"If you're interested in Cherokee culture, this is the place to spend your time," she said, her voice holding none of the coolness it had moments before.

"That's where my grandma works," Maggie said. "We go there lots of times and do dances and have fun."

"There is something going on there almost every day during the summer months," Breanna explained. "My mother thinks it's very important to continue to educate people about the Cherokee ways."

"Your father is Cherokee, too?" Adam asked.

Breanna laughed. "No. Dad is one hundred percent fighting Irish, as proud of his heritage as Mother is of hers."

"Must have made interesting supper conversations."

It was obvious speaking about her parents put her at ease. She smiled and nodded. "You don't know the half of it. Both of them are stubborn, passionate people. I should probably warn you. We rarely get through one of these family gatherings without an explosion of fireworks between them, but the fireworks rarely last long."

She pulled down a dirt lane that led to a rambling ranch house. There was not another house in sight in any direction. Cars in a variety of shapes and sizes clogged the circular driveway in front of the house.

She parked the car and turned to Adam. "Do you come from a large family?"

"No. My parents died when I was eleven and I was raised by an aunt and uncle. That is pretty much the extent of my family."

Her dark eyes flashed with a flicker of sympathy. "Oh, I'm sorry."

"Don't be. My aunt and uncle are kind, loving people."

"That's good. But I just wanted to warn you that my family is big and loud and might be quite overwhelming to somebody unaccustomed to big family gatherings."

"Mommy, let's go!" Maggie said plaintively from the backseat.

"Yes, let's go," Breanna agreed and opened her car door. "It looks like most of the gang have already arrived."

It took them only moments to get out of the car and walk down the driveway to the house. Breanna opened the door and they entered a large living room.

Adam's first impression was one of warmth and comfort. It was obvious this room, decorated in earth tones, was the heart of the house. The walls held Native American artwork, all with the common theme of Indians and bears.

"They're all the work of a local artist. Her name is Tamara Greystone. She's a teacher at the high school," Breanna explained. "You might want to look her up...you know, share techniques or whatever."

"I might just do that," he replied, although he had no intention of sharing "techniques" with an artist, who would see through his false claim with ease.

Maggie danced ahead of them and out a sliding glass door. Breanna motioned for Adam to follow her outside.

Nothing Breanna had told him had prepared him for the cacophony of sound coming from the throng of people on the large patio. Breanna had mentioned an older brother and sister, but it was obvious this gathering was bigger than immediate family members only.

He saw Rita James standing with a group of people around the large, brick barbecue. Her gaze caught his and she immediately left the group and approached him and Breanna with a warm smile.

She grabbed his hands in hers. "Adam, I'm so glad you came."

"I appreciate you inviting me," he replied.

She released his hands and smiled at her daughter. "Breanna, why don't you take Adam around and introduce him to everyone."

"All right," she agreed easily.

Over the next few minutes Adam was introduced to enough people that his head spun, trying to remember names and faces. He was introduced to Thomas James, Breanna's father, a tall man with graying red hair and bright blue eyes.

He stood duty over the racks of ribs that sizzled on the barbecue grill. He greeted Adam with a firm handshake and exuded a vigor and energy that belied his age.

Adam was then introduced to Jacob Kincaid, an older man who was Thomas's best friend and the president of the largest bank in Cherokee Corners.

"Jacob is our resident collector," Breanna said. "His house is filled with antiques to die for and he has a wonderful art collection and some of the most exquisite Fabergé eggs you'd ever want to see."

Jacob smiled at Breanna with obvious affection. "I certainly hope Mr. Spencer isn't a cat burglar because if he is, you've just given him a road map to the riches in town."

"Oh, and did I mention his state-of-the-art security system?" Breanna added and both men laughed. After visiting a few minutes with the banker, Breanna excused them and led Adam to a woman seated in a lawn chair. He instantly knew it was Breanna's sister.

The two women looked remarkably alike, except that Savannah's dark, glossy hair was cut short. That, coupled with a profound sadness in her eyes, gave her a look of intense vulnerability. Although she was pleasant, Adam found Breanna far more interesting.

He told himself his only interest was the fact that his

life and hers would forever be bound by the child she'd had...Kurt's child.

After they visited with Savannah for a few minutes, Adam was introduced to Breanna's brother, Clay. Clay had brooding good looks, his eyes radiating the intensity of a driven man. Although friendly, he seemed distracted, as if he found his inner thoughts more interesting than those of others.

Breanna introduced him to cousins and aunts and uncles and more friends of the family. It was easy to see that the James family was not only well liked in the town, but also highly respected.

"There's one more person I have to introduce you to," Breanna said, "then it probably won't be long before we eat and you can visit with whomever you please." She led him to another pretty young woman who sat slightly alone on a stone bench surrounded by early blooming spring flowers.

"This is my cousin, Alyssa Whitefeather. Alyssa, this is my new neighbor, Adam Spencer."

Alyssa stood and offered her hand to Adam. "Hello, Mr. Spencer."

Adam took her hand in his and started to return the greeting, but before he could say a word, Alyssa's blue eyes rolled upward and she collapsed in Adam's arms.

CHAPTER THREE

Breanna sat on a chair next to her parents' bed where Alyssa lay pale as a ghost against the dark blue bedspread. Adam had carried her in here, then Breanna had shooed everyone out of the room and closed the door.

She knew the family would return to their activities. Over the years they had all become accustomed to Alyssa's occasional "spells" and knew she would be unconscious for a few minutes, then would awaken and be fine.

What Breanna wanted to know was what had brought on this particular spell? Had it been the touch of Adam's hand? And if that had been it, then what had her cousin "seen"?

She knew there was no point in trying to rouse Alyssa. She'd awaken when she was ready and nothing Breanna did or said would bring her around sooner.

Minutes ticked by, indicated by the tick-tock of the old

schoolhouse clock on the wall. It was a sound as familiar as Breanna's mother's heartbeat. Many early mornings, the James's bed had been filled with her parents and the kids, greeting the day with soft talk, giggles and the rhythmic beating of that clock.

Breanna leaned forward as Alyssa released a soft, audible sigh. Her eyes fluttered open and shut...open and shut, then remained open.

"Hi."

Alyssa sat up and looked around as if to orient herself. "Hi."

"Are you okay?" Breanna frowned with concern. Usually when Alyssa came out of one of these spells, she appeared refreshed and alert. This time she appeared fragile and her hand shook as she worried it through a strand of her brown hair.

She hesitated a moment, then nodded. "I'm fine." Once again she swept a strand of her hair behind her ear and frowned. "I haven't done that in quite some time."

"What brought it on? Anything specific? Was it my neighbor?"

Alyssa's frown deepened. "No...I don't think so." Her blue eyes were troubled as she gazed at Breanna. "I felt something dark...something evil from the moment I stepped into the house today." She placed a hand over her heart. "I have a horrible feeling of dread and I don't know what's causing it."

"Have you seen anything?" Breanna asked, referring to the various visions Alyssa had suffered with since she was a small child.

"Blackness. Just blackness." She shivered. "I've never had anything like this before." She swung her legs over the side of the bed and drew a deep breath. "Whenever I've had a vision in the past, it's always been like watching a snippet of a movie in my head. But not this time. This time there was just the blackness and a sense of horror like I've never experienced before."

A slight chill worked up Breanna's spine. "Are you sure you're okay?"

Alyssa drew another deep breath, then offered a tentative smile. "I'm fine, just a little bit embarrassed. I can't imagine what your poor neighbor thinks. You introduce me to him and I faint in his arms."

Breanna offered her a reassuring smile. "Don't worry, I'll tell him you're hypoglycemic and just needed a little sugar boost."

Alyssa leaned across and grabbed Breanna's hand. "Don't look so worried. My feelings and visions don't always mean anything. Stress sometimes triggers an event and things have been really crazy down at the bed-and-breakfast."

Alyssa owned and operated a bed-and-breakfast on the square, along with an ice-cream parlor that was a favorite gathering place.

She stood and released Breanna's hand. "Now, we better get back to the party before we miss all the good food."

Breanna stood as well and opened the door, then stumbled into the solid chest of Adam. Worried blue eyes gazed at her as he grabbed her by the shoulders to steady her. "Is everything all right?" His gaze moved from her to Alyssa, who stood just behind her.

"Everything is fine, Mr. Spencer," Alyssa assured him and he dropped his hands from Breanna's shoulders. "I should apologize. I don't normally faint when introduced to a new person. I'm afraid I haven't been eating right and..." She allowed her voice to trail off.

"And it's done and over," Breanna said firmly. "Why don't we all rejoin the party. I'm sure they're probably serving up the food now." As she moved past Adam in the hallway, she smelled his cologne, a woodsy, masculine scent that stirred something feminine in her.

It irritated her, how this man affected her on some primal level that had nothing to do with intellect and everything to do with sex appeal.

As the three of them walked through the house and out the sliding glass doors to the backyard, she decided she had done her duty and introduced him to everyone. He was now on his own for the remainder of the day.

Sure enough, the food was being served and Breanna left Adam in search of her daughter. She found her sitting on her Aunt Savannah's lap.

"Hey, sweetie. Why don't you go get yourself a plate of food and let me visit with Aunt Savannah for a minute."

"I'm starving," Maggie exclaimed as she jumped down from Savannah's lap. "Bye, Aunt Savannah, we'll talk more after I eat."

"It's a deal," Savannah replied, the darkness in her eyes momentarily lifted as she smiled at Maggie.

"How are you doing, sis?" Breanna asked as Maggie scampered away.

"Good," Savannah replied, but the sadness in her eyes that had been present for the past year was an indicator to Breanna that the heartache of losing Jimmy still consumed her.

"You look tired. Are you working too many hours?" Breanna asked. The entire family had been after Savannah to take some time off, to get away from the misery of seeing murders up close and personal.

Savannah shrugged. "It's been a long week.

"Still no break in the Maxwell murder?"

"Nothing. Poor man is found naked and dead in front of the public library. Clay has been pulling out his hair because the crime scene was contaminated by dozens of gawkers and we've all been stymied by the fact that Greg Maxwell seemed to be loved by everyone who knew him."

"Something will break. It always does," Breanna said.

"Your new neighbor seems very nice," Savannah said.

Breanna looked over to the patio where Adam was talking to her father. The khaki slacks Adam wore hugged his slender hips and long legs and the short-sleeved dress shirt emphasized the width of his chest and the muscles of his biceps. "I guess. I really don't know him that well. It was Mother who invited him."

Savannah smiled. "Big surprise. She's always inviting strays home."

Breanna looked back over to Adam. He didn't seem like a stray. In her brief acquaintance with him, he appeared to be a man who knew exactly who he was and where he was going. There was a quiet confidence about him she found intriguing, despite the fact that she had no intention of developing any kind of a relationship other than that of good neighbors.

"Come and get a plate," Breanna said and pulled her sister to her feet. Breanna fixed herself a plate and joined her daughter at one of the picnic tables that were scattered across the backyard.

"Aunt Savannah said maybe she'll take me to a movie next week," Maggie said.

"That would be nice, wouldn't it?" Breanna replied.

"I like the movies." Maggie grabbed the little horse on her necklace. "I think Thunder would like them, too."

"Mind if I join you?" Adam stood next to the picnic table, his plate in hand.

Breanna wanted to tell him to go sit someplace else, but of course she didn't. "Not at all." She wondered exactly what it was about him that set her so on edge.

He scooted onto the bench next to her, their shoulders bumping as his scent filled her head.

She knew then why he set her on edge, made her uncomfortable and wary. Something about the way he affected her reminded her of those first few weeks with Kurt. Adam Spencer made her feel that same rush of heat, a lick of lust that she'd never felt before Kurt...or since...until now.

Kurt had been a disastrous mistake and so it was only natural that a man who stirred the same kind of feelings would evoke a defensive wariness in her.

"You have a wonderful family," he said.

"They are very special," Breanna replied. "I'm not sure what I would have done without them in the past five years. Being a single parent isn't easy."

"I imagine not." He frowned and focused on his food.

"What about you? Do you eventually want a wife and children?" She assumed he was in his late twenties or early thirties. Didn't most men of that age start to think about creating families?

"Not me," he said firmly. "I much prefer to be footloose and fancy-free."

"Your foot is loose?" Maggie eyed him with a touch of childish horror. "Does it hurt?"

"No, honey, my foot isn't really loose. That's just an

expression." Adam smiled at Maggie. "My feet work just fine."

"Rabbits' feet are good," Maggie said after a moment of thought. "And frogs' feet. They help jump…jump…jump."

As Adam and Maggie engaged in a conversation about various animals and their feet, Breanna couldn't help but think it was a shame Adam had no intentions of becoming a father.

He showed a natural ease with Maggie, not talking down to her or at her, but rather with her. Maybe he's just on his best behavior and being kind and patient to the granddaughter of his host and hostess, she thought. That was the socially correct thing to do.

She was relieved when Savannah and Jacob Kincaid joined them at the table.

It was dusk when Breanna drove them back home. Maggie, overwhelmed by the food, fresh air and play, immediately fell asleep in the backseat.

"Thank you for letting me ride with you today," Adam said as they pulled out of the James's driveway.

"No problem," she replied.

"I noticed an old grill in the shed behind the cottage. If I get it out and clean it up, maybe you and Maggie could join me for hamburgers one evening next week."

Now was the time to draw boundaries, Breanna thought. For the time that he was renting the cottage they would share a backyard, but she had no intention of being anything more than nodding-acquaintance-type neighbors.

"Thanks, but we usually keep pretty busy between my schedule and Rachel's."

"Rachel?" In the glow of twilight his eyes appeared more silver than blue.

"Rachel is my live-in nanny," Breanna explained. "She has been my helping hand ever since I hired her two years ago."

"Must have been hard to find somebody to trust to live in your home and caretake for your child," he observed.

"Rachel was special from the first moment I met her. She came into the police department to file a complaint against an old boyfriend who was stalking her. I took the complaint and could immediately tell she was bright, good-hearted but had made the mistake of hooking up with the wrong kind of man." Breanna turned into her driveway, shut off the car engine then turned to Adam. "Having made that mistake myself, I instantly empathized with her."

"What happened with her and her boyfriend?" Adam asked.

"He caught up with her one night and beat the hell out of her, used a knife to cut up her face. He's now serving time and Rachel and I have become best of friends."

Adam reached out and placed his hand on her forearm, his gaze so intense it momentarily seemed to stop her heart. "You said you'd made the same mistake...your ex-husband...he didn't hurt you, did he?"

His hand was warm, filled with energy and far too pleasant against her cool skin. She moved and he drew back his hand as if surprised to have found himself touching her.

"You want to know if my ex-husband beat me?" she asked. "Absolutely not. He knew better than to ever lay a hand on me." She was vaguely surprised by the bitterness that rose in her voice with each word. "You asked if he ever hurt me? He promised undying love and fidelity. He played at building dreams, then he broke the promises

and shattered the dreams. Did he hurt me? Unbearably...
irreparably." She threw open her car door. "And now I'll
just say good night." She got out of the car and slammed
her door, surprised by the depth of emotions the conversation had stirred.

"Breanna," he said as he got out of the car. "I'm sorry
if I upset you."

As quickly as it had swept over her, the anger died. She
drew a deep, calming breath. "No, I'm sorry. I'm afraid
talking about my ex puts me in a bad mood. I didn't mean
to take it out on you."

She opened the back car door, unbuckled her sleeping
daughter and pulled her up and into her arms, then closed
the door.

"Would you like me to carry her inside for you?"

"No, thanks. I've managed on my own for the past five
years. I can manage to get her inside under my own steam.
Good night, Adam."

"Good night, Breanna," he replied. He turned and
walked across the grass toward the cottage.

It took Breanna a moment at the door as she shifted her
daughter's weight from one hip to the other so she could
free up a hand to dig her keys out of her purse.

Once inside she carried Maggie directly to bed. She
took off the little girl's socks and shoes, then drew the
sheet up around her and kissed her on the cheek.

She went back downstairs where she found a note from
Rachel. The picnic with David had been a success and they
had gone to the movies. She would be home later.

Breanna smiled as she read the note. She was glad
things had gone well at the picnic. Rachel deserved happiness and love in her life.

She set the note aside and put a kettle of water on the stove for tea. She loved Sunday nights. Sundays and Mondays were her favorite days and nights because she was off duty. She didn't have to be back at work until Tuesday afternoon.

The phone rang and she picked it up, figuring it was probably her mother wanting to hash over the events of the day.

The recording began immediately, before Breanna even got a chance to say hello. It was the same as the night before, the woman singing "Rock-A-Bye Baby."

"Who is this?" she demanded when the song had ended but the phone line remained open. "What do you want? I really think you have the wrong number."

"You bitch."

The voice, gravelly deep and filled with malevolence shot a sweeping icy chill through her, but before she could make any reply, the line went dead.

The plastic of the phone felt cold in her fingers and she quickly slammed it down into the receiver, trying to shake off the chill that had taken possession of her body.

Two nights. Two phone calls. Who was making them? What did they mean? And what could they possibly have to do with her? She quickly punched *69, but got a recorded message that the number she requested was unavailable.

Like a shriek of alarm, the teakettle whistled. She jumped and stifled a scream, then quickly moved the kettle off the hot burner.

With shaking fingers, she fixed herself a cup of tea, then sat down at the kitchen table, her thoughts racing and chaotic in her mind.

A new wave of horror swept through her as she thought

of her cousin Alyssa and the visions she'd seen that afternoon. Was it possible Alyssa had seen danger that concerned Breanna? Was it possible the darkness Alyssa had seen had something to do with these phone calls?

"It was a nice barbecue," Thomas James said as he helped his wife wash and dry the last of the pots and pans.

"It was, wasn't it?" Rita smiled at him, the beautiful smile that had captured his heart thirty-nine years before. That smile still had the power to make him feel like the luckiest devil on the face of the earth.

He took the last pot from her and dried it with a dish towel as she rinsed out the sink. "Bree's new neighbor seems pleasant enough," he observed.

Rita sat at the table. "Very pleasant...and very single."

"Now, honey, you know matchmaking isn't a good idea." He joined her at the table. "The kids are all grown and they have to find their own way."

She frowned, the gesture doing nothing to diminish her beauty. "But, Thomas, what worries me is that all of our children seem to have lost their way. Breanna clings to Maggie and to her rage over Kurt's desertion. Savannah clings to her grief as if it is her best and only friend. And Clay...he clings to his job as if it can fulfill all his needs as a man."

He reached out and took her hand in his. "And there's nothing we can do about it but let them find their way on their own."

"I know." She sighed and squeezed his hand. He grinned and she raised a dark eyebrow. "What are you smiling about, old man?"

"I was just thinking about what a lucky man I am. Must

have been the luck of the Irish that made my car break down in front of your parents' house thirty-nine years ago."

"And I was just a young sweet nineteen and you were such a dashing older man."

Thomas laughed. He was eight years older than his wife. Although the eight years didn't seem so important now, he'd spent many sleepless nights at the beginning of their relationship worrying about them.

"I thought you were the most beautiful woman I'd ever seen," he said softly. "And I still feel the same way."

"Why, Mr. James, I do believe you're trying to seduce me." Her dark eyes gazed intently into his.

"Is it working?"

"Absolutely." She stood and pulled him to his feet. "Come to bed, old man, and let this old woman show you how much you are loved."

She might make him crazy at times with her stubbornness—she fought with him like a banshee—but he never lost sight of the fact that he was the luckiest devil on the face of the earth because Rita Birdsong loved him.

As twilight transformed into darkness, Adam remained seated on the sofa in his living room, thinking about the past day and what he'd learned about Breanna's family.

It was obvious it was a family built on the foundation of love and respect for one another. If Maggie had no other family in her life, he had a feeling the James family would be enough to make her feel secure and loved.

But she did have other family. She had Kurt's parents, who would merely add another layer of love in Maggie's life. He frowned and rubbed the center of his forehead as he thought of Breanna's reaction when the conversation had turned to her ex-husband.

What would her reaction be when he told her he was Kurt's cousin? And why did the thought of her reaction to that news bother him?

He was here at Kurt's request, to make certain Breanna and Maggie were doing okay, and they appeared to be doing just fine. All he needed to do was tell Breanna that Kurt's parents wanted a role in little Maggie's life, then leave Cherokee Corners and get back to his life in Kansas City.

With a new resolution, he turned on the lamp on the end table and picked up the phone receiver. He punched in a Kansas City number.

"Randolf residence."

Adam recognized Miriam Walder's voice. She'd been the housekeeper for his aunt and uncle for as long as he could remember.

"Miriam, it's Adam."

"Oh, Mr. Adam. It's good to hear your voice."

"It's good to hear yours, too," he replied. "Is my aunt or uncle at home?"

"Mr. Edward is at a meeting this evening, but Mrs. Anita is in the sunroom. If you'll wait just a moment, I'll take her a phone."

"Thank you, Miriam." As Adam waited, he wondered if it might not be better to give them the news that they had a grandchild when they were together. His aunt had suffered heart problems in the past and even though this news was good, it would be a shock nonetheless.

"Adam, my dear." His aunt's gentle voice filled the line. "How are you?"

"I'm fine, Aunt Anita. How are you doing?"

"All right. I'm hoping as time goes on the days and nights will get easier, that the grief will ease somewhat."

Tell her. The words boomed inside Adam's head. Tell her about Maggie. But something held him back.

"Are you having a nice getaway?" Anita asked. "You've been working so hard over the past five years, Adam, and you've accomplished so much. I'm glad you decided to give yourself a little vacation. Where exactly are you?"

"I'm in a place called Cherokee Corners," he replied. "It's about one hundred fifty miles south of Tulsa."

"Whatever made you decide to go there?"

"It sounded like an interesting place, and it's rich in Native American culture."

"I never knew you were interested in that."

Adam thought of the lovely Breanna. "Neither did I. But I'm finding it more and more interesting now that I'm here."

"You'll keep in touch while you're out of town?"

"Of course. Give my love to Uncle Edward," he said. They said their goodbyes and Adam hung up.

He leaned back against the sofa and thought of his aunt. Her grief over the loss of her son was still thick…raw in her voice. But Adam realized exactly why he hadn't told her about the existence of a granddaughter.

After seeing Breanna's reaction to her experience with Kurt, he wasn't at all sure that she would allow Maggie to have anything to do with Kurt's family. The minute she mentioned Kurt, it was like a noxious poison released into her blood. It was obvious she hated him.

He had no idea what Kurt had told Breanna about his family. He knew that in the past, when it had best served his needs, Kurt had painted his parents as unloving, un-caring people. What stories had Kurt told Breanna? How black had he painted his mother and father?

Adam needed to find out what Breanna knew about his aunt and uncle. He needed to make her see that they would be a loving, caring presence in Maggie's life.

His desire to stay and get to know her a little better had nothing to do with the fact that her scent made him just a little bit dizzy, that the liquid depths of her dark eyes made him feel a little like he was drowning.

It was crazy. He had to remind himself that she was one of Kurt's women, and his job here was simply to clean up the mess Kurt had left behind…just as Adam had done so many times in the past.

His interest in Breanna had nothing to do with the fact that she was a beautiful woman, but rather with the fact that he had made a vow to a dying man.

He rubbed a hand across his lower jaw, unsurprised to feel the scrub of whisker stubble despite the fact that he'd shaved that morning. Thoughts of the day and Breanna continued to fill his head.

She'd asked him if he wanted a wife and children and he'd told her definitely not, and that was the truth. Well, a wife wouldn't be too bad…as long as she didn't want children.

Adam had seen firsthand the grief, the utter ripping and tearing children could do to their parents' hearts. He'd grown up hearing his aunt crying in the night, seeing his uncle's hollow eyes when Kurt had disappointed or hurt them yet again.

There was no way in hell Adam intended to go through that with children of his own. He'd done everything in his power to be the kind of son that would make his aunt and uncle proud, but it hadn't counted because their own son had been such a mess.

He stood, suddenly too restless to sit. If he intended to stay here a little longer and not tell Breanna exactly who he was, then he probably needed to buy some art supplies to continue the illusion of his subterfuge.

The kitchen was dark as he walked in, but light shone through the window and he knew the it was from Breanna's kitchen.

He'd noticed the night before that her kitchen window faced his with a scant eight feet or so between them. He certainly didn't want to peep, but found himself drawn to the window in spite of his good intentions.

Sure enough, her light was on, but there was no sign of her. However, what he saw outside her window fired a burst of adrenaline through him. A man stood on the top of her air-conditioning unit, framed against the house, obviously looking in.

Adam tore across his kitchen, through the living room and out his front door. He rounded the corner of the house, crashing through a bush.

The man whirled around at the noise and fell off the air conditioner. "Hey," Adam exclaimed as he raced toward him.

Adam never saw what the man used to hit him in the head. He only saw the man's arm arc out, then felt the tremendous blow that knocked him backward and to the ground.

He was vaguely aware of footsteps running away and an array of stars swimming in his head as he struggled to sit up.

"What in the hell is going on?"

The stars receded and he followed the sound of the voice to see Breanna, gun drawn and pointed at him.

"You've got to stop pointing that at me," he said, surprised that his voice seemed to be coming from some distance away. "One of these times you're going to shoot me and I'm a good guy."

The stars spun faster in his head, then blinked out and Adam knew no more.

CHAPTER FOUR

Breanna held tight to her gun and walked to where Adam lay flat on his back, his forehead bleeding profusely.

She had no idea what had happened. She'd entered her kitchen in time to see the back of a man's head at her window, then heard a commotion that had prompted her to grab her gun and check it out.

The blood on Adam's forehead didn't concern her as much as the large lump that was rising up, and the fact that he appeared to be out cold.

"Adam…" She leaned down next to him and tapped the side of his cheek. She divided her focus between him and the surrounding area.

It was obvious he hadn't done this to himself and she was aware that danger could still be anywhere, hiding in the shadows of the night.

She tapped him on the cheek again, this time a bit more forcefully. "Adam…wake up." He stirred and his eyes fluttered a couple of times, then remained open. With a groan, he sat up, his hand reaching for his head.

"We need to get you inside. Can you get up?" She wasn't about to relinquish her hold on her weapon. If he wanted some medical attention he was going to have to get up under his own steam.

"Yeah...I'm fine." He pulled himself up and to his feet, but it was obvious by his ghostly, pain-racked features that he wasn't fine. A deep moan eased from his lips.

She grabbed hold of one of his arms. "Come on, let's get you inside."

He didn't attempt to answer, but stumbled forward toward her place. The minute they entered her house, Breanna tucked her gun into her waistband, locked the front door, then led Adam into the bathroom off the foyer.

"Sit," she commanded and pointed to the stool. As he eased down, she opened the cabinet beneath the sink and pulled out a washcloth and some antiseptic cream. "What happened?" she asked as she wet the cloth.

"Somebody was looking into your kitchen window. I happened to look out my window and saw him. Ouch!" He jerked as she applied the cloth to the wound. "I ran out to see what was going on and he hit me with something."

"I think it was a broken brick. There were a couple next to the air-conditioning unit." She tried to focus on cleaning his wound and not on the fact that somebody had been looking into her house, not on the fact that Adam's body was warm and smelled so clean and male. "We should call a doctor. You were out for a minute or two. You probably have a concussion."

"I'm fine," he replied. "I think instead of calling a doctor, you should call the cops."

"Adam, I am a cop," she replied dryly. She finished

cleaning off the blood, revealing a small cut and a healthy sized goose egg. She applied some of the antiseptic cream to the wound. "I think you're going to live."

"Thanks, I was hoping that would be the prognosis." He smiled and suddenly she was aware of the small confines of the bathroom.

"Let me just get you a bandage. Head wounds are notorious for bleeding a lot." Once again she opened the cabinet under the sink and withdrew a Band-Aid. "I'm afraid cartoon characters are all I have."

He took it from her and smiled again. "I've always been fond of cartoons." He stood, still a bit unsteady on his feet.

"You put your Band-Aid on and I'll be out in the kitchen." She fled the bathroom, glad to get some distance from his overwhelming nearness. Even woozy and wounded, he was still far too attractive for her peace of mind.

And she needed to think...not about the length of Adam's dark eyelashes, not about the width of his broad chest or the evocative warmth of his skin, but why somebody would be peeking in her window.

For the first time since she'd moved into this house two years before, she walked into the kitchen and drew the curtains so they covered the window. She sat at the kitchen table and stared at the window.

Had he been there, watching her as she drank her tea? Had he peeked into other windows as well? Had he watched her as she curled up on the sofa and read or as she viewed her favorite television programs? She'd never thought of having an alarm system installed, but suddenly it didn't seem like a bad idea.

Thank goodness the bedrooms were all upstairs, making

it virtually impossible for anyone to peep unless they climbed the big tree in the front yard.

Adam entered the kitchen, looking rakish with the Band-Aid across the left side of his forehead. "I feel like a pirate with a cartoon character fetish," he exclaimed as he sat at the kitchen table.

"We probably should go down to the station and make an assault report," she said.

"Is that really necessary?"

She shrugged, then asked. "Did you see what he looked like?"

"Afraid not. It was dark and I didn't have a chance to discern features or even hair color, but I can tell you he wasn't quite as tall as me…maybe five-ten or five-eleven."

Breanna jumped up and got a pad and pencil from a drawer, then returned to the table. "It's probably nothing… maybe just a teenager or a nut…but I'll just jot down a few notes. Can you tell me what kind of a build he had?"

He frowned, the frown quickly becoming a wince as one hand shot up to touch his head.

"Maybe we should do this tomorrow," she said worriedly. "You really should see a doctor."

He dropped his hand. "I'm fine. I just have one hell of a headache, but that's to be expected after being smashed in the head with a brick. Maybe some ice would help."

"Of course." She got up once again and grabbed a dish towel from a drawer, then several ice cubes from the freezer.

She was self-consciously aware of his gaze following her movements and was grateful she hadn't yet changed into her nightshirt before the commotion had begun.

She handed him the makeshift ice pack, then again

returned to the chair opposite his. He pressed the towel against his head. "You asked me about his build."

She nodded. His eyes were the purest blue she thought she'd ever seen. Like drowning pools, they seemed to beckon her closer...deeper. A flood of warmth swept through her and she stared down at her notepad, trying to remain focused on what he was saying.

"...not fat, just kind of stocky. At least, that's the impression I got before I saw stars."

"So, about five-ten or so and rather stocky." She looked at him again. "Doesn't tell us much, does it? But, as I said before, it was probably just some kid." She frowned as she thought of the phone calls she'd received. Surely the two weren't connected, or were they?

"What?" Adam leaned forward and set the ice pack on the table.

"Oh, it's nothing," she said quickly, as if by convincing him she would also convince herself.

"Breanna." He reached across the table and covered her hand with his. Pinpricks of heat sparked in her hand and shot warmth up her arm. "You have a very expressive face," he said, "and right now it's telling me that there's something else that has you worried."

It worried her that she liked the feel of his big, strong hand over hers. It bothered her that through the mere touch of his hand, she somehow felt safe...protected.

"I've gotten a couple of strange phone calls the last two nights," she said and pulled her hand from beneath his.

He leaned back, a furrow of concern creasing his forehead. "What do you mean by strange?"

She explained to him about the two calls she'd received, about the woman singing the lullaby and then earlier that night when the man had called her a bitch.

She'd thought Adam's eyes to be the clear, crisp blue of a cloudless autumn sky, but when she finished speaking his eyes were a slate blue...darker...harder.

"Have you told anyone else about the phone calls? Anyone down at the police department or any of your family?"

"No. When I got the call last night, I just assumed it was a wrong number or a silly prank." She fought against a shiver as she thought of the hatred...the utter malevolence in the man's voice as he'd said that single word.

"Can you think of anyone you might have ticked off lately?" he asked.

She smiled wryly. "Adam, I'm a cop. I tick people off on a regular basis." Her smile fell and she frowned once again. "But I can't think of anyone I've ticked off that would play a tape of a woman singing a child's lullaby, then peep into my window."

Adam stood and grabbed the makeshift ice pack that was beginning to puddle on the table. He carried it to the sink, then turned back to look at her.

"What worries me about the window peeping is how easily the guy resorted to violence to get away. There was no warning, no hesitation when he swung that brick at my head."

"I know," she said. "That worries me, too." A pounding began in her head, a dull thud that threatened to intensify at any moment.

She pushed away from the table and stood. "Adam, I'm sorry you got hurt and I really appreciate your help, but we aren't going to solve this little mystery tonight and I'm exhausted."

Together they left the kitchen and walked out the

front door and onto the porch. "If you were a really good neighbor you'd offer to sleep with me."

She stared at him, certain she'd misunderstood what he'd just said. "Excuse me?"

He grinned. "You know, so that you could wake me up every hour and look at the pupils of my eyes. Isn't that what you're supposed to do with somebody who might have a concussion? What else did you think I meant?" His eyes held a knowing twinkle.

"I knew that's what you meant," she replied, wondering if her cheeks appeared as red as they felt. "But if you're that concerned about it, I highly recommend an emergency room at one of the local hospitals."

"I like my idea better." The twinkle in his eyes faded and his smile fell. "Breanna." He reached out and touched her cheek with his warm fingertips. "I'm right next door if anything happens or if you just get afraid. I can be over here in mere seconds."

He dropped his hand, murmured a good-night, then turned and disappeared into the shadows of the night.

Breanna stepped back inside and carefully locked the front door. Gazing at her watch she realized it was after eleven.

She should go to bed. Maggie was usually an early riser and Rachel wasn't officially on duty for the next two days. Sundays, Mondays and Tuesdays were Breanna's days off, then she worked four ten-hour shifts on the other days. However, those ten-hour shifts often became twelve- or fourteen-hour shifts when she was in the middle of a case.

She climbed the stairs and checked in on Maggie before going into her own room. As she changed into her night-shirt, her four-poster bed beckoned to her, but her head was too jumbled for sleep.

Instead she shut off her bedroom light and curled up in the overstuffed chair by the window.

From this vantage point she could see part of Adam's front yard and a portion of her own. The huge oak tree that brought birdsong and the sound of scampering squirrels into her window each morning obscured the rest of the view.

She still couldn't help but believe the phone calls were some kind of crazy mistake of some kind. Why would anyone play her a tape of a woman singing a lullaby? It made absolutely no sense.

What made even less sense were the thoughts that filled her head where Adam Spencer was concerned.

Why was she wondering what it would be like to sleep with him? She knew his skin would be warm against hers, knew that his scent would surround her. By even mentioning it in jest, he'd let her know that he was attracted to her.

With a sigh of irritation she got up from the chair and stepped closer to the window. She leaned her forehead against the glass pane. What would it be like to make love to Adam?

The question came unbidden to her mind, along with a tumble of related questions. Would he be a slow and sensual lover, relishing each touch, every caress?

Kurt had been the only lover she'd ever had, and although she'd believed herself to be deeply in love with him, she'd found their lovemaking to be vaguely unsettling...unfulfilling.

He'd always made love quickly, as if eager to get to the ultimate destination instead of enjoying the scenery along the way. She'd always been left with an emptiness inside. Would making love with Adam fill that emptiness?

She whirled away from the window and got into bed.

She was thinking crazy thoughts. Anyone would think that she'd received a blow to the head that had shot all rational thought straight out her ears.

She'd only known Adam for less than two days. She knew very little about him and certainly had no idea what kind of a man he was.

Yes, you do, a small voice whispered in her head. You know he's the kind of man to put himself at risk when he suspects trouble. She reached up and rubbed her cheek in the same place he'd caressed it. You know he has a gentle touch, the voice continued.

"Shut up," she said aloud. At that moment she heard the sound of car doors shutting, then a moment later the sound of her front door opening, then closing.

Footsteps whispered against the carpeting on the stairs as Breanna reached over and turned on her bedside lamp. A second later Rachel appeared in the doorway.

"Did I wake you?" she asked. "I was trying to come in quietly."

"No, you didn't wake me." Breanna sat up and patted her bed. "Come in and tell me all about your date."

With a wide smile, Rachel flew to the bed and bounced on the mattress, looking far younger than her twenty-five years. "It was the best day and night of my life," she exclaimed.

Thoughts of Adam receded as Breanna listened to Rachel telling about her date with David. "The picnic went beautifully. We ate, then went for a walk in the park. He's so easy to talk to. We talked about anything and everything."

"I told you that you'd have a great time."

Rachel's smile was beatific. "We did. In fact, when

the picnic was finished, we weren't ready to call it a day. That's when he suggested we see a movie."

"So, when are you seeing him again?"

"Next Sunday. We're going to church together, then out to dinner afterward."

"That's great," Breanna replied. "We had a bit of excitement around here tonight." She briefly told Rachel about the window peeper and Adam getting hit in the head.

"Oh, my gosh...is he all right?"

"He's fine. We iced his head and he insisted he didn't need to see a doctor. You haven't received any strange phone calls lately, have you?"

"Strange phone calls?" Rachel eyed her curiously. "What do you mean?"

"The past two nights I've gotten calls where I answer and somebody plays a tape recording of a woman singing 'Rock-A-Bye Baby.'"

Rachel gasped and one hand rose to the scar on her cheek as her eyes filled with tears of horror. "It's Michael...it's Michael and he's calling to torment me." She burst into tears.

Breanna quickly put an arm around Rachel's shaking shoulders. "Rachel, don't cry. As far as we know Michael is still in jail. Besides, why on earth would he be playing that song to torment you?"

"Because of the baby...because of our baby." Rachel grabbed for a tissue from the box on Breanna's nightstand.

"What baby?" Breanna asked in surprise.

Rachel wiped her eyes and drew a deep breath. "When I finally got up the nerve to leave Michael, I was three months pregnant. It was the baby that gave me the strength, the courage to finally leave. I'd allowed him to be abusive to me, but I couldn't allow him to hurt our baby."

"And so you left him," Breanna said.

She nodded and dabbed at her eyes with the tissue. "Somehow he found out I was pregnant and that's when the stalking began. Three weeks later I miscarried. The doctor told me it was possibly stress related. Anyway, I told Michael there wasn't a baby, that I'd miscarried."

"But, he didn't believe you," Breanna guessed.

"He thought I'd had an abortion. That last night when he caught up with me in the grocery store parking lot, he beat me up because I'd left him, but when he cut me, he said he was doing it because I'd let a doctor cut his baby out of me." She began to cry once again.

Breanna held her close and murmured the same kind of soothing sounds she did when Maggie cried. Her heart ached with the pain of what Rachel had been through.

She let Rachel cry until her tears were finally spent, then she placed her hands firmly on Rachel's shoulders and eyed her with all the confidence she could muster.

"Okay, here's the plan. First thing in the morning I'll get on the phone and find out if Michael Rivers is still a guest of the Oklahoma Department of Corrections. If he is, we'll find out if he has access to a phone, and if he is indeed making these calls. If he is, then we'll see to it that his telephone privileges are revoked."

"And what if he's not still in jail?" Rachel asked, fear darkening her eyes.

"Then I'll find out exactly where he is and what he's up to. One thing you have to remember, Rachel. You aren't the same woman you were two years ago. You're stronger, strong enough to deal with whatever you have to."

Breanna grabbed Rachel's hand and squeezed tightly. "The next thing to remember is that you aren't alone this time. You're living with a cop and there's no way in hell

I'm going to let anything happen to the best baby-sitter in the world."

A tentative laugh escaped Rachel. "Thanks, Bree."

The two women hugged, then Breanna stood and pulled Rachel to her feet. "Don't you worry about anything. We'll have some answers in the morning and will figure it all out then."

A few minutes later Breanna shut off her bedside lamp and settled into bed. Now that she knew about the baby Rachel had lost the phone calls made more sense. They were sick…and wicked, but they made sense.

It had to be Michael. He was about five foot ten and although he'd been on the thin side when he'd been convicted, Breanna knew the starchy prison food could quickly transform a thin man into a stocky one.

He'd been sentenced to three to five years and that had been almost two years ago. With good time served he could conceivably be out now.

It was a proven fact that he had a penchant for violence. He wouldn't have thought twice about hitting Adam over the head to save his own skin.

If he was out then he was probably on parole and hunting down Rachel, peeping in windows, would get that parole revoked in a second.

It has to be Michael, she thought. That was the only thing that made sense. If it wasn't Michael and the phone calls weren't meant for Rachel, but rather for herself, then it didn't make sense. And things that didn't make sense worried Breanna. They worried her a lot.

CHAPTER FIVE

"Tell the truth, Adam. You like taking care of my women after I dump them because it allows you to get close to women who otherwise would never give you the time of day. Face it, you're boring and you'll always be second choice when I'm around."

Adam bolted upright in bed, his heart thudding rapidly. The image of Kurt faded as sleep fell away. Sunshine streamed into the small bedroom, letting Adam know he'd slept later than usual.

He raised a hand to his forehead, pleased to discover the goose egg from the night before had diminished to a small lump.

As he got out of bed, he thought about the dream he'd had just before awakening. It wasn't so much a dream as it was a memory...a painful memory of the fight he and Kurt had had the last time they'd seen each other before Kurt's accident.

Adam had been giving Kurt hell for his treatment of his latest girlfriend, a young woman named Renata. Kurt had gone out with her three times, finally managing to sweet talk her into his bed. He hadn't called or spoken to her after his night of pleasure.

Renata had called Adam, distraught. She'd begged him to talk to Kurt, to see what she'd done wrong, how she could fix it. It was obvious her heart was broken, and Adam had confronted Kurt and an argument had ensued.

A few minutes later, Adam stood beneath a hot shower spray and resolutely shoved thoughts of Kurt away.

Instead, thoughts of Breanna blossomed in his head. He'd actually attempted flirting with her the night before with his little comment about her sleeping with him. He had no idea what had possessed him. He had no intention of forming any kind of permanent relationship in his life.

He shut off the shower and dried off. There was no denying the fact that he was intensely drawn to Breanna on a physical level. Her scent enticed him, the feel of her skin intoxicated him and the thought of tasting her lips electrified him.

However, to follow through on his physical attraction to her, knowing he would be offering her only a few nights of pleasure and nothing more, made him no better than Kurt.

Physical attraction aside, he was concerned about Breanna. The incident last night with the peeper had been bad enough, but coupled with the odd phone calls she'd received, he couldn't help but be concerned.

He pulled on a pair of jean shorts and a polo shirt, then went into the kitchen to make some coffee. He was surprised to see it was after nine. He'd definitely slept in.

He poured himself a cup of the fresh-brewed coffee

and carried it through the tiny living room and out the front door.

It felt odd not to be heading for his office, where phones rang, faxes transmitted and businesses depended on his firm to keep their books straight.

He couldn't remember the last time he'd sat and enjoyed a cup of coffee with the pleasures of a spring morning surrounding him. Most mornings he was up and at the office by six or six-thirty.

The sounds of an awakened neighborhood filled the air. A dog barked cheerfully in the distance as a bird sang a melodic tune overhead.

Adam's place in Kansas City was an apartment at the top of a high-rise building. He never heard neighborhood noises and now found himself enjoying the novelty of utter relaxation.

A slam of a door sounded from Breanna's place and he looked over to see Maggie exiting, her arms laden with a variety of items. She deposited her load in the shade of the big oak tree, then went back into the house only to return a moment later with another armful of things.

Adam sipped his coffee and watched curiously as she made three more trips in and out. By the time she was finished it appeared she'd brought every toy she owned from her room to the front yard.

She spread a sheet on the ground and began to organize the items on the sheet. As she worked, he could hear her singing. Although he couldn't quite make out the song, he found the sound of her sweet, childish voice infinitely charming.

He finished his coffee and set the cup on the porch. At that moment she saw him. "Hi, Adam." She waved at him with a bright, friendly smile. "Come on over."

Why not, he thought. He got up and ambled over to her. "I'm playing house," she said. "Wanna play?"

He was going to decline, but a wistfulness in her eyes called to him. "All right," he agreed. "What do you want me to do?"

"First you have to say hi to Mr. Bear." She gestured to the big brown stuffed bear that sat in a doll's high chair.

"How do you do, Mr. Bear?" Adam shook one furry paw. "It's nice to make your acquaintance."

"He says it's nice to make your 'quaintance, too. This is my table," she said and pointed to an overturned cardboard box. "Would you like to have a cup of coffee?"

"That sounds nice." He sat cross-legged on the sheet at the end of the box.

Maggie dug into a little pink duffel bag and withdrew a plastic cup and saucer. "Be careful," she said as she placed them before him. "It's very hot."

"Thank you." Adam pretended to sip from the cup. "You make great coffee."

Maggie's little smile faded as she gazed at him. "You have a boo-boo on your forehead. Does it hurt?"

"Only a little," he replied.

To his surprise she walked up to him, placed a tiny hand on each of his cheeks and soundly kissed his boo-boo. "There," she said with obvious satisfaction. "Kisses are like magical Band-Aids. They take the hurt away."

As she stepped away from him, Adam's heart expanded in a way it never had before. Oh, Kurt, he thought. You have no idea what you missed in not knowing this sweet little girl.

"Do you like ice cream?" Maggie asked as she set a cup and saucer in front of Mr. Bear.

"Sure. It's one of my most favorite things to eat."

"Alyssa has an ice-cream parlor in her bed-and-breakfast. She has chocolate marshmallow ice cream."

"I like strawberry," Adam replied.

"She has that, too." Maggie grabbed a cup and saucer for herself and sat at the opposite end of the box from Adam. "My friends, their daddies take them for ice cream sometimes." She sighed heavily. "But I don't have a daddy to take *me* for ice cream."

"Maybe I could take you for ice cream some time." The words left his mouth before he'd thought them through. What was he doing? The last thing he wanted was to become personally involved in Maggie's life. The last thing he wanted was to have any sort of emotional investment where she was concerned.

Her gray eyes sparkled brightly and she clapped her hands together. "For real? Do you promise?"

How could Adam deny her? "Sure, I promise."

"That would make me happy."

At that moment Adam saw Breanna seated on the front porch. He wondered how much of the exchange between him and Maggie she'd heard. "I think I'll go say hi to your mommy now," he said.

"Okay."

Adam pulled himself up and ambled to the porch, unable to help but notice how lovely Breanna looked in a colorful sundress that emphasized her bronze skin tones and dark eyes.

"Good morning," he said.

"I see you survived the night," she said and motioned to the wicker chair next to where she sat. Her eyes were dark, fathomless and Adam wished he knew what thoughts were flittering through her mind.

"Yeah, I survived."

"You realize you just made a fatal mistake."

He eyed her curiously. "What are you talking about?"

"You actually sat down and drank a cup of pretend coffee with Maggie. Now she'll expect you to play every time she sees you outside."

"I suppose there are worse mistakes I could make," he replied.

"You realize she won't forget that you mentioned taking her for ice cream. Kids have amazing memories and Maggie can be as tenacious as a pit bull."

"I made a promise...and I don't break my promises."

"How refreshing, a man who doesn't break promises," she said dryly. But, before he could reply, she continued. "Actually, I was going to go over to your place to talk to you this morning. I think maybe we've solved the mystery of the phone calls and the peeper."

"Really?" He listened with interest as she told him about Michael Rivers and Rachel and their suspicions that it was him who had been making the calls and spying on Rachel. "What have you found out about him?" he asked when she was finished explaining things.

She frowned. "He's out of jail. He got out a month ago. Apparently he moved to Sycamore Ridge, a little town just north of here." She gestured to the cordless phone on the chair next to her. "I'm waiting to hear from his parole officer to find out exactly where he is and what he's doing."

"Then what?"

"Then I go have a little talk with him. If he did these things, then he'll be back in jail so fast his head will spin." Her jaw was set with fierce determination.

"You won't go talk to him alone, right? You have a partner or somebody who goes with you on things like this?"

Logically, he knew she was a cop, trained to encounter

dangerous criminals and situations, but the thought of her confronting the man who'd hit him in the head with a brick, caused a stir of anxiety to fill him.

"I have a wonderful partner named Abe Solomon. He's a great guy and I trust him with my life." Her affection for her partner was evident in her voice.

Adam was surprised to feel a flicker of an alien emotion wing through him...an emotion that felt remarkably like jealousy. "So, you and your partner...you're tight?"

She nodded. "You have to be tight with your partner when you're a cop. It's kind of like a marriage...without the heartache and without the sex." Her cheeks pinkened slightly.

"You've been partners with this Abe for a long time?"

"For almost five years. He's planning on retiring in the next year or so and I hate to even think about it. It will be like losing my favorite uncle."

A wave of relief rushed through him. A favorite uncle... retirement...Abe Solomon was obviously considerably older than Breanna and definitely not a love interest.

What do you care, he mentally chided himself. She isn't a love interest of yours, either. She had been one of Kurt's women and that was the end of the story.

"I'd better get back," he said and stood, suddenly needing to be away from her.

"How's the painting? Have you started anything yet?"

He stared at her blankly for a moment, then remembered. "Oh...the painting...no, I haven't started on anything. I'm waiting for inspiration to hit." He stepped off the porch. "You'll let me know what you find out about this Michael Rivers guy?"

"Sure," she agreed. She stood and he couldn't help but notice how the dress clung to her curves.

"I'll see you later." He turned to escape, but nearly ran into Maggie, who looked up at him with a sweet smile.

"How about we go get some ice cream tonight?" she asked.

He wanted to say no. He felt off balance, torn between his attraction to Breanna and the knowledge that he didn't want to be attracted to her. But Maggie's eyes held the eagerness of anticipation and no matter what his personal baggage, he couldn't disappoint her.

He looked questioningly at Breanna, who frowned thoughtfully. "Of course, when I told Maggie I'd take her for ice cream, I intended you to go along as well," he said.

"I wouldn't allow it any other way," she replied.

"Mommy, you can't say no," Maggie exclaimed as if horrified by the very thought. "We'll have ice cream and it will be such fun!"

Breanna gazed at her daughter and in her eyes Adam saw the enormous love of mother for child. She looked from Maggie to Adam and he had the feeling that she felt just like he did…somehow reluctant to go and yet equally reluctant to disappoint Maggie.

"I suppose we could go for ice cream after dinner tonight," she finally said.

"Yea!" Maggie jumped up and down and clapped her hands together.

"Shall we make it about six or so?" he asked.

"That would be fine."

"I'll see you then." It's just ice cream, he told himself as he walked back to his house. It wasn't like he'd invited Breanna for a date or anything like that. This was about buying ice cream for Maggie.

As he picked up his cup and went back into the cottage, he wondered why it somehow seemed so much more complicated than just an ice-cream cone.

It was ridiculous. Breanna stood before the mirror in her bedroom and looked at her reflection. This was the third outfit she'd pulled on just to go get ice cream.

First the shorts had been too short, then the blouse had been all wrong. Now she wondered why she was spending so much time worrying about what she had on. She finally settled on a salmon-colored "skort" and matching sleeveless blouse. Brown sandals adorned her feet and although she had put on a little mascara, she refused to put on lipstick. That would make it too much like a date.

Checking her watch, she realized it was almost six. She left her bedroom. "Maggie, it's almost time to go." She found her daughter sitting on the foot of her bed putting on her shoes.

"This is going to be fun, isn't it, Mommy?" Maggie's eyes shone brightly. "It's gonna be just like having a daddy."

Breanna's heart constricted. More and more frequently Maggie mentioned the lack of a father in her life and Breanna ached with the void her daughter felt, a void she didn't have the power to fill.

"Maggie, you know Adam is just a neighbor, not your daddy," Breanna replied.

"I know. But I can pretend...just to myself."

"But no amount of pretending is going to make him your daddy."

"Mommy, I know that," Maggie replied with a touch of impatience. She got her last shoe on and stood. "I just sometimes wish I had a daddy."

As they walked down the stairs, Breanna thought about

Kurt and her heart grew hard and cold. How could a man so easily walk away from parenthood?

He'd left her when she was seven months pregnant, confessing that he'd jumped into the marriage and wasn't ready to be a husband or a father. She tried never to think about the other hurtful things he'd said when he'd walked away.

He'd left her a post office box number in Platte City, Missouri, and told her to send him the divorce papers there.

She'd sent him the divorce papers and every year at Christmastime she'd sent him a picture of the little girl he'd sired. She'd never heard a word from him and she hated him for not being man enough to be a father, and hated herself for choosing so badly when it came to a husband and father for her baby.

As she and Maggie left the house, she shoved away thoughts of Kurt, knowing that thinking about him always put her in a foul mood.

She and Maggie sat in the wicker chairs on the porch, waiting for six o'clock and Adam to appear. Maggie's face held the sweetness of childish anticipation as she wiggled in the chair.

Breanna leaned back and thought about that morning. As she'd sat here and watched Adam with Maggie, a bittersweet pang had exploded in her heart. As he'd pretended to drink Maggie's coffee she'd seen what life might have been like for her daughter if Maggie had had a daddy.

If Maggie had a daddy, there would be father-daughter moments that Breanna couldn't provide for her child. But Adam Spencer couldn't provide those moments, either.

He'd made it clear he wanted no children and he was only in town on a temporary basis. Besides, she wasn't in the market for a husband. She'd never again trust her own judgment where a man was concerned and refused to go through the process of finding not only a good man for herself, but a good stepfather for Maggie as well.

Speaking of men... Adam's door opened and he stepped outside, looking far too handsome in a pair of worn jeans and a short-sleeved blue pullover shirt.

"Adam!" Maggie cried as she jumped down from the chair. "We're ready for ice cream!"

"Good, so am I," he replied with a warm smile that made sunbursts of smile lines radiate from the outside corners of his eyes. His smile remained as he gazed at Breanna. "You want me to drive or can we walk?"

"Walk!" Maggie exclaimed.

Breanna stood and shrugged. "It's about ten blocks to the square, but it's a nice evening for a walk."

"Then walk it is," he replied.

Breanna and Adam fell into step side by side on the sidewalk as Maggie danced just ahead of them. The approach of evening brought a slight breeze that was pleasant and filled with the scent of spring flowers.

"Beautiful evening," he observed, as if reading her mind.

"We'd better enjoy them. Summer gets hot in Cherokee Corners. But, of course, you probably won't be here to suffer the heat of the late summer months."

"That's true. By July I'll probably be cooped up in my office in Kansas City, all dreams of being an artist dashed by a lack of any real talent."

She cast him a sideways glance, noting how his blue shirt brought out the clear blue of his eyes. "You don't sound too upset about the prospect."

"What? Of being back in my office? To tell you the truth, I like my work as the owner of an accounting firm.

I know most people think account work is boring, but I like not having surprises when it comes to my livelihood." He smiled again. "I'm sure your work in law enforcement is much more exciting."

"You'd be surprised at how much drudge work there is." She felt herself relaxing with each step they took and the easiness of the conversation flowing between them. "Much of my time is spent writing reports and reading files."

"But you work a prostitution detail. Doesn't that get a little dicey?"

"It hasn't yet," she replied. "Maggie, wait for us before crossing the street," she instructed, then looked back at him. "I've never had any problems working undercover prostitution. Sure, some of the men we arrest get really angry, but I've always got plenty of backup and I don't do any of the real arresting on those nights."

They caught up with Maggie, who was waiting for them at the corner. "Hold my hand," Breanna said and held out her hand to her daughter.

"I want to hold Adam's hand," Maggie replied and smiled up at Adam.

Adam looked surprised, but took Maggie's hand in his and the three of them crossed the street. "When you were little, did your mommy make you hold her hand when you crossed a street?" Maggie asked.

"Always," Adam replied.

"And did your daddy take you for ice cream?"

"Not that I remember. My daddy died when I was eleven years old," Adam said.

"That's sad," Maggie replied. "We don't know where my daddy is. He went away before I was borned and we haven't seen him since."

"So what kind of ice cream is everyone going to get?" Breanna asked, uncomfortable with the conversation's direction and attempting to change the subject.

"Strawberry," Adam replied, the expression on his face letting her know he knew what she was doing.

"Chocolate marshmallow with some sprinkles on top," Maggie exclaimed. "What about you, Mommy? What kind are you going to get?"

Breanna pretended to frown thoughtfully. "I don't know...maybe some artichoke ice cream."

Maggie's giggles rode the breeze. "That's silly, Mommy."

"Nobody eats artichoke ice cream," Adam added.

Breanna laughed. "Then maybe I'll just get vanilla."

As Maggie ran ahead, Breanna felt Adam's gaze lingering on her. "What?" she asked.

"Vanilla ice cream? That surprises me. I'd have figured you for something more exotic, more adventurous."

She laughed again. "Then you definitely have the wrong impression about me. I'm neither exotic nor adventurous. I'm just a vanilla ice cream kind of woman."

She fought a sudden edge of bitterness as she remembered that had been the problem with her marriage. Kurt had been disappointed to discover she was a vanilla ice cream kind of woman.

They entered the city square and the red-and-pink awning of the ice-cream parlor came into view. The ice-cream parlor comprised the bottom floor of the three-story building. The upper two floors were The Redbud Bed and Breakfast, so named after the state tree.

Tall, round glass-topped tables dotted the interior, but Maggie clambered up on a stool at the counter, behind which Alyssa stood dipping up ice cream and old-fashioned charm in equal doses. Breanna slid onto the stool next to Maggie and Adam took the one next to Breanna.

"Hey, what have we here?" Alyssa leaned across the counter and tapped Maggie on the nose. "I'll bet somebody is ready for a two-story chocolate marshmallow cone."

Maggie giggled. "Yup," she exclaimed. "And Mommy wants vanilla and Adam wants strawberry."

Alyssa smiled at Breanna, then at Adam. "How are you two doing?"

They small-talked for a few minutes, then Alyssa served them their cones. Maggie got hers first, then Breanna and finally Adam. As Alyssa handed Adam his, her smile wavered slightly and Breanna thought she saw a whisper of worry darken her cousin's eyes. It was there only a moment, then gone.

As they ate their ice cream, they visited both with Alyssa and with the people who came into the shop. But Breanna couldn't stop thinking about that look she'd seen in Alyssa's eyes.

"Would you mind watching Maggie," Breanna asked Adam when they'd finished their cones. "I'd like to talk to Alyssa alone for just a minute."

"Sure," he agreed. "Come on, Maggie, let's go outside and you can tell me what kind of stores there are around here."

When they were gone, Breanna leaned over the counter and eyed her cousin intently. "You felt something when you handed Adam his cone," she said. "And don't try to deny it. I saw it in your eyes."

"It was nothing really," Alyssa protested. "Just confusion...I felt confusion. Honestly, Bree, I don't think it's anything to worry about...at least where Adam is concerned." She frowned.

"But…?" Breanna pressed.

Alyssa's brown eyes seemed to grow darker. "I still have a feeling of something bad happening…something horrid." She forced a laugh and waved her hand as if to dismiss the entire topic. "I've been feeling off-kilter for days now. I can't figure it out."

"Is there anything I can do to help?" Breanna asked.

Alyssa smiled and shook her head. "Unfortunately, no." She grabbed a sponge and wiped down the counter. "I keep thinking maybe the moon is in a weird phase or my hormones are out of whack."

"You aren't pregnant, are you?"

Alyssa laughed. "That would be a little difficult since I'm not even dating anyone right now." She reached across the counter and touched Breanna's hand. "Just be careful, Bree. I've got a bad feeling and I don't know what it's about or who it concerns."

"I've got to go," Breanna said, worried by Alyssa's warning and realizing her daughter was outside with a man she knew little about, even though she could see them from where she stood.

"Call me," Alyssa said as Breanna ran out the door.

She approached where Adam and Maggie were seated on a bench. Maggie was pointing to various shops and chatting like a magpie and Adam had a bemused smile on his face.

He stood as she approached. "I now know which store sells the best toys, who has the cutest clothes and what clerks are cranky."

"I told him about Mrs. Clairborn," Maggie explained. "I told him she was a witch!"

"That's not nice to say," Breanna replied, although secretly she agreed with her daughter. Katherine Clairborn was a mean-spirited witch.

But her head was still filled with Alyssa's warning. Be careful. Be careful of what? Of Adam? Now that she thought about it, she'd received the first strange phone call the night he'd moved in next door. Coincidence? Or something more sinister?

"Breanna?"

She flushed, realizing she'd been staring at him. "We'd better start back home. It's getting dark."

"Are you okay?" he asked softly as they headed for home.

"Fine," she replied in distraction. It made no sense for Adam to have made those calls to her, and he certainly hadn't hit himself over the head with the brick the night before. It was all so confusing.

"I'm worried about Alyssa," she finally said, watching as Maggie hopscotched ahead of them.

"What about her?" he asked.

She frowned, wondering how much to say, how foolish it might be to trust him given Alyssa's words of caution. But, no matter what her head said, her heart told her he was a man who could be trusted.

"Alyssa is special…or cursed, depending on what school of thought you come from."

"I don't understand. What do you mean?"

They walked slowly as night fell, casting shadows outside of the pools of light created by the streetlamps they passed.

"Alyssa has suffered visions since she was a small child."

"You mean like psychic stuff?" Even in the darkening of night she could see his eyes holding a hint of incredulity.

"You can believe it or not, but I can tell you that it's very real," she said defensively.

"I have an open mind when it comes to the possibility of such things," he replied. "Is that what happened at the barbecue the day I met her?"

"Yes. Usually immediately after having a vision she falls unconscious for several minutes." They turned onto the street where their houses were midblock.

"Did she have some sort of vision about me?" he asked.

She shot him a quick sideways look. He almost sounded guilty. "Why do you ask? Do you have something to hide?"

He laughed, but she thought it sounded rather forced. "Only the usual human weaknesses. I just figured if Alyssa had a vision of my unexpected demise, then I should know so I can get my things in order."

Maybe I'm reading too much into Alyssa's warning and seeing boogeymen where there are none, Breanna thought to herself. "Actually, Alyssa did warn me to be careful. She isn't getting any specific visions, but she has some bad feelings."

"About you and Maggie?" All laughter was gone from his voice.

"She isn't sure who or what it's about. Maggie...slow down," she exclaimed.

"Does she get these bad feelings often?"

Breanna sighed and fought against a wave of anxiety that suddenly threatened to overwhelm her. "The last time she had these kinds of bad feelings, my brother-in-law crashed his car through the guard rail of the Sequoya Bridge. He drowned in the Cherokee River."

"You don't think her bad feelings now have anything to do with the phone calls you've been receiving, do you?" He placed a hand on her arm and they stopped in place.

His eyes held her gaze intently. "What did you find out about Michael Rivers?"

A blood-curdling scream rent the air.

"Maggie!" The scream ripped through Breanna's heart as she ran toward the house.

Maggie stood on the sidewalk and pointed to the big oak tree, her eyes huge and her lower lip trembling. "Look, Mommy."

Hanging from the branches was a pink plastic cradle. On the branch just beneath it, strung by a noose around his neck, hung Mr. Bear.

CHAPTER SIX

Instinctively Adam scooped Maggie up into his arms and pressed her head against his neck in an attempt to shield her from the sight of her beloved stuffed bear.

"Rachel," Breanna whispered softly and ran to the front door. Adam watched as she fumbled in her purse for her keys and her gun.

A wave of helpless frustration raked through him as he fought his desire to grab the gun from Breanna and go inside. He wanted to protect her from whatever horror or danger that might be in the house.

Maggie wept against his neck. He patted her back, his gaze intent on the front door as he willed Breanna to reappear unharmed.

When the bough breaks, the cradle will fall, and down will come baby, cradle and all. The words from the old standard lullaby played and replayed through his head.

He glanced back at the tree with its gruesome

ornamentation. It took a sick mind to do something like that…a twisted, sick mind.

Relief flooded through him as Breanna stepped out onto the porch. "She's not here and it doesn't look like anything has been disturbed inside."

"Mommy, can we get Mr. Bear down?" Maggie asked as she raised her tear-streaked face. "He doesn't like it up there."

"We can't take him down right now, honey. We're going to let Uncle Clay look at him first," Breanna said. Adam noticed she'd brought a cordless phone with her out of the house.

"Besides," Adam said, "maybe Mr. Bear was up in that tree looking for a bee's nest filled with honey."

"Bears like honey," Maggie said softly. Her lower lip trembled ominously. "But, Mr. Bear is so scared."

Adam sat down on the porch and cuddled her on his lap as Breanna sat next to him and began to make phone calls.

She called Rachel's cell phone first and reassured herself that Rachel was really okay. Apparently the young woman had left the house with friends soon after the three of them had left.

Breanna then called her brother, Clay, and her sister, Savannah. By the time she'd finished making her calls, Maggie had fallen asleep in Adam's arms.

"Want me to take her?" Breanna asked.

"No, she's fine," he replied. He'd never held a sleeping child in his arms before and the utter trust that Maggie had displayed in him by allowing herself to fall asleep touched him. Besides, he enjoyed the sweet smell of her, the snuggly warmth of her little body against his.

"I don't want to take her up to her room until Clay has

a chance to look things over. When we left here to get ice cream, Mr. Bear was on Maggie's bed."

"So somebody got into your house." A rush of anger filled Adam.

"The back door lock is broken," she replied.

"Why don't you have an alarm system?" Adam asked. "I would think as a cop you'd have one."

She sighed. "This is a small town, Adam. I only know a handful of people who have alarm systems. I've never had a problem, never felt afraid..." Her voice trailed off.

He wondered if she'd been about to say "until now."

For a few moments they sat silent, the surrounding night silent as well, as if holding its breath in anticipation of what might come next.

"What did you find out about Michael Rivers?" he asked.

"I spoke to his parole officer and got his address. The parole officer said he's doing quite well, has a full-time job and is keeping his appointments. He's even gone through an anger management program."

"But that doesn't mean he isn't trying to terrify Rachel," Adam said.

"No, it doesn't. I had planned on getting my partner to drive to Sycamore Ridge with me tomorrow to meet with the parole officer and talk to Michael, but apparently Abe is out of town."

Before Adam could reply, a car roared down the street and into Breanna's driveway. Rita was out the passenger door and on the porch before Thomas had shut off the engine.

"Savannah called and explained everything," she said as Adam and Breanna stood. "We thought we'd come and take Maggie home with us." Rita looked at the tree, then turned back to them, her dark eyes glittering in the silvery moonlight. "Perhaps it is Raven Mocker come to take a life."

"Don't start with Indian ghost stories," Thomas said to his wife as he held out his arms to take the sleeping Maggie from Adam. He looked at Breanna. "We'll keep her with us for a couple of days. I put in a call to Glen and told him to get the guys on the force on this."

"Dad, you didn't need to call the chief," Breanna protested. At that moment another car and a van sped down the street toward them.

"We'll get this little one out of here," Thomas said. "Call us in the morning." He and Rita went back to their car as Savannah and Clay arrived on the scene.

Clay said nothing, but immediately pulled out a pad and a pen and gazed up at the tree. Savannah walked over to where Adam and Breanna stood. She gave her sister a kiss on the cheek, then offered a small smile to Adam. "Nothing like a little excitement to top off an evening, right?"

"I could live with a little less excitement," Adam replied.

They all turned as a patrol car pulled up against the curb. A big, burly man stepped out of the driver door and a second officer got out of the passenger side. Adam instantly felt Breanna's tension level rise.

"That's Chief Glen Cleberg," she said softly as she left the porch to greet her boss.

"What have we got here?" Cleberg's voice was like a boom of thunder in the otherwise silent night. He placed his meaty hands on his hips and stared up at the tree, then eyed Breanna with dark, beady eyes. "Looks like you've managed to stir up somebody."

In that single instant, Adam decided he didn't much like

the chief of police. He joined Breanna, fighting a sudden impulse to throw his arm around her shoulder in a show of solidarity.

"I can't imagine what I would have done to instigate this," Breanna replied. Cleberg grunted.

Adam decided to step into the conversation. "Adam Spencer," he said and held out his hand to the chief. "I'm staying in the cottage next door."

"Haven't seen you around town," Cleberg said as he gave Adam's hand a firm shake.

"I've only been here a couple of days," Adam replied.

"Adam's an artist. He's staying here for a while to soak up some of the Native American culture," Breanna explained.

Glen frowned, the gesture creating a deep furrow in his broad brow. "Hope you don't think this kind of nonsense is normal in our town."

"Not at all. From what I've seen, Cherokee Corners is a charming place."

Glen grunted again, this time a grunt that implied satisfaction. He looked at Breanna once more. "You want to tell me about this?"

Adam remained silent as Breanna explained about the phone calls, the incident with the peeper and her suspicions that it might be Michael Rivers trying to terrorize Rachel.

"I thought he was in prison," Glen said.

"He's been out for a month. He's living in Sycamore Ridge," Breanna replied.

"That little punk better not be coming into my town and pulling any stunts." Glen drew a deep breath and looked back at the tree, where Clay had finished taking pictures and was in the process of climbing up to remove the items from the branches.

He looked back at Breanna. "You know there's not a lot we can do about a couple of phone calls and a Peeping Tom that nobody got a good look at."

"What about this?" Adam gestured to the tree.

Glen shrugged. "I suppose we could arrest whoever did it on a trespass charge, maybe stretch it to vandalism, but I got to tell you, we don't really have the manpower to follow up on this." He raked a big hand through his salt-and-pepper hair. "The town has grown faster than our police department, and unfortunately more people means more crime."

"I know how understaffed we are," Breanna said. "I hadn't intended to bother you with this. Dad shouldn't have called you."

"He was right to call me. I need to know what's going on with my officers."

"Whoever did this got into Breanna's house," Adam told the chief. "She said the back door lock has been broken."

"Why in the hell didn't you tell me that to begin with," he replied with more than a touch of irritation. "Savannah…Joseph, get inside and clear the house. The perp was inside at some point."

"I already checked the house," Breanna said.

Cleberg frowned. "Maybe you missed him. Maybe we'll get lucky and he's still in there. I'm in the mood for an arrest tonight."

Breanna's sister and the officer who had arrived with Chief Cleberg drew their weapons and entered the front door. By this time Clay had retrieved the items from the tree and had placed them in paper bags. He drew off his gloves and joined them.

"I might be able to pull off some fingerprints on the plastic of the cradle and if I'm lucky maybe some fiber evidence or something off Mr. Bear," he said.

Breanna frowned. "Be careful with Mr. Bear. Maggie will be devastated to learn that he's not here."

Clay nodded. "There doesn't seem to be any footprint impressions around the base of the tree. The ground is too dry and the grass too thick." He held up the two paper bags. "I'm going to put these in my van, then try to lift some prints around the back door lock."

"Looks like you Jameses have this scene under control. When Joseph finishes up, we'll be on our way. Make sure you write up a report on this," Cleberg said to Breanna.

A few minutes later as Joseph and the chief were leaving, Rachel arrived home. Adam watched as Breanna hugged her.

"Go pack a bag," Breanna instructed her. "I don't want you staying here for the next couple of days until we can sort this all out."

Savannah walked up and grabbed Rachel by the arm. "You can stay with me, Rachel. I've got plenty of room and would enjoy your company."

Rachel looked shell-shocked as Savannah led her into the house to pack her things. It didn't take them long, then together they left.

Adam and Breanna went into the house where Clay was just finishing up dusting the back door. "A lot of smudges," he said, "and not a single clear print or partial. I'm ready to take a look at Maggie's room."

Adam followed brother and sister through the living room and up the stairs to Maggie's room. Adam glanced across the hall and into the room he suspected was Breanna's.

Decorated in earth tones with splashes of sky blue accents, the room emanated peace and serenity. The bed was rumpled and unmade and a vision flashed in Adam's mind...a vision of a doe-eyed Breanna, her body warm and supple with slumber.

He yanked his gaze away from the room, afraid his visions would career out of control. Instead he turned and watched as Clay examined the room with the eyes of an expert crime scene investigator.

Adam found himself entranced by the childhood magic that surrounded him. This was a place of innocence, of sweet dreams and fairy tales. It smelled of Maggie, that curious blend of peaches and sunshine.

But Adam knew better than to be fooled by the aura of innocence. Children were like ticking time bombs, just waiting for the trigger that would detonate a heartful of sorrow for their parents.

He'd just about decided while they were having ice cream to tell Breanna who he was and why he was here. He'd also made the decision to call his aunt and uncle and tell them about Maggie. But this changed everything. He wasn't going to do anything until they got to the bottom of who was tormenting Breanna. Until this mess was cleared up, he intended to go nowhere and tell nobody anything.

Clay spent several moments just looking around the room, then turned to Breanna. "Are you certain Mr. Bear was in here before you left the house?"

Breanna frowned and raked a hand through her long, shiny hair. "I thought so...but now I'm not so sure."

"Is it possible she left him outside after she played house earlier?" Adam asked.

"I don't know...I guess it's possible," she admitted hesitantly.

"Bree, I don't want to tear up this room looking for evidence of an intruder, given the fact that nobody has been hurt and you believe this all has to do with Rachel," Clay said.

"I don't want you to tear up the room," she replied. "It would upset Maggie, but it would definitely upset the chief if you use the lab for something like this."

"I'll dust the cradle for fingerprints and let you know what I find. There isn't much else I can do here."

The three of them left the bedroom and went back downstairs to the front door. Clay leaned over and kissed his sister on her forehead, nodded to Adam, then left.

"A man of few words," Adam observed.

She nodded. "Clay has always been the silent type. Mom worries about him because he has no life outside of his work."

"It must be fascinating work."

"He keeps busy. He's only one of three crime scene investigators." She looked around in distraction.

Adam wasn't sure whether she expected him to leave, or wanted him to stay. He hated to leave her alone, knew that despite her calm facade the sight of Mr. Bear and the cradle had shaken her up badly.

"We need to see about bracing up that back door until you can get the lock fixed," he said.

"You're right." She frowned, suddenly looking vulnerable and exhausted. She sat in one of the chairs at the table.

"Why don't you put on some coffee and I'll go check in the shed. I think there are some boards in there we can use," he suggested.

"You don't mind? I mean, you don't mind staying for a little while?" she asked.

Mind? If he could, he'd stay the night, hold her in his

arms and keep her safe. If he could, he'd kiss away the worry on her brow, stroke the tension from her cheek. He'd make love to her so sweetly, so gently, she'd forget about everything but being in his arms.

Stupid thoughts, he scoffed inwardly. "Not at all," he replied. "I'll just go get that lumber."

He went through the broken back door and with the aid of the back porch light, entered the small shed. What was he thinking of? Why would a woman who had married a man like Kurt ever want anything remotely romantic from a man like him?

"You've always wanted to be me." Kurt's voice filled his head. "You've always wished you were my parents' son, you've always wished you had my life and you've always wanted my women."

Adam frowned with irritation and pulled out a board that could be used to brace the back door. "Shut up," he muttered to the ghost in his head.

He wanted to dismiss the words that Kurt had once said to him, but somehow, in a deep, dark place in his heart, he was desperately afraid that they were true.

Breanna was grateful for Adam's presence as she made a pot of coffee. She had never spent a night alone in the house. She'd always had the company of her daughter and now the silence pressed in on her…the empty silence devoid of Maggie's very breath.

She'd seen a lot of terrible things in her short career as a vice cop, but nothing had prepared her for the sight of Mr. Bear hanging from the tree. She was both angry and more than a little bit afraid. What did it all mean? Why would somebody do something like that?

"I think I found the perfect board," Adam said as he

came through the back door. "I can brace it against the cabinet, then just hammer in a couple of nails into the wall. After you get the lock fixed, I can patch the nail holes for you."

"A jack-of-all-trades," she said.

He grinned. "And master of none."

As he got to work on the back door, she poured them each a cup of coffee, then sat down at the table and watched him work.

She could smell him, that male scent that she found so attractive. It was funny, although she didn't miss Kurt, there were little, silly things she missed about having a male in the house...like the fragrance of minty shaving cream lingering in her bathroom, or a sleepy early-morning cuddle against a warm, strong body.

She missed pouring two cups of coffee instead of one in the mornings, missed the small talk just before drifting off to sleep.

"There," Adam said as he finished with the door. "I hope you intend to call a locksmith first thing in the morning."

"I do." She gestured to the chair opposite hers where his coffee awaited him. "Would you like cream or sugar?"

"No, this is fine," he assured her as he sat and wrapped his hands around the mug. "Are you all right?"

His eyes were filled with such sweet concern that she felt a sudden sting of unexpected tears in her own eyes. She swallowed hard against them. "It's funny, I've seen some horrible things in my time as a cop, things much more horrid than a stuffed bear hanging from a tree. But I have to confess, seeing Mr. Bear hanging from that noose shook me up."

"Of course it did." His soft, deep voice flowed over

her like a welcome balm. "These bad things you've seen before…they were never so intimately personal, they were never an implied threat to people you love."

"I just can't help but believe this is intended to harass Rachel and that Michael Rivers is behind it. It's the only thing that makes any sense." She took a sip of her coffee, then continued. "I'm going to go to Sycamore Ridge to-morrow morning and have a little chat with Michael."

"Then I'm going with you."

She looked at him, surprised by the firmness in his statement. "Adam, I can't ask you to do that."

"You didn't ask." He leaned back in the chair, looking perfectly at ease and filled with confidence. "You said your partner is unavailable. I can at least tell by looking at Michael if he resembles the size and shape of the man who slammed me over the head. Besides, I can't let you go confront him alone. I can stand next to you and look menacing."

Despite the seriousness of the events of the night and Breanna's worry, his statement struck her as funny. A burst of laughter escaped her lips. "I'm sorry." She shook her head and drew another deep breath. "You're such a nice man, Adam. I just can't imagine you looking menacing."

The blue of his eyes darkened as his jaw muscles clenched, transforming his features into something hard and dangerous. "If somebody is threatening the people I care about, then I can not only look menacing. I can *be* downright menacing."

Breanna's breath caught somewhere in the center of her chest. He looked so intense…almost dangerous, then he smiled and the threatening danger on his features trans-formed back to simply deadly handsome.

"You realize you can't do anything to him. In fact you shouldn't even speak to him."

He shrugged. "That's fine. We can let him think I'm your strong, silent, slightly-pissed-off partner."

Breanna laughed again, enjoying the release of tension the conversation brought. "All right, then as soon as the locksmith comes and fixes the lock, we'll take off for a drive to Sycamore Ridge."

For a moment they sipped their coffee in silence. "I like your house," he said, breaking the silence before it became too long and uncomfortable. "Your decorating is so warm and inviting."

A flush of pleasure swept over her at his words. "Thank you. I wanted to make it nice, but it was also important to me that I make it a home for Maggie. I didn't want her raised in an apartment and I managed to make a nice arrangement with the landlord." She looked at him curiously. "You mentioned that you were raised by an aunt and uncle. Did they have children of their own?"

"A son." He shifted positions and took another sip of his coffee.

"That must have been difficult, at eleven years old trying to become part of a family."

"They were good people...still are. The first couple of years were a little rocky. I missed my own home, my room...my parents."

She tried to imagine what that would be like...to be eleven years old and have everything you know and love ripped away from you. She'd been so lucky to have the support, the love of her family both throughout her childhood and now. "And were you easy to raise or tough?"

"Easy," he said without hesitation. He frowned, a touch of pain darkening his eyes. "As good and loving as my aunt and uncle were, I worried that if I gave them any trouble or heartache, they'd send me away." His frown melted away as his lips curved up in one of his sexy grins. "I know now that it was a totally irrational fear, but it was one my cousin liked to play on."

"That doesn't sound nice," she observed.

He shrugged. "That's enough about me," he replied. "I heard in town that there's some kind of a powwow next weekend at the Cultural Center. Are you involved in that?"

"Minimally, in that I will be there. Actually Maggie is part of the ceremony. She'll be one of the shell-shaker girls on Sunday." She smiled at Adam's bewilderment. "The traditional dance of the Cherokee is the Stomp Dance. There is a leader, assistants and a couple of shell-shaker girls. The girls wear leg rattles made out of turtle shells filled with pebbles."

"Sounds fascinating," he replied. He leaned forward, bringing with him his wonderful scent. "And were you once a shell-shaker?"

She smiled. "Both Savannah and I were shell-shakers."

"And what about Clay? Did he have a role in the ceremonies?"

Her smile faded as she thought of her brother. As much as she loved him and as supportive as he'd always been, she didn't feel like she really knew him. "When he was young he took part in the ceremonies and events, but when he was a teenager he refused to do anything that spoke to his Cherokee blood."

"Why?"

Breanna laced her fingers around her mug. "We aren't sure why. It's been a great source of pain for my mother and I think it's a source of torment for Clay, but it's something he won't talk about."

"When your mother arrived this evening, she said something curious…about a raven?"

"Raven Mocker." As she told him the legend about the most dreaded of all the Cherokee witches, who robbed the dying of their life, she couldn't help but notice that his curly dark hair looked like it would be soft and silky to the touch.

She fought the impulse to reach out and tangle her fingers in his hair, pull his lips to hers and enjoy the excitement, the splendor of a first kiss.

"I've kept you way too long," she said and stood. "It's getting really late." She suddenly needed to be away from him, was afraid that tonight she was too vulnerable, felt too alone.

To her relief, he stood as well and together they walked to the front door. He opened the door and stepped out on the porch. She joined him there, her gaze automatically going to the big tree now devoid of strange fruit.

"Are you sure you're going to be okay?"

"Sure. I'm a single parent and a cop. I'm strong and capable."

He placed two fingers beneath her chin, forcing her to look up at him. "I know all that," he said softly. His eyes were silvery from the illumination of the nearby streetlamp as he gazed at her intently.

In that instant she knew he was going to kiss her. She knew it was foolish to allow it, knew it was a complication she didn't need in her life. However, even knowing all this, she leaned forward, lips slightly parted to accept what he offered.

Tentatively at first, his lips touched hers, almost reverent with whisper softness. It wasn't enough. She wanted more. She reached up and did what she'd thought about doing earlier…tangled her fingers in his silky hair.

His arms wrapped around her and pulled her closer as his kiss became more confident. Masterfully, his mouth plied hers with heat as he pressed her more intimately against the length of his body.

The sensation of his strong, warm body holding her tight, and the cool night air surrounding them was erotic and as his tongue touched hers a ball of heat burst into flames in the pit of Breanna's stomach.

His tongue swirled with hers as his hands moved up and down her back. As his hands cupped her buttocks and pressed her into him, she felt that he was fully aroused. Her knees weakened and her entire body felt like it was nothing more than liquid fire.

It was as if foreplay had begun the moment they met and now a single, first kiss had exploded into a well of desire that threatened to consume her.

His mouth left hers and trailed down her neck. She dropped her head back to allow him better access to the hollows of her throat, the sensitive skin beneath her ears. Each nip and teasing touch of his lips spun her desire higher…deeper.

She wanted him. It was as simple as that. She wanted him in her bed, holding her, making love to her. She trusted him, this man who had appeared out of nowhere. A man who had taken a brick in the head for her protection, who, when he looked at her, reminded her that she wasn't just a single parent and a cop, but a woman as well.

It was obvious he wanted her, too. Pressed so intimately against her, it was impossible to ignore his desire. His lips captured hers once again, this time hot and hungry.

In the back of Breanna's mind was the knowledge that

the house was empty. If he came inside and stayed the night, nobody would know. Rachel was gone…Maggie wasn't home. This single night could be theirs.

"Adam," she gasped breathlessly as the kiss ended. "Come back inside with me." She leaned back to look at his face and what she saw in his eyes only confirmed that he wanted her as much as she wanted him. "Come inside and spend the night. Make love to me."

He seemed to stop breathing as his hungry eyes searched her face. He stepped back from her and drew a deep breath of the cool night air. "Breanna, there is nothing I'd rather do at the moment than come inside and spend the night with you."

He dropped his arms from around her and stepped back. Immediately Breanna felt bereaved, as if his embrace had been giving her the very air she breathed and now she was lacking in oxygen.

"But I don't want to make love to you on a night when you've had a shock and might not be making the decision under the best of circumstances." He leaned forward and brushed her lips with his, then stepped back, regret darkening his features. "Believe me, Breanna, if I was certain I wasn't taking advantage of you, I'd be in your bed in a heartbeat."

If she'd wanted him before, his words merely increased her desire for him. But she knew he was right, and a wave of embarrassment swept through her as she realized how forward she had been. "You're right," she said, looking away from him. "I'm not myself and I'm not thinking as clearly as possible."

Again he placed fingers beneath her chin and forced her gaze to his. "I don't know about you, but the moment I met you I was attracted to you. But I don't want us to make a mistake in the heat of a moment when you aren't yourself and thinking clearly." His blue eyes were so earnest, so filled with caring, she found it impossible to maintain any embarrassment.

Although she believed she'd wanted to make love to him, there was a part of her that was grateful he'd called a halt to the prospect. She had ridden an emotional roller coaster from the moment she'd seen Mr. Bear hanging from the tree. She wasn't sure that wasn't playing into her desire for him to stay the night.

"We're still on for tomorrow," he said and dropped his hand from her face. "Going to Sycamore Ridge and finding Michael Rivers."

She nodded. "As soon as the locksmith gets finished."

He leaned forward and kissed her gently on the cheek. "Then I'll see you tomorrow." With those words, he turned and left her porch.

She watched until he disappeared into his house, then she went back inside and carefully locked the door. Once again the silence of the house pressed in around her as she walked up the stairs to her bedroom.

The house was silent, but her head was filled with chaotic noise, the sound of confusing thoughts banging against one another.

As she undressed, she tried to make sense of her thoughts. There was no denying she was vastly attracted to Adam Spencer. From the moment she'd encountered him in her driveway in the middle of the night, she'd felt drawn to him.

She'd felt the exact same way when she'd first met Kurt, although not quite as intense as with Adam. And, like Adam, she'd thought Kurt was a nice guy, a man of moral fiber, a man who could be depended on through thick and thin.

She'd been horribly wrong about Kurt, and how did she know she wasn't horribly wrong about Adam? She had told herself she would never again get her heart involved with a man, she had promised herself she would never subject Maggie to a stepfather.

He wasn't offering a lifetime commitment, a little voice whispered in her head. It was one night of desire shared, one night of passion spent. What was wrong in allowing herself that much?

She got into her nightshirt and got into bed. Closing her eyes she replayed those moments spent in Adam's arms, with his lips so hot and hungry against her own. It had been so long since she'd allowed herself to remember that she was a woman with a woman's needs. Adam had made her remember.

She stretched against the sheets, exhaustion weighing heavy now that her hormones had settled down. She closed her eyes and had almost drifted off to sleep when the telephone rang.

CHAPTER SEVEN

Walking away from a warm, willing Breanna was the most difficult thing Adam had ever done in his life. But he knew he couldn't make love to her without her knowing the truth about him. And the truth was he was the cousin of a man she hated.

He entered the cottage and sank down on the sofa, waiting for the blood to stop pulsating in his veins, for his heartbeat to return to a more normal pace.

Deciding he was better off pacing than sitting, he stood and began to move back and forth across the tiny living room floor.

He couldn't remember the last time he'd wanted a woman as badly as he wanted Breanna. Kissing her, holding her in his arms had only managed to flame the fires of desire higher and even now he wanted nothing more than to complete what they had begun…to make love to her.

What had Kurt told her about his family? Had he

mentioned who his parents were…that he had a cousin who'd been raised with him like his brother? Adam knew Kurt often rearranged the reality of his family to suit his personal interests.

It didn't matter what Kurt had told Breanna. Adam had to tell her the truth. The longer he put it off, the angrier she would be when he finally did tell her.

Although he had no intention of forming any lasting relationship with her, he wasn't the kind of man to sleep with her under false pretenses. Once he told her the truth, he'd probably never have a chance to make love to her. But he'd rather never have the opportunity to be with her than to be with her with a secret between them.

He flopped on the sofa and raked a hand through his hair in frustration. There were times he wished he could be more like his cousin, times he wished he could take his pleasure as he pleased and never suffer consequences or a pang of guilt. But he couldn't. It simply wasn't in his makeup.

He got up from the sofa and went into the bedroom. He needed to stop thinking and just go to sleep. Tomorrow he would tell Breanna the truth and face whatever consequences came.

It didn't take him long to fall asleep and his dreams were filled with visions of Breanna. In those dreams he was in her bed and her naked skin was pressed against his. Her scent had eddied in the air, driving him half-insane.

They'd made love with a feverish need, a wild abandon, and he awakened with the taste of her lips on his, the scent of her filling his head and the memory of his erotic dreams as vivid and fresh as if they were reality.

It was just after six and the sun was just peeking above the horizon. He grabbed a cup of fresh-brewed coffee and sat outside on his front porch, trying to forget the dreams of the night before.

It was hard to believe that it was just the night before that he and Breanna and Maggie had gone for ice cream. If somebody had told him a month ago that he would take a woman and her child out for an ice-cream cone and he'd enjoy it, he would have laughed in their face.

But he had enjoyed it. Watching Maggie maneuver a double dip of chocolate marshmallow ice cream had been a delight.

As she'd licked and savored the frozen treat, she'd shared little bits of herself with Adam. Her favorite color was pink, but she loved purple as well. Her favorite food was chicken nuggets and, of course, ice cream.

As she chatted, it was obvious that despite her young age she was already well educated in the ways of the Cherokee. She told him about a Cherokee marble game called *Di-ga-da-yo-s-di,* which was played on a field and used marbles the size of billiard balls.

Watching Breanna eat her ice cream was a delight of another kind. With each lick of her tongue on the cone, Adam had felt his blood pressure rise just a little bit more.

He stood and went back into the kitchen for a second cup of coffee, trying to shove sensual thoughts of Breanna from his mind.

He returned to the porch and was still seated there sipping coffee when a panel truck with the words Lock, Stock and Barrel pulled up in front of Breanna's house.

A thin, gangly young man got out of the driver's side and loped to Breanna's front door. He was invited inside and returned to his van a few minutes later. Armed with a toolbox, he went back inside.

Adam stood and stretched, working out the kinks that

had appeared while he'd sat. It wouldn't take long for an expert to change out the broken lock on Breanna's back door and when the locksmith was finished, Adam knew she'd be ready to make the drive to Sycamore Ridge.

A half an hour later the locksmith pulled away and Adam walked over and knocked on Breanna's door. When she opened the door, concern instantly washed over him.

She looked exhausted, with shadows beneath her eyes and her features taut and drawn. "Good morning," she said with what appeared to be a forced smile.

"What's wrong?" he asked as he followed her through the living room and into the kitchen.

"Coffee?" She gestured him to the table.

He nodded in distraction. "Breanna, has something happened?"

She poured two cups of coffee, then joined him at the table. "I got another phone call last night."

"The same as before? The lullaby?"

She nodded and wrapped her hands around her mug, as if seeking some kind of warmth. "Only, when the song finished playing, a man's voice asked me if I liked the presents he'd left for me."

"You didn't recognize the voice?"

She shook her head. "It sounded raspy and muffled, like he was trying to disguise it."

"Is that all he said?"

"That's it. He hung up before I could say anything."

Adam frowned thoughtfully. "I'm assuming you don't have caller ID."

A faint smile curved her lips. "I don't have cable television or caller ID or an answering machine. My father teases me about being stubborn when it comes to welcoming technology into my home."

"You can't afford to be stubborn right now," Adam observed. "While we're out today we'll get you a caller ID box."

"But can't people do something to block their numbers from showing up on those things?"

"Sure, but I'm hoping this nutcase isn't firing on all cylinders and will make a call without blocking the number."

"I guess it's worth a try," she agreed, then looked at her watch. "It's about an hour's drive to Sycamore Ridge. I guess we could go ahead and take off."

"Fine with me," Adam agreed. He finished his coffee and stood. "Are you sure you're up to it?"

She smiled again, this time fully. "I will be. In the best of times I'm not a morning person. I don't really fully wake up until about ten."

"Then I think it's best if I drive to Sycamore Ridge. I don't want a half-asleep woman behind the wheel of the car when I'm a passenger."

"It's a deal. Just let me get my purse and I'm ready to go."

Minutes later they were in Adam's car headed away from Cherokee Corners. The scent of her perfume filled the small confines of the car and he found himself drawing deep breaths to savor the attractive smell.

In spite of the dark smudges beneath her eyes that indicated a lack of sleep the night before, she grew more animated with each mile that passed.

Adam realized it was going to be difficult keeping things light and easy between them when all he wanted to do was touch her warm skin once again, taste the sweet honey of her mouth.

"Maggie called me first thing this morning and told me that Grandma and Grandpa were fighting over what to have for breakfast. Apparently my mother had already thrown the frying pan at my father."

Adam glanced at her in surprise. "And that doesn't upset you...upset Maggie?"

"My parents' battles are legendary in Cherokee Corners. Maggie knows they fuss and fight and that's just the way they are. By the time she hung up the phone Mom was using the skillet to fry up bacon and eggs."

"I never heard my aunt and uncle exchange a cross word with one another," he said. Although he couldn't count the times he'd heard his aunt cry and his uncle curse over Kurt's antics.

"Different strokes for different folks," she replied. "Some people like the stimulation of good-natured arguments and fighting. Personally, I'd prefer a relationship more like your aunt and uncle's...if I was looking for a relationship, which I'm not."

"Why not?" he asked and cast her another curious glance. "I mean, you're young and beautiful and I'm sure there are lots of men in Cherokee Corners who would like to have a relationship with you." As these words left his lips, he felt a pang of jealousy as he thought of her with any man other than himself.

"I tried the relationship thing once and found it distinctly unpleasant."

"But that doesn't mean another relationship would be unpleasant," he protested.

"Logically, I know that," she agreed softly. She stared out the passenger window for a long moment, then continued. "The idea of doing the dating game is repugnant to me, especially as long as Maggie is so young. I don't want her to be a kid that has 'uncles' drifting in and out of her life."

She turned back to look at him, her dark eyes hinting at inner pain. "Even though logically, I know not all men are like Kurt, I gave him my heart and my trust and he betrayed me. It's hard to trust again, to put your heart on the line and be vulnerable." She cocked her head and eyed him curiously. "So what's your story? You've said you have no plans for a wife or children. Did your heart get kicked by a hard-hearted woman?"

"No, nothing like that." He frowned, trying to figure out how to reply to her, trying to look deep within himself to find the answer. "I don't know, I guess I haven't had much time for any kind of a real relationship. My aunt and uncle loaned me the money to start up my accounting firm and my focus for the past several years has been on that. I finally managed to pay them back last year."

"But that doesn't answer why you don't want a wife and kids." She grinned teasingly. "You're young and handsome. I'm sure there are lots of women who would want a relationship with you."

He laughed. "Maybe there'd be women chasing me down if I was a little more exciting. Women seem to like bad boys. I'm an accountant, for crying out loud."

She laughed as well, her gaze warm on him. "I think bad boys have been greatly overrated."

"Definitely," he agreed and once again focused his attention on the road.

How could he begin to explain that he'd decided long ago never to have children who could break his heart, dash his dreams, destroy his hopes for them?

How could he explain to her that there had never been time for women of his own, that in the hours he wasn't at his office or sleeping, he was dealing with Kurt's messes. Bailing him out of jail, helping him pay legal fees, hiding him from jealous husbands, Adam had had no chance to have a life of his own, he was too busy trying to keep Kurt out of trouble.

So what was stopping him now? He had no answer and was somehow grateful when they pulled into the city limits of the tiny town of Sycamore Ridge, forcing him to concentrate on directions to Michael Rivers's apartment rather than the deep-seated reasons he refused to get a life—a woman—of his own.

Adrenaline raced through Breanna as Adam parked down the street from Michael Rivers's apartment building. Sycamore Ridge was a dusty, depressed town. Half of the stores on Main Street were boarded up, their facades weathered to the color of the dust that blew in the air.

The apartment building where Michael lived was a depressing row of flat-roofed living establishments. Trash littered the front, flowing out of metal trash cans that sat near the cracked sidewalk.

Breanna made a courtesy call on her cell phone to Michael's parole officer, letting him know she intended to question Michael about some threatening phone calls. The parole officer let her know it was his day off and it was fine with him as long as he didn't have to be there.

"Now remember, you can't say or do anything. You just leave it to me," Breanna said to Adam as they got out of the car. She reached for the navy blazer she'd brought with her and put it on over her jeans and white blouse. She pulled her gun from her purse and tucked it into the blazer pocket.

"Are you expecting trouble?" Adam asked, worry lines creasing his forehead.

"No, but I know better than to go into an unknown

situation unprepared." She smiled. "Don't look so worried. This is just routine stuff."

However, as she and Adam approached apartment 3D, Breanna knew this was anything but routine. She was an off-duty cop taking a civilian with her to question an ex-con without her boss's permission.

She knew the crime wasn't big enough to warrant this, but she'd be damned if she'd allow Michael Rivers to cause Rachel and herself another day of fear.

She was intensely aware of Adam next to her and she shot a surreptitious glance his way and saw that his jaw was clenched tight and his eyes were narrowed as if in anticipation of trouble. She had a feeling that despite his easygoing, good guy appearance, Adam was a man who could handle anything that came his way. He made her feel protected despite the fact that she was the one who had a gun in her pocket.

The door to apartment 3D had once been a burgundy color, but age and abuse had turned it into the brownish red of old blood. Breanna knocked briskly as tension ripped through her.

Michael would know her on sight. She had been instrumental in his arrest for the assault on Rachel. She'd testified at his trial. He would not be happy to see her again.

There was no answer to her knock. "Maybe he isn't home," Adam said.

"He's probably still in bed. His P.O. said he works the evening shift at a convenience store." She knocked once again more forcefully.

"Hang on," a disgruntled deep voice yelled from inside. A moment passed then the door flew open. Michael Rivers stood in the doorway, clad only in a pair of jeans he'd obviously hastily pulled on. His dark eyes narrowed as he saw Breanna.

"Hello, Michael," Breanna said. He was just as she'd remembered him, except on the day he'd been sentenced he'd had shoulder-length dark hair. Now, his head was shaved. A tattoo of a skull and crossbones decorated his upper left arm.

"What the hell do you want?" He glanced behind him, then stepped half-out of the doorway, the door held firmly in his hand.

"I just want to talk to you for a minute or two."

Michael's gaze shot to Adam. "And who the hell are you?"

"If I wanted you to know my name, I would have introduced myself," Adam said, his voice hard as Michael's gaze.

Michael snorted. "Cops...they got all the answers. So what the hell you bothering me for?"

"You been visiting Cherokee Corners? Maybe having some phone contact with Rachel?" Breanna asked.

He raised his eyebrows. "You think I'm stupid? If I go to Cherokee Corners, it's a violation of the condition of my parole and as far as getting in touch with Rachel..." He snorted again. "Not interested. I got me a new life and a new woman." He opened the door and looked back inside. "Hey, Alison, get out here."

A young, hard-looking blonde appeared in the doorway. Michael slung an arm around her slender shoulder and pulled her tightly, possessively against him. "This is Alison. We're gonna get married in a couple of months... once I'm on my feet. I don't need to talk to Rachel and I never want to step a foot into Cherokee Corners again."

"Where were you last night between the hours of seven

and midnight?" Breanna asked. There was a sinking feeling deep in her heart, in her soul.

"At work. Check it out, lady cop. I worked from 5:00 p.m. until after one. If you're trying to pin something on me, you're out of gas."

"I will check it out," Breanna said coolly. "But if I find you're causing problems for Rachel or if I see the end of your nose in Cherokee Corners, I'll have you back behind bars so fast it will take two weeks for your tattoo to find you."

"You done hassling me?" he asked arrogantly.

"For now," she replied.

"But that doesn't mean we won't be back," Adam added.

Without another word, Michael pulled his girlfriend back into the apartment and slammed the door shut.

"Pleasant fellow," Adam said as they walked back to his car.

"Yeah, I guess Rachel proves your point about women having a weakness for bad boys...only in Michael's case there were no redeeming qualities whatsoever." She tried not to show her distress as she played and replayed in her mind every nuance of her conversation with Michael Rivers.

She slid into the passenger seat as Adam got in the driver's side. He started the engine, then turned to look at her. "I'm assuming you want to check out the convenience store where that punk works."

She smiled at him. "Keep this up, ace, and you'll be an excellent candidate for the police academy."

"Thanks, but I think I'll keep my day job."

"You wouldn't want to be a cop anyway. The hours are awful and the pay stinks. Besides, one day you'll paint a picture that will earn you great riches and respect in the art community."

"So where's this convenience store?" he asked abruptly.

"It should be just ahead on the left," she replied, her thoughts going back to the conversation with Michael. As much as she wanted to believe he was lying, that it had been him who had made the phone calls and hung the things in her tree, her gut instinct told her Michael had told her the truth.

"You know, I'm pretty sure Michael wasn't the man peeking into your windows," Adam said. "The man I saw was taller...bigger. Is it possible the window-peeper has nothing to do with the calls? Maybe some horny teenager or just your ordinary creep?"

"I guess it's possible," she said. "But a horny teenager or an ordinary creep wouldn't have been so quick to hit you upside the head with a brick. Whoever it was, he could have killed you."

Adam pulled into the convenience store parking lot. "It looks like we're the only customers," he said. "Maybe I'll help the local economy and buy a soda. Want one?"

"Why not?" They got out of the car and walked into the gas station quick stop. Adam went directly to the coolers in the back while Breanna asked the kid behind the counter if a manager was in.

"Hey, Joe...somebody out here wants to talk to you," the kid yelled.

A big man, belly hanging over an ornate turquoise belt, lumbered out from the back room. He offered Breanna a big smile until she flashed her badge, then his smile fell and he emitted a long-suffering sigh. "Yeah, what can I do for you, Officer?"

"Michael Rivers...did he work for you last night?"

"Yeah, he was here. Worked from about five until after one."

"Were you here as well?" Breanna asked as Adam joined her at the counter, two soft drink cans in his hands.

"What's the point of having help if I got to be here all the time with them?"

"Then, how do you know he was here?" Breanna countered.

He pointed a pudgy finger to a camera in the ceiling. "Every night I load a tape and every morning I watch it. You'd be surprised how some of the hired help will try to rob you blind."

"You had problems with Rivers?" she asked.

"Nah. He shows up on time and stays late if necessary and so far he seems honest enough." He scratched his belly. "Sodas are on the house," he said to Adam, then looked back at Breanna. "Anything else I can do for you?"

"You have a copy of this past week's schedule for Michael?" she asked.

"Hang on, I can get you one." He disappeared into the back and returned a moment later with a sheet of paper.

"We appreciate your help," Breanna said and she and Adam left the store.

The minute they were back in the car and on the road to Cherokee Corners, Breanna stared at the copy of the work schedule for the convenience store. A knot of apprehension twisted in the pit of her stomach.

"According to this, on the nights and at the times I got those phone calls, Michael was at work."

"Is it possible he might have called from work?" Adam asked. She could tell by the tone of his voice that he was thinking the same thing she was…if it wasn't Michael Rivers tormenting Rachel, then was it possible it was somebody trying to torment *her?*

CHAPTER EIGHT

The drive from Sycamore Ridge back to Cherokee Corners was accomplished in relative silence. Adam felt Breanna's worry wafting from her, but he had no soothing platitudes to offer her.

"It's after eleven," he said as they entered the city limits. "How about we grab some lunch out, then we can pick up that caller ID box for you."

"That sounds good," she agreed.

"You need to direct me to the best place in town for lunch."

"I'm assuming you're talking about someplace between a drive-up window and coat and tie required."

He smiled at her. "You're reading my mind." He was glad to see her return his smile, her features less tense than they'd been moments before.

"Red Rock Café on the city square has a really nice lunch buffet," she offered.

"Then Red Rock Café it is," he agreed.

Twenty minutes later they faced each other across a table, plates heaped high in front of them. "I always eat too much when I come here." She looked at her plate as if she had no idea how all that food had gotten on it.

"I'm obviously no slouch when it comes to the 'my eyes are probably bigger than my stomach' department," he replied and gestured to his overfilled plate.

As they began to eat, it was as if they'd made an unspoken pact not to discuss anything unpleasant.

They talked of the books they had read, surprised to discover they both shared a voracious appetite for mysteries. She shared with him some of the Cherokee legends and they discussed the tragic history of the Trail of Tears.

Adam loved watching her as she talked, her features animated and her eyes shining. He envied her her strong sense of identity, the pride she took in belonging to a group of people who saw themselves as caretakers of the earth.

They lingered over coffee and he wondered if she was as reluctant as he was to walk out of the restaurant and back into the complications of life.

"Thank you," she said as they left the restaurant.

"For what? You insisted we go dutch."

"Thank you for letting me ramble on about nothing to keep me from thinking about everything."

"It was purely selfish on my part," he assured her. "I enjoy listening to you."

Her gaze was soft and warm. "You're a nice man, Adam Spencer."

He wasn't a nice man, he thought a few minutes later as he watched her talking to a salesman in the phone department of a discount chain store.

He wasn't a nice man at all. As she listened to the

salesman going over the features of the various caller ID products, Adam wondered when he would have the chance to kiss her lush lips again.

As she was paying for the machine they hoped would lead to the man making the phone calls...the man who had hung poor Mr. Bear by a noose, Adam wondered what it would be like to make love to her, to caress every inch of her body until she writhed with want...with need.

Despite her quietness on the way home, he'd been intensely aware of her in the small confines of the car. Her fragrance, the combination of clean mingling with the evocative scent she wore filled the car. It had been impossible for him not to have been affected by it.

"Want some help connecting this?" he asked as they pulled into his driveway.

"If you don't mind. I've already confessed to you that I'm technology-challenged."

He didn't tell her that connecting it was simple. They got out of the car and went into her house. He carried the sack with the caller identification machine. "The first thing you need to decide is what phone jack you want it hooked up to."

She frowned thoughtfully as she took off her blazer and laid it across the back of the sofa. "Both times he's called it's been late...minutes after I've gone to bed. Maybe we should put it on the phone jack in my bedroom."

Adam thought of the bedroom he'd seen the night before, the rumpled bed sheets that had momentarily filled his head with hot visions of lovemaking.

He steeled himself for the sensual barrage of entering the intimacy of the room where she slept...where she dreamed.

"Excuse the mess," she said as she entered the room

ahead of him and hastily pulled up the bedspread. "After years of being told to make my bed, my secret rebellion is that once I left my parents' home, I stopped."

"Don't apologize," he replied. "I don't care what your bedroom looks like." Which of course wasn't true. He found everything about the room fascinating and wondered what secrets about her he could glean by looking around. The walls were a light beige and held an array of paintings he guessed were by the woman she'd told him about. A large, intricate dreamcatcher hung on the wall over her bed.

Although the bed was unmade, the rest of the room was in impeccable order. The only item on the dresser was a wooden jewelry box neatly centered on a sky-blue scarf, letting him know she was a woman who didn't like clutter.

She slept on the left side of the bed. The nightstand on that side held a small reading lamp, a copy of a newly released mystery paperback, the telephone and a clock radio. The nightstand on the other side of the bed held a stunning array of silk flowers in an earthen vase.

"Adam?"

"Oh...sorry." He realized she was waiting for him to get to work. He sat on the edge of her bed to pull the caller ID from its carton, his fingers feeling clumsy and awkward.

Here, amid the covers where she slept, the scent of her seemed to waft in the air with enough potency to seep into his very pores.

"Is there anything I can do?" she asked.

"Just stay out of my way," he said more brusquely than he'd intended. If she came too close he was afraid he might grab her and tumble with her to the bed to finish what they had begun last night.

He was both grateful and disappointed that she did as he bid, moving across the room to lean with her back against the dresser.

He finally managed to get the caller ID box out of its carton and quickly plugged it into the wall jack and the phone into the back of the box. "That's it," he said.

She eyed him dubiously. "Are you sure? That seemed terribly easy."

"Actually, it was all very difficult. Only a man of my expertise and intelligence could have done it and made it look easy." He strove desperately for a lightness of tone to stymie the rising tide of desire that threatened. "I hope you're quite impressed."

"Oh, I am." She pushed off from the dresser and walked toward him. The look in her eyes, her loose-hipped saunter as she approached where he stood at the side of the bed made his heartbeat quicken.

She stopped when she stood no more than an inch away from him. "Thank you, Adam. Thank you for hooking up my caller ID box and for going with me to Sycamore Ridge." She leaned into him and he was lost.

Despite every intention he had to the contrary, his arms wound around her and pulled her tight against him. It was impossible not to kiss her eagerly parted lips, impossible not to fall head-first into a vortex of desire too powerful to avoid.

Her heart beat with the rhythm of his own... fast...frantic. They tumbled on the bed and Adam had the sensation of drowning, as if he were utterly powerless against the waves of passion that pounded him.

Her mouth was hungry against his as her hands moved up beneath his shirt to caress the bare skin of his back. It was as if fire resided in the tips of her fingers and Adam was lost in the flames.

He moved his hands down her back until he got to the bottom of her blouse, then back up again inside her blouse. Her skin was velvety soft and a moan ripped itself loose from deep in his throat.

The kiss, that seemed to last not long enough, ended as she pulled slightly away from him and began unbuttoning her blouse.

Someplace in the dark recesses of his mind a small voice whispered a warning, but at that moment her blouse fell open and the sight of her perfect breasts clad only in a pale pink lace bra stifled the tiny voice.

Moments later she was in his arms once again, this time her blouse and lacy bra on the floor next to his shirt. His hand cupped one of her breasts, his thumb raking over her turgid nipple.

His mouth kissed down her jawline, lingered in the sweet hollow of her throat, then moved to capture one of her nipples.

She gasped and her fingernails bit into his back. He teased her with his tongue, laving first one then the other breast.

He pressed his hips against hers and she arched up to meet him, the friction of her jeans against his half stimulating and half tormenting.

It wasn't until her fingers touched the top button at the waistband of his jeans that he suffered a single moment of clear, rational thought.

He grabbed her hand and groaned, not moving a muscle for a long moment. She froze as well. The room was silent except for their rapid, openmouthed breathing. "Adam?" she finally said.

How he didn't want to halt what had been about to happen. How desperately he wished he could make love to her and not worry about any consequence. "Breanna... we need to talk."

She looked at him incredulously. "Now? I mean... it can't wait?" Apparently the expression on his face answered her question. She moved away from him and reached down to grab her blouse, a frown of worry furrowing her brow.

He didn't answer for a moment, but instead got up from the bed and grabbed his shirt. He pulled it on, then looked at her, trying not to notice that her breasts were fully visible through the sheer white material.

"Adam...what is it?" she asked.

He averted his gaze and drew a hand heavily across his jaw, wondering how in the hell to tell her who he was and what had brought him to Cherokee Corners. It suddenly struck him that not only did he have to confess who he was, but he was the one who was going to tell her that the man she had married and divorced, the man who was Maggie's father, was dead.

She had no idea what was going on, but dread raked through her as she waited for Adam to talk to her. Her heart still pounded with the memory of his kisses, his sweet touch. Her body still experienced the languid warmth of imminent lovemaking. What could he have to tell her that was so important it had caused him to stop what they had been about to do?

"Why don't we go downstairs," he said, his gaze still not meeting hers.

"All right," she agreed, disquieted by the fact that

124   LAST SEEN...

whatever he had to tell her, he didn't want to do it in her bedroom.

He followed her down the stairs to the living room where she sat anxiously on the edge of the sofa and he remained standing by the fireplace hearth.

She felt oddly disconnected, as if half of her was still upstairs in his arms and the other half was waiting for a shoe to drop soundly on her head. She just couldn't imagine what form the shoe would take.

He rubbed a hand across his lower jaw, a gesture that had become familiar to her in the brief time she'd known him. It indicated deep thought...and stress. She wanted to scream at him to speak, wanted to demand he tell her what was so important it had interrupted their lovemaking.

He drew a deep breath and looked at her, his eyes a dark, slate blue. "Remember I told you that my parents died when I was eleven and I was raised by an aunt and uncle?"

She nodded with bewilderment.

He moved from the fireplace to the opposite side of the sofa and sank down wearily, as if the weight of the world had crashed down onto his shoulders.

"Adam?" She leaned forward and placed a hand on his arm. "What is it? Tell me."

"The people who raised me were Kurt's parents."

For a long moment his words didn't compute. Kurt? Why was he talking about Kurt? When the connection was made, it crashed through her with a thunderous roar. She jerked her hand back from him and jumped to her feet, myriad emotions ripping through her.

Confusion was the emotion most readily identified, but just beneath the surface simmered a stir of anger along with an overwhelming sense of betrayal. "You're Kurt's cousin?"

He nodded and a rolling dread poured through her with a nauseating intensity. "What are you doing here? What do you want? Why in the hell are you here? And why didn't you tell me who you were from the very beginning?"

He jumped at the sharpness in her voice and stood, his hands out as if to appeal to her. "I'm sorry I didn't tell you," he said. He drew another heavy sigh. "I wanted to get to know you and was afraid you wouldn't give me the chance if you knew who I was."

Dropping his hands to his sides, he sat back down and patted the sofa next to him. "Please, Breanna, give me a chance to explain."

She didn't want to hear what he had to say. He'd lied to her, perhaps not outright, but through omission by not telling her immediately of his relationship to Kurt. Knowing now who he was changed everything she'd thought about him, tainted every moment she'd spent with him. "You haven't told me why you're here," she said. She didn't move from her standing position, refused to sit next to a man whose actions were now all in question.

"I'm here because I promised Kurt I'd look in on you and Maggie and make sure you both were all right." His gaze seemed to caress her and in their depths she saw a sadness she didn't understand. "I made the promise to Kurt moments before he died."

The shock of his words forced her to sink back down on the edge of the sofa. "Before he died?" she echoed the words faintly.

"Two weeks ago Kurt died from injuries he sustained in a motorcycle accident."

He fell silent, as if to allow his words to sink in. Dead.

Kurt was dead. How was that possible? She'd always some-how believed that Kurt was the kind of man who ran too fast through life for death to ever catch up with him.

She was surprised to feel a sudden sting of tears as she thought of the man she had married and divorced.

A well of grief swept through her, not for herself, but for Maggie, who would now never have the opportunity to have any kind of a relationship with her father.

It was also grief for Kurt. Even though he had walked out on her and told her he didn't care about having a rela-tionship with his child, someplace deep in Breanna's heart she'd hoped he'd change his mind, but death had stolen that possibility away.

He'd missed out on knowing the wonder and delight of his daughter. She drew a deep breath and quickly swiped at the tears that had fallen.

"His last wish was that I come out here to Cherokee Corners and check on you and Maggie," Adam continued.

She embraced a new anger as she gazed at him. "Fine. You're here. You've checked. And as you can see we're both just fine." Her sense of betrayal emerged as she stood once again. She'd trusted him and once again she realized her trust in a man had been sadly misplaced. Bitterness ripped through her. "Tell me something, Adam. Was it the way you and Kurt were raised that made you both want to bed a half-breed?"

He gasped and his eyes widened in shock. He jumped up from the sofa. "Don't talk that way," he exclaimed.

"Why not? That's the way your cousin spoke to me." She stopped herself from going back to that time, back to the hurtful things Kurt had said to her. She didn't want to go back there. "Just go, Adam," she said wearily. "You've done what you promised Kurt you would do. Your mission is complete."

"Not exactly," he said, not moving from his position. "There's the matter of Kurt's parents. Aunt Anita and Uncle Edward don't know about Maggie yet, but I'm sure…"

Breanna held up a hand to stop him. "Anita and Edward? Anita and Edward Randolf are Kurt's parents?"

He nodded and once again shock ripped through her. She knew who Anita and Edward Randolf were…she'd read articles about the dynamic millionaire and his wife. They were high-society, benefactors of the arts and a variety of charities in Kansas City.

"Kurt told me his parents were dead," she said numbly. He'd told her a lot of things about his parents, none of it good. "He told me they died in a car accident the year before I met him." God help her, she didn't know what to believe about anything and anyone…especially Adam Spencer.

"They're alive and grieving the passing of their only son. Knowing about Maggie would help ease some of their pain."

Breanna felt as if she'd been cast into a dark, fathomless sea where nothing was familiar and as it should be. Kurt was dead…his parents were alive… Adam was his cousin and now each and every one of Adam's actions since she'd met him took on new meaning.

Again she reached for the anger as she thought of Adam's kisses…his caresses. He'd made her think he cared about her, but he'd obviously had ulterior motives. He didn't want her. He wanted Maggie for his grieving aunt and uncle. And everything she knew about the Randolfs frightened her.

"I don't want you telling them about Maggie. Maggie and I are doing just fine. We don't need them in our lives…." Her heart hardened with anger…with fear.

"Breanna…" he protested.

"And I want you out of here now." She walked to the front door and opened it. "Get out, Adam. We have nothing more to say to each other."

He stood, obviously reluctantly. "I have a lot more to say," he countered. "I need you to know that I regret not telling you the truth the night that I met you in your driveway. I need you to know that no matter what you're thinking now, I didn't mean to hurt you. That's why I couldn't make love to you…not without you knowing the truth."

"Gee, I'm glad you cleared it all up. Thanks," she said coolly. "And now, get out."

He advanced toward the door and she stepped aside to allow him to pass. She didn't look at him, found that it hurt too much.

He stopped directly in front of her and she knew he wanted her to look at him, wanted her to see the appeal in his eyes. Exhaustion overwhelmed her…sheer mental exhaustion. "Please…" she said softly without raising her gaze from the floor. "Please…just go."

She held her breath and expelled it only when he walked out the front door. She closed the door after him and leaned on it heavily, tears once again burning hot in her eyes.

Too much…her head ached from trying to wrap around all the information she'd learned. And most of that information had been positively stunning.

She shoved off from the door, locked it, then went back to the sofa and sank down on the cushions. She grabbed a throw pillow and hugged it to her chest, as if the cushioned softness could staunch the ache in her heart.

Kurt was dead. The love she'd once believed she had for him was long gone, banished beneath the weight of broken dreams and unfulfilled promises. But just because she didn't love him anymore didn't mean she didn't grieve over his death.

She'd always held out a tiny modicum of hope that eventually Kurt would grow up and be a man, take responsibility not for her, but for their daughter. The crushing of that hope was painful.

The information that Kurt's parents were not only alive and well, but were the renowned businessman Edward Randolf and his wife, Anita, filled her with fear.

Over the nine months that she had known Kurt, he had occasionally spoken about his parents. He'd told her that they had been people who worshipped their money, who liked to possess things, but had little use for people.

On the day he'd left her, he'd mentioned that it was a good thing his parents were dead because they'd never stand for a half-breed raising their grandkid.

It was the memory of these words that now stirred a fear deep in her soul. The Randolfs had enough money to get what they wanted and if they decided they wanted Maggie, she had a feeling they'd find a way to get her. This thought was so terrifying, she shoved it away as more tears flowed.

Instead, she thought of Adam, who had come here with a specific purpose in mind and had woven his way into her life under false pretenses.

In just three short days, he'd made her care for him, made her believe that she could trust him as she'd never trusted a man, other than her father, before. She'd trusted him so much she'd been willing…eager to make love with him, share an intimacy she'd guarded intensely since Kurt's defection.

It had all been lies. He was in her life not because he cared about her, but because he'd been doing a duty, fulfilling a promise to a dead man. He was in her life because he wanted to give his grieving aunt and uncle the gift of her daughter.

She swiped at her cheeks, bitterness filling her. Four days ago her life had seemed so uncomplicated. She worked her job, assured that Maggie was well cared for by a loving nanny. On her days off she spent time with her daughter and her family and the biggest worry she had was whether she'd ever be able to get Maggie to try something other than chicken nuggets when they ate out.

She closed her eyes, wishing away the disturbing phone calls, the news that Kurt's parents were alive and most of all, Adam Spencer.

The ringing of the phone awakened her. She grabbed up the receiver next to the sofa and sat up. "Hello?"

"Bree, it's Clay."

"Hi," she said and attempted to shake off her sleep. "What's up?"

"I just wanted you to know that I dusted the cradle thoroughly for prints and it yielded nothing. I would guess that the perp wore gloves."

"Thanks, Clay. I can't say I'm surprised." Although she was bitterly disappointed. It would have been nice had Clay been able to lift prints and the mystery of the phone caller had been solved.

"Are you okay?" he asked after a moment of hesitation. His question surprised her. Clay rarely seemed attuned to feelings or if he was attuned, he rarely asked about other people's emotions.

"I'm all right," she replied. "Why?"

"I don't know...you just sound sort of funny."

"I was napping and your call woke me up."

"Oh, okay. Let me know if there's anything else you need," he said briskly. She could tell his mind had already moved on.

"I will...and thanks, Clay." She hung up the phone and looked at the clock. It was already after five. She must have been asleep for over an hour.

The night stretched out before her...empty...lonely. With Rachel and Maggie gone, the house felt cold and alien. She mentally rebelled at the thought of sleeping in her bedroom, which she knew would now smell of Adam's scent.

She got up and stretched and decided what she really wanted to do was go to her parents' house and spend the night there, in the comfort of the three people who loved her most, her mother, her father and sweet Maggie.

Tomorrow she would deal with her life. Tonight she just wanted the company of her family around her and no thoughts of Adam Spencer to intrude.

CHAPTER NINE

Adam had known telling her the truth would be difficult. He'd known what he had to tell her would be a shock, but he hadn't expected it to be as difficult as it had been.

Even a full day later, the image of her lovely face with her expressive eyes as he'd told her the truth about Kurt, about himself, was permanently emblazoned in his brain. As his words had sunk in, her features had fallen and her eyes had radiated myriad emotions—anger—and pain.

He'd left her and had been angry with himself, his own heart aching in a way he'd never felt before. He'd never meant to hurt her. Dammit, he should have told her who he was and why he was here in Cherokee Corners the moment he'd first met her.

But on that night when they'd first met, the belief that she might be a prostitute had thrown him for a loop. The other thing that had thrown him for a loop was her comment about bedding a half-breed.

It had been ugly and shocking and he couldn't help but wonder if Kurt had left far deeper scars on her than Adam had initially suspected.

He'd watched her drive off and had known instinctively that she wouldn't be back for the remainder of the night. He'd give her a day or two to cool down, then he'd hope to have a rational, nonemotional talk with her. Hopefully he could make her see that Edward and Anita deserved a chance to be a part of Maggie's life. Hopefully he could make her understand that he'd never meant to hurt her in any way.

She came home the next day just before three and by four was getting into her car again. He assumed she was going to work. He was seated on the porch when she left and she gave no indication she saw him there, although he was certain he couldn't be missed.

He decided to walk into town for dinner, not finding much appeal in cooking for himself and eating alone in the shabby little kitchen.

As he walked toward the city square his thoughts turned to Kurt. His love for his cousin had always been unconditional, but as he thought of Breanna's pain and anger when she spoke of him, as he thought of the little fatherless Maggie, he felt the edge of an emotion that was both alien and distinctly uncomfortable.

He focused on the scenery he passed instead. He wasn't ready to evaluate the emotions he now felt when he thought of Kurt.

It was a perfect early May night. The air was cool and scented with sweet-smelling flowers and as he passed people working in their yards or sitting on their porches, they waved with small-town friendliness. Nice, he thought...much nicer than his sterile apartment where he had no idea who his neighbors were or what they did.

He ate at a café on the city square that advertised a stupendous daily special. It was meat loaf. He people-watched while he ate, finding other people's actions and chatter far less disturbing than his own thoughts.

After his meal he walked to the Redbud Bed and Breakfast and into the ice-cream parlor where Alyssa worked. Once again she was behind the counter and she greeted him with a reserved smile as he slid onto a stool at the counter and ordered a cup of coffee.

"So, you're Kurt's cousin," she said as she set the cup and saucer in front of him.

"You must have spoken to Breanna," he said with a grimace as tension rose inside him. "You didn't poison my coffee, did you?"

"No. The way I see it, you can pick your friends, but you can't pick your relatives."

"I guess if we could pick our relatives, nobody would have a crazy Uncle Harry who always ended up with a lampshade on his head at family gatherings," he said wryly.

She smiled and some of his tension dissipated. "In our family it's crazy Uncle Sammy. He's Uncle Thomas's brother and definitely the black sheep and most fun of the family."

He took a sip of his coffee and eyed her curiously. "So you knew my cousin?"

"For the brief time he was here. I'm afraid I didn't think much of him even though Bree was crazy about him. They married after just a month of knowing each other, far too quickly. I knew he was going to break her heart from the moment I met him." She eyed him intently, her dark gaze appearing to look deep inside of him. "And I have a feeling if you aren't careful, you could break her heart as well."

He laughed, although with little amusement. "No chance of that. I've been quite clear with Breanna that I want no ties, that I'm not interested in a relationship. Besides, at the moment she isn't even speaking to me."

Alyssa tilted her head to one side, not taking her gaze from him. "Then perhaps she'll break your heart."

He laughed again, distinctly uncomfortable. "That isn't going to happen, either. Breanna is a loose end in Kurt's life that I needed to tie up. That's all."

"Loose ends have a way of snarling you all up if you aren't careful," she replied.

He took another sip of his coffee, then eyed her curiously. "Is this one of your visions talking or just idle speculation?"

She frowned. "The only vision I have at the moment is one where I see that my darling cousin talks too much."

"She was worried and mentioned to me about your visions. She said you've been having some bad feelings lately."

Her eyes darkened, but she shrugged. "It's a curse from my grandmother on my mother's side. She, too, suffered from visions."

"If you hold my hand, will you be able to see my future?" he asked, genuinely curious.

She shook her head, obviously not offended by his question. "It doesn't work that way. I wish it did, but it doesn't."

"Then how does it work?" Although he was intrigued, he also knew in the back of his mind that what he was doing by talking with Alyssa was keeping a connection to Breanna.

"I don't know how it works. Most of the time I get a bit

of a headache and I know I'm about to have a vision. The vision itself is kind of like seeing the coming attractions of a movie...a flash of scenes that don't always initially make sense."

"Like what...? Tell me about a vision you've had in the past."

She looked around, as if hoping somebody would need her attention, but the only other people in the place was a young couple sharing a banana split. They were too engrossed in each other to be paying any attention to Adam and Alyssa.

She sighed and looked back at him. "Six months ago I was eating dinner in my apartment and I got a vision. In it, my father was telling me the story of Raven Mocker." She looked at him questioningly.

"The witch who comes to take a life," he said.

She nodded and continued. "Anyway, I couldn't understand why he was telling me a story I'd heard a hundred times before. Then I realized as he spoke that I was cold...colder than I'd ever been in my life. When the vision passed I tried to tell myself it meant nothing, but I decided to try to get in touch with my father."

"And...?" Adam found himself completely caught up in her story.

"And he wasn't home. My mother said she'd been expecting him for the past two hours, but hadn't heard from him and just assumed his last job of the day had been a bigger one than he'd expected. My father works as a heating and refrigeration repairman. When I thought about the cold I'd felt during my vision I was suddenly afraid."

She paused and grabbed the coffeepot and refilled his cup. When she continued speaking, her eyes were darker than he'd have thought possible. "I got hold of Dad's boss and insisted he meet me at the location of Dad's last job of the day, a butcher shop. The shop was closed, but we found Dad there. He'd been accidentally locked inside a walk-in freezer. He was suffering frostbite and hypothermia. The doctor said if he'd been in that freezer another hour or so we might have lost him."

"So your visions can sometimes save lives," he said.

"Sometimes…if I can figure out what they mean. The torment is in figuring them out too late, in knowing that something horrible is happening or about to happen and not being able to stop it.

"Do you always pass out after a vision?"

"No, only after a particularly bad vision."

"Is that what happened on the day of the barbecue? You had a bad vision?

He didn't think it was possible for her eyes to grow darker, but they did. "Yes and no," she replied softly.

She broke her eye contact with him and looked around the parlor. He didn't know if she was checking to see if any of the patrons needed anything or if she was merely grounding herself in the here and now.

When she looked back at him her eyes were still as dark as night and filled with what appeared to be fear. "I'm not sure what happened at the barbecue. It wasn't like my usual visions. It was like death…a feeling of loss, of emptiness too great to bear."

"What do you think it means?" Adam asked as a chill walked up his spine.

"I think it means somebody close to me, somebody I love is in grave danger." They both jumped as the bell over the front door tinkled and a family of four walked in.

She freshened up his coffee again, then stepped away from him to wait on the newcomers. Adam had a feeling she wouldn't be back to talk to him about her visions, or Breanna or anything else of importance.

He finished his coffee, waved a goodbye and left the ice-cream parlor. As he walked toward the cottage, thoughts of Breanna filled his head.

Perhaps it was a good thing he'd made her angry. He'd been getting too close to her, had been seduced by her beauty and charm, her strength and her wit. Telling her the truth had put distance between them, and that wasn't a bad thing.

If he was smart, he'd get the hell out of Dodge, pack up his things and get back to his own life. He'd done what he'd promised Kurt he would do, he'd found Breanna and Maggie and they were doing just fine. He'd never intended to get caught up in Breanna's life, hadn't anticipated being charmed by her family.

He should return to Kansas City, tell his aunt and uncle about Maggie and let them deal with Breanna to gain some sort of grandparent rights. He could step away now and remain uninvolved in the whole mess, he told himself.

He knew he was lying to himself. Despite all his protests to the contrary, he was already involved. Perhaps if he had never tasted the sweetness of Breanna's lips, maybe if he'd never held her warm and willing body against his own, he might have been able to convince himself that he wasn't involved.

But he had tasted her mouth and he had caressed her heated body and there was no way he could pretend to himself that he could just walk away and not look back. Especially not with Alyssa's ominous words ringing in his ears.

He halted in front of Breanna's house and stared up at the big oak tree, remembering the shock of seeing the pink plastic cradle and Mr. Bear hanging there. His stomach knotted with anger and a touch of fear.

Again Alyssa's words resounded in his head. "I think it means somebody close to me, somebody I love is in grave danger."

Was it Breanna? Was Alyssa's feeling coming from the same place as the phone calls and implied threat of a hanging stuffed animal?

He entered his cottage, knowing that he wasn't leaving Cherokee Corners, he wasn't going anywhere. There was no way he could leave knowing she might be in danger. He moved to his kitchen window and stared out at her house.

He wasn't going anywhere until he knew they weren't in any danger. If she never spoke to him again, then so be it. He would be a silent sentry watching over her, keeping her and her daughter safe from harm to the best of his ability.

Breanna was having a bad week. She'd arrived at work on Wednesday to discover that drug-trafficking charges against a repeat offender had been dropped that day in court due to a legal technicality. Although she and Abe hadn't been participants in the actual arrest of the creep, they had both logged long hours in surveillance on him.

Every day when she left for work Adam was seated on his porch, and he was there once again when she returned home after work. She was grateful he didn't try to speak to her because she certainly wasn't ready to talk to him. She spoke to Maggie and Rachel every day at her parents' house and was surprised that the strange, lullaby phone calls appeared to have stopped.

She figured one of two things, either the phone calls had truly been made by Michael Rivers and their little visit to him had scared him off, or they had been the result of somebody's idea of a sick joke and the joker had gotten bored and moved on to another game. In either case she was grateful that the disturbing calls had ceased.

By Friday night she was starting to feel a little bit better. She'd made arrangements for both Maggie and Rachel to return home Sunday after the festivities at the Cultural Center. It would be good to have them back where they belonged, good to have their lives back to some semblance of normal.

Her positive thinking lasted until her partner, Abe, delivered the bombshell that he'd be leaving the force for retirement.

They were seated at side-by-side desks in the station house, catching up on paperwork when Abe told her he'd put in his two-weeks' notice.

"You knew this was coming, Bree," Abe said. "I've been telling you for months that retirement for me was right around the corner."

"I know. I just didn't realize the corner was so close." She was beginning to feel as if her life would never be the same again. Kurt was dead, Adam was a liar and betrayer and now her partner was leaving her.

"Ah, don't look so glum," Abe said sympathetically. "You've got a great career ahead of you, Bree. You don't need an old coot like me hanging around your neck." He scowled, his grizzly gray eyebrows nearly meeting in the center of his forehead. "I just wish I was going out on a bang."

"What do you mean?"

"I dunno. I wish we were breaking a major prostitution ring or putting the finishing touches on a multimillion-dollar drug bust. I hate to think that the last job I'll ever do as a cop is arrest some hapless John with his pants half-down."

Breanna grinned at him. "One John at a time, that's how we clean up the streets of our fair city." She noticed a blond hair shining on the collar of his dark jacket. She leaned over and plucked it off. "Have you got some sexy blonde who's going to help you spend your retirement years?" she teased.

He laughed. "Yeah, a gorgeous little blonde. She weighs about three pounds and I call her Miss Kitty."

"You got a cat?"

"It's more like she got me." He threw his pencil on the desk and reared back in his chair. "She showed up at the house yesterday morning. I was sitting on the porch having a cup of coffee and there she was, the scruffiest little tabby cat I've ever seen. Looked like she was half-starving, so I opened a can of tuna and gave it to her."

"You know what they say…feed a cat and you own a cat."

Abe shrugged. "It's all right by me. She's obviously a stray…like me. We can keep each other company in the years I've got left."

"Oh, for heaven's sakes, Abe, you sound like you're dying instead of retiring," she exclaimed.

"I've got to admit that change isn't easy at my age. My whole life has always been the job."

"So what plans do you have?" She was so grateful to have something, anything, to keep her mind off thoughts of Adam.

"I wouldn't mind doing a little work in the private sector…maybe consulting or a little private investigation."

Breanna wished she'd had a private investigator on her payroll the night she'd met Adam. She would have had

Adam checked out upside down and inside out before she offered him a word, a glance or a smile.

But it was too late now. She'd already given Adam far more than a smile and she didn't know how to get him out of her thoughts now.

She'd spent the past three days thinking of everything he'd told her. Her heart had ached with the knowledge that now Maggie would never, ever have a connection with the man who had sired her.

And even though Breanna had told herself for a long time that she hated Kurt, she'd been surprised to realize there was a small piece inside her that mourned him, too. That mourning place inside her didn't come from any lingering love, but rather from the compassion of one human being for another.

She was at least grateful for one thing…she was grateful Adam had stopped their lovemaking in order to tell her the truth about who he was and why he was in town. But it disturbed her that knowing the truth did nothing to staunch the hunger he'd awakened inside her. Knowing the truth did nothing to erase the desire she still felt to be with him intimately.

She was equally conflicted when it came to the knowledge that Kurt's parents were alive and well and had enough money to buy the entire town of Cherokee Corners. She couldn't just forget all the things Kurt had told her about them and the things he'd had to say weren't particularly pleasant.

She wondered if Adam had already told them about Maggie, wondered if at any moment she would be served with legal papers or get a phone call demanding some sort of visitation.

The thought of sharing Maggie with people who would

be ashamed of her heritage stirred a rebellion in Breanna that would not be easily overcome.

She told herself Maggie didn't need anyone else in her life, and what the Randolfs didn't know wouldn't hurt them. Let them grieve for their son and let them leave her and Maggie alone. They had nothing that Breanna and Maggie needed, and Breanna certainly had nothing to give to them.

It was after one when she pulled into her driveway and saw Adam seated on his porch. She kept her gaze carefully averted from him as she got out of her car and approached her front door.

She'd just reached her front porch when she heard his footsteps coming toward her. She tensed and reached into her purse.

"Please don't tell me you're getting your gun," he said from just behind her. "I keep telling you if you point that at me often enough one of these times you're going to accidentally shoot me."

She turned to look at him as she pulled her keys from her purse. "And what makes you think it would be an accident?" she asked coolly.

She unlocked her door then turned back to face him. It was difficult to look at him and not remember how masterful his mouth had felt against hers. It was difficult not to remember how his naked chest had felt against her own. It was hard to forget how much of a support he'd been to her in the brief time they'd known each other. "What do you want, Adam? It's late."

"We need to talk, Breanna. Can I come in for just a few minutes?"

She wanted to tell him no, she wanted to tell him to just go away and leave her alone, but she knew that sooner or later he would want to talk and decided to just get it over with. "I really can't imagine what you might have to say to me, but I'll give you fifteen minutes."

He followed her inside where she dropped her purse on the sofa, then turned to face him, arms crossed defensively over her chest. "You said we need to talk...so talk."

He frowned, as if aware that she wasn't open to hearing anything he had to say. He took a step forward, his arms stretched out toward her, but stopped as she took a step backward. His arms fell helplessly to his sides

She didn't want him close enough to her that she would be able to smell his distinctive scent, feel the heat from his body. She didn't want her brain muddied by the desire for him that refused to die despite her wish to the contrary.

"Breanna," he began softly. "Nothing I did from the moment I arrived here was done in an effort to cause you pain in any way."

She eyed him accusingly. "You lied to me by not telling me who you were."

He nodded. "I guess that's true, but the first night I met you, I thought you were a prostitute. I decided to wait to tell you who I was and why I was here until I knew more about you."

"By the next morning you knew I wasn't a prostitute, that I was a cop and came from a good family," she countered.

"I know," he agreed. He dragged a hand across his lower jaw, then raked it through his curly hair. "And I should have told you then, but I didn't. I wanted to make sure you would be open to having a relationship with Uncle Edward and Aunt Anita."

"Have you told them about me...about Maggie?" Fear surged up inside her.

"No. I don't want to tell them until I have your agreement that you'll let them be a part of Maggie's life."

"Then you're going to wait a long time." Exhausted, she sank to the edge of the sofa.

He eyed her in obvious frustration. "Why? Why would you deny a couple the opportunity to bond with their only grandchild? And why would you deny Maggie the opportunity to have more love in her life? Is your hatred for Kurt so great that you would seek revenge on his parents…on your own daughter?"

"I'm not seeking revenge on anyone," she scoffed irritably. "I'm protecting myself…and Maggie."

"From what?" he asked incredulously. He sat down next to her on the sofa, not so close as to be a threat, but as if her words had taken the strength out of his legs. His beautiful blue eyes eyed her searchingly. "What are you afraid of, Bree? For God's sake, tell me what is going through your head."

To her horror, tears stung her eyes. She had tried so hard to forget the horrible things Kurt had said to her when he was leaving. She'd shoved his words deep into the dark recesses of her mind where she believed they would no longer have the power to hurt her. But Adam's questions brought all the pain, all the fear back to the forefront of her mind.

She turned her head away from him, angry that the tears appeared to be out of her control. She felt him move closer to her on the sofa and she wanted to scream at him to get away, to leave her house and allow her the privacy she suddenly needed.

"Bree." His voice was achingly soft and he placed a hand on her arm.

She jerked her arm away, swiped at her falling tears and

turned to glare at him. "What difference does it make to you? Why do you care?"

"Because I love my aunt and uncle, because they've lost their only son and I know the knowledge that they have a grandchild will help ease some of their grief, will give them a reason to go on." His eyes grew dark. "My God, Breanna. Where's your compassion?" His voice took on a hard edge that stirred the anger in her.

"Where's *my* compassion?" She jumped up from the sofa and faced him. "Excuse me if my compassion is spent on my daughter rather than two wealthy people who will probably only make her ashamed of her heritage!"

"Ashamed of her heritage?" Adam stood as well, confusion twisting his features. "What in the hell are you talking about?"

"I'm talking about the two people who raised Kurt." Tears raced frantically down her cheeks. "Before Kurt left, he told me that it was a good thing his parents were dead, that it would kill them if they knew their grandchild was going to be a little papoose from a half-breed.

"Don't you understand? Leaving me wasn't the worst thing Kurt did, but making me ashamed of who I am was, and I won't let his parents do the same to my daughter. I won't!" Sobs choked in her throat at the same time Adam reached out and roughly pulled her tight against his chest.

CHAPTER TEN

Adam held her as she cried with a depth of pain that horrified him. He'd always believed his love for his cousin was unconditional.

But as he felt Breanna's pain racking her body with deep sobs, as her words echoed around and around in his head, he realized there was a part of him that didn't like his cousin at all. There was a part of him where a rich anger had been growing for years and now threatened to explode.

This wasn't just a nasty mess Kurt had left behind. This was a real woman, with real emotions and real pain intentionally inflicted by a man Adam had believed he'd loved.

He held her tight, as if the circle of his arms could somehow staunch the pain, stop her tears. He didn't try to speak to her, knew she was beyond listening. He also knew instinctively that the tears she spilled now had probably been balled up inside of her for years.

She cried with her arms around his neck, her face buried in the front of his shirt as she leaned weakly against him. As his shirt grew damp, he wondered how many tears a woman could cry...a thousand...a million?

As the minutes passed, her sobs became less intense and she finally pulled away from him and once again sank down to the sofa. Her eyes were red-rimmed and utterly hollow.

Adam sat next to her and took her hand in his, grateful when she didn't fight him and pull her hand away. "Over the years, my aunt and uncle and I used many adjectives when describing Kurt. He was flighty and unfocused, adventurous and easily bored. We should have been using the truthful adjectives...like irresponsible and lazy and cruel."

The truth seared through him, destroying any illusions he'd ever entertained about Kurt. It was one thing to grieve a man who had died, quite another to grieve for a man who had never existed.

"I've spent my life following behind Kurt, cleaning up whatever chaos he'd left behind...and there was always plenty of chaos."

A deep-seated anger rose to the surface as he thought of the time, the energy that was spent on Kurt's life. "I tried to be a mentor, a role model of sorts, but instead I became his keeper. But you can't blame my aunt Anita and uncle Edward for the kind of man Kurt was. They are good, decent people who would be appalled by Kurt's words to you."

She sighed and pulled her hand from his. "Kurt told me his parents were dead, but he also told me they had been selfish, mean people who only believed in the almighty dollar. He told me that, before their deaths, they had tried to control him and if they'd been alive when Maggie was born, they would have used their power and influence to take her away from me, to make her into the image of themselves."

"I neglected to mention another adjective that obviously described Kurt." Pain shot through Adam. "He was a liar who used lies to manipulate people into doing what he wanted."

Breanna leaned her head back and closed her eyes. "I don't know what to believe. I've read articles about Edward and Anita Randolf. I know they're wealthy and high-society. How can I trust that they aren't the people Kurt thought they were." She opened her eyes and gazed at Adam once again.

"I'm not going to lie to you. They are wealthy...incredibly wealthy, but that doesn't make them bad people. I was a grieving eleven-year-old when they opened up their house, their hearts to me. They loved me like a son and made me a part of their family."

He could see she still didn't believe him. "Breanna, Kurt lied about them being dead, he apparently lied when he said his marriage vows to you, how can you believe anything he told you?"

She sighed again. "I don't know, Adam. I don't know what to believe about anything anymore."

Once again he reached out and took her hand in his. "I'll make you a deal. I won't tell my aunt and uncle about Maggie until you give me the okay. But, in the meantime, I want you to consider it. They need her, Breanna, and I promise you won't be sorry if you give them a chance to be a part of her life."

"I just...I need some time," she finally said.

He nodded, then tightened his grip on her hand. "I've missed talking to you the past couple of days."

"I've been very angry with you."

"As you should have been," he agreed. "I just need you to understand that I didn't mean to betray your trust. I didn't mean to hurt you."

She said nothing, but the hollow look in her eyes seemed to fill with a touch of warmth. "The phone calls have stopped," she said, changing the subject.

"They have?" He eyed her in surprise.

"I didn't receive another one after I hooked up the caller ID."

"That's odd, isn't it? Who did you tell about the ID?" She seemed to have forgotten that her hand was still in his. He liked the feel of her hand, so small and dainty and swallowed by his bigger one.

"My family...my partner. Why?"

"I just think it's weird that the calls stopped the minute you got the ID box."

"I figured either it was Michael Rivers and our little discussion with him backed him off, or it was somebody pranking and they got bored. I don't care exactly what happened, I'm just grateful the calls have stopped." She pulled her hand away from his and stood. "It's late, Adam, and I think we've said everything that needs to be said."

He stood and followed her to the front door. She looked small and vulnerable and when he thought of the things Kurt had said to her, his blood boiled hot in his veins.

When they got to her front door, he paused just inside, wanting...needing to touch her in some way, erase the memory of Kurt's hurtful words.

She looked up at him, her eyes dark and achingly beautiful. "You said before that you've spent your life cleaning up

Kurt's messes. Is that what I am to you? A mess that needs to be taken care of, a problem that had to be resolved?"

A swift denial leaped to his lips, but didn't make it out of his mouth. "I came to Cherokee Corners with that in mind, that you were the final loose end...the final mess that Kurt had left behind." He saw that his words cut her and he quickly continued, "But it took me exactly one day to realize you were far, far more than a mess for me to clean up."

Cautiously, he reached out a hand and touched a strand of her shining hair. "The warmth of your family touched me and Maggie has utterly charmed me. And you...from the moment I saw you, you took my breath away. If I could, I'd take away all the things Kurt said to you that caused you pain. If I could, I'd make it so nobody would ever hurt you again."

She was in his arms then, her lips raised to his and he kissed her with a fervor he hadn't known existed inside him. Her mouth was hot and eager against his, but she broke the kiss abruptly and stepped back from him.

She shut the front door and locked them inside, then looked up at him, her eyes filled with a want that made him weak inside.

"I don't know if I really even like you anymore, Adam Spencer," she said softly. "And I certainly don't completely trust you. But I want you, and I haven't wanted a man since Kurt left me years ago. Still, I need you to understand that if we sleep together, it will just be sex...it doesn't change my mind about anything where you are concerned."

For a moment Adam was speechless. "That's fine with me," he finally said. "I told you from the very beginning the last thing I want is any sort of a long-term relationship. But I do want you."

He barely got the words out of his mouth before they were in each other's arms, kissing with a depth of emotion that made second thought impossible, threw caution to the wind.

As his lips possessed hers, he knew nothing and nobody was going to stop them tonight. The world could crash down around their heads, but he was going to make love to Breanna James.

Breanna would like to believe that she'd been gripped by some sort of temporary insanity, but the truth was she hadn't made love with a man since Kurt had left her nearly six years before. Her body ached with the need to be held, to be caressed, to be loved, and in the six years since Kurt's desertion no man had tempted her in the least... until Adam.

As their lips clung together, he started moving them out of the foyer and toward the stairs, but she stopped him. She didn't want him in her bed, didn't want the implied intimacy of him in her personal space.

Instead she kicked off her shoes and led him into the living room, where she turned out all the lights, leaving the room illuminated by a shaft of moonlight that danced through gauzy curtains.

Their kiss broke and she sank to the floor, motioning him to join her on the soft, lush carpeting. She didn't have to motion twice. He sank down to his knees facing her and cupped her face with his hands. In his eyes she saw a feverish need that would have wiped away any lingering doubts she might have entertained.

It was obvious he wanted her, but she was doing this for herself. It was a selfish act, feeding her own need to be held, to pretend for just a little while that she was loved.

His hands moved from her face down her shoulders, then cupped her breasts. She could feel the heat of his hands through her wispy bra and thin T-shirt. Her nipples tingled and hardened in response to the intimate touch.

She ran her hands across the broad width of his shoulders, over the muscles of his chest and down the flat of his stomach. He sucked in his breath, as if finding her touch a delicious torment.

In one smooth movement, he reached down, grabbed the bottom of her T-shirt and pulled it off over her head. Her heart raced and she felt as if she were burning up with fever as his lips claimed hers in a deep, hot kiss.

She tugged at his shirt, wanting to feel his naked skin beneath her fingertips. He quickly unbuttoned the shirt and shrugged it off his shoulders, then reached around her to unsnap her bra.

As the wisp of lace fell away, he pulled her tight against him and she reveled in the feel of her naked skin against his. His skin was hot and she felt herself melting into him, as if they were fusing together.

Gently, he laid her back on the carpeting then his fingers worked the snap fastener on her slacks. As he pulled down her slacks, she aided him by raising her hips. He stood, leaving her there clad only in her pink silk bikini panties.

She watched as he kicked off his shoes, pulled off his socks, then tore off his pants, leaving him only in a pair of briefs that did nothing to disguise the extent of his desire for her.

He rejoined her on the floor, gathering her in his arms as his mouth hungrily devoured hers. His hips moved against hers, the friction of his hardness even through the barrier of their underclothing driving her half-wild with desire.

He raised his head to look at her, his eyes filled with a wildness that thrummed through her. "You are so beautiful," he said, his voice deep and husky.

"So are you," she replied. Her hands splayed across the width of his back, loving the way his muscles bunched and played beneath her fingertips. "I love the way your skin feels against mine."

He slid his mouth down the length of her throat and captured one of her nipples. As he rolled his tongue over the tip, pinpricks of fire exploded in her veins, radiating out from her breast deep into the very center of her being. He looked at her once again. "I love the way you taste," he said, then tasted her some more, moving his mouth to her other breast.

By the time he was finished nipping and licking her skin down to the waistband of her panties, she was delirious with want. But he seemed to be in no hurry to complete the act.

"Breanna," he said, his voice seeming to come from far away. "I...I don't have anything with me."

She frowned, trying to surface from the dizzying haze to understand what he was talking about. When realization set in, rather than upset her, it relieved her. He hadn't come here with a condom in his pocket, which indicated seduction hadn't been on his mind.

"It's all right," she replied. "I'm on the pill." She mentally thanked the doctor who had placed her on the pill three years ago due to irregular periods.

She barely got the words out of her mouth when he touched her through the thin material of her panties and she cried out in exquisite pleasure.

Then her panties were gone and he touched her bareness with quick light strokes that swept her higher and higher,

moved her to a release that left her shuddering and clinging to him with panting gasps. Her body felt like liquid,
boneless and spent, but more than anything she wanted to
return the pleasure.

She plucked at his briefs and he pulled them down and
kicked them off, leaving him as naked as her. She gripped
him, reveling in his throbbing hardness and as she stroked
her hand up the length of him, he moaned deep in the back
of his throat.

His mouth sought hers again, hot and hungry as she continued to move her hand over him. He groaned and shoved
her hand away, then rolled over on top of her, poised to
possess her completely.

Before he entered her, his eyes held hers and she felt
as if he were making love to her there first…with those
beautiful blue eyes of his. Then he slipped into her and she
closed her eyes, unable to hold them open as wave after
wave of pleasure suffused her.

Slowly at first, he moved deep within her, then pulled
back, each stroke a pleasure that threatened to shatter her
into a thousand pieces.

She clung to him like a drowning woman, meeting his
thrusts with a need of her own. It had never been this way
for her before. She'd never felt so lost…and so found, so
needy and yet so fulfilled. The depth of emotion, both
mental and physical that filled her both frightened and
excited her.

Faster and faster he moved against her, into her, stoking
the flames of her passion higher…higher. A new tension
built inside her as her muscles tensed in expectation…an-
ticipation.

He cried out her name and she loved the sound of his
voice, graveled and thick with emotion. Just as she reached

the peak of a second release, he stiffened against her and shuddered with his own.

For a long moment they remained in each other's arms, the only sound in the room their breaths working to slow to a more normal pace.

He finally leaned up and gazed down at her, his eyes warm as the sky on a sunny day. Gently he swept a strand of her hair from her cheek, then leaned down and kissed her lips lingeringly.

The sweet gentleness of his kiss touched her as much as anything else they had shared and she tried to throw up mental defenses against him.

When the kiss ended he smiled at her. "I feel like a teenager."

"What do you mean?" Her heart was finally finding a normal rhythm although she loved the feel of his skin against hers.

"I feel like your parents are upstairs in bed and we're sneaking a bout of lovemaking on their living-room floor. I've even got the rug burns on my knees to prove it."

She laughed. "This would never have happened in my parents' house. All the boys in town knew my father was chief of police and wouldn't hesitate to shoot them if they tried something like this." She rolled away from him and sat up. "I'm going to go take a shower."

"I'm a great back scrubber," he said.

Breanna had intended her statement to indicate to him that it was time for him to go. But, it was obvious he wasn't ready to call it a night and looking at the heat in his eyes, she realized neither was she.

"A woman can always use a good back scrubber," she replied, surprised to discover she was half-breathless again.

Within minutes they were standing beneath a hot, steamy spray of water in the bathroom off Breanna's bedroom. She had never showered with a man before, had no idea what to expect. But he led the way, soaping up a sponge and running it across her back.

At first it seemed he intended to do just what he'd said... scrub her back. But it didn't take long before he was raking that sponge not just across her back, but across her breasts, over her thighs and down her legs. And then the sponge was gone and it was his soapy hands exciting her back to a fever pitch.

They made love again with Breanna pressed against the glass enclosure, the warmth of the water and steam and the slickness of their soapy bodies enhancing the pleasure.

Afterward, Breanna pulled on a robe as Adam redressed. Regret swept through her as she silently watched him. She'd thought she could make love to him and enjoy the physical release it would bring without being touched emotionally.

But she realized now this man had managed to crawl beneath her defenses. Despite the fact that he'd kept his real identity a secret from her, in spite of the fact that he'd come here simply to tie up any loose ends Kurt had left behind, he'd managed to get inside her heart in a way that frightened her.

He made her almost willing to believe in the dreams she'd once entertained...the dreams of love forever, of a strong and happy marriage...of a family all her own. Fool's illusion, she reminded herself. Illusions bred in the afterglow of beautiful lovemaking.

What she needed most now was distance from him and from the foolishness of her own thoughts. She was grateful he didn't mention spending the night. She didn't want to spend her sleeping hours in his arms, didn't want to awaken in his warm embrace.

"You know this changes nothing," she said as she followed him downstairs to her front door.

"What do you mean?" He reached the door and turned to look at her.

"I mean I still don't want you to tell your aunt and uncle about Maggie." She pulled her robe closer around her, threatened by how much she wanted to grab him by the hand and lead him back up to her bedroom. To sleep, to dream in his arms would be heaven, but it would only make things more difficult in the end...and there was an end.

"Breanna, I told you I wouldn't tell them until you're ready for me to, but you're wrong when you say that nothing has changed."

"What do you mean?" She eyed him curiously, wondering how it was possible he could look so devastatingly handsome with his hair in curly disarray and a five o'clock shadow decorating his jaw.

He opened the front door, then leaned over and kissed her on the cheek. As he straightened up, in her eyes he saw the flames of a fire not yet sated. "As far as I'm concerned everything has changed. Now I don't have to imagine what your body feels like against mine, I know. And I don't have to try to imagine the sound of your sweet sighs while I make love to you, because I know. And most important of all what's changed is that I now know how much I love making love to you and I know I want to do it again...and again."

His words made her heart flutter with a combination of sweet anticipation and anxiety. "Adam, tonight was wonderful…beautiful, but wouldn't it be foolish for us to repeat the experience?"

"Why would it be foolish?" His eyes held her gaze intently.

Because I'm falling in love with you, she wanted to say. Because ultimately it would be like Kurt all over again… only this time it would be worse because Adam was on the verge of capturing her heart in a way Kurt never had. But the end result would be that he'd walk away, just as Kurt had done.

She grabbed the ends of her belt and pulled it tighter. "Adam, it's late and at the moment I'm too tired to think."

Once again he leaned down, this time to kiss her gently on the temple. "Good night, Bree," he said softly. "May sweet, happy dreams be yours." With these words he turned and left her house.

She closed the door after him and knew she didn't have to worry about the danger of any strange phone calls. The danger to her was much closer…right next door in the form of one handsome Adam Spencer.

CHAPTER ELEVEN

Sunday was one of those picture-perfect spring days. The morning sky was cloudless, but there was just enough of a breeze to keep the sun from feeling overly warm.

Adam dressed in a pair of jeans and a light blue polo shirt, then climbed into his car and headed out for the Cultural Center. He wasn't sure what time the festivities would start there, but he didn't want to miss anything.

More than anything, he didn't want to miss seeing Breanna. He hadn't seen her at all the day before. Her car had been gone when he'd gotten up yesterday morning and she hadn't come home after work.

With Alyssa's premonition of danger still in his head, he'd gotten worried when she hadn't come home after work. On a hunch he'd driven by her parents' home, relieved to see her car parked there. He went back to the cottage, knowing she was safe.

She was safe, but obviously avoiding him. He frowned

as he rolled down the window to allow in some of the fresh, sweet scented spring air. Maybe she regretted their love-making. While he thought making love had not been the wisest decision they could have made, there was no way he could regret what had been so fantastic, so magical.

Making love to her had filled an emptiness he hadn't realized he possessed. She'd been an eager participant, a generous lover. But he knew all about dawn regrets and suspected that's what had kept her from her home the day before.

Hopefully when he saw her today there would be no awkwardness between them and he wouldn't see the darkness of regret in her lovely eyes.

The parking lot of the Cultural Center was already nearly full when he arrived. He spied Breanna's car parked in one of the spaces nearest the building and was surprised to feel his pulse quicken.

The Cultural Center building was void of people, but large doors opened to allow entry to the back of the property where Adam realized the festivities were taking place.

A large crowd of visitors were gathered around a huge open area. At the far end of the area was a deep pit and he could see the flames of fire coming from within the pit. There were seven arbors encircling the fire and he wondered about the significance of them.

He joined the crowd of spectators just as the drums began beating rhythmically. His gaze shot around, trying to catch a glimpse of Breanna and Maggie. He saw them standing on the other side of the large expanse of dirt and he took a moment to drink in Breanna's stunning appearance.

She wore a dress in a calico print material. Bright blue material formed a series of diamond shapes around the yoke and on the skirt. The dress had three-quarter-length sleeves and ended at her calves. Her feet were bare and her hair was braided in two thick shiny braids, the ends of which rested on her breasts.

She looked proud and strong and achingly beautiful and he wondered how in the hell Kurt had been able to turn his back on her and walk away. Adam knew with a certainty it had been a flaw in Kurt, not Breanna, that had ruined their marriage.

Maggie stood next to her mother, clad in an outfit identical to Breanna's, except on Maggie's little legs were the shells that Adam knew would be part of one of the ceremonial dances.

It was Maggie who saw him first and her smile was as bright as the sky. She waved, then tugged at her mother's dress and pointed to him.

Breanna raised a hand in a greeting, then returned her attention to the dancers who had begun to perform. Adam tried to watch the dancers, but found his attention wandering again and again to Breanna.

He felt the rhythmic bang of the drums thrumming deep in his veins. It was a primitive beat of timelessness, of a proud people with a rich culture and traditions.

He could tell that Breanna felt the drums inside her as well. Her slender body swayed slightly with each beat and one of her feet tapped on the ground. He wanted to go to her, to move with her to the beat that sang in her soul, to learn the mysteries of her heritage.

When the dance ended and the drums had stilled, Rita stood in the center of the circle. Like her daughter she was clad in a traditional dress and the crowd stilled as she raised her hands for silence.

For the next few minutes she educated the group, explaining to them that the seven arbors surrounding the ceremonial fire represented the seven clans, Wolf, Wild Potato, War Paint, Bird Clan, Long Hair, Deer and Blue. She then entertained with several legends Adam found fascinating. When she was finished, more dancing resumed.

Adam made his way around the ceremonial circle to where Breanna and Maggie were standing. "Adam, did you come to watch me dance?" Maggie asked eagerly when he'd reached them.

"I wouldn't have missed it," he replied, obviously to the little girl's delight. He then smiled at Breanna. "Hi."

"Hi, yourself," she replied. Before they could say anything else to each other Rita arrived to greet Adam.

"Adam, it's nice to see you here," she said. "Are you enjoying everything?"

"Definitely. I'm finding it both entertaining and educational."

Rita smiled in obvious satisfaction. "That's exactly what we're hoping for with these festivals. We want people to enjoy them, but we'd like to teach a little of the Cherokee ways at the same time."

"You're doing a remarkable job," Adam replied, noticing that Breanna had moved with Maggie closer to the circle apparently in preparation of Maggie's performance.

"And what are you doing, Adam Spencer?" Her dark eyes held his gaze and in those eyes he saw the love of a mother worried for her daughter.

He didn't pretend not to know what she was asking. He was fairly certain Breanna would have told her mother everything...at least up to the point of their lovemaking.

"I'm not sure," he admitted softly, his gaze once again seeking Breanna. "It seemed clear-cut and simple in the beginning. Find Breanna, make sure she and Maggie were doing all right, then go back to Kansas City and let Kurt's parents know they have a grandchild."

"And now it isn't so simple?"

He looked back at Rita and sighed. "No, it isn't. She doesn't want me to tell Kurt's parents about Maggie."

Rita's eyes were suddenly filled with sad wisdom. "Your cousin took much more from my daughter than her heart. He took her pride as a Cherokee, her pride as a woman and left her with an anger that still burns far too bright."

"But she's angry at the wrong people," Adam said. "She's denying two loving people the chance to love her daughter."

"Give her time," Rita said. "She's had almost six years believing Kurt had no family, that his parents when alive had been bad people. She's only had a week to process the fact that he lied about something so basic."

Adam nodded, but there was a part of him that was afraid to give her too much more time. He felt himself being drawn closer and closer into her life, into her family and into a world he'd never wanted for himself.

At that moment the Cherokee Stomp Dance began and Adam watched as Maggie participated in the ceremonial dance of her people. Several times during her performance she smiled at Adam, as if she were performing specifically for him alone. Breanna had disappeared and Adam returned his attention to little Maggie.

When she was finished, she came running to his side. "Did you see me, Adam?" She took hold of his hand. "Did you see me be a shell-shaker?"

"I did." He returned her smile, finding it impossible not to. Her eyes sparkled with excitement and her round cheeks were flushed with color.

"Did you like it?" she asked.

"I thought you were the best shell-shaker I've ever seen."

She tugged his hand, forcing him to lean down closer to her. "If you wanted to, you could tell me that you're proud of me." He looked at her in surprise, finding her words odd. "When my friend, Jenny, dances for her daddy, he always tells her he's proud of her."

Adam's heart constricted in his chest as he gazed at Maggie's pretty little face and the hungry look in her eyes. "I am very proud of you, little one," he said softly. "But you know I'm not your daddy."

She leaned against him and nodded. "I know. My mommy told me my daddy died. I feel sad about it, but I think the best thing to do would be to get another daddy."

She gazed up at him with serious gray eyes. "My daddy wasn't really that good anyway…I mean I never saw him or talked to him. The next one I get I want him to live with me and talk to me and maybe sometimes even give me a hug and tell me he's proud."

Adam's heart swelled up in his chest, momentarily making speech impossible. What simple things would make a little girl happy, make her feel as if her life was complete. It was positively criminal, what Kurt had left behind.

"Until you find that new daddy, how about I give you a hug and tell you I'm proud of you." Adam leaned down and Maggie wrapped her arms around his neck. He squeezed her tightly, then released her and straightened up.

Eventually, Breanna would find a man to be a part of her life, to become a loving, caring stepfather for Maggie. But that man wasn't him. Still, he knew somehow he would never be the same when he left Cherokee Corners and this family behind.

Breanna had been helping the other women set food on the long tables near the back of the building. She looked up just in time to see Adam give Maggie a hug. The sight of the big, handsome man hugging her daughter brought forth a pang of pain in her heart.

When Kurt had left her, she had closed her heart to the possibility of ever again having a man in her life. But in doing that, was she being unfair to her daughter, who seemed to be so hungry for a father figure? Was she ultimately punishing Maggie by guarding her own heart?

She shoved away these disturbing thoughts and went back to work, setting out platters and dishes of both traditional and contemporary fare to feed the spectators. Coleslaw sat beside the traditional grape dumplings, a loaf of French bread was next to a platter of fry bread. There was fried chicken, roast beef, macaroni salads and beans. The women had been busy for the past week preparing dishes for this event.

Within minutes the food was ready and the spectators moved around the tables filling their plates. "Are you going to avoid me all day?"

She whirled around to see Adam standing just behind her and was irritated at the way her heart leapt in her chest. "I'm not avoiding you, I've just been busy," she countered.

He smiled knowingly and to her surprise she felt a blush

warm her cheeks. "Okay," she admitted, "perhaps I've been avoiding you a little."

"Why?"

She couldn't tell him the truth, that she was falling in love with him and needed to distance herself from him. "I don't know," she hedged. "I guess a bit of morning-after embarrassment."

"There's nothing to be embarrassed about," he returned. "We're two consenting adults who shared something special. And what I'd like to do now is share the day with you and Maggie."

She wanted to say yes…she wanted to say no. She wanted him to stay, she wanted him to leave. Before she could reply, Maggie raced up between them and grabbed his hand and hers. "Are you both going to watch me play *A-ne-jo-di* after lunch?"

Adam looked at Breanna questioningly. "It's a form of stickball. The young people play several games this afternoon."

He looked down at Maggie. "I'd be delighted to watch you play your game, especially if your mother will watch with me."

"You will, right, Mommy? You and Adam together and you can cheer for me."

Breanna shot a quick glare to Adam, knowing he'd intentionally manipulated her. "Yes, Maggie, we'll watch you together…now go get something to eat so you have plenty of energy to play." As Maggie ran off to fix a plate, Breanna looked at Adam once again. "That wasn't very nice."

"What?" His clear blue eyes held a teasing pretense of innocence.

"You know what," she replied. "You manipulated me by using my daughter."

"You're right," he agreed with an irritating, dashing smile. His smile faded and he gazed at her with naked honesty. "Breanna, can't we just spend some time together today? I enjoy your company and it won't be long before I'll be returning home to Kansas City."

His words shot through her. Of course he would be leaving Cherokee Corners and returning home. He'd never indicated anything to the contrary. He'd made it more than clear on several occasions that he had no intention of getting married, of having any children.

But why not just enjoy the day, a little voice said inside her head. Why not just take this day to enjoy his company?

"Fine," she finally said. "The first thing I intend to do is eat. You're welcome to join me."

Ten minutes later they sat at one of the picnic tables to eat. All around them people chatted to one another and the whoops and hollers of kids at play filled the air.

"I saw my mother talking to you earlier," Breanna said. "Did she give you one of her standard educational lessons?"

He grinned, looking achingly handsome with the sunshine playing on his hair and emphasizing the sculptured planes of his face. "No, no lessons, we just visited for a few minutes. Your father had a little talk with me, too."

Breanna looked at him in surprise. "About what?"

He smiled wryly. "The gist of our conversation was that if I hurt you in any way, the wrath of the entire James family would come down upon my head."

Breanna groaned. "I can't believe he did that."

Adam shrugged. "He's your father. He wants the best

for you and doesn't want to see anything make you sad or unhappy."

"I'm twenty-seven years old...old enough to take care of myself," she replied. "Besides, you don't have the power to hurt me. You've made it clear you aren't in the market for a relationship and I've made it clear that I'm not, either."

"Good," he replied. "Then I don't have to worry about anyone from your family meeting me in a dark alley with a gun?"

She smiled. "It depends on what you're doing in that dark alley."

"You told me your sister usually takes part in these festivities, but I haven't seen her here today," he said.

"Apparently there was a break in the murder case she's been working on so she couldn't come." For the next few minutes they ate in silence, although she noticed Adam taking in the ambiance of the gathering.

"There's such a strong sense of community here," he said later as they walked toward the field where the *A-ne-jo-di* games would be played. "You mentioned the other night that the worst thing Kurt had done to you was make you ashamed of your heritage. What did you mean?"

Breanna sighed and stared out to the field where the players were gathering. In her mind's eye she saw Kurt on their wedding day. They'd married at city hall, a spur-of-the-moment action that Breanna would later regret.

On that day Kurt's gray eyes had glittered with a sense of adventure that had been infectious, and in his eyes she thought she had seen the promise of a lifetime of love and commitment.

Aware that Adam was waiting for her to say something, she searched through her mind to find the right words to explain the depth of the trauma his cousin had left behind.

"At first, Kurt seemed to take a genuine interest in the Cherokee culture. He encouraged me to tell him about our belief system, our legends and our way of life both now and in the past."

She looked at Adam, surprised to discover that the pain that had once lingered in her heart whenever she thought of Kurt, was far less intense, rather like the echo of a song she'd heard long ago. "I was thrilled to share with him, felt as if his interest was because he loved me. I didn't realize that to him it was simply a weapon to later use against me."

"What do you mean?" His question was nearly drowned out by the crowd's cheers as the game on the field began.

She waited for the cheers to die down and continued to stare out at the field. "It wasn't long before he was making fun of our legends, scorning our belief system and mocking our ceremonies. He began to call me his little savage, his squaw woman." The memory of her humiliation warmed her cheeks.

"I have never been so ashamed in my life." Adam's voice was sharp and she looked at him in surprise. "It sickens me to think that I had any kind of a connection to a man who would be capable of doing something like that."

He grabbed her hand. She could tell by the expression on his face, the desperate empathy as he squeezed her hand, that he meant what he said. He looked ill with disgust, revolted by what she'd just shared with him.

"By the time he finally left, I felt as if there was something wrong with me...like I was a dirty savage."

Adam's gaze turned to one of surprise. "But you're such a strong woman, such a smart woman. How could he make you believe those kinds of things about yourself?"

She pulled her hand from his and waved to Maggie.

"I don't know." She looked at him once again. "Lots of smart, proud, strong women become the victims of mental abuse. I was pregnant, probably hormonal and desperate to maintain a relationship with the father of my baby. Besides, Kurt's mental abuse began subtly and built over the months."

Once again she directed her gaze to the field. "If he hadn't left when he did, eventually I would have left him."

"I'm sorry, Bree. Dear God, I'm so sorry." His deep voice was laced with pain.

She smiled at him ruefully. "You cleaned up his messes, you tried to keep him out of trouble, you even feel bad about the things he did. Tell me, Adam, what did you get out of it?"

He frowned at her in bewilderment. "What do you mean?"

"I mean, in any kind of a relationship there is give and take. It's obvious Kurt did a lot of taking, so what did you get from your relationship with him?"

He laughed and in the laughter he sounded distinctly uncomfortable. "This is far too serious a conversation to be having on such a beautiful day in the middle of a festival."

"You're right," she agreed. She wasn't even sure why she'd told the ugly details of her marriage to Kurt, and she certainly couldn't figure out why she felt the need to understand his relationship to Kurt.

Too close. She was already far too close to him for comfort and she wasn't thinking about his physical proximity at the moment.

He had gotten far too deep into her heart, far too much under her skin. It was far too easy when she was with him to remember the dreams she'd once entertained, the dreams of a happy, passionate marriage and a loving family of her own.

Already she knew that when he left he would leave her heart in pain. Each day, every moment, every second he remained only cut her heart more deeply. It was time to put an end to whatever it was the two of them had been sharing. It was time to say goodbye.

CHAPTER TWELVE

It was almost ten when Adam got into his car to follow Breanna and Maggie home from the Cultural Center. As he kept their taillights in his sight, the enjoyment of the day filled his soul.

After the stickball games there had been more dancing, more singing and celebration. More legends had been told, more education given on the Cherokee people and their past. There had been much laughter and talk as old friendships were renewed and new friendships were made.

Watching Breanna interact, talking with animation, laughing in abandon and joyously singing had been a delight.

By evening it seemed that all the town of Cherokee Corners had come to the Cultural Center to join in the fun. Adam saw many of the people who had been at the James's barbecue.

Jacob Kincaid, the owner of the bank, had sat for a little

while with them and they had talked about the growth of the city. They'd been joined by Glen Cleberg, the chief of police, who had bemoaned the fact that the city was outgrowing the police department.

Savannah arrived late in the evening, disappointed that the lead they'd received in their murder case had gone nowhere. The police were back to square one, with the naked body of the murdered Greg Maxwell found in front of the city library and no clues as to the perpetrator of the crime.

He and Breanna had not had any time for personal conversation the rest of the day, but her question to him about Kurt had played and replayed in his mind.

What had he gotten from his relationship from Kurt? What had kept him cleaning up after him, trying to take care of him, and keeping him out of trouble for so many years?

It hadn't been his love and respect for his aunt and uncle that had kept him bailing out Kurt. More than once they had told him to get on with his life, to stop being his cousin's keeper.

Certainly Kurt had never seemed particularly grateful for Adam's support and help. Nor had he ever seemed the least bit contrite for his bad behavior.

So what had Adam gotten out of his relationship with his cousin? He felt as if discovering the answer was important, but it remained just out of his reach no matter how hard he tried to figure it out.

He pulled into the driveway of his cottage as Breanna parked in front of her house. He exited his car, then walked over to where she was getting ready to lift a sleeping Maggie from the backseat.

"Here, let me." He gave her no opportunity to reject his

offer but instead gently moved her aside and leaned into the backseat and picked up Maggie in his arms.

The little girl instantly molded herself to him, her arms around his neck and her baby breaths warming his neck.

"Thanks," Breanna murmured, then hurried ahead of him to unlock the front door. "I can take her from here," she said as they walked into the foyer.

"Don't be silly," he countered. "I can take her upstairs for you." Maggie murmured something unintelligible against his neck and he patted her back to reassure her as he walked up the stairs to the second story.

Breanna followed close behind and when he turned into Maggie's room, she quickly pulled down the spread on the bed and motioned for him to place Maggie there.

As he laid Maggie down, her eyes opened and she gave him a sleepy smile. "Hi, Adam," she said.

"Hi, Maggie. You can go back to sleep now. You're home safe and sound."

"Are you going to kiss me good-night?"

Adam leaned down and kissed her softly on her cheek, but before he could stand up again, Maggie placed her hand on his cheek. Her gray eyes were filled with the smiles of youth. "If you ever need a little girl to be a pretend daughter, you could borrow me." Her eyes drifted closed again.

Her words wrapped around Adam's heart and squeezed tight. "Thank you, sweetie, I'll keep that in mind," he whispered softly. He straightened up and turned to leave, his gaze meeting Breanna's. He found her expression positively inscrutable.

He watched as she kissed her daughter good-night, covered her with the sheet, then he followed her back down the stairs.

"Where's Rachel?" he asked when they were in the living room. "Is she still staying with your sister?"

"She was until yesterday. She left early yesterday morning to go to Tulsa. Her father is in a nursing home there. She'll be back sometime tomorrow." She hesitated a beat. "Want some coffee?"

The question caught him by surprise, but he instantly nodded his agreement. "Sounds good." Of course, what he wanted was far more than coffee.

He wanted a repeat of what they'd shared two nights before. He wanted to unbraid her hair and work his fingers through the strands. He wanted to slide her dress from her body and make love to every inch of her silken skin.

He had enjoyed casual, intimate affairs in the past, but he couldn't remember ever wanting a woman with the intensity that he wanted Breanna.

However, during the last hours of the festival, he'd thought he'd felt her withdrawing from him. She'd grown quiet...distant and he'd wished he'd had the capacity to read her mind. He wished it again as he sat at the kitchen table and watched her preparing the coffee to brew.

"I had a great time today," he said. "It seemed like everyone in town was there."

"We usually get good turnouts for the festivals." She reached in the cabinet and withdrew two mugs. "We have three each year, one in the spring, the summer and the fall." She set an empty mug in front of him as the scent of coffee filled the air.

"You okay? You seem sort of quiet."

"I'm fine," she replied. She leaned with her back against the counter and stared at some point just over his head. "I've just been thinking."

"Thinking about what?"

She didn't reply immediately, but instead turned around to grab the coffeepot. She filled his cup, then one for herself, then returned the pot back where it belonged.

"Tell me about being raised by your aunt and uncle." She sat across from him at the table. "Tell me about those years."

He leaned back in the chair and frowned thoughtfully. "I think I already told you that initially when I arrived at Uncle Edward and Aunt Anita's house I was miserable. I was mourning my parents, missing my home, my room… my life. It was summer and I spent a lot of those first days sitting at my bedroom window, certain that I'd never, ever be happy again."

"Did you and your parents live in Kansas City?" she asked.

He shook his head. "St. Louis. It was a five-hour drive from our home in St. Louis to my uncle Edward and aunt Anita's in Kansas City, but for an eleven-year-old kid, it felt as if I'd been transplanted from one country to another."

She wrapped her slender fingers around her coffee mug. "My roots are so firmly entrenched here, I can't imagine what it would be like to have been moved to a new city…a new family at such a young age."

"I was lucky in that there was no way my aunt and uncle were going to allow me to spend my life staring out a window and feeling sorry for myself." He felt the smile that curved his lips as he thought about the lengths his aunt and uncle went to in order to involve him once again in life.

"What did they do?" she asked curiously.

"The first thing they did was sign up Kurt and me for a baseball team. I don't think Uncle Edward had ever even watched a game before in his life, but suddenly he was helping coach and Aunt Anita was providing refreshments and it became a family thing. Kurt hated it, but that summer of baseball games is what made the transition of old life to new easier for me."

"You and Kurt were immediately close?"

Adam frowned thoughtfully. "Even then Kurt was filled with a crazy energy that was both invigorating and exhausting. I was fascinated by him and embraced him as I would have a younger, rather spoiled brother of my own." He cocked his head and looked at her quizzically. "Why all the questions?"

"I've been thinking about Maggie," she finally said. She took a sip of her coffee, her eyes dark. "I've just been thinking about the fact that a child can never have too much love in their life."

Adam said nothing, but he saw the conflicting emotions that swept across her lovely face. She stared into the dark brew of her cup and continued, "There's an old saying about an acorn never falling far from the tree and when I think of that, I'm afraid to allow Kurt's parents into our lives."

She raised a hand to still Adam's protest. "Wait...I'm not finished," she exclaimed. She paused a moment and took a sip of her coffee. "Then, I have to remind myself that Anita and Edward Randolf also raised you and you're nothing like Kurt."

"Well, thank you for that," he said dryly.

She drew a deep breath. "You can tell them, Adam. You can go back to Kansas City and tell them about Maggie."

He heard the whisper of fear in her voice, knew she was conflicted about her decision. He reached across the table and covered her hand with his. "Are you sure that's what you want?"

"No. I'm not sure of anything, except that I have to trust you…to trust your judgment where Kurt's parents are concerned. If what you've said about them is true, then it would be selfish of me to keep them from Maggie…to keep Maggie from them."

"I promise you won't be sorry." Happiness filled Adam as he thought of his aunt and uncle and the joy they'd feel in Maggie's existence. His happiness was quickly followed by the realization that now there was really nothing keeping him here other than Alyssa's vague feeling of danger.

Breanna pulled her hand from his. "So I guess this means you'll be returning to Kansas City very soon."

"Yeah, it will take me a day or so to pack up my things." A hollowness resounded in his chest. He shoved it away and stood, suddenly needing to get out of her kitchen, away from her. "Thanks for the coffee," he said. "I think I'm ready to call it a night. It's been a long day."

She stood as well, obviously surprised by his hasty retreat. She followed him to the front door. "You'll come around and say goodbye to Maggie before you leave?"

"Of course." Goodbye…he'd never dreamed it would be so hard to say to anyone. What was it Alyssa had said… that sometimes loose ends could snarl you all up?

"Good night," he said and quickly walked through the front door, afraid that if he lingered a moment, a mere second, he would want to take her in his arms and kiss her sweet lips. And that would only make goodbye that much more difficult.

And he did intend to say goodbye. He had a life to get back to, a life without the complications of any relationships with any women or children.

He walked into the cottage and sank down on the sofa. Leaning his head back he closed his eyes and remembered little Maggie's bright smile, the offer that if he ever needed a temporary daughter he could borrow her.

It would be easy to love a child like Maggie, whose eyes shone with the promise of the future, who offered love so easily. Had Kurt's parents felt the same way about him when he'd been young?

Had they looked into his bright baby eyes and imagined all the great things he might become, all the wonderful things he might do? Had they lain awake nights dreaming of Kurt's life, with no idea how many tears, how much heartache he would eventually bring to them?

There was no way Adam intended to live what his aunt and uncle had lived, no way in hell he would ever put his hopes, his dreams on a child who would probably only smash them all in the end anyway.

He opened his eyes and stood from the sofa, his thoughts drifting from Maggie to her mother. Who would have thought that in just a little over a week a woman would have managed to get so deep beneath his skin?

Kurt's woman. The words played through his head, taunting him. Breanna had fallen in love and married a man who had been bigger than life, filled with energy and excitement.

Adam couldn't compete with that. He was an accountant, a man who always played it safe, a man who always did the right thing. And the right thing now was to leave Cherokee Corners, leave Breanna and Maggie to their wonderful family, their rich culture and the full life they had here without him.

It took Breanna a very long time to fall asleep that night. She stood at her bedroom window in the dark, watching the moonlight play on the leaves of the big oak tree just outside.

Thoughts of Adam filled her heart, filled her soul as no man had ever done before. How was it possible in just the brief time she'd known him? And how was it possible that she felt as if she'd known him forever?

Her physical attraction to him had been instantaneous and her trust in him, in his good character had quickly followed.

Sharing the day with him at the Cultural Center had held its own special brand of magic. He'd seemed eager to learn about her people, their customs and beliefs and unlike with Kurt, she'd wanted to share it all with Adam.

She'd watched him interacting with people and found herself admiring his easygoing nature, his openness and friendliness that drew others to him.

It had been while watching Adam interact with Maggie that she had decided to trust his judgment about Anita and Edward Randolf. A man as naturally gentle as Adam, a man as affectionate with Maggie wouldn't do anything to put her at risk either physically or emotionally. She trusted Adam enough to believe his sentiments about his aunt and uncle.

She turned away from the window and got into bed, wondering how long it would be before the Randolfs contacted her. Had Adam already called them to tell them the news? Maggie would never know her father, but hopefully she would know the love of his parents.

She'd known in telling Adam that he could tell Kurt's parents she was effectively sending him on his way. It was the final loose end he had to clean up. Now there was nothing to keep him from getting back to his real life.

She'd known all along there would be a goodbye. She

just hadn't realized how difficult that goodbye would be. Was he packing already? Maybe preparing to leave with dawn's light? A sharp pain pierced through her.

She'd told him she didn't want a relationship, but she hadn't anticipated falling in love with him. She'd thought she could handle a casual affair with him and not be touched emotionally. She'd been so wrong.

It had been ill-fated from the beginning. He had come to Cherokee Corners to clean up a mess. She and her child had been that mess. His job was done here and it was time to say goodbye.

She was surprised by the tears that burned hot behind her eyes...unexpected tears, unwanted tears. She had sworn to herself that a man would never make her cry again. But she hadn't counted on Adam and the tears that she shed were for the life they'd never have together, the dreams she'd never build with him.

She'd thought she was just on the verge of falling in love with him, but she'd been wrong. She'd fallen head over heels in love and the ache of knowing there was no happy ending for them ripped her up inside.

She fell asleep with tears still staining her cheeks, and awoke with the sun shining full in her face. When she looked at the clock she was surprised to realize it was almost nine. It was unusual for Maggie not to awaken her long before now.

A peek into Maggie's room showed the little girl still sleeping soundly. Apparently the festivities the day before had exhausted her.

Breanna pulled on a robe and went downstairs, eager for coffee. She studiously refused to think about Adam Spencer, but she did notice his car was still in the driveway of the cottage.

No more tears, she told herself firmly. Her life would return to exactly the way it had been before she'd met Adam Spencer. She had a job she loved, a child she adored, a terrific nanny and a wonderful family.

She'd just sat down at the table and started sipping her first cup of coffee when the child she adored bounded down the stairs.

"Good morning, sweetness," she said.

"Hi, Mommy. I'm hungry." Maggie slid into the chair across from Breanna and smiled winsomely. "I think it's a nice morning for pancakes."

"You do?" Breanna smiled at her daughter. "And who do you think should make these pancakes?"

"Maybe you and me?" Maggie looked at her pleadingly.

This is what's important, Breanna thought moments later as Maggie stirred the batter for the pancakes and chattered like a magpie. This was all that was important in life, her daughter. Not a man, not a relationship, not love or sex, just quality time spent with Maggie.

They ate breakfast, then while Breanna was cleaning up the kitchen, Maggie ran upstairs, dressed for the day, then came back down stairs with a blanket in hand and announced she intended to play house in the front yard.

"But it won't be the same without Mr. Bear," she said.

Breanna leaned down and gave her a hug. "I'll call Uncle Clay and ask him if later today we can go pick up Mr. Bear."

"Since I don't have Mr. Bear, would you play house with me?"

"Sure, just let me get dressed and I'll be happy to play with you."

It was a perfect way to spend some of the time on her day off, playing house with her daughter, Breanna thought moments later as she changed from her nightshirt and robe into a pair of shorts and an old T-shirt.

As she brushed her hair and carefully braided it into one thick braid down her back, she heard Maggie running up and down the stairs and knew she was taking half her stuffed animals and toys out to the blanket on the front lawn.

Before she went back downstairs, she placed a quick call to Clay and made arrangements to meet him at his lab at two that afternoon to pick up Mr. Bear. She should have gotten the bear the day after Clay had told her it had yielded no information. Mr. Bear had been with Maggie since the day she'd been born.

She went back down the stairs, poured herself a fresh cup of coffee and was about to go outside when the phone rang.

"Your father is annoyed with me," Rita said the moment Breanna said hello.

"What is it this time?" She walked through the kitchen to the living room window and peered out to see Maggie busily setting up her "house" on the blanket.

"He wants to take me on a cruise."

Breanna laughed and walked back into the kitchen for her coffee. "I wish somebody would get annoyed with me and offer to take me on a cruise."

"He's annoyed because I don't want to go," Rita exclaimed.

"Why ever not?"

"He wants to go next month. He knows how busy I am in the summer months at the Cultural Center."

"Mother, I'm sure somebody could take over your duties there for a week or two." Breanna shut off the coffeepot and emptied the last of the coffee down the sink.

"That's beside the point," Rita replied indignantly. "The fact that he would even think about going then shows his utter lack of respect for my work."

"I'm sure you two will work it out," Breanna replied. "I've got to go, Mom. Maggie's waiting for me. We're going to play house."

"All right. Give her a kiss for me and tell her I'll do my best not to kill her grandfather."

Breanna laughed. "I'll give her a kiss for you." The two women said their goodbyes and hung up.

Breanna walked through the living room and out the front door, surprised to see that Maggie wasn't in the front yard. Thinking she must have come back into the house while Breanna had been on the phone, she went back inside and stood at the bottom of the stairs.

"Maggie, I'm ready to play. There's no need to bring out everything you own."

She waited a moment, then two for a reply. When there was none, she walked up two of the stairs. "Hey, kiddo, what are you doing up there?"

Still no reply. Breanna walked up the stairs and peered into her daughter's bedroom. There was no sign of Maggie.

I must have missed her outside, Breanna thought as she ran lightly back down the stairs and out the front door. But there was still no Maggie anywhere visible in the front yard.

"Maggie!" Breanna yelled as she started around the side of the house, thinking perhaps her daughter had gone around to the back for something.

She ignored the quickened pace of her heart, telling herself not to panic. Maggie was probably playing with her, giggling as Breanna walked within inches of her hiding place.

"Maggie, answer me! Where are you? Honey, you're scaring me. Come on and let's play house."

Breanna's heartbeat boomed like thunder in her chest as there was still no sound of Maggie's voice, no sight of her anywhere.

She ran back to the front of the house, a sense of panic welling up inside her. The blanket was there, the stuffed animals were there, the little plastic dishes were there, but where was Maggie?

Dear God...where was Maggie?

CHAPTER THIRTEEN

Adam had slept late, having tossed and turned all night until dawn streaked the sky.

He got out of bed, showered and dressed and was seated at the table having his first cup of coffee for the day when somebody banged on the front door.

He hurried to the door and peeked through the peephole. It was Breanna. He pulled the door open and was about to greet her when she slammed her fists against his chest. "Where is she?" she demanded. "Where have they taken her?" She drew back her fists, her eyes wild. He anticipated her hitting him again and grabbed her by the wrists.

"Calm down," he exclaimed.

She struggled to get free of his grip. "Don't tell me to calm down. Where's my daughter...where have they taken her?"

"Where has who taken her?" Adam asked in bewilderment.

"The Randolfs," she practically screamed as she managed to wrench her wrists from his hold.

"Breanna, what in the hell are you talking about? I haven't even told my aunt and uncle about Maggie yet."

"Oh...I thought...maybe..." Her eyes were stark with panic. "I can't find her, Adam." She grabbed one of his hands and squeezed tightly. "I can't find Maggie."

Quickly, in halting words, she explained to him that the last time she'd seen Maggie, she'd been in the front yard setting up for a game of house.

"Come on, let's go look again," Adam said, refusing to panic until there was a good reason.

Maggie wasn't in the front yard as they hurried to the house. "Maybe she's hiding," he suggested. "Why don't we check out the house first. You take the downstairs and I'll take the upstairs."

As he took the stairs two at a time he could hear Breanna calling for her daughter in the downstairs. There were four bedrooms in the upstairs of the old Victorian. He checked Maggie's first, peeking into the closet, under the bed, anywhere a little girl could squeeze into.

From Maggie's room he went into Breanna's, trying not to remember the near-love scene that had taken place on her bed the day he'd plugged in her caller ID box. He also checked in the closet and beneath the bed, all the while softly calling the little girl's name.

He was trying not to panic, trying not to feed off the sheer panic he heard in Breanna's voice as she checked the downstairs.

Children hid from their parents all the time, didn't they? Hide-and-seek was one of their favorite games.

From Breanna's room he went down the hall to a bathroom, then into the next bedroom which apparently belonged to Rachel. Across from Rachel's room was a spare room containing only a couple of boxes of what appeared to be Christmas decorations.

He hurried back downstairs and met Breanna in the foyer. Never in his life had he seen such desperation on anyone's face. Her eyes were black with it and her entire body appeared to be trembling.

"Come on, let's look outside again," he said, trying to remain as calm as possible. "Would she have left the yard?" he asked as they stepped outside.

"No. She knows never to leave the yard," she replied emphatically. "It's one of our rules and Maggie doesn't break the rules." She gazed at him beseechingly, as if pleading with him to make everything all right.

"Check under your porch and mine," he instructed. "I'll go around the back and check my shed. Maybe she decided to do a bit of exploring."

She nodded, as if relieved to have something, anything constructive to do. Adam hurried to his backyard, his heart double-timing it with anxiety.

Maybe she decided to check out the shed and something fell and hit her on the head. The shed was nothing more than an accident waiting to happen.

Where else could she be? What could have happened to her? Alyssa's words of foreboding echoed sharply in his brain as he ran toward the old ramshackle shed behind his house.

She didn't break the rules, Breanna had said, but as he checked the shed and found no sign of Maggie, he told himself that even the best of kids occasionally broke the rules.

He hurried back to Breanna in the front yard. The expression of hope that lit her features fell as she saw him returning empty-handed. It broke his heart.

"Oh God, Adam, where is she?"

He frowned and drew a hand through his hair in frustration. "Maybe she saw a cat running by, or a dog...or even a squirrel and decided to run after it. A five-year-old wouldn't have to get far from home to be utterly lost."

Again a shine of hope lightened the darkness of her eyes. "You're right, that's probably it. She loves animals. And just because she's never broken the rule before doesn't mean she didn't now."

"I'll do a quick canvass of the neighborhood," Adam said. "Maybe one of the neighbors saw her go by."

"I'll go, too. We can find her twice as fast with both of us looking."

He shook his head. "No, you need to stay here. She may come back, or maybe she'll stop at somebody's house and tell them she's lost. You need to stay here and by the phone."

He knew she'd rather be out actively searching instead of passively sitting and waiting and he reached out and squeezed her icy cold, trembling hand. "If I find her, I'll call you immediately."

He didn't wait for her reply, but dropped her hand and hurried off. There was a bad feeling in his gut...a sickening feeling that he knew wouldn't go away until Maggie was found safe and sound.

Alyssa's feeling of danger to someone she loved echoed again through his head as the thought of the disturbing phone calls Breanna had received joined in.

He hoped neither had anything to do with Maggie's disappearance. He desperately hoped that it was as he'd speculated…Maggie had left the yard and was too young to find her way back home.

He had no idea which direction to pick and so arbitrarily went in the direction the three of them had walked the night they'd gone into town for ice cream.

The first two houses he stopped at his knocks on the doors went unanswered and he assumed nobody was home. In the driveway of the third house, a teenage boy was washing his car. He told Adam he hadn't seen a little girl pass by, but he'd only been outside for about ten minutes. Adam hurried on.

Two doors up from where the boy was outside, Adam saw an older man trimming bushes in his front yard. "Have you seen a little girl?" Adam asked.

"You got one that's lost?" The old man put down his clippers and approached where Adam stood on the sidewalk.

"We've got one we can't find," Adam replied.

"Well, I've been out here working in the yard all morning and I haven't seen any little ones around, but good luck finding her."

They needed more than good luck, Adam thought as he hurried back the way he had come. There was no point going any farther in this direction if the old man had been in his yard all morning and hadn't seen Maggie pass by.

As Breanna's place came back into view, he saw her seated on the front porch and knew the phone was clutched tightly in her hand.

She stood as she saw him, her body taut with tension. He heard the deep, wrenching sob that broke loose from her. She ran to him, reaching him on the sidewalk and instantly he wrapped his arms around her and pulled her tight against his chest.

Her familiar scent wrapped around him, but this time it was tinged with the odor of fear. "We'll find her," he whispered into her ear. "But I think it's time we call the police."

"I already have," she replied, then drew a deep breath and stepped out of his embrace. "Somebody should be here any minute." She offered him a smile that was aching in its desperation. "I'm sure everything is going to be just fine." She turned to walk back to the porch and wait for the authorities.

Adam was about to follow her, but stopped, frozen in place as his gaze drifted down and locked on something in the grass by the curb.

It was something pink...something hot pink. Without taking a single step closer he knew what it was. An icy chill took possession of his blood.

Thunder. The pink plastic horse that Maggie wore around her neck was no longer around her neck, but rather in the grass by the curb.

On wooden legs he stepped forward until he was close enough to see that was, indeed, what it was. He started to bend down to retrieve it, but quickly changed his mind, knowing it was important for the police to see exactly where it was...right next to the street curb...right next to where a car might have parked.

He hurried toward Breanna, deciding not to mention it to her. Time enough for that when the police arrived. Adam didn't have to be a psychic to know that things looked bad...things looked very bad.

Adam had just joined her on the porch when the first patrol car pulled into the driveway behind Breanna's car. For Breanna, time had lost all meaning. One minute was like the next…an agony of uncertainty without her precious daughter.

Before she could rise to greet the officers who climbed out of the patrol car, Adam hurried to meet them. She saw him pointing to something in the grass and she raced toward them.

When she saw what Adam had pointed at, a cry tore from her throat as agony ripped through her. Before anyone could stop her, she reached down and grabbed the plastic charm. The chain was still on it, broken in half as if yanked off forcefully.

She was a cop and the implication of the broken chain along with where it had been found wasn't lost on her. Maggie wasn't just missing. She wasn't going to be found in the neighborhood. Somebody had taken her against her will and put her in a car and driven off.

"Don't jump to conclusions," Ben Larsen, one of the responding officers, said as if he could read her mind. "We don't know how that necklace got there." He held out his hand for the necklace.

Breanna dropped it in his palm, although her instinct was to hold tight to it…and keep holding it until Maggie was back safe and sound in her arms.

She didn't realize she was crying until she tasted the salt of tears in her mouth, then she quickly swiped her tears. Now was not the time to cry. They had to find Maggie.

Adam placed an arm around her. She wanted to lean in to him, to give way to the sheer terror that gripped her heart. But she couldn't. Not now.

"I'll call for a couple more cars," Ben said. "We'll start canvassing the neighborhood. Breanna, what was your daughter wearing when you last saw her?"

Wearing? As a cop, she knew how important it was that

all the officers get an accurate description of Maggie, but for a moment her mind faltered as she tried to think of what Maggie had put on that morning.

Had she worn her pink shorts set, or a pair of jeans and a T-shirt? Why, oh why hadn't she paid more attention? Pink, she remembered now. Maggie had spilled some syrup on her shirt and Breanna had washed it off.

"Pink shorts and a pink flowered short-sleeved blouse," she said.

Ben nodded and got on his radio. Fred Macon, his partner eyed Breanna sympathetically. "We'll find her, Bree," he said. His gaze turned apologetic as he drew a pad and pen from his pocket. "You know there's certain questions I need to ask you. But first," he looked at Adam, "could I get your name, sir?"

"He's Adam Spencer. He lives next door." Breanna gestured toward the cottage.

"Could I speak with you, Mr. Spencer, alone?" Fred asked.

"Okay," Adam agreed.

"That isn't necessary, Fred," Breanna said impatiently. "He had nothing to do with Maggie's disappearance. I don't beat my child so he wouldn't have seen anything or heard anything that might lead you to believe I harmed my child. Maggie doesn't run away and Adam isn't the neighborhood pedophile." The words tumbled from her in frustration.

She knew the game, but they didn't have time to play this one by the book, knew that precious minutes were slipping away with unnecessary questions.

Before Fred could reply, another patrol car squealed to a halt before the house and Savannah got out of the driver's side. The sight of her sister set off her tears again and she ran to Savannah with arms outstretched. A million times in the past the two sisters had found solace in each other's arms.

It had been Savannah who had been at her side when she'd given birth to Maggie, Savannah who had bought the child her first teddy bear, the favorite stuffed animal, Mr. Bear.

But Savannah's arms held no comfort this time. Just as Breanna knew the night Savannah's husband had died, Breanna's hug had done nothing to ease Savannah's heartbreak.

Savannah hugged her tight for a long moment, then released her and held her at arm's length. "Tell me what's going on," she said, her lovely features taut with strain.

Quickly Breanna filled her in, the darkness in Savannah's eyes mirroring the darkness in Breanna's heart. "Then let's get busy and find her," Savannah said.

Within minutes two more patrol cars had arrived and officers were out canvassing the neighborhood, talking to people, trying to learn if anyone had seen little Maggie.

Glen Cleberg, chief of police, arrived and led Breanna and Adam into her living room where he made her recount the morning activities yet another time.

"Glen, for God's sake. We've got to do something," she exclaimed, knowing that if somebody had abducted Maggie, the first couple of hours were critical. Already the officers had grilled her on Maggie's friends and acquaintances and asked about Kurt.

"We're doing everything we can," he replied. "What I need from you now is a recent photo of Maggie. We'll put an amber alert into motion immediately. We'll have the whole city looking for her."

His words should have brought her some sort of comfort,

but Breanna was beyond comfort. She felt curiously numb, but knew that when the numbness wore off she would fall into an abyss of darkness and terror that would consume her. The terror already whispered to her, beckoning her to fall into its icy grip, but she fought against it.

She got her purse and pulled out her wallet. Inside was an identification card with a photo of Maggie. She held it for a moment, staring down at the beloved face of her daughter until her vision blurred with tears.

In the photo Maggie was wearing a T-shirt with a happy face on the front. Her smile was full, her soft gray eyes twinkling with good humor.

Breanna remembered the day they had gotten the identification card done. An organization devoted to child safety had set up in a chain discount store and Maggie, who loved to have her photo taken, had been delighted to go through the process. They'd been shopping for a night-light that day for her room.

"Bree." Adam's voice was a soft intrusion into her memory. She looked up to see him watching her, his eyes filled with worry. Gently, he took the card from her and handed it to Glen.

"I'll see that copies of this are dispersed to the press," Glen said. "In the meantime, you stay here next to the phone. I'm having Brutmeyer hook up a recording device so if a ransom call comes in we'll be able to tape it."

A ransom. The word shot a gripping fear through Breanna. A ransom couldn't be made unless somebody had been kidnapped. Oh God, please don't let Maggie be kidnapped, she prayed.

"It's just a precaution," Glen said. "Of course, we're hoping she'll turn up safe and sound someplace in the neighborhood. Why don't you put on some coffee for the officers who are going to be here until we find her," he suggested.

She knew all about making coffee. It was what was suggested to the members of every victim's family during an investigation, an action that would keep them busy and out of the investigators' hair. She'd make coffee, but there was no way she was going to stay out of anyone's hair. She didn't intend to stand around and serve the officers as they drifted in and out of her kitchen.

She wasn't simply a citizen, a victim of crime. She was a cop and her daughter was missing and she intended to do what she did best...be a cop.

As the coffee brewed, Adam hovered nearby, as if at any moment he expected her to collapse. "I'm not going to pull my hair out or faint from stress," she exclaimed to him.

"I know that."

"Well, you're hovering," she said with a touch of irritation. Then she looked...really looked at his face. His features were drawn with worry and his eyes radiated a whisper of fear. It hit her hard, in the center of her heart. He cared about Maggie.

"I'm sorry," he said, averting his gaze from hers. "I didn't mean to make you uncomfortable. I just...I just feel so damned useless." His sharp voice spoke of frustration.

She walked over and stood mere inches in front of him. She placed her hands on either side of his face, feeling the faint burr of whiskers on his jaw. "You love her, too, don't you, Adam? It's impossible to know Maggie and not love her."

His gaze met hers again and in the dark blue depths of his eyes she saw the answer to her question. "Yes, I love her." The words sounded as if they were ripped reluctantly from someplace deep inside him.

She leaned into him then and allowed herself the weakness of weeping against his chest. He held on to her as if they were both standing on the edge of a dangerous precipice and he was the anchor keeping them safe.

"Breanna?"

Reluctantly she left Adam's arms and swiped at her hot tears as Ben Larsen stepped into the kitchen. "Any news?" she asked hopefully. The young officer's expression answered her question.

"Your parents are outside and Clay has arrived."

Together Adam and Breanna followed Ben to the front porch. Breanna watched her brother taping off the entire front yard with bright yellow tape. The sight of the familiar crime scene tape sent a frigid chill up her spine.

Her parents and Alyssa stood in the driveway, each of their faces reflecting the horror that Breanna felt. She walked over to fill them in on what was going on.

Thomas placed an arm around Rita's shoulder as silent tears oozed from her eyes. Through the veil of tears, a steely strength shone through. "You tell us what to do and we'll do it."

"Maybe you could go inside and see that the men who are helping have something to eat and coffee to drink," Breanna suggested.

Rita nodded, then reached out and hugged Breanna tightly. "We'll find our little doe."

As her parents went into the house, Breanna turned to Alyssa, whose face radiated a tortured pain. "Oh, Bree. I'm so sorry. I wish I'd known more...could have warned you...I knew something bad was coming...but I never dreamed it would be Maggie."

"Shhh." Breanna stilled her by pulling her into a hug. "Nothing bad is going to happen. We're going to find Maggie safe and sound." She said the words fervently, desperately wanting to believe them.

"If only I'd seen something that might help." This was the torture of the visions Alyssa suffered and Breanna knew what her cousin was feeling, that somehow she should be able to help, that the damned visions should come when they were most needed.

"Alyssa, if I even think that you're feeling guilty, it will only makes things worse. Now, go help Mom and Dad in the kitchen." She squeezed her cousin's hand and forced a smile. "It's going to be all right…truly."

"Keep those people off the lawn." Clay's stern voice rang in the air as he pointed to a couple of neighbors who were obviously curious about the commotion. Two uniformed cops hurried to comply with his order.

"He doesn't want the scene contaminated," she said to Adam who had suddenly appeared at her side. "Now his team will search by grids, looking for anything that might be a clue. It might be a footprint…or a discarded piece of chewing gum. He'll take her blanket and all the items she was playing with to the lab and check them for hairs and fibers, for a trace of anything somebody might have left behind."

She knew she was rambling and her gaze lingered on the pink blanket on the grass. Maggie…her heart cried out. Maggie, where are you? Hang on, baby. Please hang on because I can't imagine my life without you in it.

"Breanna." Adam's sharp voice pulled her from the edge of madness. She looked at him blankly. "There's nothing you can do out here. Let's go back inside and let Clay and his people do their jobs. They want you in there to answer the phone. People have started calling and you need to keep the line clear."

The numbness was wearing off. She looked at her clock, shocked to see that it was almost two in the afternoon. Maggie had been missing for at least three hours. Three hours. Her mind screamed in protest.

She allowed Adam to lead her into the house and to the sofa. Somebody had turned on the television and she sat down next to the phone that now had a recording device on it. The technician explained to her which button to push before she answered, then left her and Adam alone.

When the phone rang it jangled every nerve in her body, but it was just a neighbor wondering what was going on. The next five phone calls were all the same, concerned friends and acquaintances wondering what was happening. Breanna got them off the line as quickly as possible.

It wasn't until she saw the amber alert on the television screen that the stark reality struck and the last of her numbness shot away. The amber alert was an immediate official response when a child went missing.

Maggie's picture was in a small box at the bottom of the screen, following by a trailer that gave her name and age and what she was wearing. Breanna read it as Adam grabbed her hand tightly. "Last seen playing in her front yard," the trailer read.

"Last seen." Breanna spoke the words aloud. "Those are words a parent should never have to see or hear about their child. Last seen." She covered her face with her hands and wept, no longer feeling like a cop, but rather simply a mother in the worst kind of pain imaginable.

Adam held her as she wept tears of fright, tears of uncertainty. Her arms ached with the need to hold Maggie. She needed to smell the scent of her baby girl, feel her wiggly warmth in her arms. She needed to hear Maggie's laughter filling a room, see those beautiful baby eyes that always held a magical sparkle.

The phone rang yet again and she jerked away from Adam's embrace. She punched the button to begin the recorder, then picked up the phone and breathed an exhausted hello.

The music started immediately, the woman singing the familiar lullaby. Breanna's gaze shot to Adam's, panicked. He quickly motioned to one of the officers as Breanna placed the call on speakerphone.

The lullaby filled the living room, the woman's voice sweet and soft. When the music stopped, there was a pregnant silence. "Hello? Who's there?" Breanna asked, wishing she could crawl through the line and discover who was on the other end.

"Now we're even," a male voice said. Deep, dark laughter filled the line, then silence.

CHAPTER FOURTEEN

"The call came from 555-2314," the technician said as he punched things into a laptop computer.

"Come on, Tom. Where's the phone," Cleberg asked.

"Wait…I got it…Tenth and Main. It's a pay phone."

Before the words were out of his mouth, Breanna was out the door. She surprised Adam by running toward his place, then he realized what she was doing. Her car was blocked in by other cars. His was not.

"Breanna," Cleberg shouted after them. "Officer James! You are not working this case as a cop. Get back here."

She ignored him and instead got into the driver seat of his car. "Give me your keys," she said, her eyes wild with urgency.

"I'm not letting you drive anywhere," he protested. "You want to get to that phone, you let me drive." She sighed in frustration, but moved over to the passenger side. He slid in and pulled out of his driveway with a squeal of his tires and pointed the car in the direction of Main Street.

He looked in his rearview mirror and saw two patrol cars behind him, their lights flashing and sirens wailing. "Ignore them," she said tersely.

"You really don't think anyone is going to be at that phone, do you?" he asked. She didn't reply and he realized then that her hope was irrational, the hope of a mother clinging to straws.

Adam stepped on the gas, driven by his own irrational hope that maybe the bastard who took Maggie had stopped to make the call and his car had broken down, or he'd parked illegally and somebody was towing the car away, Maggie sleeping comfortably in the backseat.

Funny, how love could mess with your mind. Love. Despite his desire never to love a child who could break his heart, somehow Maggie had managed to crawl beneath the defenses he'd tried to erect. He loved her, and with every minute that passed his heart was breaking in a way he hadn't thought possible. He couldn't imagine the pain Breanna must be feeling.

She pointed just ahead of him. "There."

The phone booth was an old-fashioned kind that was rarely seen anymore. Adam squealed to a halt in front of it as Breanna jumped out of the passenger side and looked around, her gaze sweeping from side to side as she checked out the area. "Don't touch the phone," she instructed Adam, although he had no intention of doing so.

The other officers surrounded the phone booth with the intention of keeping out everyone. Adam figured eventually one of the crime scene people would be out here to check for evidence…something…anything the perpetrator might have left behind.

"I knew there wouldn't be anything here," she said bitterly. "But I couldn't take just sitting in that house another minute."

He understood her need to do something, but what could they do? They had nothing but a disembodied voice on the phone to go on.

"Breanna, the officers will keep an eye on things here. We really need to go back to the house," he said.

She nodded, her shoulders slumping forward. Without any argument, she got back into his car. They drove in silence and Adam tried to think of something...anything to say that might help. But he recognized that words held no power to soothe in a situation like this.

She'd already amazed him with her strength. The tears she'd shed had been brief and instead what he felt now from her was a restless energy to do something...anything to help.

When they returned to the house, Clay was gone, along with the blanket and the items that had been on the front lawn. The other two crime scene investigators who worked with Clay were still combing the front yard, looking for clues.

"Dammit, Breanna," Glen Cleberg met them at the front door. "I know how you feel, but you can't go off all half-cocked like that."

"You don't know how I feel," she replied. "Somebody has taken my daughter and I'm not about to sit here twiddling my thumbs. I'm a cop, Glen, and if you keep me out of the loop I'll go crazy. And now I'm going upstairs." She shot Adam a pointed look. "I'd like a few minutes alone."

Without waiting for a reply, she climbed the staircase and disappeared into her bedroom.

Glen Cleberg looked at Adam and shook his head. "This

entire investigation has been taken over by the James family and by rights none of them should be working the case. But they're stubborn, and all three of them are the best I've got on the force." He rubbed a hand over his meaty jaw. "I never thought I'd see the day that children couldn't play in their own front yards here in Cherokee Corners."

"It only takes one bad person in a town to make everyone afraid," Adam replied, his gaze going up the staircase, his thoughts on Breanna. What must be going through her mind? How much uncertainty could one mother stand?

"I've got to say, Mr. Spencer, I got a bad feeling about this one. We got nothing to go on. So far nobody has turned up a witness who saw a suspicious car around here, or anyone who has seen little Maggie."

"Maybe Clay will find something on the blanket that will help," Adam offered.

"Maybe," Glen replied, but he didn't sound too hopeful. "But only if the perp was on that blanket. If he grabbed her out by the curb where her necklace was found, then he won't find squat."

"What about Michael Rivers?" Adam asked.

"We already checked him out. He's been at work all day. I talked to his boss and had one of the local cops check it out. I wish to hell it would have been that easy."

Without waiting for Adam's reply, the chief of police turned and disappeared into the kitchen. The phone rang and the technician answered. It was obvious by his words that it was yet another acquaintance wanting information.

Adam sat in a chair in the living room, feeling more helpless than he ever had in his life. He'd just sat down when Alyssa came out of the kitchen, something clutched in her hand.

He stood. "What's up?" he asked.

She held out a photo of Maggie. "I'm going to get flyers made and see that they get distributed all over town."

He could see the remnants of tears, the red-rimmed lids around eyes that held fear...pain...and guilt. "Alyssa, there's nothing you could have done to prevent this."

"Logically, I know that," she replied. "But emotionally I keep wondering if there is something I missed... some vision that I didn't see clearly that might help." Tears sparked in her eyes, but she drew a deep breath and straightened her shoulders. "I've got to go. At least I have something constructive to do."

The minutes ticked by, broken only by officers coming in and out of the house and the ringing of the telephone. Adam sat in the living room thinking of Breanna...thinking of Maggie.

Maggie, who had wanted him to tell her he was proud of her because that's what daddies did. Maggie, who had told him if he ever needed a temporary pretend daughter, he could borrow her.

And now she was missing...apparently taken by a stranger and the pain that pierced his heart was all encompassing. That's why he hadn't wanted to have children...because they always broke your heart.

He sat on the sofa until the scent of hamburgers cooking filled the air. Rita must be cooking up something for everyone. Breanna had eaten no lunch. He needed to get her back down here to eat something.

He climbed the stairs, afraid of intruding, yet unable to spend another minute without seeing if Breanna was okay. Of course she's not okay, his brain screamed at him. She may never be okay again.

She wasn't in her bedroom, although he was surprised

to see the clothes that she'd been wearing on the bed. He peeked into Maggie's room and there she was, sitting on the edge of Maggie's bed.

It was the first time he'd seen her in her official uniform. The khaki shirt and slacks should have looked masculine on her, but instead seemed to emphasize her utter femininity.

She looked up at him as he entered. Her eyes were tearless, but hollow. "It's going to be dark soon," she said. She didn't look at him, but rather stared down at the stuffed rabbit she held on her lap. "I hope she got to eat lunch… or at least will get dinner. She gets so cranky when she's hungry."

Adam said nothing and she stroked the rabbit fur and continued. "When she gets back, I'll take her out for chicken nuggets. That's her favorite. I worry sometimes because that's all she ever orders when we go out. She never tries anything new. But when she gets back I'll let her order all the chicken nuggets she wants and I won't say a word."

He leaned against the doorjamb, letting her ramble, knowing this moment would haunt him for years to come. "She's afraid of the dark. That's why she always sleeps with a night-light." For the first time since he'd entered the room she looked up at him. "We have to find her before dark."

He nodded, his chest so tight he couldn't speak, couldn't move. He wanted to wrap her in his arms and never let her go, wanted to hunt down whomever had caused this pain and kill him. Adam wasn't normally a violent man, but a blood thirst filled him as he gazed at Breanna.

"Your mother is cooking some dinner." He finally found

his voice. "Why don't you come down and get something to eat?"

She shook her head negatively. "I'm not hungry."

He didn't press the issue, had known before he spoke that food for herself would be the last thing on her mind. Her cell phone rang and she leaned over and picked it up from Maggie's nightstand.

"James," she said as she answered. "Yes, Clay." She stood and her tension filled the room. "Yes…okay…got it. And Clay…thanks." She clicked off and looked at Adam. "He checked the blanket and found several things. Dirt… grass stain…Maggie's hair…just what you'd expect to find on a blanket where a little girl played. But, he also found a bit of concrete, some tar and several feline hairs."

She frowned. "Feline hair…cat hair," she said softly, more to herself than to him. Her eyes flashed to his, wide with shock. "I think I know who has Maggie." She ran past him and down the stairs. He hurried after her, his heart racing as he wondered why cat hair had given her a name?

"Turn left here," Maggie instructed Adam. She was horribly afraid she might be wrong and equally horrified that she might be right. They'd left the house without anyone knowing where they were going. She knew Glen would pop a cork if he knew what she suspected and where she was going.

She also knew she was a fool for involving a civilian and going in without backup, but it couldn't be helped. Adam's car was easily accessible, hers was not. And she knew instinctively Adam would have never allowed her out of the house without him.

"You want to tell me where we're going?" Adam asked as they flew past the Cultural Center.

"My partner's place."

Adam eyed her sharply. "You think your partner has Maggie?"

"Yes…no…I don't know," she replied miserably. Abe, her heart cried. Is it possible? Could you really do something like this to me?

"What makes you think he'd do something like this?" he asked dubiously.

"He's retiring and the other day he was talking about how he wished he was going out with a bang…some big bust of some kind. Turn right up here at the intersection."

"I'm not sure I understand."

Breanna sighed in frustration. "I don't know, Adam. Maybe he took her and has her hidden away someplace, then he'll be the cop who finds her alive and well. It would be the perfect way to retire, as a hero."

"It sounds just a little bit crazy," Adam replied.

"I know." She chewed her bottom lip thoughtfully. And it would be out of character for the man who'd been her mentor, the man she'd trusted with her life more than once. She'd thought she'd known him, but she'd thought she'd known Kurt as well. Maybe she was just a bad judge of character.

"He also has a cat," she said, then added in desperation. "I can't not check him out, Adam. Even if I don't want to believe it."

She stared out the window, absently noting the thick stand of trees beyond which flowed the river. She touched the butt of her gun, hoping she wouldn't have to draw it against a fellow officer…against her own partner.

"Slow down," she said to Adam, her gaze locking on the copse of trees beyond which Abe's home stood. Dusk was beginning to fall, painting the trees with pale gold light and creating purple shadows amid the trees.

Was Maggie there? Dear God, she wanted her to be there and she didn't. She wanted her daughter more than anything, but she didn't want her partner to be the one responsible for her being missing.

"Turn right on the next dirt road. It will lead up to Abe's house." Adrenaline roared through her. "At least we aren't in a patrol car. He won't recognize this car."

"Why don't I go up and knock on the front door...kind of get a feel for things," Adam suggested as he slowed the car to a crawl.

"Absolutely not," she replied. "You stay in the car. I'll be in trouble for having you with me. The last thing I need is for you to get hurt."

Again he eyed her sharply, his blue gaze hard and cold. "If you think you're going in there alone, then you have another think coming." There was a stern, implacable edge to his voice she'd never heard before.

"Adam, please don't argue with me," she replied impatiently.

He stopped the car and turned in the seat. "I told you, Breanna. You are not going into that house alone. You'll have to shoot me to keep me in this car."

"All right, all right," she exclaimed, not wanting to take the time to fight with him. "The house is just around the corner. Let's go ahead and leave the car here and walk in."

Together they got out of the car and started walking down the dirt road that led to Abe's place. "Do you have a plan?" Adam asked quietly.

"None," she admitted. "I just intend to get inside and see if my daughter is there." She was grateful he didn't say anything more. She pulled her gun as the house came into view.

It was a small, two-bedroom cottage tucked amid the trees. Breanna had visited Abe here on many occasions. She'd eaten dinner with him, brought her daughter here to fish with Uncle Abe in the river that ran across the back of his property.

As she stared at the house, she reviewed the floor plan in her mind and tried to figure out the best way to approach. "I'm going straight in," she said aloud. "I'm just going to knock on the door and see what happens."

Adam simply nodded, apparently trusting her judgment. Drawing a deep breath, she started across the yard toward the front door. Adam walked next to her and strangely enough she felt as if he was all the backup she needed.

He exuded strength and energy and she knew he would have her back. He reached the front door before her and knocked. Even the sound of his fist on the wooden door sounded strong and capable.

They waited a moment or two for a reply and when there was none, Adam knocked again, this time more forcefully.

"I'm coming…hold your horses," Abe's voice came from inside the house.

Breanna tensed, knowing a confrontation was imminent. Abe opened the door and his face wreathed into a surprised smile. "Bree!" His smile faded as his gaze swept over her uniform. "Don't tell me I'm confused on my days and I'm supposed to be working."

"Can we come in, Abe?" she asked.

He frowned, obviously sensing the tension ripe in the air. "What's going on?" His fingers tightened on the door.

"We'd just like to come in and ask you a few questions," Adam said.

Abe eyed him suspiciously. "Who the hell are you, and hell no, you aren't coming in until somebody tells me what is going on."

Breanna's heart sank. As she saw the hurt confusion in Abe's eyes, she realized she was wrong. He'd never do anything to hurt her or Maggie. "Maggie's missing, Abe."

"Missing? What do you mean?" He looked at her with what appeared to be obvious confusion.

"She was in my front yard this morning and disappeared."

"What can I do to help? You need me at the station?"

Breanna hesitated. She had a feeling she was about to break an old man's heart. "No...we're just checking everything...everyone," she said vaguely.

Abe stared at her, then at Adam, then back again at her, the dawning of betrayal darkening his eyes. "You thought she might be here? You thought I had something to do with this?"

"There were cat hairs, Abe."

"Half the people in Cherokee Corners have cats." Abe threw open his door. "But don't take my word for it. Hell, Breanna, come in. Search my house. Do whatever you have to do, then get the hell out of here."

Breanna promptly burst into tears...because she knew she wouldn't find her daughter here...and because she'd just destroyed a relationship with a man she loved.

CHAPTER FIFTEEN

Something had broken inside her. Although Abe had consoled her and insisted he wasn't angry with her, something had broken inside Breanna. It was as if all the grief she'd been holding in had surfaced and exploded into uncontrollable tears.

All the strength had seeped away from her and she didn't look like a cop anymore. She looked like a victim… slumped down in the seat…the inconsolable mother of a missing child. And darkness was falling.

Her wrenching sobs had finally ceased, leaving behind silent tears that continued to ooze down her cheeks as she stared out the passenger window.

Adam tried to think of something to say, anything to ease her pain. It filled the car, seeped into his pores and constricted his heart.

"It's got to be somebody I know," she finally said. The words surprised him. He'd thought she was lost in a sea of grief, but apparently she wasn't so lost that her brain wasn't working. "It isn't a stranger abduction." She sat up straighter in the seat and wiped her cheeks with the back of her hand. "Now we're even, that's what the voice said on the phone. Now we're even." She frowned thoughtfully.

"So, whose kid have you taken lately?" he asked half-jokingly.

"I don't know." She sat up even straighter in the seat. "Take me to the station, Adam. I need to pick something up."

He didn't ask questions, he merely did as she bid. When she reached the station house, he followed her inside. Fellow officers who offered their commiseration and aid greeted her.

They learned that while they'd been away from the house posters had been distributed and Jacob Kincaid had put up a ten-thousand-dollar reward for information leading to the whereabouts of Maggie.

Breanna took in all this information stoically, then disappeared into a storage room and came out carrying a heavy box of files. Adam quickly took the box from her. "What's this?" he asked.

"All the cases I've worked on since I started in the department. I can't help but think that the man who has Maggie is hiding in these files." Her eyes burned with a renewed sense of purpose.

"Then let's get them back to your place and get busy on them."

Darkness had fallen completely as they once again parked in Adam's driveway, although every light in Breanna's house was on and several patrol cars were still parked out front.

The technician manning the phone greeted them as they came back inside. "Anything?" Breanna asked him.

"Nothing."

They went into the kitchen to find the table laden with food. Several officers were filling plates and Breanna's mother was fussing over them like a mother hen. Her father was washing dishes, his face a stoic mask.

They both stopped what they were doing long enough to hug Breanna and again, the loyalty and love this family had for one another struck Adam.

"Neighbors have been bringing food," Rita said. Adam looked at the table where there appeared to be at least six different kinds of casseroles. The universal language of support and caring...the casserole.

Glen came into the kitchen, his face showing the wear of the day. "Where in the hell have you been?" he asked Breanna.

"It isn't important now," she replied.

He eyed the box Adam still held in his arms and frowned. "That looks like official police paperwork."

"It's my files, Chief," Breanna responded. "It's got to be a revenge thing. Maybe somebody we busted for drugs who lost their children to child welfare."

"Need some help going through them?" Glen asked. "I'll assign some men."

"I'll help," Savannah said from where she stood drying dishes.

At that moment Abe walked through the door. "Whatever it is you're talking about, I'll help." He looked at Breanna and even Adam could see the forgiveness in his eyes. "It's what a partner does."

Breanna's eyes moistened and she nodded.

They took the file box into the living room and got to

work. Abe, Savannah, Thomas, Breanna, Adam and two officers each took a handful of the files and began reading the cases, hoping for something that might jump out at them.

Breanna had told them to look for cases where the person being arrested had been violent, where the arrest record showed a family and employment that might pertain to working with concrete and tar.

Adam made sure Breanna was facing away from the windows, not wanting her to see the deepening darkness of night. The television was on, although the sound was muted. But every time Adam looked at it he saw the amber alert running along the bottom of the screen. *Maggie James... Last seen...* The words haunted him.

Adam had never realized before that desperation had a scent, but it did and it filled the living room as everyone read file after file of arrests Breanna had made or had been a part of.

Breanna's reports were meticulous and neatly typed. It was slow, painstaking work. There was no place on the arrest sheets to indicate a family. The only way to discern that was to read the handwritten notes Breanna had taken and included with each of the arrest forms.

Reading file after file, Adam got a taste for what Breanna's work life was like and his admiration for her grew. It was obvious that she was good at what she did. He glanced at her, noting the dark circles beneath her eyes, the slump of her shoulders, the redness of her bottom lip where she had been chewing.

The minutes ticked by...minutes that left Maggie in the hands of a possibly revenge-crazed violent man. Adam couldn't forget the blow he'd received on his head and he hoped...prayed that the person who'd been capable of almost killing him with a brick wasn't the same person that held Maggie captive.

Was it already too late for little Maggie? Was she already lying in a ditch by the side of the road? He shook his head to dislodge such a horrendous thought, surprised to feel the burn of tears.

Not Maggie, he prayed. Please God, don't take Maggie... not now...not like this. He refocused on the files, wondering if they were merely spinning their wheels while a kidnapper took Maggie farther and farther away from Cherokee Corners.

It was midnight when they finally got through all the files. Each person had a small stack of possibilities for Breanna to look through.

Adam moved to sit next to her as she perused each file. He thought he could hear her heartbeat, feel it pounding as if her heart was in his chest. Find Maggie. Find Maggie. That was the rhythm of the beats—find Maggie...find Maggie.

"I don't know...I just don't know," she said softly. She looked at him, sheer agony reflected in her eyes. "There isn't enough information here. I don't remember half these cases. How am I supposed to do this? How am I supposed to find Maggie?"

He took the files from her and pulled her against him. "Calm down," he said as he stroked the length of her hair. "We'll find her. I swear, we'll find her." He prayed as he'd never prayed before, wishing he could do more for her.

She held tight to him, as if he were her lifeline to sanity. "It's so dark outside, Adam. It's so dark and she has to be so frightened. I can't stand the thought of her being afraid." She pulled away from him and reached for the files once again.

"Breanna, the phone calls started about ten days ago. Maybe you should take out all the old files, concentrate on the ones only a week or two before the calls started," he suggested.

She nodded and for the next few minutes weeded through the files until she had a total of ten in her lap. "Now, take them one at a time and tell me about them."

As she did, people drifted in and out of the living room, but nobody interrupted them by speaking. Adam listened as Breanna went through the cases. As she studied the files and spoke aloud, she seemed to remember more than she'd initially thought she would.

"This guy was a newlywed...two weeks married and he was trying to pay me for sex." She shook her head ruefully. "He went a little crazy when we arrested him, screamed that we were ruining his marriage."

"What happens when these men are arrested for soliciting prostitution?" Adam asked.

"They're taken down to the station, fingerprinted and photographed, then given citations and they have to appear in court," Breanna explained. "It's only a misdemeanor charge...really not a big deal."

"Unless the little woman finds out and the marriage ends. His loss in exchange for yours?"

The slump disappeared from her shoulders as she sat up straighter on the sofa. "How can we find out quickly if his wife left him?" she asked.

"Easy enough. Give me your cell phone." There was a phone number on the arrest report and Adam quickly punched in it. "Could I speak to Mrs. Jennings?" he said into the receiver.

"What are you crazy? It's the middle of the damned night. She's sleeping. Who the hell is this?"

Adam hung up. "The little lady is in bed where she belongs."

Breanna dug out another file. They made eight phone calls before they hit one that counted. "May I speak to Mrs. Duncan?" Adam said into the cell phone to the gruff hello.

"She doesn't live here anymore. Who is this?"

Adam clicked off and turned to the young officer standing nearby. "We need to get some information on Eddie Duncan," he said. "When he was arrested he said he was unemployed. We need to know immediately where he's working and the circumstances of his family life."

"I remember him," Breanna said as the officer hurried out of the room. "He was a tall, burly guy. He was another one that went crazy when we arrested him. Called me all kinds of names, told me if his wife found out his life would be ruined." Her eyes held an edge of wildness. "One ruined life for another? Now we're even?"

It seemed to take forever for the officer to return to the living room. "Eddie Duncan. Address is 5981 Cypress Road. Currently employed with the highway department. It will take a little longer to find out about his family status."

"Highway department. Tar…concrete…it's too coincidental to ignore." She jumped up from the sofa, but Adam grabbed her arm.

"You aren't doing this without official backup," he said firmly. "If this guy is the same one who hit me in the head with that brick, then we know what he's capable of. You don't want to put Maggie at risk by going in alone."

"You're right." She got on her cell phone and called Cleberg who was at the station waiting for a break in the case.

Within minutes a team of police officers was being dispatched to check out the situation. Despite the fact that

Cleberg had put another officer in charge, everyone looked to Breanna for guidance, knowing she was the one with the most at stake.

"His house is off the beaten track," Breanna said, apparently knowing the area. "If it's the one I'm thinking of, it's surrounded by trees. We'll park on Highway Ten and go in on foot. Nobody approach the house until I give the go-ahead."

They all started out the door and Adam followed Breanna. She stopped him at her car. "Adam, you can't go."

"You can't stop me. I can either ride with you or I'll take my own car, but I'm going." She started to protest, but he held up his hand. "You're wasting precious time arguing a lost cause. You've forgotten...I love her, too."

She gazed at him for a long moment, then nodded and together they got into her car. "No sirens, no lights," she said into her radio. These were the last words spoken until they reached a section of dark, deserted highway where the patrol cars gathered and shut off their engines.

There were a total of six officers along with Breanna and Adam. Adam could tell that the other officers didn't approve of him being there, but Adam wasn't leaving.

He had to be here, wanted to see firsthand if Breanna was reconnected with her daughter in a happy reunion. And he needed to be here in case the reunion wasn't joyous at all.

She thought she could smell Maggie's scent as they made their way through the thick woods toward Eddie Duncan's house. It was that special blend of childhood innocence, of sweet little girl and peach bubble bath.

Of course, it was impossible that she smelled it, but she

needed to believe that she was close enough to Maggie to smell her, close enough to Maggie to save her.

She didn't even know if they were on the right trail. It was a hunch with little else behind it. It was possible that Eddie Duncan was a perfectly innocent man in all this and Maggie was a hundred miles from here.

She clutched her flashlight in her hand, although it wasn't turned on. Thankfully the moonlight cast down just enough illumination to allow them to move through the trees without artificial lighting.

Adam was right behind her and even though she knew his presence here wasn't right, she was grateful for it. He loved Maggie, too. She had to be here. Please let this hunch pay off, she prayed.

The house came into view, a small ranch. Lights shone from within, creating splashes of light on the overgrown lawn. Tall grass in the yard, dying flowers in a weed-choked flower bed gave the place an air of neglect.

She clicked on her radio. "Check in," she said softly.

"Unit one in place."

"Unit two ready."

"Three is ready, too."

The officers checked in, each from a different side of the house. Breanna and Adam remained hidden in the trees about twenty feet in front of the house.

"I'm going to check it out," she said. "Hold your positions." She turned to Adam. "You stay here. I'm just going to get closer and take a look around." She started to leave, but he grabbed her by the arm and stopped her.

"Be careful," he said, then leaned forward and covered her lips with his. It was a fast kiss, over almost before it had begun, but it warmed her as she left the copse of trees and moved closer to the house.

She avoided the pools of brightness from the lights inside the house and clung to the shadows as she made her way across the lawn.

When she reached the front of the house she paused. She couldn't take a chance on stepping onto the porch. The wood might creak or make noise that would draw the attention of whomever was in the house and she wasn't ready for that.

Instead she crept to the right side of the house where a window beckoned her to peek in. Cautiously, she raised her head just enough to look into the house. The window was in the kitchen, and the kitchen was empty of people. But her heart bucked and kicked in her chest as she saw the remnants of two TV dinners on the kitchen table. A beer can set next to one, a half-emptied glass of milk at the other.

The sight caused a wave of relief to wash over her that was almost overwhelming. If, indeed, Maggie was inside the house, then the odds were good she was still alive. Hopefully, that glass of milk and TV dinner indicated she was not only alive, but had been fed dinner, as well.

But of course there were a million other scenarios. The extra dinner could have been for a friend of Eddie's, or a relative that lived with him. There was absolutely no guarantee that Maggie had sat in that kitchen chair.

She moved around to the back of the house where there were four windows. The first was dark, but as she peered in she realized there was a hall light on and she could see that this room was probably the master bedroom. The double bed was unmade and clothes were strewn over the floor. Several coffee cups sat on the nightstand, along with balled-up tissues and a lamp with a torn shade.

If nothing else, Eddie Duncan should be cited for being

a slob, she thought as she moved to the next window, which was a bathroom.

The third window was another bedroom. She slapped a hand over her mouth to stop the cry that threatened to escape. It was a child's room. A rocking horse stood in one corner and toys littered the floor. But that wasn't what made her heart threaten to explode from her.

Maggie. She was on a single bed, her thumb in her mouth. She hadn't sucked her thumb for years and the sight of her baby made Breanna want to smash through the window, pluck her up off the bed and carry her to safety.

But it was her training that forced her to maintain control. She had no idea where in the house Eddie Duncan might be, knew that as long as Maggie was on the inside with him she was in imminent danger.

Was she okay? Was she sleeping? Breanna held her breath, watching her baby. Had he drugged her…or were they already too late? Maggie stirred restlessly and a sigh of relief escaped Breanna.

As difficult as it was, she forced herself away from the window. The last window yielded a view of a spare bedroom packed with boxes and furniture.

As stealthily as possible, she made her way back to her original position. "She's there," she whispered to Adam. "And she's alive."

"Thank God," Adam murmured.

Breanna got on her radio and let the other officers know exactly where Maggie was located and the fact that it appeared through deduction that Eddie Duncan was probably located in the living room.

"I'm going to try to get Maggie through the bedroom window, but I need two of you here in the front to provide a distraction," she said.

Plans were made and once the officers were in their new positions, Breanna worked her way back around the house and once again to the window of the room where Maggie was sleeping. She radioed her men that she was in position, then waited, heart racing, palms sweaty and gun ready.

"Eddie Duncan...this is the Cherokee Corners Police Department." A voice boomed through the night. At the same time Breanna tapped on the window.

"Wake up," she whispered. Maggie had always slept hard.

"Come out with your hands up."

The male voice once again filled the air. She knocked on the window once again, nearly sobbing with relief as Maggie stirred. The thumb came out of her mouth as her eyes opened.

Breanna, afraid to knock again without knowing if Eddie Duncan was at the front of the house or heading back to this room, willed her daughter to look at the window.

"Eddie Duncan. We have the house surrounded. Come out now with your hands over your head."

As the officers in the front of the house spoke over the bullhorn, Breanna reached up and tried to open the window. Although she didn't budge the locked window, her motion caught Maggie's attention. Breanna quickly signaled her daughter to keep quiet, then motioned for her to unlock the window. Seconds. It was all she needed to get Maggie to safety. Maggie's face was tearstained and her mouth formed the word *Mommy* as she tried to unlock the window, but she didn't have the strength to switch the lever that would unlock the window.

A gunshot exploded and full-fledged panic slammed into Breanna. She had no idea who had fired, the police or Eddie, but she knew she had to get Maggie out the window now.

"Stand back," she yelled to her daughter. She took the butt end of her flashlight and crashed it into one of the little panes on the window. When the glass was out, she reached through, flipped the lock, then yanked the window open.

"Come on, baby," she cried as another gunshot resounded.

Maggie ran to the window and climbed over the sill and into her mother's arms. At that moment Breanna saw a shadow coming down the hallway toward the bedroom.

She set Maggie on the ground and gave her a shove. "Run, baby. Run as fast as you can for the trees."

Maggie didn't hesitate, but did as Breanna told her. Breanna sobbed in relief as she saw Maggie make the cover of the trees. Only then did she turn to run. She got only a few feet away from the house, then looked over her shoulder and froze. Eddie Duncan's face appeared in the open window, along with a pointed gun.

"You bitch!" he cried, his voice filled with venom.

Breanna knew he was going to shoot and she also knew at this close range he probably wouldn't miss. At least Maggie is safe, she thought as she fumbled for her own gun.

She heard Eddie's gun roar, as if from a million miles away, then she slammed to the ground, somebody else's body covering hers.

Another shot went off and Eddie screamed. It was the scream of the wounded and Breanna knew the officers had stormed the house.

Adam's bright blue eyes gazed at her. "You okay?" he asked, his voice sounding funny.

"You saved my life, but you're really heavy," she said.

"I always thought if I ever got shot, the bullet would probably come from your gun. Guess I was wrong." His eyes rolled up in the back of his head.

"Adam!" Breanna screamed as she struggled to get out from under his dead-heavy body. It was only when she got to her feet that she saw the blood gushing from the wound in his back. "Help me!" she cried, tears blurring her vision as she tried to staunch the bleeding.

"Hang on, Adam," she whispered. "Please, hang on." They had managed to save Maggie, but she'd never be able to forgive herself if the price she had to pay was Adam's life.

CHAPTER SIXTEEN

It had been two weeks since Adam had taken a bullet in the back that had magically missed every vital organ except his spleen, which the doctors had removed.

He stood at the window of his hospital room, waiting for Breanna, who was coming to take him back to the cottage. He'd been champing at the bit for the past three days, eager to leave this medical institution behind.

For the past two weeks he'd been treated like a hero by everyone in town. It had been embarrassing as hell. He wasn't a hero, he was just an accountant who had somehow managed to get in way over his head.

Eddie Duncan's story had made the rounds. It had been a nurse who had told him that Eddie had been arrested by Breanna on a solicitation charge. His wife had found out and had left him, taking their four-year-old little girl with her. Neighbors said the little girl had been Eddie's life, and he went just a little bit crazy. According to neighbors, he'd stopped going to work, but had left the house at odd hours. He'd become secretive and furtive, and more than one source had indicated they thought he was drinking a lot.

He was in a bed in the same hospital where Adam was, being treated for a gunshot wound to the leg before standing trial on a number of charges.

Breanna and Maggie had come to visit Adam every day, as had most of her family members and half the town. His hospital room was overflowing with flower arrangements, their cloying fragrance filling the air. He'd told the nurses to disperse them around to other rooms.

"All set?"

He turned from the window to see Breanna. Her loveliness filled his heart, his soul and he knew it was time to leave Cherokee Corners behind. Today. When he arrived back at the cottage, he'd pack and leave. It was way past time for him to say his goodbyes.

"More than all set," he replied. "I hope I don't see another hospital room for years to come." He grabbed the duffel bag from the bed.

"Oh, no, you don't," a nurse said as she entered the room pushing a wheelchair. "All of our discharged patients get curbside transportation."

"That really isn't necessary," he protested.

"Yes, it is," she replied and took the duffel bag from him. "It's the rules." She looked at Breanna. "If you'd like to pull your car up in front, I'll push him to the curb."

"Okay." She disappeared and Adam reluctantly got into the chair. "We're going to miss you," she said as she pushed Adam out of his room. "You've been a terrific patient."

"The staff here has been wonderful," he replied. It was

true. He'd had good treatment by doctors, nurses and all other staff.

Breanna was waiting for him at the curb and she hurried out of the driver's seat as they appeared. "You don't have to treat me like an invalid," he protested as she opened the car door for him.

He threw his duffel bag into the backseat, then got into the car. He was irritated and he didn't know why. He drew a deep breath to gain control as she got into the car and they pulled away from the curb.

"I'm leaving today." The words fell out of his mouth without his volition.

"I'm sure it will be good to be out of the hospital," she replied.

He realized she'd misunderstood what he was saying. "No, I mean I'm leaving Cherokee Corners. It's time for me to go home."

She took her foot off the gas and flashed him an unreadable look. "Are you sure? I mean, are you sure you're up to it?"

"I'm fine." He realized the thought of leaving was what was making him irritable. But he had to leave. All loose ends had been tidied up. Maggie was safe, Breanna was fine and Edward and Anita were thrilled by Maggie's existence and had already planned a trip to meet Maggie and Breanna next week.

"Where's Maggie?" he asked.

"Spending the night with my folks," she replied.

"How's she doing?"

"All right...considering." She tucked a strand of her long, dark shiny hair behind her ear. "Thank goodness Eddie wasn't mean to her. She only had nightmares for the first two nights. She's going to be just fine."

"I'm glad." He stared out the passenger window and was grateful when she didn't say anything else. Telling her goodbye would be the most difficult thing he'd ever done, but he'd never been in the market for a long-standing relationship.

She parked in his driveway and together they got out of the car. "Can I come in for a minute?" she asked and gestured toward his cottage. "I have something I want to talk to you about before you leave."

He gazed at her curiously, but her expression gave nothing away. "Sure, come on in." It seemed that in the past two weeks of his hospitalization they'd talked about everything under the sun. He couldn't imagine what she might possibly have to talk to him about before he left.

He dropped his duffel bag on the sofa, then turned to look at her. Goodbye would have been easier if she didn't look so beautiful, he thought. But clad in a sundress of rainbow colors, her skin looked like rich polished wood and her loose dark hair beckoned him to touch it...stroke the shiny length.

"What did you want to talk to me about?" he asked.

She took a step closer to him and he tensed as her familiar, evocative scent surrounded him. "Adam...don't go."

Her simple words hit him like a blow in the gut. He suddenly recognized that the look radiating from her eyes was one of love. "Breanna...don't."

"Don't what? Don't tell you that I love you? Don't tell you that the thought of you going leaves a hollowness inside me?" She stepped so close to him he could feel her body heat radiating to him. "I swore to myself when Kurt left me that I'd never fall in love again, that I'd never share my life, my love with another man. But you changed that, Adam."

"Breanna…" He took a step back from her, desperately needing the distance. "You're grateful to me, that's what it is. We shared a trauma with Maggie's kidnapping and that has you thinking you feel something that you don't."

"Why would you believe that?" she asked incredulously. "Why would you believe that I don't love you?"

He raked a hand through his hair in frustration. "Because you loved my cousin," he replied. "Because you fell in love with Kurt and I am not like him, will never be anything like him. He was fun and adventurous, he exuded magnetism and a wildness that isn't in me."

She stared at him for a long moment. "Let me tell you something, Adam Spencer. When I met Kurt, he was pretending to be something he wasn't. He told me he was a bookkeeper on vacation. He led me to believe he was steady and responsible, caring and giving. I fell in love with the man he was pretending to be…and he was pretending to be you."

He looked at her in astonishment.

"It's true," she said softly, stepping up before him once again. "He made himself out to be a man just like you, Adam. A man who could be trusted, a man who would make me proud of who I am, a man that I could love with all my heart."

She leaned forward and he couldn't help himself, he had to kiss her. He took possession of her mouth at the same time his arms wrapped around her. He knew kissing her was a mistake, that it would only make things more difficult, but he couldn't resist having one last taste of her mouth, one final embrace to last him a lifetime.

When the kiss ended, he moved away from her. "Breanna, you know it was never my intention to hurt you. But you also know it was never my intention to share a life with you. I told you from the very beginning that I didn't want a wife or children."

"But you love Maggie," she said softly, then raised her chin. "And you love me. I know you do, Adam. You can't deny it."

He didn't try to deny it. He did love her...loved her as he'd never loved before...as he'd probably never love again. "That doesn't change the fact that I'm leaving."

"But why?" Tears suddenly appeared in her eyes and he looked away, not wanting his last memory of her to be one of her weeping.

"I have a life to get back to." It was the only reason he could give. All he knew deep inside his heart, deep inside his soul, was the need to escape...escape from her and the love she offered, escape from Maggie and the uncertainty of raising a child. He looked back at her. "I never made any promises, Bree."

Despite the tears sparkling in her eyes, she raised her chin and eyed him proudly. "I won't beg you to stay, Adam. I love you. Maggie loves you. We could have built something together, but you're more like your cousin than you think. He ran from responsibility. He turned his back on me and his unborn child. I'm not sure why you're running or from what...but I hope it's worth what you're leaving behind."

She didn't wait for his reply, but turned and left the cottage. He drew an unsteady breath, feeling as if his limbs were suddenly weighed down by the tonnage of the world.

He wasn't running away, he told himself. He was just going home. He'd taken care of Kurt's final mess and it was time to leave.

It took him only an hour to gather his things in his car. As he packed, he studiously kept his thoughts from

Breanna and Maggie. Instead, he thought of all the things he needed to do when he got back to Kansas City.

Maybe it was time to move to the suburbs, get out of his high-rise and into a neighborhood. He could move to a little ranch where he'd have a yard to mow. Maybe he'd get a dog.

Neither Breanna nor Maggie were outside when he got in his car to leave. He stood for a moment and looked at their house, wondering if he wasn't making the mistake of his lifetime.

She loved him. She loved him and Maggie loved him. He got into his car and pulled out of the driveway. As he pointed the nose of the car toward the highway that would take him back to his life in Kansas City, he told her she was wrong, he wasn't anything like Kurt.

He didn't run from responsibility, he embraced it. He met life head-on, plowing through instead of racing to the next adventure.

He was nothing like Kurt...nothing. Then why are you running away? a little voice whispered inside his head. What are you running from? And what are you running to?

She watched from her front window as he pulled out of his driveway and disappeared from sight. Her heart was broken into a million pieces, and she knew it would be a very long time before the pieces found their way back together again.

She'd had hope. Each day as she'd sat in the hospital room with him and they'd talked, she'd believed there was a chance for them.

Those hours with him had merely drawn her closer to him than she'd already been. She couldn't deny the fact that she was grateful to him. He had saved her life. The bullet Eddie Duncan had fired from his gun had been intended for her and Adam had thrown his own body in the way to save her.

But, gratitude aside, she was deeply in love with him. And now he was gone. She was glad she had the house to herself. Maggie was at her parents' place and Rachel was on an outing with David, leaving her to deal with her grief all alone.

She hadn't wanted to fall in love, had thought she was perfectly satisfied living her life alone with just her family and Maggie to fill in the empty spots. But there had been an emptiness inside her that no family or daughter could fill. Adam had filled it.

She moved through the lower level of the house like a zombie, willing herself not to spill any tears, reminding herself that he'd been honest about the fact that he didn't want a wife or a family from the very beginning.

She couldn't even be angry with him. It wasn't his fault she'd fallen in love with him. She'd survived the kidnapping of her daughter. She would survive this pain as well.

Cleaning. That's what she needed to do. She'd clean the house from top to bottom and maybe in the process exhaust herself so that she didn't have the energy to think about Adam and all that would never be.

Cleaning didn't help. Twenty minutes later she was upstairs in her room dusting the dresser with tears streaking down her cheeks.

Somehow Adam had made her believe again in the dreams she'd once entertained. He'd made her think about a happy marriage with a strong, committed man. He'd reminded her of dreams of working together, building a future, sleeping in somebody's arms.

Adam, her heart cried. Adam, I love you.

She jumped up off the bed as she heard the front door crash open. For a split second an irrational fear swept through her. Eddie! He's come to finish the job!

"Breanna!"

It wasn't Eddie's voice that called her name. It was Adam's. What was he doing back here? "I'm up here," she called and quickly swiped at her tears. She didn't want him to see her crying.

She heard him coming, taking the stairs two at a time and when he entered her bedroom he filled it with a barely suppressed energy. "We need to talk," he said.

"Talk?" She stared at him blankly, wondering what had brought him back here. What more they could possibly have to say to one another.

"I got twenty miles down the highway and realized you'd once asked me a question that I'd never answered, and it was suddenly important that I answer it."

She sat on the edge of the bed, looking at him in confusion. He remained just inside the doorway returning her gaze with intensity. "What question?" she asked.

He raked a hand through his hair and broke eye contact. Instead he stared at someplace just over her head. "You asked me once what it was I got out of my relationship with Kurt. What kept me taking care of his life and cleaning up his messes. At the time you asked, I didn't have an answer and it bothered me. I knew it was important that I discover the answer, but I didn't seem to be able to come up with one."

"And you have now?"

Once again he looked at her, his eyes so blue they made her ache inside. "I have my answer. As long as I had Kurt's life to deal with, I didn't have to have a life of my own." He took a step toward her, his brow drawn into a deep furrow. "It's so much easier, so much more self-protective to deal with somebody else's life. There's no emotional involvement, little chance for pain."

"And little chance for any real joy or happiness," she replied.

"You're right. You are so right." He walked over to where she sat, took her hand and pulled her to her feet. "I had decided I didn't want any children because I'd watched my aunt and uncle be hurt over and over again by Kurt. I didn't want anyone to have that kind of power over me."

Despite the fact that he was holding her hands, that he gazed deeply into her eyes, she was afraid to hope. "There are no guarantees with children, Adam. You can love them, but they can get sick or bad things can happen to them, or they can make bad choices. But heartache isn't all there is to parenthood. You haven't considered the joy."

"I've experienced the joy...with Maggie." He smiled, a beautiful smile that seemed to light him from within. The smile faltered a bit. "And I've experienced the pain and fear of the possibility of losing her."

"But Adam, there is more joy than pain...and not every child is like Kurt was."

"I know. Maggie fills my heart." He dropped her hands and instead placed his hands on either side of her face. "And you fill my heart. Bree, I don't want to go back to my life in Kansas City. It wasn't a life at all. You make me feel alive. You make me feel as if there is no end to the possibilities for happiness. You were a loose end that wrapped around my heart and made me captive. I love you, Bree."

"Oh, Adam." Tears of joy splashed her cheeks and then he was kissing her...a kiss filled with passion, a kiss filled with sweet love.

"Marry me, Bree," he said as the kiss ended. "I can't think of any other family I'd rather be a part of, I can't think of any other little girl I'd rather be a father to and I can't think of any other woman I'd rather share my life with than you."

"Yes," she exclaimed, laughing and crying at the same time. "Oh, yes, I'll marry you." As he pulled her closer against him and once again claimed her lips with his, the craziest thought went through her mind.

She remembered the alert that had trailed at the bottom of the television screen when Maggie had been missing and in her mind a new alert was playing. Breanna James… last seen in the arms of love…last seen in Adam's arms.

Alyssa Whitefeather had just served a double dip of Rocky Road ice cream when the headache pierced through her left eye, a warning that a vision was imminent. "Sarah, take over for me, would you?"

With the pain nearly blinding, Alyssa left the ice-cream parlor and went into the living area in the back. She stumbled to the sofa and sat down.

Blackness…waves of it consumed her. And with the darkness came the horror, a yawning greedy beast of horror that swept over her, through her. And with the horror came the certainty that evil approached and threatened somebody she loved. It was an evil so dark, so malevolent it terrified her.

She awakened fifteen minutes later to find herself lying on the sofa. Slowly, she pulled herself up to a sitting position, her heart racing with fear.

When Maggie had been kidnapped, Alyssa had thought that's what the visions had portended. But Maggie was safe and sound and the horrible darkness still haunted Alyssa.

This was the third time she'd suffered the awful blackness since Maggie had been recovered safe and sound.

Something was going to happen...something bad, and until the visions revealed something more than darkness and terror, there was nothing Alyssa could do to stop it. All she could do was wait for it to happen.

EPILOGUE

The darkness filled the bedroom, broken by streams of moonlight that danced into the window and across the bed. Adam loved the way his wife looked when she was bathed in moonlight. He loved the way his wife looked in any light.

They had married a week ago in a small ceremony at city hall. Adam had never known how rich life could be until now. He awakened in the mornings to Maggie kisses and sunshine, to challenges of opening a new office and Breanna's love and support.

She raised her head and smiled at him, her eyes shining in the glow of the moonlight. "What are you thinking, Mr. Spencer?"

He returned her smile and stroked a hand down her silky bare back. "I'm just lying here thinking about what a lucky man I am, Mrs. Spencer."

"That's funny, I was just lying here thinking about what a lucky woman I am."

"You know this is a forever kind of thing," he said to her.

"I wouldn't have it any other way," she replied. She cuddled closer to him and sighed with obvious contentment. "I've never been so happy in my life, Adam."

"I feel the same way. I never knew what it felt like to have a full heart, but you fill my heart, sweet Bree." They both jumped in surprise as the telephone rang.

"It's after eleven, who could that be?" she murmured as she reached over to answer. "Hello? Hi, Clay." A frown worried itself across her forehead and she sat up. Adam sat up as well and turned on the light on the nightstand.

"What's going on? Yes…yes…we're on our way." She hung up the phone and looked at him. "That was Clay. He said we need to get out to my parents' place right away."

"Did he say why?" Adam got out of bed and pulled on a pair of jeans.

She stood and reached for the clothes she'd thrown on a chair before bedtime. "He wouldn't say. He said we just need to get out there." She looked at him, fear darkening her eyes. "There was something in Clay's voice…something that frightened me."

Adam walked around the bed and pulled her into his arms. "There's nothing to be afraid of," he said. "Whatever is going on we'll face it together."

She smiled up at him. "Together. I love the way that sounds. I love you, Adam."

"And I love you, Bree." He claimed her lips in a kiss that spoke of his devotion, his desire, his love for her. "And whatever we face in the future, we face together."

"And we'll be fine because we have the strength of our love to support us," she replied.

As he hugged her once again, he silently thanked his cousin. Kurt hadn't left him one final loose end, rather he'd pointed him to a path that had led to a future filled with joy and love…a future filled with Maggie and Breanna.

* * * * *

DEAD CERTAIN

PROLOGUE

She crouched on a wooden support beam beneath the bridge that spanned the Cherokee River. Although it was after midnight, the full moon overhead splashed down a silvery light that danced on the river water below.

Shiny water, she thought. Shiny, treacherous water. For Cherokee Native Americans water was sacred, used for cleansing and purifying. It had been the presence of this river that had led her people to this area of Oklahoma many years before.

For her, the river no longer signified anything but death. Fourteen months ago, in a freak accident, her husband had lost control of his car and slammed through the wooden guard rail of the old bridge. He'd plunged to his death in the river below. At the moment his life had left his body, all will to live had left hers as well.

Every Saturday night when she got off work she came

here. She climbed up the wooden support beams until she was high over the river, and stared at the water below.

Beneath the bridge the river was at its most fierce, with speed and depth and powerful whirlpools that rarely spit up a survivor.

If she released her hold on the support beam over her head and leaned forward just a little bit, she would fall. The river would accept her into its depths, and she would be rejoined with the man she loved.

Jimmy, her heart cried. If she just let go and leaned forward, she and her husband would walk hand in hand through the spirit world for eternity.

"Just let go," a voice whispered in her head. "That's all you have to do…let go." But even as the voice whispered seductively in her ear, her hand tightened its grip on the overhead support.

A sob caught in her throat as she realized she couldn't release her grip on the beam. Her heart desperately wanted to, but she simply couldn't let go. She didn't understand. All her hopes, all her dreams had drowned along with Jimmy. She had no reason to live.

Once again she stared down at the river, finding the moonlit water hypnotic. Jimmy. Jimmy. Tension ebbed away from her body as she continued to gaze at the water below. Her grip on the beam loosened as her fingers began to relax their hold. Just let go. Just let go.

At that moment her cell phone jangled from its resting place inside her pocket. Instantly her fingers tightened once again around the support.

Who would be calling her now? It wouldn't be anyone from the station; they would use her radio. Who else would be calling at this hour of the night? With her free hand she wrestled the cellular from her pocket and answered.

"Get out to Mom and Dad's place as fast as you can." The familiar male voice radiated urgency.

"What's going on?" she asked.

"Just get here."

Her brother disconnected the call, and a chill of foreboding chased down her spine. What was going on at her parents' house at this time of night?

Carefully, Homicide Detective Savannah Tallfeather climbed down the wooden beams beneath the bridge. She would not be joining her husband on this night.

She wasn't sure if she was relieved or devastated by the fact that once again she was walking away. She'd have to wait for another time to join her husband in the water she thought of as the river of no return.

CHAPTER ONE

She saw the floodlights before she got to the house. They lit up the night sky as if announcing the arrival of a carnival to the town of Cherokee Corners. Savannah stepped on her gas pedal, knowing it wasn't carnival lights that strobed the sky over her parents' ranch house. It was police lights.

What was going on? She groaned, wondering if her parents' had gotten into one of their legendary fights and some passerby or well-meaning neighbor had called out the entire police force.

Even as the thought flew through her head, she dismissed it as the house came into view. Something had definitely happened, and it wasn't just a noisy spat between her parents.

Police cars lined the driveway and floodlights hit the house from every angle. Her heart smashed into her rib

cage as she saw one of her fellow officers cordoning off
the porch with bright-yellow crime-scene tape.

She parked and was out of the car almost before it
stopped running. She raced toward the house, vaguely
aware that neighbors had begun to gather around the pe-
rimeter of the scene.

As a homicide cop she knew the scent of death, knew
how the scent permeated the air at a homicide scene. She
didn't smell death as she reached the edge of the yard, but
before she could get any closer, she saw her brother, Clay,
talking with Chief of Police Glen Cleberg.

She hurried to the two men, instantly aware that her
brother was as angry as she'd ever seen him. His handsome, sculptured features were a mask of barely suppressed rage, and his black eyes glittered with a fierceness
she'd never seen before.

"I'm the best crime-scene investigator you have, Chief,"
he said, his voice deep and filled with urgency. "You've
got to let me in."

"Dammit, Clay. I told you no and I mean no."

"What's going on?" Savannah asked, looking at her
brother. "What's happened?" Her heart thudded painfully
as she turned her gaze to her boss.

"Dad's been taken to the hospital. He was attacked."
Grim lines bracketed Clay's mouth as he spoke.

"What do you mean…attacked? Where's Mom?" Savannah tried not to panic, but something in Clay's dark
eyes and in the fact that Glen didn't quite meet her gaze
filled her with fear. "Where's Mom?" she repeated.

"Savannah…at the moment we aren't sure what we've
got here," Glen said and stared for a long moment at the
house where officers were going in and out as they per-
formed their duties. "Apparently John Newman stopped

by here about a half an hour ago. The front door was open and he knocked but nobody answered. He could hear the television on, saw that your parents' car was in the driveway and so he knocked again."

He finally looked at her and in his eyes she saw a sadness that frightened her. "When he still didn't get an answer, he decided to go inside. He found your father in his recliner. It was obvious he'd been hit over the head with something and was in bad shape. He called for help, then went in search of your mother."

Savannah's hand flew to her mouth as tears burned her eyes. "Oh, God…is she…is she dead?"

"They can't find her, Silver Star," Clay said.

The fact that he'd used her Cherokee name indicated just how upset her brother was. "What do you mean, they can't find her? She's got to be here." Savannah felt as if she'd been thrust into a puzzle and none of the pieces she'd been handed made any sense at all.

"Look, I'll let you both know what's going on when *we* know what's going on," Glen said impatiently. "In the meantime I want you both to stay out of the way and let us do what we need to do." He pointed to Savannah's car. "Sit there and I'll have somebody brief you as soon as we have any more information."

Clay let his feelings be known by cursing soundly beneath his breath as he walked beside Savannah to her car. At that moment another car squealed into the driveway. It was their sister, Breanna, and her new husband, Adam.

Savannah listened as Clay filled them in with the brief information they had learned so far. "What about Dad?" she asked when he'd told them what little he knew.

"From what Glen told me he was alive when they took him out of here by ambulance. But I'm not leaving here until they find out where Mom is." He frowned and looked at the house. "And they are absolutely destroying vital information by allowing in so many officers."

"Why don't we go to the hospital and check on Dad," Breanna suggested. "You two stay here and call us the minute you hear anything about Mom."

Savannah touched her sister's arm. "Call me on my cell and tell me how Dad is doing."

Breanna nodded, and she and Adam took off. Savannah turned back to the house, her heart still pounding an irregular rhythm. Everything felt surreal—the lights, her fellow officers, the crime-scene tape flapping in the mid-June night breeze. It all felt like a terrible dream.

What could have happened? Who could have hurt her father? Had it been a robbery? If so, then where in God's name was their mother?

It felt odd to stand on the periphery of a crime scene as a bystander. Even more odd and frightening was the fact that the crime scene was the house where she'd grown up, where her parents lived.

"I can't just sit around here and do nothing," Clay said, interrupting her thoughts. "I'm going to check the outbuildings."

"I'll go with you," she said, needing to do something, anything constructive.

She was grateful nobody tried to stop them as they walked around the house and toward the barn at the back of the property. She had a feeling Clay wouldn't hesitate to deck anyone who tried to get in their way.

Savannah felt as if she'd jumped off the bridge and entered water so deep it clogged her brain, making rational thought impossible.

Somebody had hurt their father…and their mother was

missing. Her brain worked to wrap around the situation but found it impossible to comprehend.

It didn't take long for them to check the barn, which was used mostly as a storage area for Native American artifacts. Rita Birdsong James worked at the Cherokee Cultural Center at the edge of town and had slowly taken over the barn as a place to keep items for the center.

It was when they were searching the shed that Savannah's cell phone rang and she answered to hear Breanna at the other end of the line.

"It's not good, Savannah," she said, her voice choked with emotion. "Dad received several severe blows to the back of his head. The doctor isn't sure about the possibility of brain damage, and Dad is in a coma. What's up there? Have they found Mom?"

"No...nothing. They aren't telling us anything, Bree." For the first time the full awareness of the gravity of the situation hit Savannah.

Their father was in a coma and their mother was missing. She sank down on a bale of hay, tears suddenly blurring her vision. "Bree, I'm coming to the hospital. There's nothing I can do here. Glen won't let us anywhere near the house. Maybe Dad will wake up and be able to tell us what happened."

"I'll stay here," Clay said a moment later after she'd hung up with Breanna and brother and sister were walking back toward the house.

"Come with me to the hospital, Clay. Right now Dad needs us there." She somehow felt it was important that they all be together, in the same place. She felt as if her family was slipping through her fingers and what she needed was to hang on tightly to them all.

Clay raked a hand through his thick dark hair,

uncertainty twisting his handsome features. He stared at the house, tension radiating from him, the same tension that whipped through her. "What in the hell happened here tonight?"

"I don't know, Clay." She placed a hand on his muscular forearm. "But it's obvious we're out of the loop here at the moment. Come with me to the hospital. Right now we don't know where Mom is, but we know that Dad needs us." She was half-afraid that if he remained here he would do something to get himself thrown off the police force.

"All right," he replied. "I'll just check in with the chief and I'll meet you there."

As Savannah headed for her car, she noticed the crowd of neighbors and the curious had grown despite the fact that it was the middle of the night.

She recognized the Marshalls, her parents' nearest neighbors. Their house was some distance away, but they both stood by their car, worried expressions on their lined faces. Familiar faces everywhere, and they all seemed to be watching her as she made her way to her car.

She stopped to talk to nobody, having nothing to say, no way to assure anyone of anything. She got into her car and started the engine and that's when she noticed him...a stranger on the edge of the crowd.

He stood taller than most of the rest of the people, and his gaze was fixed on the house. With a cop's training, she took in his appearance before backing out of the driveway.

He was good-looking, with dark-brown hair and facial features that radiated intensity. People stood in front of him, making it impossible for her to see his build. A traveler who'd seen the lights and action, she thought as she pulled away from the ranch.

Or a perpetrator watching the aftermath of his actions,

her seasoned cop brain thought. She knew it was not unusual for the criminal to watch the unfolding drama, to even become involved in the investigation of the crime they committed.

Surely one of the officers would take names and question the people who had arrived to see what was going on. It was standard procedure.

Besides, she couldn't think about the investigation. Despite the fact that her years as a homicide detective had seasoned her to maintain a certain amount of emotional distance, her training and experience seemed to have left her the moment she'd pulled up to the house.

As she sped toward the hospital, she desperately sought that emotional distance, but her hands trembled and her chest felt heavy and a sickness she'd never felt before permeated every pore of her body.

Where was her mother? Was her father going to be all right? What on earth had happened? She stepped on the gas pedal, fear consuming her from the inside out.

Riley Frazier stood staring at the house where the bright-yellow tape contrasted with the beige house paint and hunter-green shutters and trim. The sight brought back painful memories of another crime at another house years before. As he stared at the house, snatches of conversation drifted toward him.

"…can't find Rita."

"…heard his head was bashed in."

"…you know they fight a lot…"

He listened with interest as the people around him speculated on what had happened to Rita and Thomas James. He wouldn't draw any conclusions until he heard the official word on what had happened at the sprawling, attractive ranch house.

It was possible he was here on yet another wild-goose chase. Certainly over the past two years he'd been on many. But when he'd heard the initial report of what was going on from a reporter friend in Cherokee Corners, he'd left his home in Sycamore Ridge and driven like a bat out of hell to get here.

It was possible what he was watching was the investigation of a domestic dispute gone bad, or a botched robbery attempt. It was possible it had nothing to do with what had happened to his parents two years ago.

The overbright floodlights, the swirling cherry police lights and the yellow crime-scene tape brought back nightmarish memories. The sight of his father's dead body sprawled in the middle of the living room floor still haunted him…along with all the questions the crime had produced.

That's why he was here, looking for answers to a crime nobody cared about anymore but him. This might be a wild-goose chase, but in the past two years his life had become a series of wild-goose chases.

His information had told him that there were three James siblings, and he suspected he'd driven up in time to see the three huddled together with the chief of police. The man and two women he'd seen had looked like siblings.

All had been of Native American heritage, with rich black hair and finely sculptured features. His source had even given him their names—Clay, Breanna and Savannah—and told him that each of them worked in some aspect of law enforcement.

He'd watched as one of the women and a man had left

together. Then had watched as the second woman left. Finally the man he thought was Clay James got into a car and took off as well.

Riley suspected they were probably headed to the hospital where their father had been taken. He waited around until the police began to attempt to disperse the crowd and he saw the police chief leave, then he got into his car and headed into the small city of Cherokee Corners.

The quickest way to find out what had happened at the James ranch was to speak to one of the children. It was too late for any of the details to get into the morning paper, and the police wouldn't be talking to anyone until they spoke to the family members.

He had a feeling if he wanted information, the hospital would be the place to get it. He didn't want speculation and rumor. He wanted facts, and he had a feeling the only way to get facts sooner rather than later was to go introduce himself to the James siblings.

The nightmare continued. Savannah sat in the hospital waiting room wondering when they would have some answers, when any of this would make sense.

Clay paced the floor, looking as if he would gladly take off the head of anyone who got in his way. Breanna sat next to Adam, their hands clasped together.

Savannah had been there for almost two hours, and the doctor had yet to come out and speak to them. There had been no word on their mother's whereabouts and nothing concrete from the investigation itself.

Savannah wished she had somebody's hand to hold or that she could generate the kind of anger that seemed to be sustaining Clay. Instead she was left with a disquieting numbness.

They weren't alone in the waiting room. Saturday nights always brought an influx of people to the emergency room in the only hospital in town.

As Dr. Miles Watkins, their family physician, came into the room they converged on him like a single unit. He held up his hands to still their barrage of questions. "I don't have a lot to tell you," he said when they all fell quiet.

"Your father has suffered massive trauma to the back of his head. We can't be sure of the extent of any brain damage at the moment. Our main concern has been to stabilize him. At the moment his vital signs are fair, but he's currently in a coma. I've called in a neurologist from Tulsa. He'll be here sometime tomorrow. In the meantime my recommendation to all of you is to go home. There's nothing you can do here." He sighed wearily, then added. "Go home and pray."

He'd barely exited the waiting room when the exterior door whooshed open and Glen Cleberg entered. Lines of stress surrounded his mouth, and his hair stood on end, as if it had felt a frustrated hand rake through it more than once. He motioned them to chairs in a corner and joined them there.

"I know you're all anxious to learn what we've uncovered so far." He frowned, as if dreading what information he had to impart. Every nerve ending in Savannah's body screamed with tension.

"It looks like a domestic dispute scene that got out of control," the chief told them.

"That's crazy," Clay said, voicing Savannah's initial response.

"Chief, surely you don't think our mother could be responsible for Dad's condition?" Savannah looked at him incredulously.

His frown deepened. "I'm just telling you what the initial investigation points to. There's no sign of forced entry, no indication that anything has been stolen."

"How would you know if anything has been stolen?" Breanna asked, tears shimmering in her eyes.

"Tomorrow, after the crime-scene investigators get finished, we'll do a walk-through," Glen said. "I need you all to tell me if you see something out of place. But, I can tell you right now the only things that appear to be missing are a suitcase from a set in your parents' closet and some of your mother's personal items."

Stunned. His words stunned them all. Savannah could see the shock she felt on her siblings' faces. The implication was obvious. They believed that Rita had smashed her husband over the head, then packed her bags and run.

"Glen, you know my parents, you know what you're thinking is impossible," she said.

He hesitated a moment. "I know what the evidence looks like at the moment," he replied softly.

"Then let me inside. Let me find the evidence that points to the truth," Clay exclaimed, his hands balled into fists at his sides.

"That's exactly what I'm not going to let happen," Glen said, his tone sharp. "Even though the three of you are officers of the law, you will have nothing to do with this investigation." He held up a hand to still the protests that came at him from three different directions.

"Think about it. I can't let the family members of a crime do the investigating of the case. A defense attorney would be able to rip a case to shreds under those circumstances."

Savannah knew he was right, but that didn't make the situation any easier to swallow. "But what about Mother's car?" she asked suddenly. "It was there in the driveway... so how did she leave?"

"I don't have the answers," he said with obvious frustration. "Look, we're only a couple of hours into this investigation. We have a lot of work ahead of us. It would help if your father could enlighten us about what happened."

"Dad's in a coma," Clay said, and his voice radiated with the hollowness of a person still in shock. "According to Doc Watkins he isn't going to be explaining anything anytime soon."

For the first time since she'd driven up to her parents' house a stark grief swept over Savannah. She felt almost sick to her stomach as she tried to digest what they knew so far.

The man who had held her when she'd been sick, the man who had taught her how to dance, how to shoot a gun and given her a love for law enforcement was clinging to life by a thread.

Her mother, a proud, beautiful woman who had taught her to honor her Cherokee heritage, the woman whose hands had soothed, whose laughter could light up the night, was missing.

Hold on, Daddy, she cried in her heart. Please hold on, we still need you. Where are you, Mom? What has happened to you?

"Savannah, why don't you meet me at your folks' place tomorrow at noon. We'll do a walk-through then," Glen said. "I'm putting an all points bulletin out on your mother. We need to find her. We need to talk to her. Take the next couple of days off. Your father is going to need you when he comes out of his coma, and I don't want any of you mucking around in this investigation."

"If he thinks I'm staying out of this, he's crazy," Clay said the minute Glen had left to go in search of Dr. Watkins.

"Just because we can't investigate officially doesn't mean we can't investigate unofficially," Breanna said.

"I can't stand around here and do nothing," Clay replied. "I'm going to make some phone calls, drive around and see if I can find Mom. Maybe she got hit in the head, too...has wandered off in a daze and doesn't know who or where she is."

"You know she didn't have anything to do with Dad's injuries," Savannah said.

"That goes without saying," her brother replied. He looked toward the windows. "She's out there somewhere, and she's in trouble. We've got to find her."

He didn't wait for any reply but strode out the door and disappeared into the night.

Savannah felt the darkness of the night closing in around her, filling her heart, filling her soul with fear. She turned back to look at her sister. Breanna reached out and grabbed her into a hug that kept the darkness from consuming her.

"Go," Breanna said as she released her. "Go find Mom. Adam and I will stay here."

"You'll call me if there's any change?" she asked.

"Of course we will," Adam said as he wrapped an arm around his wife's shoulder.

Although she was reluctant to leave, Savannah knew there was nothing she could do here. Her father was getting the care he needed.

She left the hospital through the emergency room doors and stopped in her tracks. Parked in a car in the closest parking space to the door was the handsome stranger she'd seen out at her parents' place.

Who was he? What was he doing here? It had been odd

enough to see his strange face among those of the neighbors at the house. Had he been involved in whatever had happened there? Had he come here in a compulsive, sick need to see the grief he'd caused? Was he here to see if her father had come awake and was talking?

A burst of adrenaline chased away grief as she pulled her handgun from her shoulder holster and approached the car. "Show me your hands," she demanded to the man in the driver's seat.

Startled blue eyes widened as he lifted his hands off the steering wheel. "I think there's been some sort of mistake." His voice was a deep baritone.

"The only mistake anyone has made around here is yours." She pulled open the driver door. "Now, get out of the car, put your hands on the roof and spread 'em."

CHAPTER TWO

Riley Frazier hadn't reached the age of thirty-four without learning when to balk and when to comply. When a woman who'd just suffered an emotional trauma pointed a gun and began to bark orders, it was definitely a good idea to comply.

He got out of his car, placed his hands on the roof and spread his legs. "There's a wallet in my back pocket with my identification in it," he offered.

She frisked him with a professional, light touch, beginning at his ankles. She patted up his legs, then around his waist. Only then did she pluck his wallet from his back pocket.

He remained in place, although there were a million things he wanted to say to her, things he wanted to ask her.

"What are you doing here, Mr. Frazier?" she asked.

He dropped his arms to his sides and turned to face her. In the bright illumination of the parking lot light overhead he got his first good look at her. A rivulet of pleasure swept through him.

Earlier at her parents' house he'd been too far away to see just how beautiful she was. Long black lashes framed dark eyes. Her hair was jet-black, and the short cut emphasized high cheekbones and sensual lips.

She stared at him expectantly and he frowned, unable to remember her question to him. "I'm sorry... What do you want to know?"

"Your identification says you're from Sycamore Ridge. What are you doing here in Cherokee Corners and what were you doing out at my parents' ranch?"

Riley suddenly realized what it looked like...why his presence had prompted her to pull a gun and check him out. "It's not what you think."

"And how do you know what I think?" she returned in a cool tone as she handed him back his wallet.

"I know what I'd be thinking if I was in your place," he replied.

"Riley!"

They both turned at the sound of the young male voice. Scott Moberly hurried toward them, and Riley thought he heard a faint groan come from Savannah.

Scott reached them, half-breathless from his run across the parking lot. "You bothering the local law enforcement, Riley?" Scott asked, a wide grin stretching across his freckled face.

Riley shrugged, and Scott turned his attention to the woman officer as he withdrew a notepad and pen from his pocket. "So, what's the scoop, Savannah? Is your father dead?"

"Scott!" Riley exclaimed as Savannah's features twisted with a combination of pain and anger.

"Oh…was that insensitive? Sorry." Scott sighed miserably. "How about an exclusive, Savannah?"

"I'll give you an exclusive. All reporters are pond scum." She turned on her heels and started toward her car.

She'd written him off as a reporter, Riley thought. He fumbled in his wallet and withdrew his business card and a copy of a newspaper clipping.

"Savannah," he shouted, and ran after her. She didn't stop walking, didn't indicate in any way that she had heard him.

He caught up with her at her car. "Savannah…wait."

She whirled around to face him, her eyes flashing dark fires of anger. "No interview, no scoop…I have nothing to say."

"Please…*I'm* not a reporter," he said quickly. She jumped in surprise as he grabbed her hand and pressed his card and the copy of the clipping into her palm. "Call me when you're ready to talk."

He backed away and watched as she got into her car and drove out of the hospital parking lot. He hoped she'd call. He hoped she'd read the old news clipping, but there were no guarantees. For all he knew she might toss what he'd given her into the trash without even looking at it.

"Did she say anything to you?" Scott asked eagerly as Riley returned to where he stood.

"No, nothing." He turned and looked at the young man he'd befriended two years earlier. "Thanks for calling me."

Scott nodded. "As soon as I heard the initial report, I knew you'd want to know." Scott glanced longingly at the emergency room door.

"Go on, Scott," Riley said. "Go see if you can get a story, but try to be a bit more sensitive. Anyone you find to talk to about any of this will be in shock…in pain."

Scott flashed him another quick grin. "Got it." As he disappeared into the hospital, Riley sat on a nearby bench, not yet ready to make the hour-long drive back to his home in Sycamore Ridge.

The late-June night air was unusually warm, more in keeping with August than June. It had been on a hot August night that his world had been ripped asunder, and for the past two years he'd felt as if his life had been in limbo.

He'd awakened each morning with unanswered questions plaguing his mind and had gone to bed each night with those same questions still begging for answers.

He'd met Scott in the dark days following the event that had shattered his life. The brash young reporter had journalistic dreams of becoming the next Ann Rule and writing bestselling books about compelling crimes.

Initially Riley had found the young man relentless and his questions an irritating breach of good manners and an invasion of Riley's privacy.

But when the cops had gone away, when the crime-scene investigators had packed up and gone home, Scott had remained. When the neighbors had stopped sending cards of condolence and the flowers on his father's grave had withered and blown away, Scott was still around, sometimes asking insensitive questions but also offering friendship and support that Riley desperately needed at the time.

The friendship had lasted, although there were times when Scott's eagerness overwhelmed his tact. And tonight with Savannah had been one of those times.

He turned his head as he heard the hospital door open and Scott walked through. He spied Riley and walked over and sat next to him on the bench.

"What did you find out?" Riley asked.

"Not much," Scott replied glumly. "Thomas James is still alive, but he's in a coma. I tried to get some information out of Glen Cleberg, the police chief, but he wouldn't tell me anything. It's going to be hell trying to get any information from law enforcement...you know, the brotherhood of cops, the blue wall and all that."

"I think that's only a myth when a cop is supposed to be bad or corrupt," Riley replied.

"Who knows what was going on with Thomas. You know he was chief of police before Glen Cleberg. Maybe somebody had a score to settle with him."

"And so they banged him over the head and did what with his wife?" Riley asked.

"I don't know," Scott admitted. "I'm just speculating here."

"I thought good reporters weren't allowed to speculate. I thought they were just supposed to report the facts."

Scott grinned widely, exposing a chipped front tooth. "Who ever told you I was a good reporter?"

"So, tell me about Savannah James," Riley asked, changing the subject.

"Her name is actually Savannah Tallfeather. She's a homicide dick and a widow. About a year ago her husband, Jimmy, crashed into the old bridge over the Cherokee River. The wood was old and rotten and his car went over the edge."

Riley frowned. There should be a law—only one tragedy in a single lifetime. The fact that she was so young and already had suffered two seemed vastly unfair.

"It's eerily similar to what happened to your parents, isn't it?" Scott asked. He wasn't talking about Jimmy

Tallfeather's untimely death. He was talking about whatever had happened at the James ranch.

"Yes…at least from the snippets of information I've heard so far." Riley sighed and looked upward toward the night sky where the stars were obscured by the bright parking lot lighting. "But I hope it's not the same."

He looked back at Scott, but his thoughts were filled with a vision of the lovely Savannah. He knew every agonizing emotion she was experiencing. He knew intimately the sensation of shock, the taste of uncertainty and the scent of your own fear.

He knew the furtive glances of people willing to believe the worst. He knew the isolation of friends drifting away, uncomfortable and somehow afraid. He wouldn't wish what he'd been through in the past two years on anyone, especially a young woman who'd already been touched by tragedy.

"I hope they find Rita James alive and well. I hope she left for a planned trip hours before her husband was attacked." Riley held his friend's gaze intently. "I hope this is nothing like what happened to my parents. But if it is like what happened to my family, then God help them all."

It was near dawn when sheer exhaustion drove Savannah to bed. She'd been up for over twenty-four hours, and although her head wanted to keep searching for her mother, her body rebelled, forcing her to rest.

The night had been a fruitless search. She and Clay had contacted half the townspeople to see if they knew anything about Rita's whereabouts.

They had contacted friends, relatives and acquaintances, all to no avail. Savannah had taken a photo of her mother to the bus station while Clay had checked all the rental car companies.

Nothing. It was as if Rita had packed her suitcase, then disappeared off the face of the earth.

Before crawling into bed for a couple hours of sleep, Savannah sat in her living room window and watched the sun peek up over the horizon as if shyly testing its welcome.

Tears burned her eyes. Was her mother seeing the sunrise? Had she left on an unexpected trip and had no idea what had happened at the ranch? Or had whomever hurt Thomas also done something awful to Rita?

Savannah had shed few tears all night, but as she watched the beauty of the sunrise, sobs choked in her throat, racked her body and ripped through her heart.

She'd believed all her tears had been depleted on the day she'd buried her Jimmy, but she'd been wrong. A river of tears escaped from her until she fell into an exhausted sleep.

Her alarm awakened her at nine. Gritty-eyed and half-asleep, she stumbled into the bathroom for a quick shower.

As the steamy hot water washed away the last of her grogginess, she mentally steeled herself for what lay ahead of her—the walk-through at the ranch house to see if anything was missing or out of place.

Savannah had been to many crime scenes in the six years she'd been a cop, but she'd never been to a crime scene where her own family members were the victims. And there was no doubt in her mind that her mother was a victim as much as her father was. They just hadn't figured out yet what her mother was a victim of.

Before leaving her apartment she called Breanna to check in on their father. There had been no change in his condition, and Breanna told her she and Adam were heading home for some much-needed sleep. Clay had no news, either.

In the brilliant sunshine of day the crime-scene tape surrounding the house looked even more horrifying than it had the night before.

Savannah got out of her car and was greeted by Officer Kyle O'Brien, a young man who'd apparently drawn the duty of guarding the house until it was released by the police department.

"The chief is on his way. I'm sorry I can't let you inside until he gets here." He looked at her apologetically.

"It's all right, Kyle." She forced a smile. "I'll just wait for him in my car." She slid back in behind her steering wheel, ignoring the look on Kyle's face that indicated he wouldn't have minded a little conversation.

She didn't feel like talking. She leaned her head against her headrest and closed her eyes as the events of the night before replayed in her mind.

He'd had the bluest eyes she'd ever seen. Her mind filled with an image of the man she'd frisked in the hospital parking lot. Yes, he'd had the bluest eyes she'd ever seen, but they hadn't sparkled; rather, they had been somber and filled with sympathy.

She rummaged in her purse and pulled out the business card he'd handed her the night before. Riley Frazier, Master Builder of Frazier Homes.

She'd heard of Frazier Homes. But why would a homebuilder think she'd want to speak with him? She wasn't in the market for a new home, and last night had definitely not been the time to approach her. It didn't make any sense.

At that moment Glen Cleberg arrived on the scene. Savannah shoved the business card back into her purse, then got out of the car to greet her boss.

"How you doing, Savannah?" he asked with uncharacteristic kindness.

When Glen had become chief a year ago, he'd seemed to be afraid that the James siblings wouldn't honor his authority after serving under their father. He'd been harder on them than on any of the other officers and it had taken several months before they had all adjusted.

"I'm fine...eager to get this over with."

He frowned. "Maybe I should have had Clay do it...but I was afraid he'd look at the scene professionally rather than as a family member."

"He probably would have," Savannah admitted. Clay was consumed by his work as a crime-scene investigator. She suspected if somebody cut him he wouldn't bleed blood, but would bleed some kind of chemical solution used in his lab to look for clues.

"We tried not to make a mess, but you know some things can't be helped," Glen said as he handed her a pair of latex gloves.

"You don't have to explain that to me." She pulled on the gloves, surprised by the dread that she felt concerning entering the home where she'd been raised by loving parents.

Glen drew a deep breath. "Let's get on with it, then." He unlocked the front door and together they stepped into the large living room.

Savannah drew in a breath as she saw the blood. It stained her father's chair, dotted the ceiling overhead and had dried on the television screen in front of the chair. She knew enough about blood-spatter evidence to realize her father had received a tremendous blow.

She struggled to find the emotional detachment to get her through this, trying to think of it as an unidentified victim's blood instead of her father's.

Fingerprint dust was everywhere and swatches of carpeting had been cut and removed. Her father's chair faced away from the front door. It would have been easy for anyone to ease into the house and hit him over the head.

"Let me guess, no sign of forced entry," she said. "My parents kept their door open and unlocked until they went to bed." Emotion threatened to choke her. She swallowed hard against it. "It would never have entered their minds to be afraid here, to think they should lock up the doors and windows."

She drew a deep breath and looked around the room carefully. "Nothing seems to be missing in here. If it was a robbery attempt, you'd think they would have taken the stereo or computer equipment."

Glen didn't quite meet her gaze, and with a stunning jolt she realized he believed her mother had done this. He wasn't seriously entertaining the thought that it had been a botched robbery or anything else.

"Glen, I know my parents fought. Everyone knew they fought. They fought loud and often in public. They were both stubborn and passionate, but they were madly in love. You know my mother isn't capable of something like this."

His gaze still didn't meet hers. "Savannah, we can only go where the evidence takes us, and until we find your mother, she's our top suspect in this case."

Knowing he thought it and hearing him say it aloud were two different things. She swallowed the vehement protest rising to her lips, aware that whatever she said would make no difference.

From the living room they entered the kitchen, which

was neat and clean and showed no evidence that anything or anyone unusual had been in the room. The only thing out of place was a pie that sat on the countertop, along with a knife and a plate. Her father loved his pies, and Rita baked them often for her husband.

The next two bedrooms yielded nothing unusual. Nothing appeared to have been touched or disturbed in any way.

As they entered her parents' bedroom, a small gasp escaped her lips. Here it was obvious something had happened. The closet door stood agape, and it was evident clothes were missing. The dresser drawers were open, clothing spilling out onto the floor as if somebody had rummaged through them quickly.

She walked to the closet and looked on the floor, where three suitcases in successive sizes had always stood side by side. Now there were only two. The middle size was missing.

She stared at the spot where the suitcase had stood, trying to make sense of its absence, but it made no sense. In all their years of marriage her parents had never taken trips separately.

It would have been extremely out of character for Rita to pack a bag and go anywhere without her husband. Just as it would be extremely out of character for her to harm the man she loved.

Clothes were missing…several sundresses, slacks and summer blouses. Empty hangers hung on the rod and littered the floor, as if items had been forcefully pulled off them. A check of the dresser drawers showed missing lingerie, sleepwear and other personal items.

She became aware of the ticking of the schoolhouse clock that hung on the wall, stared at the beautiful dark-blue floral bedspread that covered the bed.

What had happened here? She looked at Glen, whose face was absolutely devoid of expression. "I don't care how it looks. I'll never believe my mother had anything to do with my father's injuries."

"But you have to admit, it looks bad."

Savannah's heart ached as she acknowledged his words with a curt nod. Yes, it looked bad. It looked very bad. If her father didn't survive, then her mother would be wanted for murder. Either possibility was devastating.

They finished the walk-through and left the house. She'd hoped to find some sign of an intruder, some clue that somebody else was responsible for her father's condition. But she'd seen nothing to help prove her mother's innocence. And where was her mother?

She remained in her car long after Glen had pulled away, trying to piece together possible scenarios that might explain the absence of her mother's personal items, the missing suitcase. But nothing plausible fit.

So, what happened now? Where did they go from here? She dug into her purse to find her car keys and suddenly remembered that Riley Frazier hadn't just handed her a business card the night before. He'd handed her something else, as well.

Digging in her purse, she finally found the sheet of paper that had been thrust into her palm by the handsome stranger. She opened it.

It was a photocopy of an old newspaper article that had appeared in the *Sycamore Ridge News* on August 14, two years ago.

Man Murdered...Wife Missing, the headline read. Savannah's heartbeat raced as she read the article that detailed a crime chillingly similar to what appeared to have happened in her parents' house.

The victim's name was Bill Frazier and the woman missing was his wife, Joanna. According to the article a son, Riley, survived Bill Frazier.

What had happened to Riley's mother, Joanna? Had she been found and had she been guilty of the murder of his father?

She needed to talk to Riley Frazier. She needed to find out how things had turned out in this case. And she needed to know what it might have to do with her family's case.

CHAPTER THREE

He'd hoped she would call, but he really hadn't been expecting her call so soon. Riley sat in the ice-cream parlor that was the bottom floor of the Redbud Bed and Breakfast in the center square of Cherokee Corners.

He was early. She'd told him to meet her here at seven, and it was only now just a little after six. But he'd decided to come early. He'd ordered a cup of coffee, taken a chair facing the door and now waited for Savannah Tallfeather to join him.

She hadn't mentioned the news clipping in her call, only that she'd like to meet with him. He sipped his coffee, watching the people who came and went as he waited.

The ice-cream parlor was a popular place. He wondered if it was always so busy or if Saturday nights brought families out for ice cream. Certainly it was ice cream weather—hot and dry like only Oklahoma could be at this time of year.

The front page of the evening edition of the Cherokee Corners newspaper had been filled with the crime that had taken place the night before at the James ranch. Along with the facts that Thomas James was in critical but stable condition and Rita Birdsong James was missing, the article also was a tribute to the couple's contributions to the city.

Thomas James had served as chief of police for ten years, and before that had been on the force for twenty years. During his career he'd received a variety of awards, and recognitions of honor.

His wife, Rita Birdsong James, was no less visible in the community. A full-blooded Cherokee, she was the driving force behind the Cherokee Cultural Center. Her goal had been to educate through entertainment and re-creations of the Cherokee past and present. Both were described as pillars of the community.

Riley's parents hadn't been community icons to anyone but him. His father had been a simple man, a carpenter, and his mother had been a housewife who loved to crochet. In the evenings they had often worked on jigsaw puzzles together.

Two couples, seemingly very different, and yet they both had suffered a similar fate. The pain he felt when he thought of his parents had lessened somewhat with time, but it certainly hadn't gone away.

The most difficult part was that there had been no closure. Sure, the police had closed the file, branded his mother a murderer on the run. But he knew better. He knew that somewhere the real killer of his father ran free and the fate of his mother had yet to be learned.

He'd just finished his first cup of coffee when Savannah walked in. Her gaze locked with his, and in that instant he felt a connection like none he'd ever felt before.

He saw the confusion, the pain in her eyes, felt it resonate with aching familiarity inside him. He was certain it was the connection of two survivors, of two people whose lives had been turned upside down by violent, senseless crime.

His impulse was to stand and draw her into his arms, hold her tight to take away the chill that he knew wrapped tightly around her heart.

But, of course he didn't act on his impulse. She was a virtual stranger, and the last thing he wanted to do was alienate her right from the get-go. He stood as she approached his table. "Officer Tallfeather," he said in greeting.

"Please, make it Savannah," she said, and waved him back into his chair. "I'll be with you in just a minute." She walked over to the counter and greeted the woman working there. The two hugged and spoke for a minute or two, then Savannah returned to the table and sat across from him. "My cousin," she explained.

Before she could say anything else, her cousin appeared at their table. She placed a coffee mug before Savannah, then filled both Savannah's and Riley's cups.

"Alyssa, this is Riley Frazier," Savannah said. "Riley, my cousin, Alyssa Whitefeather."

Alyssa's eyes were as dark and as filled with pain as Savannah's. "Nice to meet you," she murmured in a soft, low voice.

"Nice to meet you, too," Riley replied. "I'm sorry for the pain your family is experiencing right now."

She nodded, then touched Savannah's shoulder. "Let me know if I can get you anything else."

"Thanks, Alyssa," Savannah said.

Once again Savannah directed her gaze at him as Alyssa

left the table. She wrapped her long, slender fingers around the coffee cup as if seeking warmth. "I read the newspaper article you gave me," she began.

"I figured you had when you called."

She took a sip of her coffee. "Tell me about it. Tell me about the night it happened."

Riley leaned back in his chair, for a moment rebelling at the thought of revisiting that horrible night. And yet he'd known she'd want him to tell her about it. He'd known when he'd given her that news clipping that he would have to call up everything about that night.

"Before I tell you what happened to them, let me tell you about my parents…about what kind of people they were."

"All right," she agreed.

"They were quiet people and lived an uncomplicated life. My father was a carpenter, my mother a homemaker. He liked to putter in his garden in his spare time and my mother loved to cook and crochet. In the evenings they'd either watch old movies together or work on jigsaw puzzles that they set up on a card table in the living room."

"You were close to them." Her voice was as unemotional as her beautiful features, but her eyes spoke volumes, radiating with pain. He just didn't know if the pain was for him or for herself or perhaps a combination of both.

"I was their only child and yes, I was close to them." He thought of the nights when his choice had been to go to the local honky-tonk or spend the evening at his parents' house. He'd often chosen his parents' company. "They were good people."

"So, what happened…that night?" The words came from her in hesitation, as if she was sorry to have to ask him such a question.

He raked a hand across his lower jaw and forced himself to go back to that night. "I'd been over to their house that afternoon to show my dad some blueprints of new homes. I had a six-o'clock appointment with clients and so left my folks' place about five-thirty."

He paused to take a drink of his coffee and felt himself plunging back in time, pulled back into the nightmare. "It was after eight when the clients left, and I realized I'd left some of the blueprints at my folks' house, so I drove back there."

On one of the walls of the restaurant was a beautiful painting of a redbud tree in bloom. He stared at the picture as he continued. "The front door was open, which really wasn't unusual. I walked into the living room and my father was on the floor in front of his chair. I knew in an instant he was dead."

Grief, as rich and raw as the moment it had happened, seared through him. He cleared his throat. "I picked up the phone and called for help, then went in search of my mother, certain that I'd find her dead, as well."

"But she wasn't there?" Savannah leaned forward, her eyes more alive than before.

"A suitcase was missing, along with some of her clothing, and she immediately was placed at the top of a very short list of suspects." It was impossible for him to keep the edge of bitterness from his voice as he remembered how he'd fought with the police, begging them to look for another killer. "I was also placed on the top of the list, but only for a brief time."

"Your appointment was your alibi?" she asked.

He nodded. "That and the fact that when I left my parents' place that evening both my mom and dad walked me to my car. One of the neighbors was outside and was able to verify that when I left the house my parents were alive and well."

"That was two years ago. What did you find out about your mother? How does the case stand now?" She flushed, her cinnamon skin turning a deeper shade of red. "I mean, I'm sorry for what happened to your father."

He smiled, hoping by the gesture he let her know there was nothing to apologize for, that he understood the reason for the questions before she offered any sympathy. His smile faded as he continued to look at her.

"My mother has never been found." He didn't mean the words to sound as stark as they had. Her eyes widened with surprise.

"And your father's case?" she asked softly.

"Is officially closed. The local authorities are certain my mother is responsible and probably fled the country."

Once again her fingers curled around her mug. "And what do you think?"

This time it was he who leaned forward and held her gaze intently. "I *know* my mother had nothing to do with my father's death. I know it with all my heart, with all my soul, and nothing and nobody will ever make me believe otherwise. If there's anything in this world I'm dead certain of, it's that."

He frowned and leaned back in his chair, realizing he'd become loud and had drawn the attention of the other patrons. "Sorry, I didn't mean to get carried away."

"Please, don't apologize," she replied. "I feel exactly the same way about my mother."

There was more life in her eyes now, a flash of determination Riley could easily identify with. "Are they already saying your mother is a suspect?"

"Yeah. At the moment that's what the evidence points

to, and the police will follow the evidence." She stared down into her coffee cup for a long moment.

He remained silent, giving her time to deal with whatever emotions might be reeling through her. She looked utterly vulnerable with her eyes downcast, displaying the long length of her dark lashes.

She had delicate features, a slender neck and small bones. He'd noticed her scent when she'd first sat down, a fragrance that reminded him of spring days and full-blooming flowers.

How long had it been since he'd noticed the smell of a woman? How long since he'd noticed the curve of a slender neck, the delicacy of feminine hands, the thrust of shapely breasts?

It had been since Patsy. Too long. Something long dormant inside him stirred as he sat watching her, smelling her fresh, feminine scent.

Finally she looked up, her eyes the rich brown of deep chocolate. "What do you think happened to your mother, Riley?"

A sharp shaft of pain drove through him, banishing the momentary warmth that had filled him. "I really don't know. Over the past twenty-two months I've come up with hundreds of possibilities, each one more outrageous than the last. She got hit over the head and is wandering around somewhere with no memory of who she is. She became part of the witness-protection program and had to build a new life for herself."

He flashed her a wry grin. "Hell, one night I got desperate enough, drunk enough that I checked to make sure there hadn't been any UFO sightings on the night she disappeared. I thought maybe she'd been sucked up into a spaceship as an example of a human being with a perfect heart and soul."

To his surprise, she reached across the table and placed her hand over his. Her skin was warm. "I'm so sorry for you. It must be horrible—the not knowing." She drew her hand back as if suddenly self-conscious. A fierce determination swept over her features. "But I'm sure my mother is going to turn up anytime now. It's all just been a mistake, a terrible misunderstanding of some sort."

He didn't try to contradict her. He knew how desperately she was clinging to that certainty at the moment. And he hoped she was right. He hoped it all was a terrible misunderstanding and Rita Birdsong James would be found safe and sound and innocent of the charge of attempting to kill her husband.

Savannah took another sip of her coffee, her thoughts racing. Cop thoughts and woman thoughts battled inside her. The crime that had occurred to his family was remarkably similar to what appeared to have happened to hers. Did he have any idea the power of his hypnotic blue eyes?

Was the connection she felt to him that of two people whose lives had been touched by violence, or was she drawn to him because he stirred something inside her that reminded her that she was not just a cop, not just a victim, but a woman as well?

This thought irritated her, and she averted her gaze from him. Brown eyes, that's what she had loved. Eyes the color of her own, filled with laughter, filled with love, that's what she had lost.

"Did the police attempt to find your mother?" she asked, grasping at the cop inside her rather than the lonely woman. "Usually when somebody disappears there's a paper trail of some kind."

He nodded and she couldn't help but notice the rich shine of his dark-brown hair beneath the artificial lights overhead. "The authorities checked for activity on their bank account and credit cards, but there has been none in the nearly two years since it happened."

She shoved her half-empty cup aside. "There's no way to ignore the similarities in the two incidents," she said.

"That's why I thought it was important I make contact with you last night. Scott called me as soon as he heard the first report over his scanner, and that report indicated a man attacked in his living room and his wife missing. Scott thought I'd be interested since it seemed so much like what had happened to my family."

"But, despite the similarities, it's possible one has nothing to do with the other," she added hurriedly. She couldn't imagine her mother missing for two years. Savannah couldn't stand the thought of not knowing where her mother was for another two minutes.

"I'd guess that it's far too early in your investigation to draw any kind of conclusions," he agreed. "But if you're interested, I have copies of all the records pertaining to the crime against my parents. I've got witness lists, detective notes, everything."

She raised an eyebrow in surprise. Family members rarely saw those kinds of things.

"I had a friend on the Sycamore Ridge police force," he said in answer to her unspoken question. "Anyway, you're welcome to see anything I have. Of course, nothing I have will help if it's not the same kind of thing."

"I appreciate the offer," she said. "But I really don't think it would help much." She didn't want to believe there was any connection between what had happened to his family and what had happened to hers. After all, his father had died and his mother had never been found.

Suddenly she wanted to be away from him, needed to be away from him. It was almost as if she felt that if she spent too much time here with him, his tragedy would become her own.

"Thank you so much for meeting with me," she said, and rose from her chair.

"No problem." He got up, as well. He was taller than she remembered from the night before—tall with broad shoulders and slender hips. It was the physique of a man who worked a job of physical labor. He began to pull his wallet from his back pocket, but she waved her hand.

"Please, the coffee is on me."

She was grateful he didn't try to fight her for it. She was far too tired, far too emotionally fragile to fight over something as inconsequential as a dollar cup of coffee.

"Thanks for the coffee," he said as he walked to the door of the shop.

"Thanks for the information," she replied. Together they stepped outside, where night had fallen and the surrounding stores had closed up for the night. The night brought with it a terrifying sense of loss as she realized that her mother had been missing for nearly twenty-four hours.

"Your father…is he doing all right?"

"He's hanging in there. He's a stubborn Irishman with a hard head."

He quirked a dark brow upward. "Irish, huh? I would have never guessed. You and your sister and brother don't look Irish."

"My father always teased that Mom wasn't happy unless she dominated everything, including the gene pool." She swallowed hard as a wave of emotion swept over her. "It was nice meeting you, Riley," she said, and held her hand out to him.

"I wish it had been under different circumstances." He reached for her hand, but to her surprise instead pulled her into an awkward hug. "I'm so sorry about your family," he said into her hair. "I hope...I pray that everything turns out okay." He released her as quickly as he'd hugged her, then murmured a good-night and walked away.

She stood on the sidewalk, shell-shocked, a bundle of exposed nerves and heightened sensations. It had been a very long time since she'd felt the press of a muscular chest against hers, the warmth of strong arms surrounding her. In the instant that he'd hugged her, she'd smelled him, a distinctly woodsy male scent that was quite appealing. Too appealing.

She turned and went back into the ice-cream parlor. She joined her cousin Alyssa behind the counter where she was making a fresh pot of coffee. Alyssa finished what she was doing then turned and embraced Savannah. "Is there any news?"

Savannah shook her head. "I spoke with Bree before coming here and there's no change in Dad's condition. Clay is trying to get Glen to let him into the house or at least see what the crime scene has gathered so far, but Glen is refusing."

Alyssa sank down on a stool. "This is what I saw," she said softly. "I knew something bad was coming...knew somebody was going to be hurt...but I couldn't tell who...I couldn't stop it." Tears filled her eyes, threatening to spill down her cheeks.

"Melinda, keep an eye on things, okay?" Savannah asked the young woman who worked for Alyssa. Savannah took Alyssa by the arm and pulled her through the doorway that led to Alyssa's living quarters.

She closed the door behind them, shutting off the sounds from the ice-cream parlor and led Alyssa to the cream-colored sofa where they sat side by side. She took Alyssa's hands in hers and squeezed tightly.

"Alyssa, everyone in the family knows how your visions come to you. We all know that most of the time you can't figure out exactly what they mean. Nobody blames you for not seeing this coming."

"I know that, but it's just so frustrating," she replied. She pulled her hands from Savannah's grasp and used one to push a strand of her long dark hair behind an ear. "Over the past two months, I've had a single, recurring vision, and it's been different from any other one I've ever had."

Although Savannah had heard this before, she sat patiently and listened, knowing Alyssa needed to talk about it. "What I've experienced over the past two months weren't even real visions," Alyssa continued, her eyes dark and worried. "There was never a picture…just a feeling of horrible doom, of enormous grief and emptiness. Is there any news on Aunt Rita?"

"None."

Alyssa frowned. "I had a new vision this morning… about Aunt Rita."

Savannah leaned toward her cousin, her heartbeat quickening with hope. Maybe Alyssa's newest vision could provide a clue of some kind as to where Rita was…what had happened to her. "What? What did you see?"

Alyssa frowned, a delicate furrow appearing across her brow. "It won't help," she said as if reading Savannah's thoughts. "It doesn't make any sense."

"Tell me anyway," Savannah replied.

"I saw Aunt Rita in bed. She was sleeping peacefully in her own bed, in her own room." She sighed in frustration. "I told you it wouldn't help."

Savannah frowned thoughtfully. "Are you sure it was her own bed?"

"Positive. I saw her beneath the dark-blue floral bedspread that's on their bed. I saw the Tiffany-style lamp they have on the nightstand. It was her room, Savannah. I told you it wouldn't help. We both know Aunt Rita isn't safe and sound and sleeping in her bed at home."

Savannah reached for her cousin's hand once again. From the time they had all been children together, the James siblings had known that their favorite cousin had mysterious visions. The visions were as much a part of Alyssa as her long, dark hair and gentle nature.

"But you'll tell me if you have any more visions of her?" Savannah asked.

"Of course," Alyssa replied.

"Even if they seem crazy or unimportant?"

Alyssa's lips curved into a half smile. "Even then."

"And if you think you see anything that might help find her, you have to promise me you'll tell Chief Cleberg."

The half smile fell into a frown. "Glen Cleberg is like nine-tenths of the people in this town. They all think I'm more than a little crazy."

"I know the chief has given you a hard time before when you've tried to help, but you've got to promise me you'll tell him if you see anything that might help us find Mom."

"I promise," she agreed. "You know I'll do whatever I can to help find her. She's always been like a mother to me." Tears once again sprang to Alyssa's eyes, and she and Savannah hugged.

Alyssa's mother had died when Alyssa was four, and it

had been Rita who had stepped in to fill the empty space in the little girl's life.

"Who is Riley Frazier?" Alyssa asked as Savannah stood.

"A man who had something horrible happen to his parents a couple of years ago. He was offering me his support."

"Nice-looking man," Alyssa said, also rising from the sofa.

Savannah shrugged. "I guess." A vision of Riley streaked through her mind. "I've got to get going. I want to stop by the hospital on my way home."

Alyssa walked with her to the door. "You doing okay?" she asked.

"I'm holding up," Savannah replied.

Alyssa gazed at her with warm affection. "You were always the strong one, Savannah. I've always admired your incredible wealth of strength."

Alyssa's words replayed in her head thirty minutes later as she sat by her father's hospital bed.

The sight of her father lying there, so pale, so lifeless had shocked her. Thomas James was a big man with an even bigger presence. Now, with his head wrapped in bandages and his mouth hanging slack, hooked up to a variety of monitors and machines and with deep, dark circles beneath his eyes, he looked frighteningly old and fragile.

Savannah took his hand in hers. Cold…his hand was so cold. Tears welled up in her eyes as she gazed at him. "Daddy," she said softly. Did he hear her? Could he hear her? "Daddy, you need to wake up." She squeezed his hand. "We need you…I need you."

It was all too much, she thought. Her mother missing, her father in a coma—it was all too much to survive. She released his hand and leaned back in her chair, utterly exhausted both physically and mentally.

Alyssa had been wrong. She wasn't strong. She wasn't strong at all. She wasn't strong enough to survive what had become of her life, nor was she strong enough to let go of the bridge support and join her Jimmy in the spirit world.

She felt as if she was caught in some horrible state of limbo, too cowardly to join her husband in death, but equally afraid to contemplate what lay ahead for herself and the people she loved.

CHAPTER FOUR

Every morning when Riley left his house and headed for work, he passed by his parents' house. As the early-morning light played on the neat little ranch house surrounded by trees and bushes, it gave the place a golden aura of warmth. One would never know the house had been the scene of a violent crime.

During the summer months, Riley kept the yard mowed and weeded, and in the winter months he would shovel snow from the driveway and sidewalks. But, since the day the police had released the house back to him, he hadn't been back inside it.

The house was in his name so he could sell it or rent it out if he so chose, but he couldn't. It was here, just the way she'd left it. It was here, waiting for his mother's return.

This morning as he drove past the house, his thoughts were filled with Savannah Tallfeather and the conversation they'd shared two nights before.

She'd been reluctant to completely acknowledge the unmistakable similarities between his case and hers. He understood her reluctance. If she believed the same perpetrator was responsible not only for what had happened to his family, but to hers, then she also had to accept the possibility that her mother's whereabouts might still be a mystery two years from now.

She wasn't ready to face that possibility.

A swell of pride filled him as he turned off the main road and drove through a stone entrance. Gold lettering on the left side of the entrance read Frazier Estates.

Just ahead was the trailer that had served as Riley's office since he'd begun this dream project four months ago. In the distance he could see the rooftops of the four model homes that were nearing completion.

Pride mingled with a bittersweet pang of grief as he parked in front of the trailer. For so many nights he and his father had sat at the kitchen table and planned this, plotted this, dreamed this, and now the dream was within Riley's hands. But his father wasn't here to share it with him.

He wasn't surprised to see Lillian's car already parked in front of the trailer. He'd hired the sixty-two-year-old woman six months ago as his secretary. However, in the space of those months she'd become a combination of secretary, personal assistant, friend and mother hen. There were times when she could be as annoying as hell, but he positively adored her.

The scent of fresh-brewed coffee greeted him as he entered the trailer. Lillian sat at her desk with the morning paper spread out before her.

"Morning, Lillian."

"Morning, boss. Coffee is made and there are some

muffins on the counter…bran. You should eat a couple. You young people don't get enough fiber in your diet."

"Fiber isn't high on my priority list, Lillian," he said wryly.

She quirked upward a perfectly plucked silver eyebrow. "Wait until you get to be my age, then fiber intake definitely becomes a priority."

Riley poured himself a cup of coffee, then grabbed one of the muffins from the flowered plate. "I'll eat a muffin, okay?" he said as he disappeared into his office.

The day was the usual blend of headaches and happiness: supplies arrived late; a fistfight erupted between two roofers; his foreman threatened to quit for the fifth time in as many days…they were the usual headaches that came with a big construction job.

The tension headache he'd begun to nurse by ten vanished at eleven when a young, newlywed couple stopped by to have a look around.

As he showed them the plans for the community he envisioned and saw their excitement and interest, he was the happiest he'd been in years.

In between the headaches and the joys the day brought, thoughts of Savannah intruded at odd moments. As he watched the hardwood floors in one of the model homes being varnished, he thought of her skin. A lot of women would pay a lot of money to get that beautiful cinnamon shade of her skin.

He thought of the moment when he'd told her goodbye, and spontaneously pulled her into a hug. She had been neither a willing nor unwilling participant in the embrace. It had been rather like hugging an inanimate, unemotional stuffed animal.

Eventually her numbness would wear off, he thought.

And then the grief would begin in earnest. But she wasn't a stranger to grief. She'd lost her husband a year before.

At noon he ordered a pizza to be delivered from the local pizzeria. Lillian would give him hell about his food choices, but he'd become a junk-food junkie in the past couple of months.

He'd just hung up the phone from ordering the pizza when it rang. He grabbed it up and murmured a hello.

"Riley?"

He recognized her voice immediately. The low, dulcet tones sent a wave of warmth through him. "Hi, Savannah."

"I'm sorry to bother you, but I was wondering…about those papers…those files you have from two years ago…" Her voice trailed off, as if she was reluctant to come right out and ask him for what she wanted.

"Would you like to take a look at them?"

"If you wouldn't mind."

"Not at all. Just tell me when and where."

"Have you eaten lunch yet?" she asked.

He thought of the pizza he'd just ordered…easy come, easy go. "No."

"Could you get away for a little while now?" Her voice was hesitant, as if she was afraid of asking too much of him.

"Sure," he agreed easily. "Savannah, I know what you're going through. Whatever I can do to help, just tell me."

"Could you meet me in an hour? How about at the Briarwood Truck Stop. We could have lunch while I go over the paperwork."

"Fine. I'll see you there in an hour." Riley hung up the phone and immediately got up from his desk. The Briarwood Truck Stop wasn't the snazziest place in the world, but it was located between Sycamore Ridge and Cherokee

Corners. It would be about a half hour drive for both of them.

Before meeting her he'd have to go back to his house and grab the file that held all the paperwork that had been generated in the case of his father's homicide.

"There's a pepperoni pizza coming in about twenty minutes," he said to Lillian. He threw a twenty on her desk. "Enjoy the pizza and I'll be unreachable for the rest of the afternoon."

"Wait…you've got an appointment at two with Hal Brooks from Brooks Carpeting."

"Cancel it. Set something up with him for tomorrow," he said as he flew out the trailer door.

It was ridiculous how much he looked forward to seeing her again he thought as he drove to his home to get the files. It was ridiculous that his heart was racing just a little bit faster since her call.

He told himself it was nothing more than a continuation of the strange connection he'd felt when he'd first seen her…the connection of two survivors.

He told himself that his eagerness to see her again was because maybe, just maybe, something he found out about what had happened to her parents would bring him some closure as to what had happened to his.

But, even as he told himself all these things, he knew it was more than that. Part of the connection he'd felt had been one as old as time—the response of a male to an attractive female.

It had been years since he'd felt that charge of adrenaline, the rush of possibility where a woman was concerned.

He'd thought he'd found the perfect woman three years before. Patsy Gerrard had been attractive, witty and charming, and they had dated for just a little over a year. Their relationship had been one of the casualties of crime.

During those nightmare days immediately following his father's death and his mother's disappearance, he'd discovered that witty could be shallow, that charming could grate and what felt right through the good times often became terribly wrong during bad times.

It had been a relief when Patsy had moved on and he could give himself solely to the grief of losing his parents. But now he realized he'd been alone for too long, focused too intensely on his work and fighting loneliness during quiet moments to himself.

He pulled up in the driveway of his beautiful story-and-a-half home. The house had been his first building project and thankfully had been completed before the night of the crime.

His mother had fussed that the place was too big, too sterile for her son, and his father had explained that since Riley was a builder the house where he lived was important for future business. He'd assured his wife that it wouldn't be long before Riley would have the house filled with things to make it warm and homey. Riley knew his mother was hoping he'd find a wife to warm up the house.

It was still a cold and sterile place, Riley thought as he ran into his study and grabbed the thick file from his file cabinet. Since his father's death and his mother's disappearance, he'd done little to make the place a home. Maybe it was time, he thought.

Minutes later, as he drove to the Briarwood Truck Stop, he reminded himself that Savannah was in no position to be interested in pursuing any kind of relationship with a man. Her world had been turned upside down, her mother was missing and her father was still in a coma. The last thing on her mind would be romance.

But she could use a friend, he thought. And what better friend than a person who'd already been through the same kinds of things she was experiencing? What better friend than a man seeking answers to the same kinds of questions she had?

Savannah sat in one of the red leather booths in the Briarwood Truck Stop, toying with the silverware as she waited for Riley to arrive.

She'd hesitated before calling him, stewing it over for a full day before succumbing to desperation. It had now been almost ninety-six hours since her father had been hurt and her mother had disappeared.

Although she and her brother and sister were being kept out of the investigation loop, she knew that it had stalled and was going nowhere.

She sighed and motioned to the waitress for a refill on her coffee. She'd been living on coffee for the past three days, coffee and nerves. She'd just finished her second cup when he entered the restaurant.

Her pulse quickened slightly at the sight of him. Clad in a pair of navy dress slacks and a navy-and-white-striped dress shirt, he looked every inch a successful businessman. But as he walked toward her, she noted that he had an aura of strength, of power about him. It seemed obvious to her that he was a man confident of who he was, a man more than capable of taking care of himself.

He carried in one hand a bulky manila file and her heartbeat raced as she anticipated looking at what was inside. Since she couldn't investigate the crime that had occurred in her parents' home, she was eager to look through the files detailing the crime that had occurred in Riley's parents' home.

At least it was something to do, she thought. Glen had kept her away from work, and she had nothing to do except wait for her mother to return and wait for her father to come out of his coma. The waiting, she feared, would make her go more than a little crazy.

Looking through Riley's files might be nothing more than a dead end, but at least it was something for her to do beside sitting idle and thinking.

"Savannah." His gaze was warm as he greeted her. He slid into the booth across from her and shoved the folder to the side of the table. "I heard there's been no change in your father's condition and you haven't heard anything about your mother. How are you holding up?"

"Okay, I guess." Her gaze shot to the folder.

He placed a hand over it and smiled gently at her. "We eat first, then you can look through it."

"I'm really not hungry," she replied.

"But you have to eat," he returned. She looked at him with a touch of irritation. She didn't need a virtual stranger telling her what to do, and she certainly didn't need a mother figure.

Again he smiled, as if he knew exactly what she was thinking. "I've been there, Savannah. I know how slowly the hours can creep by while you wait for answers that make sense. I know how hard it is to sleep, how the simple act of eating doesn't seem important. But you have to keep your strength up. Your father is going to need you when he comes out of his coma and your mother is going to need you when she comes back home."

Before she could reply, the waitress appeared at their

table. "I'd like a cheeseburger, fries and a soda," he said, then looked at Savannah expectantly.

His little lecture had made sense and she opened the menu and frowned at it, trying to find something that would whet her appetite, but nothing sounded the least bit appetizing. Aware of Riley's gaze on her, she closed the menu. "I'll just have the soup of the day and a dinner roll."

The waitress left, and for a moment the two of them sat in silence. As she had the last time she'd met him, she smelled his scent…clean male coupled with woodsy cologne. "Are you married, Riley?" The question surprised her. It had fallen from her lips before becoming a conscious thought in her mind.

"No. Got close once, but then the thing with my folks sort of broke us apart."

"Oh, I'm sorry."

He waved a hand and grinned. "Don't be. The biggest mistake I would ever have made in my life would have been to marry Patsy. The messiness of the crime and the fallout from my emotional craziness was just too much for her to handle. She likes things neat and tidy, and there was nothing neat and tidy about me or the situation. I'm just grateful I found out before we got married instead of after."

"Your emotional craziness…what does that mean?" she asked curiously.

"Probably what you're going through right now."

"I'm not going through anything," she said.

He lifted a dark eyebrow wryly and leaned forward. "Then, you aren't having problems concentrating? You aren't having to talk around a ball of emotion so thick in your throat it threatens to suffocate you? The little minutia of life isn't ticking you off...the laughter of strangers, the birds' chirping, the need to pay bills?"

Initially his words offended her. She felt violated, as if he'd looked into her heart, seen the anguish of her soul. Then she realized he had, in a way. He'd been through it— the pain, the uncertainty, the anger that seemed to exclude everything else in her life since the moment she'd arrived at her parents' home that night.

"You're right," she finally replied, her voice flat and hollow to her own ears. "The woman where I got my gas earlier today told me good morning, and I had the sudden urge to reach across the counter and slap her silly."

She shook her head ruefully. "I want to scream and I want to cry, and more than anything I want it all to just go away. I want my father to wake up and my mom to come back and things to go back to the way they were."

She drew a deep breath, surprised by her own outburst. "I'm sorry...I just...nobody else seems to understand what I'm going through." She stared down at the tabletop, unable to meet his gaze.

"What about your sister and brother? Surely they're going through the same things that you are. Are the three of you close?"

"We're close, but Breanna just got married and has her husband, Adam. Clay—" she frowned, then continued "—Clay is so angry right now he's not letting anyone get close to him. He's a crime-scene investigator and it's killing him that nobody will let him into the house to do his job."

He covered her hand with his own. "So, when you feel all alone and have nobody to talk to about the emotional crazies, don't hesitate to call on me. You need to have somebody who understands what you're going through."

His hand was warm, his palm callused and strong over hers, and it felt good, which made her pull her hand away. His offer of support filled her with warmth. "And just who did you have who understood what you were going through? From what you told me a moment ago, Patsy didn't. And didn't you tell me before that you're an only child?"

He leaned back against the leather booth. "Yeah, it was just me." His blue eyes darkened to the deep shade of midnight. "I didn't have anyone to help me through it and I have to tell you there were times I wasn't sure I was going to survive it."

"How did you survive it?"

"I'm still surviving it," he replied. "It isn't as difficult as it was initially, but it's still with me…the questions, the uncertainty." He stopped talking as the waitress arrived at their table with their orders.

"I have kind of a rule about dining," he said when the waitress had left once again.

"And what's that?" The darkness in his eyes had left, and again she was struck by the beautiful blue of his eyes. She'd thought that was his appeal, what made him appear so handsome. But sitting across from him, she realized the startling color of his eyes was only part of it.

He had a firm, square chin that spoke of strong convictions and perhaps a bit of stubbornness. When he looked at her there was an attentiveness in his gaze that was both engaging and slightly provocative.

His dark hair had just enough curl and not quite enough style to keep it from falling over his broad forehead. His face and forearms were tanned, indicating a man who spent a lot of time outdoors.

"The rule is that we talk of nothing unpleasant while we eat. Unpleasantness at mealtime causes ulcers."

"Is that a medical certainty?"

He grinned, exposing his straight white teeth in a charming fashion. "That's a mother certainty. It was my mother's most strict rule and I still honor it."

"Okay," she agreed, and looked with disinterest down at her bowl of soup. It was minestrone, and nothing had ever looked less appetizing.

The silence between them stretched out and she felt the weight of it pressing against her chest. She felt as if she should say something, make some sort of meaningless small talk, but she seemed to have lost the ability.

She grabbed her dinner roll and pulled it apart and shot a surreptitious glance at Riley. He caught the glance and smiled sympathetically as if he knew idle conversation was beyond her grasp.

"It must be interesting, your work as a homicide detective," he said.

She eyed him wryly. "If the conversation is supposed to be pleasant, then it's not a great idea for me to talk about my work."

"Ah, just the opening I was waiting for. Now I get to tell you about my work." Again his charming smile. "You know how men love to talk about themselves."

The burst of laughter that escaped her lips both surprised and appalled her. How could she laugh—about anything—with the situation with her parents? The laughter died on a burst of guilt and tears suddenly stung her eyes. She stared down, fighting to get her emotions under control.

"It's all right, Savannah," he said softly. "Even though something bad has happened in your life, you've got to laugh when you get the chance. God knows it can't hurt your parents."

"Logically I know that," she exclaimed.

"Trust me, I know that you can't maintain the grief every moment of every day. It makes you a difficult person to be around." He gestured toward her soup bowl.

"Were you difficult to be around?" Dutifully, she picked up her spoon and took a sip of the soup.

He popped a French fry into his mouth and nodded. "I still have difficult days."

For the next few minutes they focused on their meals. To Savannah's surprise, the soup was quite good and awakened a hunger she hadn't realized she possessed.

"You haven't really taken the opportunity to talk about yourself," she observed as she buttered her dinner roll.

He'd nearly finished his cheeseburger and he took a sip of his soda before answering. "I decided to be kind and not bore you."

She had a feeling he was many things, but boring wasn't one of them. "Consider this an invitation to bore me."

He smiled, and again she was struck by the force of his appeal. "As you probably know from looking at my business card, I'm a builder. This spring we broke ground on my biggest project to date…my dream, really."

"And what's that?" She was always interested in hearing about other people's dreams, especially since she'd lost all of hers.

"Riley Estates," he said as if those two words explained everything.

"A development," she replied.

"More than just a development." His eyes lit with life. "It's going to be a community with amenities for everyone from the very young to the very old. Along with the new homes, I've agreed to refurbish some of the stores in downtown Sycamore Ridge to induce merchants back."

"Sounds like a big job all the way around," she observed.

"It is, but I'm hoping Riley Estates will bring people, and with people more stores will open and Sycamore Ridge will become the thriving little metropolis it once was."

"You grew up in Sycamore Ridge?"

"Born and raised there."

"Savannah?"

The deep, familiar voice came from somewhere behind her. She turned, then scooted out of the bench and hugged the distinguished-looking older man who stood near their booth. "Jacob! What are you doing here?"

"I was on my way home from one of the branch offices and thought I'd stop in here and grab a bite to eat." He squeezed her hands in his. "I can't begin to tell you how upset I've been over this thing with your mother and father. Has there been any news today?"

"None," she said as he released her hands.

"I'm offering a twenty-five thousand dollar reward to anyone with information about the whereabouts of your mother or whomever hurt your father."

"You don't have to do that," Savannah protested faintly.

His pale blue eyes radiated a combination of pain and concern. "I have to do something. Your parents were two of my dearest friends. I'm not good with anything but money."

Savannah hugged the portly man. "Thank you."

He looked at his watch. "I've got to run. I have an afternoon appointment to get to."

As he left, Savannah slid back into the booth and instantly realized she'd been rude. "I'm sorry, I should have introduced you," she said to Riley. "I wasn't thinking."

"It's all right. I recognized him. Jacob Kincaid, owner of Kincaid Banks."

"And a close friend of my parents. He's putting up a large reward for information about my mother and father."

"That's nice."

She shrugged. "We'll see. It's been my experience that rewards tend to bring out every nutcase in the county. Glen won't be overly pleased. A reward usually means more work for the people working the case. But it also sometimes takes just one tip to crack a case wide open." She eyed the manila folder he'd brought with him. "Would you mind if I took that with me?"

"Actually, I would." His gaze held an unspoken apology. "I didn't think to make copies before I left home, and I'd prefer it not leave my possession. My cop buddy left the force and if anything were to happen to these reports, I'd never be able to get copies again. You can look through them now, or if you'd prefer you can read through them at my place or yours. The other alternative is that you can get copies as soon as I have some made."

She didn't want to wait, but she hadn't really thought it through when she'd asked him to meet her here. She didn't feel comfortable reading the files now…here in a public place.

"If you don't mind…maybe you could follow me to my place," she said. "I really don't feel like we should go through it all here."

"I agree, and I don't mind at all following you."

Fifteen minutes later Savannah was regretting inviting him to her place. She should have just looked through the file at the truck stop.

She clenched the steering wheel tightly and glanced in the rearview mirror where Riley's pickup was visible. He was nice...too nice. He was attractive...too attractive.

"Don't worry, Jimmy," she whispered aloud. "No man, no matter how nice, no matter how attractive, will ever take your place in my heart, in my soul."

It was about the crime and nothing more. The crime they both had suffered explained the attraction she felt for Riley Frazier.

Once she read through his reports and files concerning the crime against his parents, then she would be done with him. Her heart would still belong to the man who'd been her soul mate from the time they'd been children.

CHAPTER FIVE

Riley thought he had no preconceptions about where Savannah lived. Still, he was vaguely surprised when she pulled into an attractive apartment complex and parked. He realized that somewhere in the back of his mind he'd assumed she was a house kind of person.

He followed her up the sidewalk to her unit, the manila folder clutched tightly in his hand.

He was glad she hadn't wanted to go over the file in the truck stop. Even though he'd read the reports a hundred times in the past two years, he still wasn't inured to the emotional assault he felt when looking at them.

"Come on in," she said as she opened the door.

"Thanks." He entered ahead of her into a small foyer. The focal point was a beautiful oil painting of bears in the wilderness. "Gorgeous art," he said.

"It's the work of a local artist. Her name is Tamara

Greystone. She teaches school and paints in her spare time. Let's go into the kitchen. I'll put on a pot of coffee."

"Sounds good."

She led him through a nice-size living room decorated in earth tones. The first things that snagged his attention were the photographs. They littered the room—small ones, larger ones, all framed and all of the same man.

He wasn't a particularly handsome man. Obviously Native American, his nose was a bit large and hooked, and his face was slightly chubby. But something about his eyes and his wide smile in each of the photos radiated an innate warmth and friendliness.

It wasn't so much a living room as a shrine to the man Riley presumed had been her husband. There were also photos of him and her together. In each of those her hair was long and her face held a bright, happy smile that made his heart ache for her loss.

"I heard about your husband," he said, aware that she'd seen him looking at the photos. "I'm sorry."

"Thank you." Her lips pressed tightly together, indicating to him that she intended to say nothing more on the subject.

The kitchen was bright and airy, decorated in an apple motif and smelling faintly of cinnamon. Windows surrounded a round oak table on three sides, giving an open, airy feel to the room. She gestured him to a chair at the table while she opened a cabinet and began to prepare the coffee.

"This is nice," he said. "How long have you been here?"

"I moved in about six months ago. Do you take cream or sugar in your coffee?"

"No, thanks. Black is fine." So, she'd moved in here after her husband had died. Probably escaping memories.

A new burst of compassion for her swept through him. He'd lost his parents, and although it had been intensely painful, it couldn't compare to losing a spouse.

As the kitchen filled with the scent of the fresh-brewed coffee, she pulled cups out of the cabinet and placed them on the table as Riley struggled to come up with some benign conversational topic.

"It's sure warm for so early in the summer," he finally said.

She shot him a quicksilver smile that lit up her features and nearly stole his breath away. "When uncertain about making conversation the safe resort is always the weather."

The smile was only there a moment, then gone, making him feel oddly bereft. "I was just making idle chatter," he replied.

She grabbed the coffeepot and filled their cups. "I know. The ability to make small talk seems to have eluded me some time ago." She put the coffeepot away, then joined him at the table.

He shrugged. "The ability to make small talk is vastly overrated. There's nothing wrong with moments of silence occasionally."

"Sometimes, though, too much silence can almost send you over the edge."

"True," he agreed, then took a sip of his coffee. He thought of what she'd said, about too much silence, and wondered how much she'd suffered in the past year since the death of her husband. He wondered if she had any idea how revealing her words had been, that she'd given him an intimate glimpse of her life.

"Well, I guess it's time to get to work." She drew a deep breath, her gaze on the manila folder. He pulled his chair around to the same side of the table where she sat.

"I have to warn you, some of this is kind of graphic," he said.

"Riley, I'm a homicide cop. I've seen graphic plenty of times before."

He opened the file and despite her last words, he heard her soft gasp as she saw the photo of his dead father on the floor next to a buttery tan recliner. Despite the fact that he'd believed himself mentally prepared to see the photo once again, the vision caused his breath to momentarily catch in the back of his throat.

Dad. His head filled with images of his father at the same time his heart cried out in pain.

He cleared his throat. "Apparently he was in his recliner when he was hit from behind with a blunt object. He fell forward and tumbled from the chair to the floor."

"Was the weapon found?"

"No."

"No weapon was found at my parents' house, either." She turned the photo over and picked up the medical examiner's report.

For the next half hour Riley sipped his coffee and watched as she read page after page of reports. He liked looking at her. Her features radiated so many things—strength, yet a soft vulnerability, determination mingling with a hint of stubbornness and an exquisite femininity he found captivating.

Occasionally she would ask him questions, take in his replies, then go back to reading. It was obvious her entire focus was on the reports. That was fine with him. He was content to sit next to her and smell the sweet scent of her, feel the body heat that radiated from her and wonder what it would be like to taste her lips.

It surprised him, that something about her had awakened

a hunger that hadn't been present in him for a very long time. Something about her made him think about hot kisses and the sweet hollow between female breasts.

Her hands fascinated him. They were slender, delicate and her fingernails were painted a pearly pink. He couldn't imagine them holding a gun. They seemed much more suited to stroking a brow...or holding a baby.

He frowned, aware that his thoughts were definitely sexist. He'd seen her handle her gun the night she'd drawn it on him in the hospital parking lot. She'd been coolly efficient, as if the gun were a natural extension of her arm.

"I've read all the notes about the people the police interviewed at the time of the incident. It sounds like your parents were very nice people," she said, and looked at him.

"They were." He leaned back in his chair to get a bit of distance from her, aware that his thoughts of moments before still had half possession of his brain. "They were quiet people. They didn't have a wide circle of friends, but they didn't have any enemies, either. I think that's why it was so easy for the officials to assume it was a domestic dispute gone bad."

"Despite the fact that nobody had ever seen signs of marital discord between your mother and father?"

He smiled with a touch of bitterness. "You know what they say, nobody knows what goes on behind closed doors. I guess the cops were able to figure that just because a couple doesn't air their dirty laundry in public doesn't mean there isn't any dirty laundry."

She closed the file, a frown creasing her brow. "In my parents' case it's just the opposite. The authorities don't have to speculate about dirty laundry behind closed doors."

He leaned forward once again. "What do you mean?"

She scooted back from the table and stood, as if uncomfortable with his nearness. She leaned against the cabinets, the frown still furrowing her forehead.

"Half the people in town can attest to the fact that my parents fought and fought often. They were loud and passionate fights, but never physical." She smiled, but it was a curious mix of pleasure and pain. "I think they were two people who were stimulated by the arguments. You know there are people like that."

He nodded and found himself wondering what her relationship had been like with her husband. Had they been like her parents? Stimulating each other with fights so the make-up sessions would be more exciting and intense? Or had they been more like his parents—quiet with their passion for each other, rarely exchanging words of conflict?

It didn't really matter what kind of relationship she had shared with her husband. It was obvious from the photo display in the living room that their relationship had been a loving one.

He shook his head in an attempt to focus on what she was saying and not on how lovely she looked.

"I really appreciate you letting me see the files," she said. "I'm not sure that anything I read will help in my case, but it was kind of you to share it with me."

He sensed a dismissal in her words and in the way she crossed her arms over her chest. "Actually, my reasons for letting you look at them were not altogether altruistic," he replied. "If the same perpetrator is responsible for your crime and mine, then perhaps in helping you to solve yours, I can find out who murdered my father and what happened to my mother."

"Whatever the reasons, I appreciate it." She moved to

the table and gathered up the papers. He knew it was a subtle action to get him on his way.

He reluctantly got to his feet and wasn't surprised when she led him back through the living room and to the front door. He felt a sense of rising panic, knowing that unless something else happened he'd probably never see her again, never talk to her again.

He told himself that he hardly knew her and had contacted her strictly as one victim seeking out another, as somebody hoping to find answers. But his interest in her had quickly outgrown that particular desire.

"Thank you again, Riley," she said at the door and offered him her hand.

He took it, enjoying the feel of its delicate femininity against his harder, bigger hand. "Anything I can do, Savannah, anything at all, don't hesitate to call me." He knew he was holding her hand longer than necessary, but he was reluctant to give it up. "Even if you just need to talk, I'm only a phone call away."

"Thank you." She pulled her hand away and there was nothing more for Riley to say, nothing more for him to do but leave.

As he drove away from the apartment complex, thoughts of her filled his head. He thought again of the pictures he'd seen, the ones where she'd been smiling and there had been no darkness in her eyes, no hint of the profound sadness that darkened them now.

Would she ever find that smile again? That bright, beautiful smile that lit her features from within? If she ever did, he hoped he'd be around to see it.

"What are you doing here?" Glen Cleberg greeted Savannah with a scowl as she walked into the brick building that housed the Cherokee Corners Police Department.

"I work here," she replied.

"I told you to take some time off," he replied.

She set her purse on her desk. "Glen, it's been over a week. If I don't get back to work, I swear I'll go crazy. Don't make me go back home."

Glen grabbed her arm and steered her into his private office. He pointed her to the chair in front of his desk as he pulled the door closed behind them.

Savannah steeled herself for a war. She couldn't stand the endless days and nights anymore. She'd spent hours at the hospital watching her motionless father, and hours wandering the streets trying to think of what might have happened to her mother.

"Glen, please don't send me home," she said again before he could say anything. "I need to get back to work. We've still got an open murder case to solve."

He nodded. "The Maxwell case…I know." He frowned and rubbed his hand across his meaty jaw. "I can't have you mucking around in your parents' case." His frown deepened. "But, I'll be honest, Savannah, we do need you on the Maxwell thing. You have a better grasp of the case than anyone else working it."

The case he spoke of was one Gregory Maxwell, found naked and dead in front of the public library. Savannah had been the first officer on the scene and had been assigned lead investigator. "Anything new on it since I've been out?"

"Nothing." Glen released a puffy sigh of frustration. "And Maxwell was well liked, highly respected. Folks want to know who did such a terrible thing."

"Then let me get back to work," she exclaimed.

He hesitated a long moment and pulled his hand across his lower jaw once again. "Okay." He leaned across his

DEAD CERTAIN

desk and pointed a stubby finger at her. "But you keep your investigation skills focused on the Maxwell case. You don't bother the men working your parents' case. That's not a homicide, and we're keeping you apprised of the details you need to know."

Which was nothing, she thought with a touch of bitterness. It had been eight days and there had been nothing new on the case. Her father was still in his coma and her mother was still missing and Jimmy, her sweet Jimmy was still dead.

"Get out of here and solve the Maxwell case," Glen said. "But your brother is still on paid leave. I don't want him anywhere near the lab until the forensic work is complete on your case."

She didn't waste time arguing with him, afraid that he might change his mind about her coming back to work. Instead she left his office and headed for her desk. She was greeted by fellow officers, most of whom had already given her their regrets over what had happened to her family.

The Maxwell file was on her desk just where she'd left it the last time she'd been in the station. She picked it up and read through her notes, trying to get back into the case that had haunted her before her personal tragedy had struck.

Greg Maxwell had been thirty-two years old at the time of his murder. He'd built a successful business selling and repairing computers and writing computer programs. He'd lived in a lovely home with an equally lovely wife, but somebody had stabbed him, then had undressed him, leaving him naked in the middle of the sidewalk as a final insult.

The authorities had uncovered no financial problems, no secret vices and no marital discord in their investigation.

She studied her notes of her interview with Virginia Maxwell, Greg's wife, but she found her thoughts wandering to Riley.

Long after he'd left her apartment his clean male scent had lingered. Somehow the smell had brought back her grief and thoughts of all she had lost when Jimmy had died.

After showing Riley to the door, she'd returned to the kitchen table and breathed the air that held his scent as she'd drunk yet another cup of coffee. She'd liked the way his hand had felt holding hers. His had been the hands of a working man—strong and competent and slightly rough.

He'd been in her thoughts often in the days since she'd last seen him. She told herself her only interest in him was the fact that he'd been through what she was going through. He was living proof that not knowing the whereabouts of a loved one could be survived.

But somewhere deep inside her, she knew it was more than that, that when he gazed at her with his oh-so-blue eyes, she became aware of herself as a woman, something she hadn't felt in a very long time.

"Well, well. Look who is back."

Savannah tensed slightly at the sound of the familiar voice. She looked up to see Officer Jason Sheller. Jason was the one man she worked with whom she didn't like. He was too handsome, too slick, too confident, and something about him had always made her skin crawl. Part of her aversion to the man came from the fact that he had tried to put the moves on her mere weeks after Jimmy's death.

"What do you want, Jason?" she asked.

"I see you're reading up on the Maxwell case. Anything new?"

"Apparently not since I've been gone. I'm thinking about reinterviewing Virginia Maxwell. There's something here we've got to be missing."

"She's staying at the Redbud," he said. She looked at him in surprise and he shrugged. "The local gossip update. She couldn't stand to stay in their house alone." One of his dark eyebrows quirked upward. "And the other local gossip has it that you were seen there one evening with a handsome stranger. What's the deal, Savannah, local guys aren't good enough for you? Haven't you heard I have a big gun?"

"Go away, Jason," she said with disgust. "Don't you have a speeder to ticket or a doughnut to eat?"

"Ha, very funny," he said, but to her relief he ambled away from her desk.

She tried to focus once again on rereading the material in the Maxwell case file but realized she was too antsy to sit still. Instead she headed to the Redbud Bed and Breakfast to reinterview Virginia Maxwell.

The interview yielded nothing new except the reminder that she'd found Virginia's response to her husband's murder rather odd and nothing during this interview had changed her impression.

The pretty blond woman had cried at the appropriate times and had cursed the person responsible, but to Savannah none of it had rung quite true.

As she drove back to the station she chided herself. Not all grief manifested itself in the same way for every person. Jimmy had loved her waist-length hair, and two days after his death, in a state of profound grief, she'd stunned her family and friends by cutting it all off.

If Virginia Maxwell was dealing with her grief by shopping and getting manicures, then who was Savannah to judge her?

She'd been back at the station for over an hour when the phone on her desk rang. She snatched it up. "Officer Tallfeather."

"Savannah?"

She hadn't realized before how pretty her name was, but coming from Riley, it sounded lovely. A crazy kind of pleasure swept through her. "Hi, Riley."

"I'm glad you're back at work."

"Me, too. I needed to get away from myself, if that makes sense."

"It makes perfect sense," he replied. "The best thing you can do for yourself is to keep busy."

It was good to hear his voice, to talk to somebody who had been through it all, somebody who understood. "The reason I'm calling," he continued, "is that you mentioned last time we talked how frustrated your brother is that they aren't letting him into your parents' home."

"That's right." Clay's mood had gotten progressively worse with each passing day, and Savannah suspected he was spending too much time alone in his home and drinking.

"This is probably an absolutely crazy idea."

"What? What's a crazy idea?"

"I know it hasn't been established that what happened to your parents and what happened to mine are linked."

She released a sigh of frustration. "I spoke with Glen about your case just a little while ago, and he refused to even consider the possibility that they're linked. He said your case is closed and…" She hesitated a moment, unsure if she should continue with what else the chief had said.

"And what?" A deep sigh filled the line. "I suppose he

mentioned the speculation that my mother ran off with the local handyman."

"Apparently Glen has access to some files you don't have and had looked up the case, and yes, that's exactly what he mentioned."

Again another deep sigh. "My parents had befriended a man named John Barker who was learning disabled. He had no family and did odd jobs for people in Sycamore Ridge. About once a week or so my parents would hire him to do some little job and invite him to stay for dinner. Sometimes in the mornings John would stop by the house and have a cup of coffee with my mother. It was all very innocent, but some people tried to turn it into something ugly."

"So, what happened to this John?"

"Two days before the incident, my mom told me that John had gotten a job with a family in Oklahoma City and was very excited about it. He'd come by to tell my parents goodbye."

"So, the handyman disappeared around the same time that your mother disappeared," Savannah said.

"Yes, but I'm telling you there's no way in hell my mother killed my father, then ran off with John. I've never been more certain of anything in my life. I'm as certain about it as you are about your own mother's innocence."

She believed him, and the more she'd thought about the two cases, the more she couldn't help but think that somehow, someway they had to be connected. "So, what does all of this have to do with Clay's frustration?" she asked.

"At the time of my father's murder, of course their house was gone over by the police, but once the crime-scene people were done with it, I locked it up and it's been locked up ever since. I just thought maybe Clay would like to get inside and see if the original officers overlooked something."

Savannah's pulse rate increased at the thought. Was it possible Clay could find something in Riley's parents' home that might help them figure out what had happened to their parents? Something that might point to the whereabouts of their mother?

"You wouldn't mind us going inside?" she asked.

"Not if it would help."

She frowned thoughtfully. "Why don't we tentatively plan to meet around four tomorrow afternoon and I'll talk to Clay about it tonight."

"Sounds good to me."

"And if for some reason that time won't work for Clay, I'll call you back."

"Whatever works for the two of you will be fine with me. You've got the address. Do you need directions?"

"No, we should be able to find it without any problems."

"Then I'll see you tomorrow at four."

She told herself the excitement she felt was all about being able to reprocess a crime scene that might yield some information. She told herself it had nothing to do with the fact that she was going to see Riley again.

That evening, after getting off duty, she drove directly from the station to her brother's house. Clay lived on the outskirts of Cherokee Corners, in a small ranch house that was isolated from its neighbors by miles of dusty earth.

Silhouetted against the setting sun were several old, no-longer-working oil pumps. They resembled big-headed insects crouching in the dust.

Clay's car was out front so she knew he was home. She knocked on the front door, then pushed it open. "Clay?"

"In the kitchen," his deep voice replied.

She walked through the sterile living room, the room decorated with more lab equipment than actual furniture. She found her brother seated at the kitchen table, a handful of reports spread out before him.

"What are you looking at?" She sat across from him at the table.

"Preliminary lab reports of the forensic findings from Mom and Dad's." He didn't look up from the paper he held in his hand.

Savannah raised an eyebrow in surprise. "How did you get them?"

"Jesse brought them to me." Jesse Sampson was one of the three crime-scene investigators for the county.

"If Glen finds out you have those Jesse could get fired," she observed.

He looked up, his eyes the darkness of a cold, moonless night. "I don't intend to tell Glen…do you?"

"Of course not."

Clay threw the paper down on the table and took a long drink from a bottle of beer. "It doesn't matter anyway. So far the tests have yielded nothing to point to a suspect."

"Have you eaten anything today?" she asked, noting the empty beer bottles that peeked out of the nearly over-flowing trash can.

"I'm not hungry."

"You have to eat." She got up from the table and walked over to the refrigerator. She opened it up, unsurprised to see a variety of bottles of chemicals, solvents and items she didn't recognize but had nothing to do with foodstuff. She also spied a package of bologna and some slices of cheese.

"How about you eat a sandwich and I talk to you about something that might or might not interest you."

"What are you talking about?"

She waited until he was eating before telling him about Riley and the crime that had happened two years before. Clay listened intently, his dark gaze giving away nothing of his inner thoughts.

Although he was her brother, she'd always found him an enigma, impossible to read, difficult to know. Oh, she knew he loved her and Breanna and their mother and father...at least as much as he was capable of loving.

"So, what do you think?" she asked after she'd told him about the pending meeting with Riley the next day.

"I think it sounds like a waste of time," he said flatly. "I mean, what's the point? The scene was processed a long time ago."

"But you're the best, Clay. If the original officers missed anything, you'll find it. You always find things nobody else does. What if the two cases are linked? What if you go to Riley's parents' house and do a little work and you find out what happened there? What happened to Mom and Dad?"

He reached across the table, grabbed her hand and squeezed. His eyes held the dark pain of a tortured soul. "We fought, you know. The last time I saw Mom, we had a terrible fight."

"About what?" Savannah asked.

"It doesn't matter what the fight was about...but I keep thinking, what if I never get a chance to apologize...to tell her that I love her." He released his hold on her hand, but she grabbed it once again.

"You will get a chance to apologize," she said fervently. "And you'll get a chance to tell her how much you love her. She's just missing, Clay. If it were anything else, we'd know. If she was really gone, surely we'd feel it in our hearts."

"You don't really believe that, do you?" This time he pulled his hand away and wrapped it around his beer bottle.

"I believe she's still alive." An ache pierced Savannah's heart as she thought of her mother. "I don't know. Maybe *we* wouldn't know if she was gone, but Alyssa would."

Clay finished his beer and tossed the bottle into the garbage. "Okay, I'll process the old crime scene and see if it yields any clues." His jaw clenched for a moment. "At least it will be better than sitting around here waiting for Dad to wake up, waiting for any news."

"Good." Savannah stood, leaned over and kissed her brother on the forehead. "Why don't I meet you here about three tomorrow afternoon. We can drive to Sycamore Ridge together."

"All right," he agreed, and for the first time since that night of horror at her parents' home she saw life flicker in his eyes.

Tomorrow, she thought as she drove home minutes later. Tomorrow she'd see Riley, and perhaps tomorrow they'd get some answers.

CHAPTER SIX

Riley sat in the driveway of his parents' home, dreading the moment when he would enter it again. A hundred times in the past two years he'd dreamed of going inside to find his mother and father seated at the card table in the living room, stewing over their latest, intricate jigsaw puzzle.

He knew that particular scenario would never happen, that his father was never coming back from the grave. But he did still hope that one day his mother would return from wherever she'd been with a logical explanation for her absence.

He hadn't been parked in the driveway for long when the car interior grew too hot. He got out and walked to the porch and sat on the stoop. Although he dreaded going into the house, he was looking forward to seeing her again.

Savannah. He wasn't sure why she'd lodged in his brain the way she had, from the moment he'd met her. Even now if he closed his eyes and focused he could smell the scent of her, visualize the rich darkness of her short hair, the beauty of that smile he'd seen in the photographs.

Over the past couple of days he'd tried to tell himself that what he felt was a crazy infatuation, that his life had been so isolated for so long that of course he would be attracted to a woman as pretty as Savannah.

But, no matter how he tried to convince himself that it was simply a passing infatuation, he couldn't. He'd never been the kind of man given to flights of fancy where women were concerned. It took far more than a pretty face or a killer body to pique his interest. And he couldn't make himself believe that his only interest in her was as a companion victim.

He saw the white panel van approaching and stood. He recognized that kind of van. One just like it had pulled in front of this house on the night of his father's murder. He just hadn't expected Clay and Savannah to arrive in such a vehicle. But it was them, and they pulled into the driveway and got out.

For a brief moment Riley drank in the sight of Savannah. The white shorts she wore not only showed off the length and shapeliness of her legs, but also complemented her cinnamon-bronze skin tones.

Her blouse was sleeveless and red, tied at her slender waist and opened at the neck to expose delicate collarbones. White strappy sandals adorned her feet, and her toenails were painted scarlet red.

He forced his attention away from her and to the man who accompanied her. It was the same man he'd suspected was her sibling the night he'd seen them together at her parents' home.

"Hi, I'm Riley Frazier," he said, and held out a hand.

"Clay. Clay James."

His handshake was strong and lasted only a moment. He nodded curtly, then rounded the back of the van and opened the doors.

"Clay isn't real good with people," Savannah said as if to apologize for her brother's brusqueness.

"He seemed fine to me," Riley replied. "How are you doing?"

She shrugged. "I'm as okay as I can be under the circumstances. We're still waiting for Dad to regain consciousness and hoping he can tell us what happened." She looked toward the house. "Are you sure you're okay with this?"

He glanced at the house and felt every muscle in his body tense at the prospect of going inside. He looked back at her and forced a smile. "I'm as okay as I can be under the circumstances."

She flashed him a smile that shored up his strength, made him believe he could face going back into the scene of his father's murder if it helped her in any way.

"Are we going to do this or what?" Clay peered around the back of the van at the two of them.

Savannah touched Riley's arm and gestured for him to follow her to the back of the van. Once there Clay handed each of them gloves and plastic booties. "I don't know how much good this will do," he said. "But we might as well try not to contaminate anything that might be left inside."

Clay grabbed two steel suitcases, then the three of them walked to the front door. Riley was surprised to see his hand shake slightly as he reached out to unlock it. He hoped neither Savannah nor Clay had noticed.

He opened the door, noticing immediately that the air smelled musty…like a house that had been closed up for

far too long. He was almost grateful for the foreign scent.
The house no longer smelled like home.

Clay followed him in and set the two suitcases down
on the foyer floor. As he bent down to open them, Savannah entered the house.

Riley drew a deep breath and stepped into the living
room. Here the aftermath of murder still lingered. Fingerprint dust remained on the furniture, blood still stained
the carpet around where his father's chair had been. The
chair itself had been taken away by the police on the night
of the murder.

Riley had believed his muscles were already taut, but
now he felt them tighten even more. He needed to be
strong. He wanted to be strong. He couldn't think about
the last time he'd been in this room, when his father's
body had been sprawled on the floor, the back of his head
a bloody mass of tissue and brain matter.

He jumped as Savannah touched his arm. He turned to
look at her, hoping she didn't feel, couldn't see how close
he was to shattering into a million pieces.

"It's the natural way of things that children bury their
parents, but not like this," he said. "No child, no matter
how old, should have to go through something like this."

"I know," she said softly. "Unfortunately, as a homicide
detective I see this all too often."

He turned to look at her. "How do you get through the
days?"

"I remind myself that I'm doing something good, that
maybe with my work, a murderer will be taken off the
streets and put behind bars for the rest of their lives."

"That's what I want to happen to the person who killed
my dad. I'm not a vengeful man, but in this case I make
an exception."

She nodded. "I know exactly how you feel."

"If you don't mind, Riley, I'd like to do a complete walk-through of the house before I really get down to business," Clay said.

Riley was grateful for the all-business tone in Clay's voice. For just a moment he'd felt himself getting far too emotional for comfort. "Fine with me. Why don't we start in the kitchen."

The walk-through was difficult. In every room there was evidence of lives suspended. In the kitchen a drainer held a rack of clean dishes, a dish towel covering them. His mother had rarely used the electric dishwasher, preferring to hand wash any dishes. She called the time it took her to hand wash dishes her think time.

In the bathroom a towel hung over the shower door and Riley remembered how much his mother had hated it when his father didn't put his towel in the hamper.

Both Clay and Savannah remained quiet as he led them through the house. He was grateful for their silence, felt as if it was somehow respectful of the people who had once lived here, loved here.

Savannah was the first to speak. They entered the bedroom where Riley had grown up, the room that his parents had kept much as it had been when he'd been a teenager. She walked over to the bookcase and looked at the trophies displayed there.

"A football jock, huh?"

"I played a little ball," he replied, oddly embarrassed by her peek into his past.

"Looks like you played pretty well—All-State Champion."

"We had a good team that year. I don't think there's anything in here that can help us."

"You're probably right," Clay agreed as if sensing his discomfort.

The master bedroom was the most difficult. Here was the evidence the initial investigators had thought proved that his mother had been responsible for his father's murder. Drawers were open, clothes spilling out as if items had been grabbed hurriedly. Several empty hangers dangled in the closet, some had fallen to the floor.

There was no denying that it appeared as if somebody had packed in a hurry. "Unless my mother tells me she's responsible for this, I'll never believe she packed up and ran away," he said. "Besides, even if the worst-case scenario is true, that somehow she suffered some kind of temporary insanity and hit my father, she never would have left without her treasure box."

"Treasure box?" Savannah looked at him curiously.

He went inside the closet and from the shelf above the clothes removed a wooden container the size of an old-fashioned breadbox. He placed it on the edge of the bed and opened it, aware of Clay and Savannah moving closer to see what the box contained.

Inside were a number of items—a baby photograph of Riley, the invitation to his parents' wedding, a dried corsage from a long-ago prom. There was also money. Lots of money. "Mom and Dad never took a honeymoon," Riley said. "So, Mom was saving up enough money for them to take one, last year on their anniversary. There's a little over a thousand dollars in here." He looked from Savannah to Clay. "Why would a woman on the run not take this money with her?"

Savannah and Clay exchanged a look. "You just made me remember something about our mother," Savannah explained. "She had a secret hiding place in her headboard. She kept her good jewelry there along with some cash."

"Was it taken?" Riley asked.

"I don't know. I don't think anyone ever checked."

"Let me know what you find out. I'd be interested to know," Riley replied.

From the master bedroom they returned to the living room and suddenly Riley needed to get out, get some air. He'd thought he'd be able to handle being inside the house again, but he couldn't. A sharp grief ripped through him with jagged edges that pierced his heart.

"You do whatever it is you need to do. I'll be out back on the patio," he said. He didn't wait for either of them to reply, but headed outside through the sliding glass doors in the living room.

The heat of the sun as he sat on one of the deck chairs warmed the chill that had taken possession of him. Two years—for almost two years his mother had been missing.

He leaned his head back and gulped the air that was filled with the sweet scent of roses. The scent came from a dozen rosebushes in the backyard, each one laden with blooming, rich-colored flowers.

How long before he got some answers? How long would he keep this house just as it was…waiting for the return of a woman who might never return?

He frowned at this thought. He couldn't think that way. She would come back. Somehow, someway, she'd return. He had to hold on to that thought.

There was nothing Savannah could do to help Clay. First and foremost she wasn't trained in his field, and secondly, her brother had always worked best when left alone.

She moved to the sliding doors and looked out to where

Riley sat with his back to her in a plastic deck chair. She wasn't sure if he needed some time alone or would prefer company.

She'd seen his anguish with each step they'd taken through the house, had felt his anguish echoing inside of her. He'd given them a stiff upper lip, but his emotions had shown in the slight shake of his hands, his jaw muscles that clenched and unclenched and the pain that radiated from his blue eyes.

"I'm going outside. Call me if you need me to do anything," she said to her brother. He grunted in reply, his concentration completely focused on his task.

If Riley needs to be alone, then I'll know it and come back inside, she told herself as she slid the door open and stepped outside.

She sat in the deck chair right next to his but focused her attention on the lovely roses, giving him an opportunity to compose himself if he needed to. "The roses are gorgeous and smell wonderful," she said.

"My father planted them about six years ago after my mother complained he never brought her flowers. He said this way every spring and summer day she'd have flowers from him."

She looked at him then, saw that some of the grim lines that had etched into his face while they'd been inside the house had gone. "I'm sorry, Riley. I'm sorry you had to come here again."

He smiled, but it was a sad kind of smile. "It was my idea. You didn't force me into it."

"I know, but still…it has to be hard."

"I hadn't anticipated it being as hard as it was," he confessed. He drew a deep breath and sat up straighter in the chair. "But, it's nice out here. I've always liked this backyard."

"You like picnics?" she asked.

"Only if they include the food from the important food groups…thick sandwiches, potato salad and chocolate cake for dessert."

She laughed. "Ah, a fellow chocoholic."

"Definitely. I've been known to eat a handful of M&Ms and call it lunch, much to Lillian's disgust."

"Lillian?"

"Lillian is the feistiest sixty-two-year-old woman you ever want to meet. I hired her as a secretary six months ago, and she's become both a friend and a nagging surrogate mother figure."

"If she makes you eat more than M&Ms for lunch, then she's definitely worth her weight in gold," Savannah observed.

"And she reminds me of that every day," he replied.

His eyes had lightened, the darkness that had clung to them gone the longer they spoke of mundane things. "Tell me what else you like beside picnics," she said, wanting the pleasant conversation to continue.

He leaned back in the chair and stretched his long legs out before him, his gaze going to the rose bushes in the distance. "I like pepperoni pizza and a warm fire on a cold winter night. I like walking the land of Riley Estates and envisioning what will eventually be built there. I like getting up early enough to see a sunrise. Now, your turn."

For a moment her mind went blank. It had been so long since she'd thought about the things that brought her pleasure. "I like mushroom pizza," she began. "I like curling up with a good novel, working at the Cherokee Cultural Center and cats."

"Cats? I didn't see any cats when I was at your house."

"That's because I don't have one." She and Jimmy had talked about getting a cat many times, but had never gotten around to actually doing it. It was one of the promises they'd made for a future time…like anniversaries…and children…and love forever.

"Why not?" he asked.

"I don't know. I guess it's just one of those things you talk about but never actually take the time to do." In truth, after Jimmy's death she hadn't wanted to be responsible for any living thing.

"Life is pretty short," Riley said. "If you want a cat, you should get yourself one. They're pretty low maintenance from what I hear." He tilted his head and studied her for a long moment. "I would bet you're a low-maintenance kind of woman."

"What does that mean?" she asked, unsure if the observation should offend her or not.

"It's easier to explain if I tell you what a high-maintenance kind of woman is like. Take Patsy, for instance. She was definitely high maintenance. We couldn't go out if the wind was blowing and might mess up her hair. If it was too cold her lips got chapped, if it was too warm she felt faint. And I can't tell you how many meals got sent back to the kitchen when we ate out because they didn't meet her requirements."

Savannah laughed. "My hair is too short to get messed up in a tornado. I have chapped lips most of the time and I've never met a meal that I didn't like."

Riley grinned. "Definitely low maintenance and that's a nice thing."

They continued to talk as dusk shadows deepened and Clay turned on lights in the house that radiated out to the back patio. The dark of night finally swallowed up the purple shadows of night and still Clay worked inside and still Riley and Savannah sat outside, talking and then falling into occasional comfortable silences.

The tension she'd felt radiating from him when she'd first come outside was gone and she sought to continue with a topic that would further relax him. "What's your favorite season, Riley?"

"Any of them except winter. For a builder the enemy is always winter. What about you? What's your favorite?"

"I love the one we're in," she said without hesitation. "Jimmy used to tell me that I was probably the only woman on earth who didn't complain about the cold in the winter, the heat in the summer and the wind in the spring and fall."

"Jimmy...he was your husband." Curiosity lit his eyes. "Tell me about him."

It was odd, to have somebody ask about him. Since the time of his death nobody had wanted her to talk about Jimmy. Move on, they'd told her. Don't dwell on it. Now he wanted her to tell him about the man who had been her best friend, the man she had intended to spend the rest of her life with.

"I'm not sure where to begin," she said, fighting the grief that always accompanied thoughts of Jimmy.

"How did you meet him?"

"That's easy. When I was four, my mother and Jimmy's mother decided to do something to honor the Cherokee heritage. They were instrumental in getting the cultural center in Cherokee Corners started." As she spoke of distant days of childhood, some of the grief subsided. "Anyway, Jimmy was four years old, too. From the very beginning, we were great friends."

"That must have made his loss doubly hard," he said,

his voice so soft, so gentle it brought a sudden burn of tears to her eyes as she nodded.

Jimmy. Dear Jimmy, her heart cried. "There are times it's still so hard. He was so much a part of my life. He was such a good man…a kind man."

"What did he do for a living?"

"He'd been a salesman, but he wasn't very good at it. He didn't like to push people, wasn't aggressive enough to be in sales. So, we'd agreed he should take some time and go back to school. He was driving home from night classes the night he crossed the old bridge and hit the guard rail."

Emptiness. She could still feel the emptiness she'd felt when the officers had arrived on her doorstep to give her the news. It had been a cold, hollow emptiness that, at times, still held her in its grip.

She'd thought of taking Riley's hand to offer support when she'd first come outside. But now it was he who reached for her hand, and she welcomed the warmth that seemed to flow straight to her heart.

"There are times you wonder how much suffering the human spirit can endure."

"I guess everyone's threshold for suffering is different. There are some nights I climb up in the girders of that old bridge and stare at the water beneath and wonder if I've finally reached my threshold of pain." The moment the words left her lips she was appalled that she'd confessed such a thing.

Before she knew what was happening, Riley stood and jerked her up before him. His fingers bit into the skin at her shoulders. "My God, Savannah. Surely you don't go up there and contemplate…even entertain for one moment the desire to…to…" He broke off, as if finding the thought too horrible to be spoken aloud.

He grabbed her to his chest, wrapped his arms around her and held her tight against him. She wanted to protest, but his arms were so strong, his chest so broad, and it had been so achingly long since she'd been held.

"If you ever, ever feel desperate and as if you can't go on, you call me. I'll help you get through the dark hours until you get strong again."

His words once again brought tears to her eyes. How long had it been since anyone had cared about those dark hours? Her family members had long ago quit talking about her loss, as if to stop speaking of it would make her heal more quickly.

His body was so warm against hers, and the warmth, coupled with the pleasure of their conversation, made her linger in his arms when she knew she should move away.

His scent, that bold masculine fragrance filled her senses at the same time her fingers itched to touch the rich darkness of hair at the nape of his neck.

She fought the impulse and started to step out of his arms. But when she raised her head to look at him, her breath caught in her chest and she couldn't move an inch. Desire. It radiated from his eyes, a rich desire that drew her into the blue depths.

She knew he was going to kiss her, knew she should step away, break the moment, stop it from happening. But before she could do any of those things his lips were on hers.

Hot and hungry, his mouth demanded...and got a response from her. She was helpless against the sensual assault as his tongue touched first the tip of her teeth, then slid beyond. It was wrong—desperately wrong—but it felt so right, so wonderfully right.

The kiss seemed to last both a single moment and an

eternity. She wasn't even sure if he was the one to end it or she did. She only knew that one moment his mouth possessed hers, and the next moment it didn't.

She stumbled back from him with a surprised "Oh."

"Savannah."

"I've done everything I can here." Clay's voice boomed from the back door, interrupting whatever Riley had been about to say.

He stepped outside and looked at them expectantly. "Are we ready to take off? I've got some tests I'd like to get to right away."

Couldn't Clay feel the tension in the air...the thick, sexual tension that crackled and snapped between her and Riley? Savannah could certainly feel it. Not only could she feel the invisible tension, but her lips still felt hot and her heart pumped an irregular rhythm and she found it impossible to meet Riley's gaze.

"I'm ready when you are," she said to Clay. She forced herself to look at Riley. "Thank you for letting us in here."

His eyes held a dozen unspoken questions and the whisper of a still-simmering desire. "You'll let me know what you find?" he asked Clay.

"Of course," Clay replied.

"And, Savannah? I'll call you?"

She hesitated a moment, then nodded. "Okay."

For once in her life Savannah was grateful Clay wasn't a talker as they drove back to Cherokee Corners. She didn't want to talk. Over and over again she replayed those moments when his lips had been on hers, when his arms had held her tight. Over and over again her body flushed with heat as she remembered the bliss of his kiss.

It was nearly eleven by the time they got back to Clay's house and Savannah got into her car to drive home. She was nearly home when she realized it was Saturday night… her night to go to Jimmy.

Guilt ripped through her as she realized she'd nearly forgotten. The blackness of despair crept over her, through her. How could she have allowed one simple little kiss to make her forget Jimmy?

Riley had told her to call him when she felt like going to the bridge, but he didn't understand…couldn't understand the despair that drove her there. Nobody could understand.

Tonight her despair was worse than ever as she thought of how easily she'd fallen into the sensual play of Riley's lips on hers. She felt as if she'd betrayed Jimmy, her husband, the love of her life.

Before she knew it, she was at the old bridge, and it took her only minutes to climb the familiar path amid the girders over the dark water of the Cherokee River.

Shame washed over her, not the shame of kissing another man, but the shame of enjoying the kiss of another man. She had promised to love Jimmy through eternity, had vowed that he would always be the only man in her heart.

"You're my woman, Savannah." Jimmy's deep voice echoed in her head. "We were destined to be together… forever…for always."

For just a moment she'd allowed herself to indulge in the possibility of another relationship, another man. Jimmy deserved better than that.

"I'm sorry, Jimmy," she whispered, looking to the water beneath her.

She was overwhelmed, guilt ridden by the fact that she'd enjoyed Riley's company, enjoyed his kiss. She was twisted into knots by the trauma and uncertainty of her parents' well-being. Things had become just so hard. Life had become so difficult.

Her mother was gone, her father in a state of limbo and she was lonely...so very lonely. Why hang on? Why face another day? What was the point of getting up in the morning? Going on with her empty life?

"Jimmy." She tried to feel the same anguish she'd felt the last time she'd been here, the strong desire to jump and join him in the spirit world. She closed her eyes against the tears that burned.

If she did jump she would be in the arms of her husband forever. She wouldn't have to deal with the unanswered questions where her father and mother were concerned. She could just let go...let go of life and be released from all pain.

But when she looked down at the river, it was Riley's face she saw reflected on the water. His blue eyes shone like stars in her mind, his smile like the sun lighting up the sky. She squeezed her eyes tightly closed again, not wanting to think about him.

Jimmy...that's who she should be thinking about. Jimmy, who had loved her so deeply, who had been her soul mate. Jimmy deserved her love, her devotion.

The ringing of her cell phone shattered the silence of the night and her thoughts. She ignored the first four rings, but whoever was trying to get in touch with her was persistent, for the phone kept on ringing.

She finally answered.

"Savannah?" A subdued excitement filled the voice of her sister, Breanna. "You've got to get over here to the hospital. Daddy's waking up."

CHAPTER SEVEN

By the time Savannah arrived at the hospital, Scott Moberly was skulking around in the lobby. "Hey, Savannah." His boyish features lit up as he spied her coming through the double door. "I heard your father's waking up."

"That's what I've heard, too." Savannah didn't stop her progress toward the door that led to the patient rooms.

"Will you tell me what he says..."

Scott's voice disappeared as the door closed behind her. Ahead of her, down the distance of the long hallway, she saw a group of people gathered outside her father's door. Breanna and Adam were there, as well as Clay and Glen Cleberg.

Breanna and Adam saw her first and hurried to meet her. "Dr. Watkins is in there with Dad now."

"How's he doing? Can he speak? Has he said what happened to him? To Mom?" The bridge she'd just climbed down from seemed very far away as adrenaline pumped through her.

"We don't know anything yet," Adam said. "The doctor has been in there with him since we all arrived."

The three of them joined the others who stood just outside the closed door.

"Who called Moberly?" Savannah asked. "He was perched like a vulture in the lobby when I came in.

"The little twerp was hanging around at the station when the call came in about your dad," Glen explained. "I'd put the word in that I wanted to be notified immediately if there was any change in Thomas's condition."

Before anyone could say anything else, Dr. Watkins stepped out of the room and into the hallway. They all converged on him, and he held up his hands to silence them.

"He's awake and he's talking. But it appears he's suffered some damage to his motor control. He's confused and a bit disoriented, so we're going to make your visits brief. You can go in a couple at a time for a few minutes."

It was decided that Breanna, Adam and Clay would go in first. "I do not want him upset," Dr. Watkins said. "I know you're all eager to get some answers, but I don't want him pushed. He's quite fragile right now, and I won't have him set back by everyone demanding more than he can give at the moment."

He followed the first group into the room while Savannah and Glen remained in the hallway.

"When are you going to let Clay come back to work?" she asked her boss.

"I thought maybe he already returned to work without my notice. The CSI van was missing for several hours this evening." He cocked an eyebrow. "Want to tell me what that was all about?"

Instantly her head filled with the memory of Riley's kiss, that heavenly, hot kiss that had given her a moment of pleasure and more time of torment.

"Savannah?"

Even though she knew he'd be irritated, she told Glen about going to Sycamore Ridge and Clay reprocessing the old Frazier crime scene.

"That case is closed," Glen exclaimed. "Your afternoon there was a waste of time."

"Maybe," she agreed. "But keeping Clay out of his lab and away from his work is a waste of his talent."

"You James people hang tighter than anyone I know," Glen said irritably. "I've already heard it all from your sister when she got here."

"Clay needs to work. That's all he has at the moment to keep him sane."

"I'm releasing the house tomorrow," Glen said. "We've done all we can there. And if I know Clay, the minute I tell him the house is released he'll be over there reprocessing that scene." Glen shoved his hands in his pockets and leaned again the wall. "Who knows, maybe he'll be able to pick up something we missed."

Before they could speak further, Breanna, Adam and Clay filed out of the room. Breanna was teary-eyed but smiling, and Adam leaned over and whispered something in her ear and her smile grew brighter as love for him poured from her gaze.

A thick shaft of envy struck at Savannah's heart. How lucky Bree was to have someone to hold her hand, support her and love her.

She thought of Riley's hand...so big...so warm and with just enough rough edges to be interesting. She frowned.

Why was she thinking of Riley's hand? She should be re-membering the feel of Jimmy's hand holding hers.

Dr. Watkins appeared at the door and motioned to Sa-vannah and Glen. Savannah went in first and her heart swelled to fill her chest at the sight of her father's famil-iar blue eyes gazing at her.

"Daddy," she said, and rushed to his side as Glen re-mained standing just inside the doorway.

"Savannah…my shining Silver Star." Although the words were slurred, they were intelligible, and a vast relief swept through her. He was lucid enough to know who she was, to remember her Cherokee name, and he could talk. At the moment nothing else seemed quite as important.

She took his right hand, which remained limp and un-responsive in hers. "You've had us all so very worried."

"Sorry." His eyes held bewilderment. "Where's your mama…why isn't she here with me?"

Savannah exchanged a look with Glen, who stepped up to the foot of Thomas's bed. "Do you know how you got hurt, Thomas?" Glen asked.

Thomas frowned and with his left hand reached up and touched the swath of bandages on the back of his head. "Did I fall?"

"Don't you remember?"

Panic filled Thomas's eyes. "Am I supposed to remem-ber?" His frantic gaze went from Glen, to Savannah, then back to Glen. "Where's Rita? She'll remember. I don't…I can't…"

"Shh, it's all right, Dad," Savannah assured him, and shot a warning look to Glen. "You just rest now. You rest and get better, stronger. That's what's important."

Thomas closed his eyes as the doctor motioned them

out of the room. Dr. Watkins led them some distance down the hallway, then turned to face them all.

"I know you're all anxious for answers. But I have to warn you that there's a possibility you won't ever get any from Thomas. It isn't unusual for victims of severe trauma to have no memory of the incident that lands them in a hospital."

An intense disappointment swept through Savannah, and she knew it was the same emotion every one of them were feeling. They had so hoped that when Thomas came awake answers would quickly follow.

"That's it for tonight," Dr. Watkins continued. "I want my patient to rest. And there will be no visitors allowed tomorrow. We'll be running a full battery of tests to determine the full extent of damage and working up a rehabilitation program. You all can visit him again tomorrow evening."

Minutes later the James siblings all sat in the empty hospital cafeteria. They were seated at one of the round tables, each with a cup of stale coffee in front of them.

"Okay, so we know now that it's possible Dad won't be able to tell us anything about that night," Breanna said. "I think it's time we get more proactive about doing something to find Mom."

"What do you suggest, Bree? We've done everything we can think of," Savannah replied.

"Adam and I were talking last night and we think it might be a good idea to get some posters printed up and distributed around the county."

"Glen already had her picture flashed on the evening news," Clay said.

"But that was just for two nights, and the picture was

only shown briefly. We need posters to keep Mom's face in front of people," Bree explained.

"I'll see to the printing if you will help with the distribution," Adam said.

Clay shrugged. "I guess it can't hurt." Savannah nodded her agreement.

"Has anyone checked in at the cultural center?" Savannah asked. This was the busiest season at the tourist attraction and she wondered how they were getting along without her mother's drive, enthusiasm and organizational skills.

"I spoke with Mary yesterday. Everything is hectic, and they miss Mom desperately, but they're functioning as best they can. I'm planning on helping out whenever possible. It would be nice if you two would step up to the plate and give them some time, as well," Bree said.

"I'll call Mary tomorrow," Savannah said. Clay said nothing and both sisters knew he wouldn't be offering any of his time or services there.

Clay refusing to have any part of the cultural center had been a continuous source of friction between him and his mother, and Savannah wondered if perhaps that had been what they'd fought about before her disappearance.

In any case it didn't matter. Savannah made a mental note to herself to call and see if there was anything she could do to help with the work that was dearest to her mother's heart.

It was agreed that they would meet the following night at Breanna and Adam's house to pick up posters for distribution.

Exhaustion weighed heavily on Savannah as she drove home from the hospital.

It had been more than a full day. First she'd wrestled

with the Maxwell case for several hours at the station, trying to glean any clues that might have been missed, clues that might lead to a murderer. Then the emotional trauma of joining Riley in his parents' house...a house of death that still held the vestiges of a son's hopes.

If that hadn't been enough, there had been that kiss followed by her journey to the bridge and then the phone call that her father had come out of his coma.

The day had been a roller coaster of ups and downs, ins and outs that had left her physically and emotionally depleted.

And still they knew nothing about what had happened to their mother.

Sleep came quickly to her that night, but it was a sleep filled with dreams. She dreamed of the river, and in her dream she clung to the bridge support over water that foamed and splashed with a restless energy.

Jimmy was there beneath the surface, his brown eyes pleading, his arms stretched out to her. She knew if she went to him, the worries of the world would no longer be carried in her heart. She was just about to let go, to join him in his watery grave when Riley appeared on the ground beneath her.

"Come to me, Savannah," he said, his piercing blue eyes holding the promise of new passion, of possibility. "Forget him."

"Silver Star, you are my woman forever and always." Jimmy's gaze held the bittersweet memories of childhood friendship, adolescent sexual awakening and adult love and commitment. "Forever and always."

She awoke with the perspiration of conflict dampening her body. She turned on her bedside lamp and swung her legs over the edge of the bed, trying desperately to shove away the remnants of the dream.

One thing was certain. Riley Frazier and that kiss they had shared was messing with her mind, making her think about things she shouldn't, dream about choices that shouldn't exist.

She didn't intend to see Riley Frazier again.

"That looks like a love-struck man if ever I've seen one." Lillian's voice pulled Riley back to the here and now.

He felt the heat of a blush work up his neck and wondered how long she'd been standing in his office doorway watching him stare out the window. "I just have a lot on my mind."

"A woman. Tell me the truth, you have a woman on your mind." She smiled knowingly. "I've seen men with that expression on their faces many times before, and it's always a woman that's in his head."

"Her name is Savannah Tallfeather," he said. And three days ago I kissed her, and that kiss was the best thing that's happened to me in two years. "She's a homicide detective over in Cherokee Corners."

One of Lillian's brows raised. "A homicide cop? Is she working on your father's case?"

"Yes and no." Briefly Riley explained to her the criminal connection between him and Savannah. "I went to her because I thought maybe the person responsible for her parents' crime was also responsible for mine."

"And what have you found out?"

Riley frowned. "Nothing conclusive. The situations are the same and her mother is missing like mine, but nothing specific to tie the two scenes together."

"And so your interest in Savannah Tallfeather is strictly

professional, so to speak?" There was a distinct twinkle in Lillian's eyes.

"It might be a little more than that," Riley admitted after a moment of hesitation.

"Good," Lillian exclaimed decisively. "It's about time you got a woman in your life, time you moved away from your pain and loss and looked to the future."

"I do look to the future," Riley protested. He gestured out the window. "That's what Riley Estates is all about."

"That's your work future, that has nothing to do with your personal happiness. A man isn't all that he can be when he's alone, Riley. A man needs a woman, children to fulfill his complete potential."

Riley laughed. "For heaven's sake, Lillian, I barely know the woman."

Lillian studied him for a long moment. "Maybe so, but I haven't seen that particular spark in your eye since I've known you. Just saying her name makes your eyes light up, and if you have any sense at all, you'll pursue her with the same single-mindedness you've spent in your work."

Minutes later, with Lillian gone from the doorway, Riley once again focused his gaze out the window. In the distance he could see the dust rising in the air from the bulldozer clearing land for a new home site, but his thoughts were on Savannah.

In the three days since they had parted at his parents' home, he'd called her several times and left messages on her machine at work. She had not returned any of his calls.

The kiss had been a mistake. It had been entirely inappropriate and he half wished he could take it back. But the other half of him reveled in the memory of the sweet heat of her lips, her slender curves that had momentarily melded into him, the race of her heartbeat against his own.

He'd had no intention of kissing her when he'd pulled her into his arms, had known only a gut-wrenching fear for her when she'd confessed about her sojourns to the bridge.

She'd scared him half to death with her confession and he'd done the only thing he knew to do—pull her against him and hold her tight. If she hadn't looked up at him with her doe-soft eyes, he might have released her without the kiss. But the minute she'd looked at him, he'd been lost. And damn it, it had been too much, too soon.

He'd obviously scared her. He wanted to talk to her, to tell her that he was sorry if he'd overstepped the boundaries between them. But it was difficult to apologize when he couldn't get hold of her.

He hated to think that she was avoiding his phone calls, preferred to think that she'd simply been too busy to contact him. He'd heard from Scott that her father had come out of his coma but had been unable to remember anything about the night he'd been attacked.

Savannah Tallfeather certainly had many more important things on her mind than him and the kiss they had shared.

He stood and stretched, then looked at his wristwatch. It was almost five. Within ten minutes the crew would be knocking off for the day and he felt like a drive.

"I'm out of here," he said to Lillian as he left his office. "I'll have my cell phone with me if anything should come up in the next ten or fifteen minutes."

"I'm sure we'll be fine, boss," she assured him. "Enjoy your evening."

"You do the same, Lillian."

He thought he was going home, but was somehow unsurprised to find himself on the highway that would take him to Cherokee Corners.

He just wanted to talk to her, wanted to apologize, if an apology was necessary. He didn't want to do anything that would make her uncomfortable. He just wanted her to know that he was available to be a support to her in whatever way she might need him to be. No expectations. No strings attached.

The hour-long drive was nice. Riley felt himself unwinding from the day, putting the cares of the business behind him as he anticipated seeing Savannah again.

An officer had answered her work phone the day before and told him that Officer Tallfeather wasn't available at the moment but was working until five that evening.

It would be after six by the time he reached Cherokee Corners, and he was hoping he would find her at her apartment. If he didn't find her there, then he would drop in at the Redbud Bed and Breakfast and see if her cousin knew where she might be found.

He thought of what Lillian had said…about a woman and children making a man realize his full potential. He'd thought about children once upon a time, but the problem had been no matter how hard he tried, he couldn't imagine Patsy as a mother. The first time a baby spit up on her, or grabbed one of her perfectly coiled curls, she would have had a fit.

No, Patsy hadn't been mother material, but that didn't mean he wasn't father material. Someday, with the right woman, he'd love to have children, fill that big house of his with laughter and love. That had been his parents' dream for him, a dream he had forgotten about until now.

It was just after six when he pulled down Main Street of Cherokee Corners. On a whim he parked his truck in front of the Pet Palace. He thought of the conversation he and Savannah had shared and the desire she'd once had to own a cat.

I'll just take a look at what they have, he told himself as he entered the store. It would be highly presumptuous of him to actually get her a cat.

A cacophony of sound greeted him. Birds screeched, dogs barked and little furry critters scurried around in their cages as if seeking to capture his attention and find themselves a home.

He bypassed the hamsters, the fish and the squawking birds. He paused briefly in front of the dog cages, momentarily captivated by a white and black puppy of indeterminable parentage who shoved his food dish toward the front of the cage, then eyed Riley expectantly.

"We've nicknamed him Munch," a female voice said from behind Riley. He turned to see an older woman with a pleasant smile. "All he wants to do is eat."

Riley smiled. "He's cute, but I was actually interested in a cat."

"Ah, we have two lovely Persians that just came in."

Riley frowned. He had a feeling Savannah Tallfeather wasn't a Persian cat kind of woman. "I was thinking more like a tabby." Patsy was a Persian cat kind of woman, Savannah was definitely a tabby.

The saleslady led him to a large cage where half a dozen kittens were playing. As he moved closer they meowed loudly, as if vying for his attention, their little paws reaching out between the cage bars.

Again Riley wondered if this was a good thing to do or if it might just be a mistake, like the kiss might have been. Then he spied the kitten that sat on a perch at the back of the cage. So tiny—he knew it would fit in the palm of his hand—the yellow-striped tabby watched him silently.

"The one in the back...is it sick or something?" He pointed to the little one.

"No, she's just one of the most laid-back kittens I've ever seen."

Exactly what Savannah needed, he thought. If he bought her a cat, maybe it would keep her off that bridge. Maybe she needed something alive and solely dependent on her.

And if it was a mistake and she didn't want the kitty, then he'd keep her. Twenty minutes later he left the pet store with not only the kitten but everything a cat might need to live a comfortable life—food, toys and a super scooper litter box.

He drove from the pet store to Savannah's apartment complex, pleased to see her car parked in the space in front of her apartment.

With the kitten in the crook of his arm, he walked up to her door, surprised to find himself more nervous than he could remember being in a very long time.

She opened the door, and any nervousness he'd momentarily suffered instantly left him. She looked beautiful, clad in a rose-colored robe and with her hair tousled as if she'd just awakened from a nap.

"Riley!" It was obvious by the expression on her face that he was the last person she had expected to see.

"Can we come in?" he asked.

"We?" Her gaze shot beyond his shoulder, as if anticipating another person standing nearby.

"We." He held out the kitten.

"Oh, Riley, what have you done?" She opened the door to let him in, and he walked ahead of her to the living room and sat down on the sofa.

"Look, if you aren't interested in taking her in, it's not a problem," he said hurriedly. "I just remembered you mentioning the other day that you'd always wanted a cat."

She sat down next to him, so close he could smell the familiar scent of her, that feminine flowery fragrance that made his pulse beat just a little bit faster.

She leaned over and took the kitten from him, and as she did, her robe gaped open slightly, exposing delicate collarbones and something silky and pink beneath the robe. "Where'd you find her?" she asked.

"The Pet Palace."

The kitten curled up in her lap and as she stroked the soft reddish-blond fur, a noisy purr filled the silence. She looked tired, Riley thought as she gazed down at the cat. She wore no makeup, and purple shadows dusted the skin just beneath her eyes.

He felt like an adolescent, wondering if he should apologize for the kiss, yet dreading the idea of bringing up the subject.

"I bought everything you'd need if you decide to keep her," he said, unable to stand the silence any longer. "All she needs is a name."

Savannah looked up at him, her gaze radiating bewilderment. "Why did you do this, Riley? What do you want from me?"

What did he want from her? He wasn't sure. He wanted to spend time with her. He wanted to kiss her again, but he couldn't very well tell her that. His gaze fell on one of the pictures of her and her husband.

"What do I want from you?" He pointed to the photograph. "I want to see you smile like that…like you have the world by the tail, like you have nothing but happiness ahead of you."

She stared at the picture for a long moment, and when she looked back at him her eyes were dark, almost haunted. "I don't think that's ever going to happen again," she said softly. "Riley, I..."

He heard the protest begin in her words, and he quickly jumped in to interrupt her. "To be honest, Savannah, the last couple of years have been difficult for me. I've kept myself too isolated from people, and I like you. I could use a friend, and I think you could use one, too. No strings attached, no expectations...just friendship."

He hoped as she studied his face she couldn't see how desperately he'd like to kiss her right now, right at this very moment. "Okay," she said, her voice still soft. "I'd like to be your friend—no strings attached, no expectations."

"And my gift?" He gestured to the kitten still curled up in her lap.

She smiled. "Is accepted with many thanks."

"Good." Riley stood. "I'll just go get the food and toys and things from my car." Friendship, it was a start, and he had a feeling it was all she was willing to give for now.

And he hadn't been lying. He wanted to see that smile she'd had in the photograph with her husband. But he wanted to see that same kind of joyous, loving smile directed at him.

Yes, a friendship was a start, but he knew he would never be satisfied with just that from her.

CHAPTER EIGHT

She'd made a conscious decision not to return his phone calls over the past three days. She told herself they really had nothing to say to each other. Clay was still processing the evidence he'd gathered at the Frazier house and none of Riley's messages indicated any urgency.

Even though she hadn't returned any of his calls, she had to confess to herself that seeing him standing at her door had sent a wave of pleasure through her.

As he went out to get the things he'd purchased for the kitten, she belted her robe more tightly around her, then carried the cat into the kitchen and set her on the floor so she could make a pot of coffee.

She couldn't believe he'd bought her a kitten, and such a sweet little baby at that. She couldn't believe he'd paid that much attention to the conversation they'd had on the back deck at his parents' home. For the past year she hadn't felt as if anyone listened when she spoke.

Friends. He'd said he'd like to be friends, no strings attached. There was no fooling herself about the fact that she could use a friend. She hadn't realized until after Jimmy's death that most of their friends had been his, and they had vanished soon after Jimmy.

For Savannah, her family had always been enough, but now her family was fragmented and there were moments when her feelings of isolation threatened to consume her.

But a friendship with Riley? Was that possible? They'd already overstepped the boundaries of friendship with the kiss they had shared, a kiss she'd had difficulty forgetting.

Once the coffeepot was steaming and spewing hot brew into the glass container, she picked up the kitten. At the same time Riley came back inside, his arms laden with supplies.

"My goodness, it looks like you bought out the place," she exclaimed.

"I bought the things I thought a kitten would need to live a long, healthy life."

"Obviously a long, healthy, pampered life," she said with a small smile as he unloaded the items on the floor near the kitchen table. "Let me repay you what you spent, Riley."

He looked shocked at the very notion. "A gift isn't a gift if the recipient pays for it. And she and everything that comes with her is a gift."

"Then, thank you." She looked down at the kitten, her heart filled as it hadn't been in a very long time.

"Now all you need to do is name her."

"Happy," she said without conscious thought, for that was what she felt at the moment.

"Sounds good to me," he agreed. "And that coffee smells great."

Minutes later, with Happy contentedly eating gourmet cat food, Savannah and Riley sat down at her kitchen table, each with a cup of coffee.

"Now, how are you? You look tired," he said.

"I am," she admitted. "The last couple of days have been frantic. I've been dividing my time between the hospital, work and distributing posters of my mom all around town. I came home from work tonight ready to collapse. I promised myself a night of doing nothing, so I took a long, hot bath and climbed into my nightgown and robe." Self-consciously she tugged on her belt once again.

"Then I'm interfering with your quiet time. I should go." He started to rise from his chair.

"No, it's fine," she said hurriedly. "Besides, now you have to stay and help me finish that pot of coffee."

He sank back down. "I heard your father came out of his coma."

"Yes, and he's recovering nicely. Unfortunately, he doesn't remember anything about the night he got hurt, and he needs some rehabilitation for some resulting weakness on the right side of his body."

"Has anyone told him yet about your mother being missing?"

"We had to tell him yesterday." Her heart ached as she remembered the tears her father had shed at the news. In all her thirty years she'd never seen her father weep until yesterday.

His tears had quickly transformed to bellows of rage when they told him the authorities thought Rita was responsible for his injuries. He'd called them stupid fools, shouted that it was impossible that his Rita had been responsible. It had been a heartrending scene.

"He believes, like all of us, that there's no way Mom could have done this to him then run away."

Riley shifted positions in his chair and the displacement of air around him sent a whisper of his scent wafting to her. He wore the smell of the outdoors, the fragrance of a sunshine-drenched shirt and an underlying hint of woodsy cologne.

It was a scent that provoked memories of what it had felt like to be held tight against his broad chest, feel the beat of his heart against her own.

"My uncle Sammy arrived in town yesterday," she said, trying to keep her mind focused on her life and not the man seated next to her. "He's my father's younger brother. He's going to be staying at the ranch now that the police have released it."

"Is that a good thing?" Riley asked.

"It will be good to have somebody there. None of us wanted to leave the place empty until Dad can go home. I probably would have been the one to stay out there, and to tell the truth, I wasn't sure I was ready for that."

He nodded and she had the satisfaction of knowing he knew exactly what she was talking about. "Are you and your uncle close?"

She smiled at thoughts of her uncle Sammy. "Throughout our childhood Uncle Sammy was like this bigger-than-life hero who would swoop into our lives and turn everything topsy-turvy for a couple of days, and then disappear again. He was handsome and fun and always brought presents." She paused to take a sip of her coffee, then continued. "Now that I'm older I see him a little differently."

"How so?"

She startled as Happy jumped up in her lap. She

scratched the kitten's head and frowned thoughtfully. "Uncle Sammy is still handsome as the devil and can be a lot of fun. But I've come to realize he's also an irresponsible dreamer who has always chosen the easy way out of everything. He drifts from place to place looking for the next get-rich-quick scheme. He's had some brushes with the law, he's never worked a regular job and never has a permanent address."

"So, he's kind of the black sheep of the family," Riley observed.

"More gray than black," she replied. "What about you? Any black sheep in your family?"

"No family," he replied. "My parents were only children, and I was an only child. I guess that's why I was so close to them…because it was always just the three of us."

She doubted he even heard the depth of pain in his words, but she heard it and found it impossible not to be moved. She wanted to reach out and touch him, to stroke the back of his hand or place her fingers on the warm skin of his forearm, but she was afraid…afraid that if she touched him once, she'd want to touch him again…and again.

"Beside everything else that's going on, I'm in the middle of a murder investigation that's driving me insane," she said to change the subject.

"Want to talk about it?"

She shrugged. "Unfortunately, there isn't much to talk about. Greg Maxwell was found naked and stabbed in front of the public library on Main Street and we have no idea who's responsible."

"Oh yeah, I remember reading something about that when it happened." He stood and walked over to the coffeepot and refilled his cup, then hers. As he took the pot back to where it belonged, she couldn't help but notice how his jeans seemed to fit as if denim had been invented just for him.

She quickly shifted her attention back to the kitten in her lap, who was purring like the engine of a motorboat. He rejoined her at the table, his gaze curious. "So, no forensic clues in the case?"

"No, the scene was fairly well contaminated by the time Clay got there to collect evidence."

"What about motive? Who stood to gain something if Greg Maxwell was dead?"

Savannah raised an eyebrow. "You sound like a cop."

He grinned, the gesture lighting his eyes to an azure blue that nearly stole her breath away. "I watch a lot of television. So, any motive?"

"A fairly substantial life insurance policy for his wife."

"Ah, so there's your answer," he said. "Don't they say most homicides are committed by spouses?"

"That's the mentality that has our mothers as prime suspects," she said wryly.

"Touché." He frowned thoughtfully. "But statistically isn't it more likely than not in a homicide that the first suspect is always the spouse? And the other thing I've always heard is that cops follow the money, and that often leads to the guilty."

"Sure, and in the Maxwell case I haven't written off Virginia Maxwell as a suspect." It felt good to talk about the case with somebody who had a fresh eye, somebody she trusted completely. "There's something about her that doesn't quite ring true to me."

"What do you mean?"

Savannah stared down into her coffee cup, trying to discern just what it was about Virginia that didn't sit right with her. She looked back up at Riley, as always finding his direct blue gaze almost hypnotic.

"I don't know, maybe it's because I'm a widow, too. Her grief just doesn't feel deep enough, true enough. She says all the right things, but I just don't believe her."

"Does she have an alibi for the night of her husband's murder?" Riley asked.

"According to her, Greg had spent the evening at the library and she'd had dinner with friends. After dinner she went home and fell asleep while waiting for Greg to return home. As an alibi, it's impossible to corroborate."

"But it's also difficult to think about a woman being able to strip a man naked and stab him to death," Riley said. "Especially if that man is her husband."

"That's what Glen thinks, too," she admitted. "But, women do kill...and sometimes they kill viciously. Whomever killed Greg knew him personally, of that I'm convinced."

"What makes you so sure?"

"He was stabbed in a frenzy and that indicates rage...a personal rage. Also, the fact that he was left naked suggests the perpetrator wanted him humiliated. I'm betting on Virginia having something to do with it and I'm checking into her background. And I've bored you long enough with all this talk about my work."

He smiled. "I don't find it boring at all. I find it fascinating, but you're right, that's enough shop talk. And I've taken up enough of your evening."

This time when he rose from the table she didn't attempt to stop him. All the talk about the Maxwell case had exhausted her and had reminded her of all the unanswered questions in the cases that were dearest to both her heart and Riley's.

She stood also, gently placing Happy on the floor, where the kitten stretched, curled up in a ball and went back to sleep. She walked with Riley to the door. "I can't thank you enough for Happy," she said.

"Yes, you can," he said, and turned to face her as they reached the front door. "The way you can thank me is by making me a promise."

"A promise?" She looked at him curiously.

He reached out a hand as if to touch her, but to her relief quickly dropped it back to his side. "You can promise me you'll stay off that bridge."

A hundred different emotions attacked her from all sides at his request. Anger that he would even presume to ask for such a promise, a tiny thrill that he would care, and the frustration that he obviously didn't understand, couldn't understand the constant grief that drove her.

"I can't do that, Riley, and you really have no right to ask that of me." She focused her gaze away from him, unable to look at him without fearing she might capitulate and make the promise to him. And she wasn't ready for that.

"You're right," he said with a deep sigh. "I apologize. I was just hoping as a friend who cares about you, I'd have the right to ask you that. Anyway…good night, Savannah." He leaned forward and gently pressed his lips to her forehead. "Sweet dreams."

For a long time after he'd left, Savannah felt the sweet burn of his lips on her forehead and a curious ache she couldn't identify in her heart.

She'd just settled down in bed with Happy curled contentedly at her feet when her cell phone rang. She struggled to sit up and reach for the offending instrument on her nightstand.

"Officer Tallfeather," she said.

"Savannah…it's Glen. We've got another one."

"Another one?"

"Sam McClane was found a little while ago behind the post office. He's naked and has been stabbed."

"I'm on my way."

Although she was exhausted, adrenaline shoved her out of bed and she was dressed and out the door within minutes. Although she dreaded what lay ahead, she was relieved for any distraction that would take her mind off Riley.

By the time she arrived at the scene, the county medical examiner was already there and the immediate area had been cordoned off. Clay was there, as well, gathering evidence that would hopefully give them some clues.

"Hey, Walter, what have you got for me?"

The elderly M.E. drew off his plastic gloves and shook his head. "I'd put time of death within the last two hours. Cause of death is multiple stab wounds to the chest. At first investigation it looks just like the Maxwell scene."

At that moment Glen Cleberg joined them, his brow deeply wrinkled with worry. "Who found him?" Savannah asked.

Glen jerked a thumb in the direction of the back of the post office building where a young man stood talking to one of the officers. "Name is Burt Sheffle. He works part-time cleaning some of the offices down here. He had just finished up inside the post office and was taking trash out to the Dumpster."

"He look likely?" she asked.

"Not hardly. The kid's been puking his guts up since he found the body."

Savannah sighed. "I guess this shoots to hell my gut instinct that Virginia Maxwell killed Greg."

"Unless this is a copycat deal," Walter said.

"Let's hope it is," Glen replied. "Let's hope to hell it's a copycat."

Savannah knew what he was thinking. If it was a copycat, then that meant they had two murderers to find. If it wasn't a copycat, then it could be the beginning of something much more sinister. It could mean they had a brutal serial killer in the small town of Cherokee Corners.

The officers worked the scene until the first tentative colors of dawn spread across the sky. Only then did they finally take a break for coffee.

Savannah took her foam cup and carried it over to where her brother sat on the curb. She sank down next to him and took a sip of the hot, strong coffee.

"Hell of a business we're in," he said. "I spent all day processing our parents' house, and tonight I'm processing a new crime scene. I haven't been this busy since I started on the job."

"Did you find anything interesting at Mom and Dad's?" she asked.

"Fibers…hairs…the usual bag of tricks. I still need to separate, examine and categorize everything. I didn't find anything that looked like a sure-fire address to the perp."

She smiled ruefully. "It never is that easy."

He sighed. "No, it isn't."

"You think we have a serial working?"

"I hope not…but this scene and Maxwell's are exactly the same. Fortunately there is less contamination at this one, so maybe something will turn up to help us find whoever did this."

"Let's hope so." She finished her coffee, then got back

to work. The last of the sunrise streaked the sky when she finally headed home.

A serial killer. Was it really possible? Despite the press that made serial killers seem commonplace, they weren't all that common. And it seemed unbelievable that one would be in residence in the tiny, safe town where she had lived all her life.

Her thoughts turned to Riley and the crimes that had brought the two of them together. As tired as she was, her mind whirled with what she knew of both crimes. Despite what Glen thought to the contrary, she believed they were connected.

"If it looks like a duck and quacks like a duck...it's a duck," she murmured to herself as she pulled into the parking lot of her apartment housing.

She felt it in her gut, in every fiber of her being. The person who killed Riley's father was also responsible for attempting to kill hers. Whatever had happened to his mother had also happened to hers.

Had it happened to others? Before this moment she hadn't considered the possibility that perhaps she and Riley weren't the only ones whose lives had been ripped apart by this person or persons.

She was so tired it was difficult to even contemplate how they would go about checking into such a thing. Unfortunately, the Cherokee Corners Police Station didn't have the budget to have computers hooked into big mainframes and systems to exchange information.

Every year the police department requested a tax increase to help update and every year the voters turned them down. The area was depressed and people were eking out a living as best as they could. The last thing they wanted was more tax dollars leaving their pockets.

Most of the officers who used computers worked on laptops they had purchased themselves.

If she was going to check to see if there were other crimes like hers and Riley's, then she would need some help. It would require hours of time checking newspapers around the area, and with a brand-new murder investigation on her hands, she wouldn't have hours of extra time.

Riley would help. She'd call him later...after she got a couple hours of sleep. As she got out of her car, she looked up, the beauty of the sky overhead filling her with an ache of anguish.

Where are you, Mom? her heart cried. Are you someplace where you can see the sunrise? Are you cold? Hungry? She couldn't stand the thought of her mother suffering. Wherever you are, hang on, Mom. We'll find you. I swear, we'll do everything in our power to find you.

She headed inside for some much-needed sleep.

Rita Birdsong James felt as if she were swimming up from the depths of a cotton-filled lake. Consciousness came and went, like streaks of lightning in a blackened sky. She fought for the surface of the lake. An urgency filled her brain, but somehow didn't transmit to the rest of her body.

Something was wrong...but what? She willed her eyes to open despite the fact that she felt the darkness pressing in around her, attempting to take her back to the bottom of the lake.

Her eyes opened, but it took a moment to adjust to her fuzzy vision. She was in bed, the color and pattern of the spread achingly familiar. Her bed. The illumination in the room came from the Tiffany-style lamp that was also familiar. Her lamp.

Her hand moved to the side of the bed next to her. Empty. But that wasn't unusual. Thomas always rose earlier than her. Any minute now he'd come in to wake her, carrying her first cup of coffee for the morning.

She smiled and her eyes drifted closed, the sense of urgency dissipating. All was well. She was in her own bedroom, in her own home. She was just tired…so very tired. She allowed the darkness to reclaim her.

CHAPTER NINE

Riley hadn't expected to hear from Savannah again, not after he'd done such an incredibly stupid thing the night before. What had he been thinking by trying to pressure her into making him such a promise?

He stared out his trailer window where his crews were out in full force, clearing lots and preparing for new building sites.

What had he been thinking? He'd been thinking of her clinging to a bridge, staring into the waters below and considering joining her dead husband in some insane pact of undying love.

He'd been thinking of a world where Savannah Tallfeather no longer existed, where her heart would no longer beat, and it had frightened him.

It also frightened him just a little bit how much he wanted to be a part of her life, how jealous he was of a man named Jimmy who had died a watery death far before his time.

Amazing, really, how in the brief period he'd known her he felt so connected to her. At first he'd thought it was because they'd both shared the same experiences, the same grief because of the crimes that had shaken up their worlds.

He'd believed that this connection had created a sort of false intimacy between them. But with each moment that he spent with her, he realized there was absolutely nothing false about it.

Something about her resonated inside him, touched him as no woman ever had before. He wanted to see her happy. He wanted to see the darkness in her eyes dissipate. He wanted to be around when she rediscovered that life had possibilities.

It was just before five when she called, and he sat up straighter in his chair at the sound of her sweet, familiar voice.

"I heard you had a rough night," he said.

"How did you hear? It didn't make the morning papers."

"Scott."

"Ah, the mouth of Oklahoma," she said dryly.

"Cut him some slack," Riley said with a chuckle. "He means well."

"I only have a minute to talk. I've got to get back to the station, but I was wondering if you'd like to come to a birthday party tomorrow? My niece, Maggie, is turning six and despite all that's going on, Breanna is throwing her a little party."

He was both surprised and thrilled by her invitation. "Sure, I'd love to join you. Just let me know where and when." He quickly jotted down the address and the time she gave him.

"I have to warn you," she said. "I intend to ply you with cake and ice cream, then ask a favor of you."

"You don't have to ply me with anything. If you need a favor, just ask me."

"I'll talk to you about it tomorrow. I really don't have time now. I'm running in a hundred different directions with this new murder case. I'll see you tomorrow, Riley." Before he could say anything else the line went dead.

It was ridiculous how pleased he was that she had invited him to a birthday party, especially given the fact that she'd indicated part of the reason for inviting him was to ask a favor.

But she could have asked him a favor over the phone, or if she wanted to ask in person she could have met him in a restaurant. Instead she had invited him to a family gathering and that somehow felt like a big step forward in their relationship, such as it was.

He was surprised by how nervous he was the next day when he pulled up in front of an attractive two-story Victorian house with a big shady tree in the front yard. He checked the address he'd written down against the numbers on the house. They matched.

Savannah's car wasn't there yet and he wasn't sure if he should go ahead and knock on the front door or not. There were several other cars in the driveway, but he decided to sit and wait for Savannah's arrival.

A gaily-wrapped package sat on the passenger seat. He'd stopped in a toy store earlier in the day and had instantly been overwhelmed by the choices presented to him. Gadgets and gizmos, games and craft kits, it seemed the choices were endless.

He'd decided a doll would be appropriate for a six-year-old girl. But even then the selection was huge. There were dolls that sang and dolls that danced. There were dolls that swam and roller-skated and discoed and said prayers. He'd finally settled on a sweet-faced baby doll that did nothing.

From the time she'd called him the day before until now, he'd wondered what kind of favor she could possibly want from him. Maybe she and Clay wanted to go through his parents' house again? If that were the case, of course he'd allow them access.

He grabbed his gift and got out of the car as Savannah pulled in behind him and parked. His heart gave a little jump as she got out of the car, looking as cool and fresh as a stick of spearmint in a pastel-green sundress.

She carried a smaller gift in her hand and immediately pointed to the one he carried. "You didn't have to do that," she exclaimed.

"Of course I did," he replied. "I can't show up at a little girl's birthday party without a present. It would be positively un-American."

She smiled and again his heart did a little flip-flop in his chest. It wasn't the full, joyous smile he longed to see from her, but it was enough for the moment.

"How's Happy adjusting to life with a cop?" he asked as they headed toward the front door.

"Fine. She's already shredded two pairs of my panty hose and turned over a plant, so I've placed her under house arrest. She's also won my heart completely."

"I claim no responsibility for the damage wrought by my gift to you," he said.

Again she smiled. "I don't expect you to." Her smile faded as they reached the door. "Riley, this might be a little difficult…the party. It's the first gathering we've ever had where Mom and Dad aren't there."

"Hopefully it will be the last without them."

"I hope so," she said fervently. "And thanks for coming today." She hesitated a moment. "I didn't really want to come alone."

"I'm honored to be here."

She nodded, then knocked on the door. A pretty little girl with long brown hair and beautiful gray eyes opened the door. With a squeal of delight, she launched herself into Savannah's arms. "Aunt Savannah, I'm so glad you came to my party."

"I wouldn't have missed it for the world," Savannah exclaimed as she hugged the little girl. "And I brought a friend with me to your party. His name is Riley."

"Hi, Maggie," Riley said.

"Hi." She gazed at him with the open curiosity of a child. "Are you my Aunt Savannah's boyfriend?"

Savannah coughed in surprise, and Riley rocked back on his heels. "Well, let's see, I'm her friend and I'm a boy, so I guess I could be considered a boyfriend."

"That's nice," Maggie said, and at the same time Breanna appeared behind her daughter.

"Hi." She smiled warmly at her sister, then turned her smile on Riley. "You must be Riley. My sister has told me all about you. Please…come in."

As Riley followed the women inside, he wondered what Savannah had told her sister about him. Had she merely mentioned that he was a fellow victim of a crime or had she told him that that she liked him…that they had shared a soul-searing kiss? Did sisters exchange information like that?

The backyard was filled with squealing children and adults huddled in groups as if in defense of their offspring. Brightly colored balloon bouquets were tied to chairs and the picnic table held a huge cake decorated with white and pink icing and sugar candies in a variety of shapes.

Savannah led him to a group of people and introduced him to Adam, her brother-in-law, the infamous Uncle Sammy, and several other men who were apparently friends of the family.

It was an hour into the party before Riley began to successfully put faces to names.

As the children played games, the adults visited with one another. The talk was fairly benign...the weather, a new movie playing at the one theater in town, local politics. Riley spent much of his time watching Savannah.

He liked watching her interact with her sister. It was obvious the two were close and it was also obvious Savannah adored her niece.

Sammy James proved to be entertaining, regaling Riley with tales of travel and women and fortunes made and lost. He seemed bigger than life, devoted to his brother and sister-in-law and just a bit too slick for Riley.

Clay showed up late and distracted. He stayed only long enough to give Maggie his present, then left, murmuring that he was in the middle of processing the evidence from the latest murder scene.

Riley visited a little with Jacob Kincaid, the local banker in town, then spent some time talking to an older policeman named Charlie Smitherspoon. Charlie seemed genuinely upset by what had happened to the James family, but had few kind words to say about Thomas James.

"I ran against him for chief of police years ago, but he had it easy. He got all the Irish Catholics in town to vote for him, and his wife got all the Injuns to vote for him, too. I didn't have a chance."

Riley's blood heated but before he could comment to

the man, Savannah touched his arm and motioned him to join her away from the crowd. She held two paper plates with a generous slice of cake on each.

"Have you checked out that man's alibi for the night your father was hurt?" he asked as he took one of the plates for her.

"Why? Because he's an old, prejudiced moron? This town and the police department are full of men just like him. They think we Native Americans should go back to the reservation and sell beads and drink whiskey."

He looked at her in amazement. "How do you work with people who think like that?"

"I mostly ignore them." She gestured toward a pair of lawn chairs and they sat. "It's really not so bad. It's mostly the old-timers who are the most prejudiced. The younger guys don't have the same problems."

"Well, old Charlie there definitely seems to have a problem with your father."

"Charlie has never hidden the fact that he and my father didn't get along. Besides, if Charlie is responsible for what happened to my parents, then we have to consider that he's responsible for what happened to yours." She paused a moment and took a bite of her cake, leaving behind a tiny smudge of white frosting right next to her luscious upper lip.

Riley wanted to lean forward and clean it off with his mouth, swirl his tongue across her upper lip. He could almost taste the sugary sweetness coupled with the fiery heat of her mouth.

He'd been on a slow simmer all day where she was concerned. Watching her in that mint-colored sundress that exposed the length of her long, shapely legs and emphasized her slender waist and rounded breasts had stirred an undeniable desire in him.

He was like an adolescent, mortified more than once in the afternoon to find his body reacting to his wayward thoughts.

He focused his attention toward the children, who were playing a game of pin the tail on the donkey under the supervision of Breanna and Adam. "Thanks for inviting me here, Savannah," he said. "Birthday parties are always fun."

"When is your birthday, Riley?"

"September twenty-second." She frowned thoughtfully. "What…what's wrong?"

"I was just thinking. You mentioned that you have no family since your parents…since that night. So, who celebrates your birthday with you?"

That she would even think of such a thing touched him deeply. "You know, you get to be a certain age and it's just another day. Your niece is a cutie," he said to change the subject.

She looked at him for a long moment, then nodded. "Yes, she is. She gave us quite a scare a couple of months ago."

He looked back at her. "How so?"

"You know Breanna works vice, and usually on the weekends she works a prostitution detail. One of the men she had arrested for solicitation kidnapped Maggie. Thankfully we got her back quickly, safe and sound, and the perp is facing lots of time in prison."

"Your family has definitely been through the wringer."

She nodded, her eyes darkening. "And I hope both of my parents are at the next family gathering. Just like I hope we find your mother alive and well."

"Have you decided that you definitely think the same person is responsible for what happened to my family and what happened to yours? Did Clay find something to tie the two together?" He tried to focus on the conversation as she took another bite of her cake and found the errant smudge with the tip of her tongue.

"No, he hasn't finished with his tests to conclude that the two scenes are connected by forensic evidence. But, working this new murder scene made a thought come into my head. We're all hoping that Greg Maxwell and Sam McClane were killed by the same person, a person with a specific motive in mind, because if these were two random killings, it's a whole different ball game."

"You mean a serial killer." He took a bite of his cake to distract him from his intense desire to kiss her.

She nodded. "And thinking about a serial killer made me think about what happened to us." She set her cake down on her lap and gazed at him, her pretty brown eyes somber. "We know what happened at my parents' house and we know what happened at your parents' house two years ago. What we don't know is if these are the only two crimes like this."

All other thoughts fled from his brain as he realized the implication of her words. More? Was it possible there were more families where the fathers had been hurt or killed and the mothers had vanished?

He set his paper plate down, his appetite gone. "That's a horrible thought," he said as he pulled his chair closer to hers.

"I know." She rubbed the center of her forehead, her shoulders slumping slightly. "The problem is we don't have a computer geared to make the search easy, and it's going to require a major time commitment to find out, one that I can't make right now with this new murder on my plate."

"And that's where I come in," he said.

She frowned. "I hate to even ask, but if you have a computer and could do a little research…maybe make some phone calls."

"Why do you hate to ask?" He reached out and took her hand, finding it impossible not to touch her in some way. "We're in this together, Savannah, and I'll do whatever I can to help you find the people responsible."

For a moment he thought she was going to pull her hand away, but instead she twined her fingers with his and squeezed, and in that instant Riley knew that he was falling in love with Savannah Tallfeather.

"Tahlequah, Muskogee, Locust Grove…"

Savannah fought a rambunctious Happy as she tried to scribble down the names of cities and towns Riley reeled off.

"Wait a minute…what was that last one?" she asked, and squeezed the phone receiver tighter against her ear.

It was late, after eleven, and Savannah was in bed, papers strewn everywhere around her. The phone calls from Riley had become a ritual for the past three nights, ever since she'd told him what she needed from him at the birthday party.

While she spent her days interviewing Sam McClane's family and friends and revisiting the Greg Maxwell files, he surfed the Internet, looking for crimes that were similar in nature to theirs.

Each night he called her with the names of the cities he'd checked, either through newspaper searches or by phone calls to the various police departments. So far their search had yielded nothing.

"That's it for today," he said.

Savannah set her pen down and relaxed against the pillows, fighting the bone-deep exhaustion that had become so familiar.

"So, how was your day?" he asked.

This was the part of their nightly conversations she'd come to anticipate the most…when they shared the details, often mundane details, of their day. There was something nice about having this just-before-she-fell-asleep contact with another caring human being.

"Frustrating," she replied. "The problem with a small town is there are too many links between victims. We have one barber, so Sam and Greg got their hair cut at the same place. Jacob Kincaid has the only bank in town so the two men banked at the same establishment…and so on…and so on." She snatched her pen from Happy's paws. "How about you? Did you have a good day?"

"Yeah, actually I did. Two families went to contract on two of my homes. Lillian brought blueberry muffins this morning instead of bran, and the last person I'm talking to before I go to sleep is you. Life is good."

A pleasant warmth washed over her at his words. She wondered if, like her, he was in bed. Was he naked beneath the sheets? A vision unfolded in her head, a vision of his tanned body against white sheets. As the warmth of her body intensified, she imagined she could smell him, that provocative fresh male scent.

"Savannah…did you fall asleep on me?" His deep voice vanquished the vision.

"No…I'm here. I'm glad you had a good day."

"What are your plans for tomorrow? It's your day off, isn't it?"

"Yes, but I think I'm going to go ahead and work. If I stall on the murder investigations, I can always do a little investigating on my parents' case."

"Has Glen okayed that?"

"He's given me permission to see the reports being generated, but I'm not to actively pursue the case." She tried to stifle a noisy yawn, but was unsuccessful.

"You're exhausted. Why don't you just take the day off tomorrow and give yourself a break?"

She didn't want downtime. She needed to keep going... pushing...searching. She needed activity. She didn't want time to think because lately when she did take a moment to think, her thoughts were as troubling as the events that had shaken up her life.

"I'll tell you what," he continued before she had a chance to reply. "Be ready at noon tomorrow. I'll pick you up."

She started to protest, then changed her mind. "Okay... but, be ready for what?"

"Be ready for anything. I'll see you at noon." He clicked off, leaving Savannah with a rush of sweet anticipation that she refused to even try to analyze.

She slept indecently late the next morning, waking only when Happy batted her in the head and mewled plaintively for breakfast.

At noon she stood in her living room looking out the front window, watching for Riley's arrival. The thoughts she'd been running away from for the past week came back in a rush to haunt her.

She liked Riley. She liked spending time with him. She

liked the way his skin crinkled around his eyes when he smiled, when he laughed.

She walked over to the coffee table that held an array of photos. Her gaze lingered on one in particular. It was of Jimmy, his cheeks ruddy from the cold, and the fur of a parka framing his face.

She'd taken the picture on a wintry day just before his death. He'd protested that he looked like a polar bear in his jacket, but she insisted on taking the picture anyway. It had been the last photo she'd taken of him.

A wave of grief washed over her and she embraced it like a warm, familiar shawl. Unlike the emotions Riley stirred in her, this emotion was oddly comforting.

For months her mother had tried to talk her into packing the photos away. "How can you move on when you keep the past staring you in the face all the time?" she'd said.

And now her mother was gone as well as Jimmy.

But, it wasn't the same, she quickly reminded herself. Jimmy was never coming back, but her mother was. Savannah had to keep the faith and believe it was true—it was just a matter of time before her mother returned to them. To even entertain thoughts to the contrary was impossible to bear.

She looked at the picture of Jimmy one last time, then turned away and went back to the window to watch for Riley. Just one day, she mentally told her husband. It's just one day with Riley.

It doesn't mean anything at all. It can never mean anything. You were my soul mate, Jimmy, and nothing will ever take away from my love for you.

Riley and I have things to discuss...things about the crime. That's all it is. She closed her eyes and allowed herself another moment to wallow in the familiar grasp of grief.

When she opened her eyes again and looked out the window, she saw Riley's truck pulling into the complex. She watched him park and get out of the truck. As he approached her door, all thoughts of Jimmy seeped out of her mind.

Riley looked so handsome. He was dressed casually in a pair of jeans. His short-sleeved white shirt was open at the collar and tucked into his jeans, emphasizing his slender waist and lean hips.

She smoothed a hand down her denim sundress, a flutter of crazy nervous anxiety rippling through her. What did he have planned for the day? He'd said to be ready for anything.

He spied her through the window and his lips curved into a smile that shot a river of warmth through her. And in that moment she knew she was—she was ready for anything.

CHAPTER TEN

"Are you hungry?" Riley asked as he headed his truck out of town. He tried to keep his eyes on the road, but it was difficult when all he wanted to do was gaze at her.

She looked so pretty in her denim sundress, with her cinnamon-colored shoulders and long legs bare. She smelled as pretty as she looked, and he tightened his grip on the steering wheel, willing himself not to think about how much he wished he could kiss her again.

"Not really. I had a late breakfast. So, where are we going?" she asked curiously.

"I'm being self-indulgent and taking you to my dream."

"Ah, Riley Estates." She settled back in the seat, appearing relaxed.

"Actually, I have several things planned for the day," he said. "And there's only one rule."

"What's that?"

"I think we should make a deal that we aren't going to

talk about murders or missing mothers or crimes of any kind. We are not going to talk about Internet searches or anything else that makes us feel bad or sad. What do you say? Is it a deal?"

"Sure, but that doesn't leave us much to talk about."

He flashed her a look of incredulity. "Savannah, we aren't the sum total of the crimes that happened to us. We'll find lots of things to talk about."

She nodded, a small smile curving her lips. "All right. I'm game if you are."

"Good." Riley's main concern today was giving her a day off, some time where she wasn't thinking about or working a case.

Each night that he'd spoken with her by phone he'd been struck by how tired she sounded and he'd known it wasn't a physical tiredness, but rather a mental exhaustion. He wanted to take her cares away, if only for this day.

"I spoke with Breanna this morning. She told me Maggie has named the doll you gave her Rose."

"Rose is a nice name. You like roses?" he asked.

She smiled again, that little smile that was merely a flirtatious hint of the kind of smile her lips were capable of. "What woman doesn't? However, my absolute favorite flower is black-eyed Susans…I think because my father used to call me black-eyed Savannah which always made my mother mad because she said if he was going to call me a nickname it should be my Cherokee name."

"And what's that?" he asked curiously.

She grinned teasingly. "Ah, I can't tell you. It's a Cherokee taboo to tell anyone your Native American name. If I told you, then I'd have to kill you."

"Really?"

She laughed. "No, I just made that up." Her laughter

died and she eyed him thoughtfully. "But I don't think I'm ready to tell you my Cherokee name yet."

"Okay," he agreed. This was a side of Savannah he hadn't seen before. The coy teasing, almost flirtatious banter intensified his desire for more from her. "But, I won't be happy until I know your Cherokee name," he warned.

The drive to Sycamore Ridge seemed to take no time as they talked about all kinds of things. It was amazing how much they found to talk about, even without the mention of what he'd announced off-limits.

She spoke about some of the Cherokee traditions, enlightening him on a culture that was steeped in beautiful beliefs and ideals. It was obvious she was proud of her heritage, and he found himself wanting to learn more.

Although they had agreed not to discuss their mothers, she told him about Rita's work at the Cherokee Cultural Center and how that had been such a big part of Savannah's childhood.

By the time they reached the entrance to Riley Estates, he could tell she was more relaxed than he'd ever seen her. Her smile came frequently, and the tiny stress lines that had wrinkled her forehead seemed to have magically disappeared.

"Oh, Riley," she said as they drove through the entrance. "This is quite impressive."

Pride swelled inside him. "We still have a lot of landscaping to do around the entrance," he explained. "I want shrubs and flowers everywhere...you know, to add warmth." He parked in the driveway of one of the model homes, then smiled at her. "How about I give you the dollar tour?"

"Sounds nice," she replied.

For the next hour Riley led her around his dream. He showed her where the swimming pool would eventually be, where he intended to place a central park area. They went in and out of the model homes, climbed on equipment to see into the distance, hiked until they both were near exhaustion, then he took her to his office to meet Lillian.

"It's so nice to meet you," Lillian said as she motioned Savannah into one of the chairs in Riley's office. "Riley has spoken so highly of you. Iced tea…that's what we need. You both look parched. I suppose he had you traipsing all over the countryside."

She disappeared from the office and a small giggle escaped Savannah. Riley grinned. "Hard to get a word in edgewise when she gets going."

"She seems quite sweet."

"She is," Riley replied. "I'm not sure what I would have done without her the past six months."

"You would have done just fine," Lillian said as she reentered the office carrying two tall glasses of tea. "But, you wouldn't be as organized and you definitely wouldn't be eating enough fiber."

She handed Savannah a glass of the tea and smiled. "Nobody realizes just how important fiber is to the diet. Let me know if you two need anything else," she said to Riley, then left the office once again and closed the door behind her.

Riley sat in the chair behind his desk and grinned at Savannah, then took a deep drink of the iced tea. "And this…is my world," he said as he set the glass down on his desk.

"And a nice world it is," she replied. "I can't imagine anything nicer than being a builder, knowing that each house you build will be a family's home, the place where they live and dream and love."

She got it. She got his dream. "A lot of people assume builders go into their trade for the money and there's no denying that if you are successful there's plenty of money to be had with building homes."

She took a sip of her tea, then smiled at him. The warmth of her smile eddied through him. "But, that's not the reason why you do it, is it?" She stood and walked over to the window and peered out. "Your vision here isn't about money. It's about people." She turned back to face him.

He'd never wanted to kiss a woman as much as he wanted to kiss her at that moment. He wanted to take her into his arms, feel her warm curves against him as his mouth explored hers. In truth, he wanted to do far more than kiss her.

He cleared his throat, fighting against the desire that simmered in his veins. "You hungry?" he asked.

She nodded. "Starving."

"Me, too." He got up from his desk. "Let's go get something to eat." They finished their tea, said goodbye to Lillian, then got back into Riley's truck.

"So, where are we eating?" she asked.

"Chez Riley's." He cast a quick glance in her direction. "I thought I'd take you to my place, let you see where I live and where a meal fit for a king is waiting for us."

"Really? You cooked?"

He grinned sheepishly. "Actually, to be perfectly honest, I shopped." He hesitated a beat. "Little Doe?"

"Excuse me?"

"Just making a guess about your Cherokee name," he said.

She laughed. "Little Doe? Couldn't you at least be a little original?"

"Okay…Foolish Fawn," he teased.

Her laughter rang in the truck and he relished the sound of it. He wanted to make her laugh always, to see that glimmer of happiness shine in her eyes every day of his life.

"Not even close," she exclaimed. She grew silent as he pulled into his driveway. He shut off his motor and turned to look at her. "It's beautiful, Riley. Absolutely beautiful, and the setting is stunning."

He looked back at the house. It was a beautiful place, and there wasn't another house in sight, only trees and grass and carefully planted shrubbery. "Thanks."

They got out of the car and he led her inside, and as he saw the living room through her eyes he realized his mother had been right. It was a beautiful house, but it wasn't a home, and he felt the need to apologize for the cold, impersonal living conditions.

"I'm not here much. The place needs a little TLC."

She walked across the living room and stood before the floor-to-ceiling windows that offered a scenic view of a small brook and ancient trees. "Why hang pictures and put out knickknacks in a house that offers this kind of view?"

He came to stand just behind her, drawing a deep breath of the scent of her. "It is beautiful, isn't it?" He pointed to a spot down by the brook. "That's where we're going to eat our dinner."

"How wonderful." She turned to look at him and they were so close he could feel her breath on his face. Time seemed to come to a halt as they stood face-to-face, a mere breath apart.

Every muscle in his body tensed as desire rocked him

nearly mindless. He wanted to back her up against the window, claim her lips with his while his hands caressed up the length of her legs, up beneath her denim skirt. He wanted to press himself against her, let her feel the extent of his need for her.

Her eyes widened, as if she could read his thoughts, see inside his head and into his deepest desire. "When…when do we eat?"

He saw her mouth move, and somewhere in the back of his brain the words registered, but her voice sounded very faraway and huskier than usual.

"Riley?"

The moment shattered as Riley heard the apprehension in her voice. "Now," he said as he stepped back from her. "Now we eat."

The picnic basket he'd prepared earlier was in the refrigerator, all packed and ready to go. He handed her a neatly folded red blanket then he grabbed the basket and the jug of cold sweet tea and they headed outside.

It was a perfect evening for a picnic, warm but with a slight breeze that made the temperature comfortable. "How did you find this property?" she asked as they spread the blanket out in the lush grass.

"It was part of a ranch that belonged to a friend of my father's. He couldn't use this area for planting because it was too wooded so he sold me these three acres."

"It's beautiful," she exclaimed.

No, you are, he thought. You're beautiful and sexy and have me half-crazy with wanting you.

They both sat on the blanket and he opened the picnic basket. He was hungry, but the last thing he hungered for was food.

* * *

As they ate, Riley entertained her with stories about his job. He told her about temperamental workers, small-time thugs and crazy prospective home buyers.

He made her laugh again and again and she realized how desperately she'd needed this day away from the strife, the worry and the very torment of her life.

He made it impossible for her to think of anything but him and this moment of laughter and good food. He made it impossible for her to regret the impulse that had made her accept his invitation for the day.

Dinner consisted of what he'd once told her made a perfect picnic meal—thick ham sandwiches, potato salad and chips, and for dessert, big slices of chocolate cake.

As they talked and ate, evening shadows danced first around the base of the trees, then spread to embrace all they could find.

Savannah ate too much, and as Riley finished his meal, she stretched out on the blanket, a languid sense of well-being seeping through her. The nearby brook made little bubbling noises as it cascaded over rocks. The sound was almost hypnotically soothing.

She didn't realize she'd gone to sleep until she opened her eyes to discover the sun had fallen from the sky and the moon had taken its place. Riley was stretched out beside her, propped up on his elbow, watching her.

"Oh, goodness. I'm sorry," she exclaimed. She propped herself up on her elbow facing him, embarrassed that she'd apparently slept for a little while. "I didn't mean to fall asleep."

"Don't apologize," he said with a smile. "You were obviously exhausted."

"It was all that good food you provided," she replied.

"And the sound of the little stream." She knew she should sit up, tell him it was time to take her home, but she was reluctant to call an end to what had been a near-perfect day.

Besides, he looked so handsome in the purple shadows of night. His blue eyes glowed with an almost silvery sheen and the bright moonlight that streamed through the trees emphasized the chiseled planes of his face.

"Thank you, Riley, for a wonderful day," she said softly.

"No. Thank you," he returned. "I can't remember a day that I've found more pleasurable." The glow in his eyes seemed to intensify and he reached out a hand and stroked a strand of her short hair away from her forehead.

"I like your hair short," he said softly. "It draws attention to your beautiful face. And you are so beautiful," he murmured.

He didn't pull his hand away from her, but rather it lingered, touching her cheek, tracing down the line of her jaw.

She could feel it in the air; her senses were taut with it. Desire. It shone from his eyes, radiated from his touch and welled up inside of her. She knew he was going to kiss her and for the life of her she couldn't imagine telling him no.

He leaned forward and she met him halfway. His warm mouth moved against hers with featherlight softness, but the softness lasted only a moment before his mouth became more demanding.

She gave in to the kiss, opening her mouth to him as his tongue met hers. He was no longer inches away from her, but rather pressed against her, his arms gathering her closer...closer against him.

It felt good, to be held intimately against the length of him, her softness against his strength, her heat melding with his. The kiss went on and she reveled in the taste of him, the hot demand that was in his lips.

She tangled her hands in his hair, loving the feel of it between her fingers. Her heart pounded a rhythm to match the beat of his...racing...almost frantic.

His mouth left hers and trailed a hot rain of kisses down her jaw, then behind her ear. The sweet sensations forced a shiver of need to work through her.

She felt his fingers behind her working at the zipper of her sundress and she didn't want to stop, knew they were both beyond stopping. Her need for this human contact was too great and she wanted Riley, the man who made her laugh, the man who seemed to understand her from the inside out.

Hunger thrummed in her veins, crashed in her heart. She didn't want to think. She only wanted to feel...experience making love with Riley.

"Savannah," he whispered, his voice no louder than the babble of the nearby brook. "Sweet Savannah..." Her zipper hissed down and he pulled her to a sitting position. The opened dress fell from her shoulders and she got to her feet, letting it fall to the blanket.

At the same time he stood and kicked off his jeans, then yanked his shirt open and tore it off. Together they fell back on the blanket, guided by a frenzied need and in no time at all they both were naked.

There was a surreal feeling to the whole thing...the night air coupled with moonlight splashed their bodies. She'd never made love outside before, and there was a part of her that marveled at the abandon she felt, the utter freedom of it all.

Her head was filled not only with the male scent of Riley, but also with the sweet smell of grass, the rich fragrance of earth and the hint of woodsy wildness. She felt as wild as the landscape that surrounded them…as soft as the grass, as liquid as the stream, as warm as the ground that retained the day's sunshine.

He stroked her skin, his hands feeling fevered as they cupped her breasts, caressed down the length of her stomach, and smoothed across the tops of her thighs.

She wanted to weep with pleasure and scream at him to take her. She didn't want foreplay. She'd been ready for him since the moment of their first kiss.

"Riley," she finally managed to gasp. And that was all it took to snap whatever control he'd fought to maintain. He entered her in one smooth thrust and groaned as he remained unmoving, buried completely inside her.

She raked her fingers down his bare back and with another groan he moved his hips against hers. And in that moment they were at each other like hungry animals. Only their gasps and moans, their ragged breaths and groans, broke the silence of the night.

Almost as quickly as it had begun, it was finished. They fell apart, each trying to catch their breaths. Rational thought was still impossible for Savannah. She was a bundle of feelings, overwhelmed by sweet sensations, and in any case she didn't want to think—not yet.

He reached out and drew a finger down her cheek, his eyes glowing in the moonlight overhead. "You are so beautiful, Savannah." His voice held a softness that touched her deep inside.

"Silver Star," she said. He frowned quizzically. "My Cherokee name is Silver Star."

He smiled. "That would have been my next guess." His smile faded as he continued to look at her. "I'm sorry it was, uh, so fast."

A wave of heat suffused her face. "It was fine, Riley."

His frown deepened. "Only fine?"

"More than fine...wonderful." She was completely embarrassed now. She sat up and reached for her panties and bra.

"I never even gave you the whole tour of my house," he said as they dressed.

She was grateful for the change in subject. "I'd love to see the rest of your house."

Together they picked up the last of the picnic things and the blanket, then went back into his house. As he put on a pot of coffee, she excused herself to go to the bathroom.

In the privacy of the guest bath, she stared at her reflection in the mirror. Her cheeks were pink and her eyes sparkled and her lips were slightly swollen and red.

They'd been like two animals going at each other, she thought. It had been all about physical need, and somehow that comforted her. Her body had responded, but of course her heart hadn't been involved at all.

When she left the bathroom and returned to the kitchen she was grateful that they suffered no apparent awkwardness between them.

They drank coffee and he told her about building his house. "I'm grateful that my parents were here to see this completed and me living here," he said.

"So you've been here a couple of years," she said in surprise. By the austere living room and kitchen, she would have guessed he'd moved in only a couple of months before.

"Yeah, hard to believe, isn't it? I keep telling myself maybe I should hire an interior decorator to kind of liven up the place, but so far I haven't managed to bring myself to do it." He hesitated a beat. "Maybe you could give me some ideas for making it seem more homey."

She laughed. "Trust me, I'm the last person to ask. My mother constantly tells me my taste is all in my mouth when it comes to decorating."

He stood from the table where they had been sitting. "Come on, let me give you the whole tour."

He took her upstairs first, where there was a large bath and three nice-size bedrooms. Each room had a bed and dresser, but nothing on the walls and no specific style at all.

"You know, you might check out Tamara Greystone's work. She does wonderful paintings that would perk up your walls a bit," she offered.

"Maybe you'd go with me to see some of her stuff... help me pick out some artwork."

"Sure," she agreed as he led her back down the stairs. "Although her work is so good you couldn't make a mistake in choosing any of it."

The dining room was attractive with an elegant table and chairs and a matching china cabinet. "You have wonderful taste," she said as she ran a finger across the polished wood of the table.

"Thanks." He touched her arm. "Come on, and I'll show you the master suite."

She wasn't sure why but the thought of seeing where Riley slept, where he dreamed, filled her with a new tension, a strange, exciting tension.

The bedroom was huge and light and airy. The room held the essence of Riley Frazier. His scent hung in the air and photos of his parents in small gold frames stood on the top of the dresser, along with loose change and several sheets of paper containing doodles.

The bed was king-size and covered with a dark-blue spread and burgundy throw pillows. The curtains carried out the same color scheme, looking rich and masculine. The windows offered the same view as the living room windows—that of the brook and the trees and the utter serenity of the property.

"It's beautiful, Riley," she said. She couldn't imagine the pleasure of waking up each morning with that view in sight. How peaceful it must be.

She walked over to the photos on the dresser, aware of him coming to stand just behind her. Funny, how quickly her senses responded to his nearness.

She looked at a photo of him with his mother and father. He seemed to be about eighteen or nineteen and all of their faces shone with the happiness of love…of family togetherness.

"She's probably dead."

His words, spoken softly, shocked and horrified her. She whirled around to face him, saw the stark despair on his features.

"Don't say that, Riley," she exclaimed. "Don't even think it."

"I need to face reality," he replied, his beautiful eyes dark with pain. "I have to face the fact that after all this time without a word, without a trace, she surely must be dead."

"No, you can't think that way." Savannah placed a hand on his cheek, felt the whisper of dark whiskers against her palm.

His words frightened her. If he truly believed there was no hope for his mother, then she had to face the possibility that there was no hope for hers.

"You have to keep the faith, Riley. Nobody has found

her, there's been no body. You have to keep hoping, keep believing that eventually she'll be found alive and well."

He placed his hand over hers and closed his eyes for a moment, then nodded. "You're right. I've got to keep hoping."

She started to remove her hand, but he kept it pressed tightly against his cheek with his own. "Savannah." His voice was just a whisper, but it sent a shiver up her spine for it was filled with desire. "I want you again…here, in my bed."

"Riley, I…" She wasn't sure what she'd intended to say and in any case speech was impossible as his mouth crashed down on hers and all thoughts of protest were swept out of her head.

CHAPTER ELEVEN

The first time they had made love, it had been like two animals wanting only physical release, with little emotion, little tenderness involved. What Riley wanted now was to make love to her slowly…tenderly and with every ounce of emotion he had in his heart.

He turned off the overhead light and by the illumination of the moon drifting through the windows led her to the edge of the bed. Quickly he pulled down the bedspread, afraid that if he took too much time in preparing, she'd change her mind.

He turned back to her and gathered her in his arms. Willingly she came to him, her lips warm and yielding as he kissed her again and again. He felt as if he would never tire of kissing her, but knew eventually he'd want more… he'd want not just her lips, but all of her.

He cupped her face in his hands and stared deep into

her eyes, seeing the glazed look of desire shining back at him. "Savannah, I want you so badly."

He fought for control, not wanting to lose it as quickly as he had earlier when they'd made love. He'd been almost embarrassed by his lack of control earlier.

"I want you, too," she whispered, as if the words caused her pain.

What he wanted was to take the time to know her, to explore each and every inch of her, to discover all the secrets that led to her passion.

Once again they undressed, then slid beneath the sheets. He was pleased to realize that long after she'd gone, his sheets would retain the scent of her, that indelible, unforgettable, delectable scent of warm sexy woman and sweet flowers.

As he claimed her lips again, his hands stroked down to capture her breasts. She had perfect breasts, not too big but not too small. As he rubbed his thumbs across her turgid nipples a deep moan issued from her throat. The moan shot fire through his veins, and he replaced his hands with his mouth, moving from one nipple to the other. She tasted so good and he loved the feel of her against his tongue.

Her hands clutched his shoulders and stroked his back, igniting tiny flames wherever she touched. His lips moved down her flat stomach as her fingers tangled in his hair.

He wanted to taste every inch of her, feel her writhe against him in mindless passion. He wanted to love her as she'd never been loved before, as she'd never be loved again.

Someplace in the back of his mind he knew he wanted to love her deeply enough, passionately enough to banish any thought, at least for the moment, of a man who could never, would never be in her life again.

Silver Star. Her Cherokee name sang through his head. She was like a shining silvery star in his heart, filling him with heat and light after years of darkness and despair.

Before this moment he'd only imagined what she would look like in his bed. Her dusky skin glistened in the moonlight, stoking his need for her to a near-fever pitch.

"Riley," she cried out as he found the center of her, stroked her with his hand, then with his mouth. It wasn't a cry of protest, but rather one of exquisite pleasure. Shudders racked her body, and only then did he move back up, raining kisses as he went.

Then it was her turn to explore his body and he trembled beneath the heat of her hands and the warmth of her mouth. She was a bold lover, matching him caress for caress, kiss for kiss.

"I love touching you…tasting you," he murmured into the hollow of her neck.

She stroked her hand up the hard length of him. "I love touching you, tasting you, too."

Once again his fingers found her warm moistness and he saw her eyes widen as her hand fell away from him. As he moved his fingers against her, she clutched at the sheets, her hips rising to meet his as her body grew taut.

As she moaned her delight, he felt his own desire growing harder…higher…reaching heights he hadn't thought possible.

A series of shudders swept over her and he knew she was riding the crest of a tsunami that left her weak and gasping. It was only then, when he knew she'd had complete and total pleasure, that he entered her.

She wrapped her legs around his hips, bringing him into her completely at the same time his lips possessed hers in a fiery kiss of both dominance and submission.

Riley felt his control slipping. He was surrounded by her warmth, imbibed with her scent, and capable of only one single thought…Savannah…Savannah.

She sang inside him, heating his blood, permeating his veins, and filling up every corner of his heart. He loved her, and words of love begged to be released, but he had enough sense left to know it was too soon.

And so he loved her in every other way that he could, stroking her sweet skin, whispering sweet, loving words in her ear as he moved in and out of her.

As much as he wanted to take it slow, to make this act last forever, he couldn't. She was too much for him, too hot, too soft, too overwhelming to fight the natural impulse of his body to race to completion.

His movements became faster, but she met him thrust for thrust. Moans filled the room and he wasn't sure if they came from her or from him. All he knew was that he was lost…lost in Savannah, and he never wanted to be found again.

Afterward, he held her in his arms, unsure what to say. Making love to her had only confirmed what he had already known—that he loved her as he'd never loved a woman before, that he wanted to spend the rest of his life with her.

But he knew, more than anyone did, just how fragile she was, the turmoil of her life right now. Was she ready to welcome love? He wasn't sure and he was afraid of risking everything by moving too far too fast. They'd made beautiful love, but that didn't mean she was ready for a lifetime commitment.

"I've got to go," she said, breaking the silence that had lingered between them. "I've got a lot of things to do tomorrow."

He tightened his grip around her, reluctant to let her go. "Stay the night. I can take you home as early as you need in the morning." He'd love to wake up with her nestled in his arms. "There's nothing that can be accomplished tonight. Sleep here…with me."

She tensed, then pushed out of his arms and sat up. "No, I really need to go home now." She raked her fingers through her short hair, her gaze not meeting his. "If you don't feel like driving me home I can call a friend or a cab. It's no big deal."

"Don't be silly. Of course I'll take you."

She grabbed her clothes from the floor and disappeared into the master bathroom. Riley sat up and finger combed his hair, disappointment like a stone heavy in his chest.

He'd lost her. The closeness, the intimacy that had transcended a mere physical level had vanished. She'd distanced herself from him in the blink of an eye. He'd thought he'd known loneliness over the past two years, but in that instant he felt a loneliness he'd never experienced before.

Reluctantly, he got out of bed and turned on the bedside lamp. He would have loved to have her in his bed all night long. He would have loved to open his eyes with the sunrise and see her next to him.

But what he wanted didn't matter. He knew he had to be patient with her, and he had to find the patience within himself to give her time. They'd known each other for only two weeks. Although that was enough time for him to know his feelings for her, it was obviously not enough time for her.

He had just finished dressing when she came out of the bathroom. The first thing he saw on her face was regret. "Savannah…don't," he said softly.

"Don't what?" Still her gaze didn't quite meet his.

"No regrets," he said. "Please don't regret what happened here tonight." He took a step toward her. He wanted to reach out to her, take her in his arms. But he could tell by her posture and the shuttered look in her eyes that she wouldn't welcome any touch from him at the moment.

"I have no regrets," she said, but her body language said otherwise as she headed for the bedroom door. "I just have a lot on my mind."

Riley followed behind her, wondering how something that had been so beautiful, so moving, could have been a mistake. It was odd. He felt as if he was losing her and yet wasn't sure he'd ever really had her.

As Riley and Savannah got into his car, Rita Birdsong James came awake once again. Her head pounded with a headache the likes of which she'd never suffered before. The dim light from her nightstand only made it worse, and she closed her eyes and fought against the pain.

She reached out a hand to Thomas's side of the bed. "Thomas?" His side of the bed was cold. He'd always been an earlier riser than she had. Thomas loved the early mornings, and Rita didn't really come alive until midmorning.

Wincing, she opened her eyes once again. She had no idea what time it might be, felt the grogginess of too much deep sleep. Surely it was time to get up, but where was the sun?

Her gaze shifted toward her nightstand, searching for her clock radio, but it wasn't there. She frowned. That was odd. Why would her clock be gone? But her lamp was there, the Tiffany-style shade in reds and greens and deep blues.

She clutched a handful of the familiar bedspread, a

flutter of disquiet coursing through her as she frowned and once again squeezed her eyes tightly closed. There was something…some nebulous memory just out of reach begging to come to the surface.

Her chest tightened and her headache intensified as she tried to think, but she felt as if her head had been stuffed with wads of cotton.

Maybe if she got up, opened the curtains and oriented herself as to the time of day. "Thomas?" she called as she carefully swung her legs over the edge of the bed.

Where was Thomas? The disquiet that had been with her moments before transformed into something deeper, more frightening.

Thomas. Something had happened to Thomas—but what? She managed to stand despite the fact that she felt weak and wobbly as a baby attempting first steps.

She clung to the nightstand for a moment, then stumbled to the curtains. Sunshine. Surely sunshine would make her feel better. Sunshine and a nice hot cup of coffee. Where was Thomas with the coffee?

She opened the drapes, but no sunshine greeted her. She stared uncomprehending at the concrete wall behind the curtains. Where was the window?

Jerking around, she looked at the room that she'd thought was her own. But now she saw that it wasn't really her room at all. It was a facade, like a set constructed for a play.

The bed was like hers, the bedspread exactly like the one she had in her room. The nightstand was the same, as was the lamp that sat on it. The walls were the same beige and the pictures hanging on the walls were very similar to the ones she owned. But, this wasn't her room.

Panic welled up inside her, a panic verging on sheer

hysteria. As the cotton in her head fell away, she moved away from the curtains, trying to get a handle on exactly where she might be.

It was a room made to look like hers, but there were no windows. A door led to a bathroom where there were fluffy towels on a shelf, her favorite scented powders and lotions on the countertop and her bathrobe, hung from a hook on the back of the door.

Was this a hospital? Certainly her head hurt badly enough for her to believe she'd been hospitalized. And somewhere in the dark places of her mind, she remembered being taken to the bathroom, being helped in and out of bed.

But what kind of a hospital provided rooms that looked almost exactly like the patient's bedroom at home?

There was another door, a strange steel door with what appeared to be a panel that could be opened and closed in the center. She made her way over to it and gripped the handle. Locked.

The instant she tried to turn the handle, the memory that had been niggling at her mind crashed open.

She'd been in the kitchen preparing to cut a piece of apple pie for Thomas when she'd heard him cry out. She'd smiled, thinking he was voicing his objection to a referee's call in the baseball game he'd been watching.

She'd just sliced the pie when she was grabbed from behind, and a large, gloved hand clamped across her nose and mouth. A strange smell burned her eyes, and she tried to hold her breath, fought desperately to get free. But darkness descended, and just before she lost total consciousness she caught a glimpse of Thomas sprawled facedown on the living room floor. Blood was everywhere...too much blood.

She now cried out and fell weakly to her knees as she thought of her beloved husband. "Thomas... Thomas." She wept his name over and over again. He was dead. He had to be dead...there had been too much blood and he'd been so still.

Raven Mocker. That's who had come into their home and killed Thomas. Only Raven Mocker, the most evil of Cherokee witches, could be responsible.

She thought of all the stories her mother had told her about the dreadful Raven Mocker. According to the ancient stories, Raven Mocker flew through the night with his arms outstretched like wings and went into the house of somebody that was sick or dying and robbed them of their life.

But Raven Mocker was just a legend, like the Anglo bogeyman, her mind protested. Despite the fact that she was a modern woman, she couldn't deny the power of the stories she'd been told about the dreaded witch of her people.

Although she and Thomas were not ill, there was no doubt in her mind that only the evil Raven Mocker would be powerful enough, evil enough to kill Thomas and take her.

She rose to her feet and tried to open the door once again, but she couldn't. She made her way back to the bed and sat on the edge, fighting against the grief that threatened to rip her apart. Not only was she fighting her grief, but she also felt so very tired and realized she must have been drugged.

Shaking her head to try to get the fog out, she looked around the room once again and noticed the open closet. The clothing that hung inside was familiar. They were all hers...the dresses, the blouses, the skirts...all had hung in her closet at home.

What was going on here? What was happening? Her gaze darted frantically around the room. No windows—a locked steel door.

Raven Mocker had stolen Thomas's life and now held her as a prisoner. For what? Grief battled with terror and she curled up on the bed, wondering how long before she learned what her fate was to be.

He watched her on four screens, the images transmitted from the dozen cameras built into the ceiling of the room. Each screen gave him a different bird's-eye view and with the flick of a switch he could turn the camera's eyes so she would never be out of his view no matter where she was in the room.

She was weeping and he'd heard her cry her husband's name again and again. That was natural. He understood her grief and knew eventually it would pass.

He'd stopped the drugs, eager to see her awake and moving instead of inert and lifeless on the bed. He knew he'd have to tolerate her grief for several days to come, perhaps even a week or two, but if there was one thing he was, it was a patient man.

Soon she would come to understand that she belonged here...with him. She'd come to realize that she was special...a chosen one.

He hoped she didn't disappoint him.

He'd been disappointed so many times in the past.

"Good night, Riley," Savannah said and jumped out of his truck before he could even offer to walk her to her door. If he walked her to her door he'd want to kiss her good-night, and she was afraid a kiss from Riley at this moment would shatter her into a million pieces.

She hurried to her apartment door, unlocked it, then went inside and slammed the door shut behind her. She locked it again, then sagged weakly against it.

The drive home had been silent, filled with tension and for her, filled with regret. She'd made love with Riley not once, but twice. Once, she could chalk up to raging hormones or a lack of control. She could have told herself he'd seduced her, that she'd been weak and vulnerable and he'd taken advantage of her.

But no matter how hard she tried she couldn't excuse or explain away the second time. She'd gone willingly to his bed, wanting the pleasure of being naked and intimate with him between his sheets.

She had been a willing participant in their lovemaking—lovemaking that had gone beyond the boundaries of mere physical pleasure.

She pushed herself away from the front door and stepped into the living room where the photos of Jimmy seemed to stare at her in accusation.

Tears burned at her eyes and she raced into her bathroom, stripped off her clothes and got into the shower. She scrubbed herself in the near-scalding water, needing to remove every trace of Riley.

She only wished there was some way to take out her memories and rinse them clean of him, as well. But his smile remained in her head, the sound of his laughter rang in her ears, and the warm light of his eyes bathed her in a heat that had nothing to do with the shower water.

As she dried off and pulled on her nightgown, she thought of her mother. How Savannah wished her mother was here right now, to talk to, to hold her and make all the madness of her life go away.

From the bathroom she wandered back into the living

room and picked up the frame with the photo of Jimmy in his parka. She curled up on the sofa with the photo in hand, staring at the man who had been friend, companion, lover and husband.

Life had been so easy when Jimmy had been with her. There had been no murders, no missing mother, no lonely nights and no torturous feelings of guilt.

His brown eyes were so gentle...so kind. But so were Riley's blue ones, a little voice whispered. Jimmy had made her laugh. Riley makes you laugh, too, the voice whispered.

And Riley had made her body sing as it never had before. He'd made her feel alive for the first time in over a year. Even now, just thinking about their lovemaking sent a shimmering wave of heat through her.

She grabbed the photo of Jimmy tighter and clutched it against her chest. He'd been her destiny, her soul mate. She closed her eyes in an attempt to stanch the hot tears that threatened. But the attempt was futile, and tears spilled down her cheeks as she realized she couldn't remember her soul mate's kiss. Her head was too filled with Riley.

CHAPTER TWELVE

She'd stopped taking his calls. Every night for the next three nights Riley called her at the same time, as had become their habit. And each night he got her answering machine. He suspected she was home, listening to his messages, but refusing to pick up and actually talk to him.

It killed him. After what they had shared, it killed him to know she was now attempting to push him right out of her life.

She was in love with him, he knew it in his heart. He knew she wasn't the kind of woman who could make love with somebody she didn't care about or wasn't falling in love with. Yes, he believed she was falling in love with him but was bound heart and soul to a dead man.

How could he ever hope to compete with a marriage that would never suffer any more discord, a marriage that would forever be happy in the memories of the woman left behind?

How could he ever hope to compete with a man who could now never disappoint or hurt her in any way?

The messages Riley had left for her had been lists of additional cities and towns where he'd checked records to see if he could find a case like theirs. So far there had been nothing, but in every minute of his spare time he got back on the Internet and the telephone to search some more.

That's what he was doing when his other phone line rang. He snatched it up, hoping, praying it was Savannah. But instead it was her brother, Clay.

"Found something interesting," he said without preamble.

"And what would that be?" Riley asked.

"Pebbles."

"Excuse me?" Riley shut down his computer to better focus on the conversation.

"Pebbles…little rocks. There were two in the carpeting at your parents' house and three in the carpeting at my folk's place."

Riley frowned, not understanding the significance. "I would expect there to be pebbles in everyone's carpeting. There are all kinds of rocks and gravel around."

"But not like these," Clay replied. "These aren't your garden variety pebbles. They're polished, decorative rocks used for landscaping."

"Can you tell where they come from? Who sells them?" Adrenaline pumped through him. Maybe finally…finally they had gotten a break in the cases.

"Unfortunately there are three rock quarries in this county that sell them and a dozen quarries throughout the state. I'm in the process now of requesting customer lists from all of them, but I'm not sure if we'll learn anything from them or not."

"So, we're back to square one," Riley said, fighting a wave of disappointment.

"Not exactly. I'd say with this evidence, it's possible that whoever killed your father also tried to kill mine."

"Possible, but you can't be certain."

There was a moment of silence and Riley felt the other man's frustration radiating across the line. "I couldn't testify in a court of law unequivocally that the two crimes were committed by the same person based on this evidence alone."

"But what do you think, Clay?" he pressed, wanting a definitive answer.

"I don't think. That's not my job. I analyze trace evidence. It's just intriguing, that's all, that the same kind of rock was found at both places. I thought you'd like to know."

"I appreciate it. Have you told Savannah?"

"Yeah. It was her idea that I call and let you know."

Riley's suspicion that Savannah was avoiding him was confirmed by Clay's words. A week ago there was no way in hell Savannah wouldn't have been on the phone to him to share this piece of news. But a week ago they hadn't made love.

He rebooted the computer and stared at the screen. How could making love to her screw everything up between them? He hadn't forced himself on her. She'd been a willing participant both times.

He'd never experienced the kind of pleasure he'd had making love to Savannah. It hadn't been just the act itself, but the beauty of looking deep into her eyes, feeling the beat of her heart against his, knowing a bond was being cemented between them that went beyond the mere physical act of lovemaking.

At least that's what he'd thought. He suspected he knew what had chased her away—the memories of a man now dead. Jimmy Tallfeather must have been a hell of a man to still have such a hold on his wife a year after his death.

Riley wanted to break that hold. He didn't want Savannah to forget the man she'd loved and married, but he wanted her to open her heart to the possibility that she could love and marry and be happy once again.

He shut off his computer, realizing it was impossible to work with her filling his every thought. Instead he decided to knock off from work altogether, take a ride into Cherokee Corners and see if he could find Savannah.

If he could just see her, speak with her in person, then he hoped he could convince her there was no reason to feel bad or guilty about what they had shared. He hoped he could convince her they belonged together.

"Lillian, I'm taking off for the rest of the afternoon," he said as he left his office.

"You might as well," she said. "You've been here all day, but you haven't been here, if you know what I mean." She tapped the side of her head to make her point. "If I was to guess, you've got woman problems," she added.

Riley smiled at her, surprised by her astuteness. On impulse he sat in the chair opposite her desk. "Lillian, you're a widow."

She nodded. "It's been five years since I lost my Joseph."

"And you've never remarried," he observed.

"That's true," she agreed. "What's with all these questions? Is this about your Savannah?"

Your Savannah. He loved the way that sounded and he desperately wanted to make it so. He hadn't realized until these last couple of weeks with her how utterly lonely, how desolate his life had become.

Before meeting Savannah he'd just been going through the motions, enduring each day without real pleasure. She'd changed all that for him. She'd filled his days with joy, given him a new hope for his future. She'd made him believe happiness was possible again despite the tremendous loss in his life.

"Riley?" Lillian looked at him expectantly.

"Sorry, yes it's about Savannah. Why haven't you remarried?" he asked.

Lillian blinked, as if finding it difficult to track the conversation. "I don't know. I haven't met anyone since Joseph that has made me think of marrying again. I've grown accustomed to being alone and it's not like I *need* to remarry.

"I have my gentlemen friends. I go to dinner or whatever, then send them on their way."

Riley frowned, trying to think what this might have to do with Savannah's widowhood.

"But you have to remember, Riley, I'm an old woman. I've had my children, I was married for thirty-five years."

"She clings to the memory of her husband, and I think she's refusing to even give us a chance. I respect the fact that she misses him, but I can't believe she intends to hold on to memories for the rest of her life."

Lillian leaned back in her chair and gazed at him sympathetically. "I don't have any answers or words of wisdom for you, Riley. Maybe the timing just isn't right for you and Savannah. Maybe if you'd met her ten years ago or two years from now." She shrugged helplessly and Riley stood.

"Thanks, Lillian, but as far as I'm concerned, the timing is right now. All I have to do is figure out a way to con-

vince her of that." With those words, he walked out of the
trailer and got into his truck.

As he headed for Cherokee Corners, he thought of Lillian's words about the timing perhaps being all wrong.
He'd never believe that, not in a million years. He felt as
if some strange sort of serendipity had been at work from
the moment he'd first met Savannah.

He'd come looking to see if the crime that had taken
place in the James home was like the one that had taken
place in his parents' home. He could have made initial contact with the newlywed Breanna or with Clay. But fate had
led him to Savannah, a woman as needy as he had been.

It had to mean something. The timing had felt intrinsically right when they'd been making love. He'd looked
deep into her eyes as he'd taken possession of her, and
what he'd seen shining from the brown depths of her eyes
had been love…love for him.

He knew there was turmoil in her life, that the recent
murders and what had happened to her parents had created havoc. But he needed to make her see that he could
be her shelter in the storm, her rock to cling to. He had to
convince her that he was what she needed in her life.

The problem was he couldn't find her. When he got to
Cherokee Corners, he drove by her apartment first to see
if her car was there. It wasn't. Then he drove to the police
station, past her parents' place and by the hospital parking lot. Her car was nowhere to be found.

There was only one other place he knew to look for her,
and the thought that she might be there chilled his blood.

He drove to the old bridge where her husband had
plunged off the side to his death, where she'd confessed
to him she sometimes climbed up in the girders and stared
down at the water below.

There was only one area where a car could be parked and a person could get to the girders to climb up, and it was to that spot that he went. Relief flooded through him as he saw that her car was nowhere in sight.

Unsure where to go next, he found himself pulling in front of the Redbud Bed and Breakfast. Maybe Alyssa, her cousin, would know where he could find her.

It was early enough in the afternoon that apparently the lunch group had gone and the after-dinner crowd hadn't yet started in. The place was empty except for Alyssa, who sat behind the counter sipping a cup of coffee.

She began to stand as he came through the door, but he waved her back down and slid onto a stool opposite her. "Hello, Mr. Frazier," she greeted him.

"Please...make it Riley."

"What can I get for you? A double-dipper cone? A hot-fudge sundae? Banana split?"

"No, no thanks. I was just wondering if maybe you knew where Savannah might be? I've been looking for her this afternoon."

"I heard from her earlier this morning, and she said she was heading into Tulsa to follow up on a tip in the Mc-Clane murder. She said that she didn't expect to be back home until late tonight."

Riley couldn't hide his disappointment. He'd hoped to talk to her now...this minute. The love he felt for her burned in his heart, in his soul and he felt the need to tell her before another hour passed, before another day went by.

"I guess you knew her husband, Jimmy," he finally said.

Alyssa nodded, her gaze holding his with a disquieting intensity. "I knew Jimmy all my life," she said. "He was a nice boy who grew into a nice man, rather quiet and utterly devoted to Savannah."

She broke eye contact with him and gazed down at the counter. "I don't know if Savannah mentioned it to you, but I have visions." She looked at him again, as if to gauge his reaction.

"Visions? You mean like psychic stuff?"

Her nod was almost imperceptive. "I've had them since I was a young child."

"So, you can see the future?" Riley was open-minded enough not to discount the possibility. After all, it was the era of people talking to the dead and psychics solving crimes for police departments. He'd never personally been touched by anything remotely paranormal, but that didn't mean he didn't believe it was possible.

She shrugged. "I see visions and sometimes they are of the future, and sometimes they are from the past. Sometimes they're about people I've never met and sometimes they're about people I love."

"And have you seen visions about Savannah?" A new tension filled Riley.

She frowned thoughtfully. "I don't have to see visions about her to know what's going on with her. When Jimmy died, something inside her died. We Cherokee believe that when people die their souls becomes spirits who walk among us." She worried a hand through her long hair, her frown deepening. "I think Savannah walks too close to Jimmy's spirit."

"I love her." The words fell from his lips before he realized he intended to say them aloud.

Alyssa smiled. "I know."

He looked at her in surprise. "You saw a vision or something?"

She laughed. "You wear your feelings for my cousin on your face, in your eyes. I don't need a vision to tell me how you feel about her." Her laughter faded and she eyed him sympathetically. "I don't know what to tell you, Riley. Savannah has been closed off from life…from love for a long time. I don't know if anyone is capable of opening her heart again."

Riley stood from his stool and raked a hand through his hair. "Wish me luck, because I intend to try."

He left the Redbud Bed and Breakfast and headed home, knowing there was nothing he could do that night. He didn't intend to give up. There was always tomorrow…or the day after…or the day after that, but sooner or later, he intended to be the man to open Savannah's heart to life… to love once again.

The week had seemed interminably long. The trip to Tulsa the day before had exhausted her, and so far the morning had been no less tiring.

Savannah drove fast toward her parents' house, hoping to arrive before Breanna and Adam brought Thomas home. She suspected Uncle Sammy wasn't the neatest of house-keepers and wanted to make sure the place was in good shape before her dad arrived home.

It was going to be difficult enough for Thomas to come home to a house where his wife wasn't there. Seventeen days. It had been seventeen long days since Rita Birdsong James had disappeared.

Although Thomas had made great strides physically since awakening from his coma, his mental state was pre-carious. She now arrived at the ranch and parked behind her uncle's car, then raced to the door and knocked.

Her uncle Sammy opened the door and pulled her into

a bear hug. "Hi, sweetheart." He released her and stepped back to allow her in. "I heard your dad was being released, so I've been doing a little cleanup." He grinned at her, his features still retaining a boyish charm. "I'll bet you came over to make sure the place wasn't a pigsty."

She smiled ruefully. "It did cross my mind that you might need a little housekeeping help." She followed him into the kitchen, which was spotlessly clean.

"Nah, I got myself to work, decided the last thing my brother needs is to come home to a dirty place. It's bad enough he's coming home without Rita."

As always her mother's name evoked both grief and fear inside Savannah. Where was she? What was happening to her? Seventeen days felt like an eternity.

"I'm glad you're here, Uncle Sammy," she said, refusing to dwell on her mother. Right now she had enough on her mind worrying about her father. "It's nice to know you're here for Dad."

He sank down at the kitchen table and gestured for her to do the same. "I'm glad to be here. It was time for me to change my circumstances. To be honest, I was in a bit of a money crunch and was about to get kicked out of my apartment, anyway. Besides," he flashed her a wide grin, "I've always said that Cherokee Corners has the best-looking women in the world."

"Uncle Sammy, you're incorrigible," Savannah said with a laugh. At that moment they heard a car door slam out front.

Savannah and her uncle went to the door to see Breanna and Adam helping Thomas out of the car. Savannah ran outside to see if she could help.

Breanna and Adam looked incredibly stressed, which meant her father was probably in one of his moods. In the past week he'd alternated between deep depression and rage. The doctor had told them this was to be expected, but it didn't make it any easier to deal with.

"Daddy," Savannah said and hugged him tight as he got out of the passenger seat, using a cane for support. "How are you doing?"

"How do you think I'm doing?" he replied angrily. "This isn't right. This just isn't right. I shouldn't be here without her." He waved Savannah away from him with the cane as she attempted to help him toward the house. "I can walk fine on my own. I don't need any damned help."

Breanna shot Savannah a helpless look. Together Adam, Breanna and Savannah followed Thomas as he slowly made his way toward the house where Uncle Sammy stood at the front door watching their progress.

When Thomas got to the door, he grunted a hello to his brother, then went on into the living room. He stood and stared around. "My chair is gone."

"Daddy, the police took the chair. They were looking for evidence."

Tears welled up in Thomas's eyes, and the anger that had carried him inside seemed to leave him. He slumped down on the sofa. "She should be here. Where is she? What are you all doing to find her?"

"Daddy, we're doing everything we can," Savannah said. She sat next to him and placed her hand on his knee. Breanna sat on the other side of him.

"Clay is busy analyzing trace evidence, and we're following leads as fast as they develop," Breanna said. "But there just aren't that many leads to follow."

"Everyone is doing everything they can, Thomas," Uncle Sammy said.

"You have to be strong, Daddy," Savannah continued.

"You have to stay strong for when she comes home. She's going to need all of us."

"She will come home, won't she?" He looked from one daughter to the other. "She'll come home and we'll all be a family again. She has to…she absolutely has to."

Savannah nodded, and the three of them hugged as Savannah prayed that what he'd said would come true.

She went from her parents' home back to work, still chasing leads on the two murder investigations that remained unsolved and without any real viable suspects.

It was after seven when she walked into her apartment and was greeted by a meow from Happy who was apparently hungry for a little quality time.

She scooped the furry bundle up in her arms and sank down on the sofa. It was impossible to hold Happy and not think about the man who had given her to Savannah.

For the past week it had been impossible to draw a breath and not think about Riley. The feel of his skin still burned into hers, the taste of his mouth lingered. But thoughts of him were more than just about their lovemaking.

As she thought of him showing her around Riley Estates, she couldn't help but remember the beautiful sparkle of his eyes as he spoke of building a community, his enthusiasm that had been infectious.

She thought of the stories he'd told her, stories intended to make her laugh and how gentle he'd been when he'd offered her emotional support.

Each night for the past week he'd called, and she'd had to fight with herself not to pick up the receiver. After all, what was the point of talking to him anymore? What was the point in seeing him again?

She had no intention of allowing herself to be drawn

in again. She'd been weak. Her heart belonged to Jimmy and nothing and nobody could ever change that.

It would be wrong to pretend otherwise. Jimmy walked with her every day in spirit and that would be enough for her for the rest of her life.

Still, it was difficult to ignore the messages left by Riley each night. He was still searching for similar crimes in the state, and each of his phone messages began with a list of the cities and towns he'd checked out.

After he'd finished with the list, he left a more personal message…asking about her, wondering why he hadn't heard from her…hoping she was doing all right. It was the final parts of his messages that ached in her heart, his attempt to connect with her on a personal level, the memory of the nights when they'd shared those right-before-sleep telephone talks.

"Come on, sweet, let's get something to eat." She carried Happy into the kitchen and sat her on the floor near her food dish, then opened the refrigerator and stared at the contents without interest.

She couldn't remember the last time she'd been grocery shopping, and the pickings the fridge offered were slim. She finally decided to make a quick omelet. As she prepared the ingredients she studiously ignored the flashing red light on her answering machine. She knew it was probably a message from Riley. In the past two days he'd left messages for her both at the station and here at home.

She didn't want to play it. She didn't even want to hear his voice, for if she did, she'd miss him and she'd think about making love with him and she'd get excited and scared and filled with emotions she didn't want to feel.

The sound of a television game show accompanied her

as she ate her dinner, but beneath the television noise she was aware of the profound silence of the apartment.

It was an absence of noise that seemed to reverberate in her head, echo deep in her heart. It created an ache inside her, the ache of loneliness.

It irritated her, because before Riley she'd had her grief to keep her company, her memories of Jimmy to make noise in her head.

She'd just finished placing her plate in the dishwasher when her phone rang once again. She knew it was Riley, felt it in her bones. She stood by the answering machine and stared at it as she waited to see who would speak to leave a message.

"Savannah…are you there?"

Riley's deep, sweetly familiar voice filled the line, and she closed her eyes, fighting the urge to pick up the phone.

"I need to talk to you," he said. "It's important…I found something." There was a long moment of silence. "We really need to talk, Savannah."

She told herself the only reason she was picking up the phone was because he'd said he'd found something important. But she also knew she couldn't spend the rest of her life avoiding him.

Besides, in the time she had known him he'd been too kind, too generous to now ignore. She at least owed him something—an explanation of why she no longer wanted to see him.

She picked up the receiver. "I'm here, Riley."

"Savannah," he said her name with relief. "I was beginning to think I'd never talk to you again."

"I've been really busy. What's up?"

He hesitated a moment, as if put off by her businesslike

attitude. "I found something in my search, but I'd rather not discuss it over the phone. Can I see you?"

She frowned thoughtfully. Had he really found something important or was this just a ruse to see her again? Still, she had no reason to believe that Riley would lie to her.

"I can be there in forty-five minutes," he continued. "You'll really want to see this," he added as if recognizing she might need further incentive.

"All right. Come on over," she agreed, and she was filled with a combination of anticipation and dread at the same time.

CHAPTER THIRTEEN

Riley hadn't been kidding when he'd told her that he'd found something that was of interest to their cases. But his driving need to see her went far beyond the information he had to impart to her.

He pulled into her apartment complex, anxious to tell her what he'd discovered, but more anxious to tell her of his feelings. He felt an urgency, somehow, that if he didn't tell her of his love for her soon something terrible might happen.

He'd learned from what had happened to his parents not to take a moment of time, of life, for granted. In a single split second of the past, he'd realized that every moment was a gift and shouldn't be wasted. He didn't want to waste another minute without telling Savannah how very important she'd become to him.

When she answered the door, his heart swelled with his love for her. Although she was dressed in a pair of jeans and a short-sleeved button-up red blouse and had a look of exhaustion on her face, he thought she'd never looked lovelier.

He'd been so hungry to see those beautiful brown eyes, watch the fleeting flicker of emotion that danced through the brown depths. He'd been starving for the scent of her, the nearness of her, but it was obvious from her body language that she was defensive and distant.

She motioned him into the kitchen and when he sat she took the seat opposite his, obviously having no intention of sitting right beside him.

"I heard you drove into Tulsa yesterday on a hot tip on your murder case. Did anything come of it?" he asked.

"Unfortunately, it was a waste of time, although I managed to confirm the rumor that Sam McClane was a ladies' man despite the fact that he'd been married for ten years. He had a mistress in Tulsa."

He noticed that she offered him no coffee, nothing to drink. Apparently, she didn't want him to linger and didn't see this as a social visit. His heart fell at the knowledge that she'd withdrawn so far from him.

"Does that help with the investigation? Knowing that he was a ladies' man and had a mistress?"

"Yes and no. We now have several women to question concerning Sam's murder, but it doesn't help in tying the two murders to the same perpetrator, and we're all pretty convinced they were killed by the same person." Her gaze had yet to meet his fully. "So you said on the phone you had some information for me."

He refused to be disheartened by her distance. He would take care of business first, but then they were going to have a personal talk whether she liked it or not.

He reached to open the folder he'd carried in with him

and handed her a sheet of paper he'd printed off an Internet site. Shoving it across the table toward her, he wondered how she could so easily pretend that nothing had happened between them, that they hadn't been as intimate as a man and a woman could be.

As she read the paper he'd handed her, she sat up straighter in the chair and her eyes widened. "Where is this from?" she asked, finally looking fully at him for the first time.

"A town called Sequoia Falls…it's just outside of Oklahoma City."

"But it's just like what happened to us," she said, a spark of excitement shining in her eyes.

"Yeah, except it took place a year before the crime against my folks. I called the detective who was in charge of the case at the time. He's retired now, but remembered the case well."

"What did he say?" She leaned forward, and he wished she were leaning forward to be closer to him instead of in eagerness to hear what he had to say to her about the case.

"He said it was the first time he recognized that women could be as vicious as men when it came to killing. Apparently the man had been hit over the head from behind with a blunt object. The blow killed him instantly. By the time his body was found, his wife was gone. Some of her clothing and toiletries were missing, and she went to the top of the suspect list."

"What happened with the case?"

"Still open. I found it on a site called Cold Cases in Oklahoma. The woman has never been found, dead or alive. She disappeared without a trace."

"Just like your mother and mine," Savannah said softly. She stared down at the paper in her hand once again.

"The only difference between this case and ours is that the couple apparently was having some marital problems at the time that the crime occurred, which made it easier for the police to write it up as a domestic homicide."

He'd never wanted to take anyone in his arms as much as he wanted to her at the moment. A tiny wrinkle furrowed her brow as she once again read the newspaper account of the crime that had taken place three years earlier.

When she gazed back at him, her expression was troubled. "If we're to believe that this crime is also related to yours and mine, then what is going on here? Where are these women disappearing to?"

"I wish I knew," he said soberly.

She sighed and scooted the paper across the table back to him, the wrinkle between her eyes growing more pronounced. "What if this is some kind of a serial thing? Somebody sneaks into a house, bangs the male occupant over the head, then does something with the women? But what?"

Riley didn't reply. He had nothing to say and saw that she wasn't finished yet, that the wheels of her detective mind were still whirling.

"A crime…then the passing of a year and another crime…then the passing of two years and another. Exact same crime scene and three missing women." She sighed once again. "I don't know, maybe I have serial killers on the brain and there's nothing except a strange coincidence where these three crimes are concerned."

"Do you really believe that?"

She offered him a small smile. "No." Her smile fell. "I think it's something far more sinister than mere coincidence. Tomorrow I'll see if I can get all the official records of this particular case and see where that leads. There has to be some sort of connection…something we're missing."

"Clay told you about the pebbles he found in my parents' house and at yours?"

She nodded. "It's not a lot to go on, but we're checking out the quarries in the area, seeing if we can find who sells and who buys that kind of decorative rock." She pushed back, away from the table and he sensed a dismissal coming.

"Thanks, Riley, for bringing by the information. Who knows, maybe it will lead to something substantial." She stood and eyed him expectantly, but he remained seated.

"We need to talk, Savannah," he said.

He saw the flash of knowledge in her eyes, somehow knew that she'd been expecting this. She stared at the wall just over his left shoulder.

"Riley, I'm tired. It's been a long day. I appreciate you coming by to tell me what you found, but I really need to call it a night." She backed away from the table, until she bumped into the countertop across the room.

He stood. "We need to talk now, tonight because I have a feeling that if I walk out your door now we're never going to have the discussion we need to have."

She raised her chin and stared at him, resolve in her eyes. "What do you want to talk about, Riley? You want to talk about the fact that we had sex? Okay…we had sex. It's over and done and that's that."

"That's that?" He stared at her incredulously. "That's that?" In three quick strides he stood before her, so close he could smell the scent of her, see the dread that darkened her eyes. He placed his hands on her shoulders, felt the tension that made them rigid as steel.

"Honey, we did more than have sex. We made love.

Having sex is what I've done throughout my adulthood. I've only made love twice…and both times were with you."

He didn't know how it was possible for eyes as dark as hers to grow even more dark, but they did. "Riley… please…I don't want to do this." She twisted from his grasp and went into the living room.

He followed behind her, but stood his ground in the center of the room, refusing to go another step toward the front door. Here he was surrounded by the photos of Jimmy…the man who held her heart captive and refused to let go.

"You don't want to do what?" he asked. "You don't want to hear that I love you? Well, you're going to hear it anyway. I love you, Savannah Tallfeather."

She winced, her eyes nearly black with pain, and she waved a hand as if to still the words that had ached for too long inside him.

He sat on the sofa and raked a hand through his hair in frustration. Somehow, some way, in his dreams, he'd thought that by confessing to her that he loved her, she'd fall into his arms and admit her love for him. He'd thought hearing the words spoken aloud would make it real for her, right for her.

But the look on her face was anything but love…it was horror and fear and a touch of anger. "Savannah," he said softly. "The one thing my mother and father wanted for me more than anything else on this earth was love. Oh, they wanted me to be successful, financially stable and all that, but more than anything they wanted me to find a woman to share my life. I found her in you, Savannah."

"No…no you haven't," she exclaimed, her eyes liquid as if she were fighting back tears. "We've been thrown together because of the crimes that wrecked our lives. That's all it is, Riley."

"That's not all it is," he protested. He got up, feeling at a distinct disadvantage sitting while she stood halfway across the room. He took a step toward her. There was a knot in his chest as he gazed at her. "I love you, Savannah. Marry me and share my life."

This was the conversation she'd hoped to avoid. Only it was worse than she'd anticipated. She hadn't expected a confession of love…a proposal of marriage.

She hated him at that moment, hated him because there was a part of her that wanted to throw herself into his arms, there was a part of her that longed to agree to share his life, his future.

There was a part of her that wanted to forsake Jimmy, and she knew it was a wicked, selfish part of her. And she didn't know if she hated him or hated herself.

"No, Riley. I can't marry you."

He approached where she stood, and what she wanted more than anything was to run away, to disappear. She didn't want him close enough to touch her, didn't want him near enough so she could smell the wonderfully male scent of him. She didn't want him to weaken her resolve.

"Why not? Why won't you marry me?" He stopped only when he stood close enough to her that she felt his breath warm her face, his body heat radiate through her.

She wanted to melt into him, seek the warmth and shelter of his arms, and that sickened her, for what kind of woman did that make her?

"Savannah," his voice was a soft plea filled with emotion that tugged at her heart. He reached out and took one of her hands in his. She tried to pull away, but he held tight, refusing to grant her the distance she so desperately needed.

"I know you feel as if your life is in turmoil right now. I know you have the murders on your mind, and the pain of your mother's absence. But let me be your sanity. Hang on to me when things get crazy…let my love for you sustain you."

His eyes, those beautiful blue eyes of his were filled with such longing, with a depth of love she'd only seen in one other man's eyes before. Jimmy's eyes.

With a sharp pull, she yanked her hand from his grasp. "Don't make this hard for me, Riley." She took a step backward, tears momentarily obscuring her vision. "I've had my love, Riley. His name was Jimmy Tallfeather, and he was my soul mate. I gave my heart to him and now there's nothing left for me to give to anyone else."

His gaze remained soft and tender as it lingered on her. "I'm not asking you to forget Jimmy and the love the two of you shared. I would never try to take that away from you. But surely there's room in your heart for me, too."

Room in her heart? She had a whole houseful of him in her heart. But it wasn't real. It couldn't be real. It was love based on sheer emotion, on raging hormones and the commonality of their situations.

She couldn't look at him, was afraid that if she gazed into his eyes once again she'd be lost. "I'm sorry, Riley," she said, staring down at her feet.

She gasped as he grabbed her by the shoulders. "Look at me, Savannah. Look at me and tell me that you don't love me."

"I don't," she said as tears splashed down on her cheeks. Still she refused to look at him.

"I don't believe you. You can lie to me with your mouth,

but you can't lie to me with your eyes, and when you look at me, I see love there. You can't lie to me with your kisses, because when I kiss you I taste love. And you can't lie with your heartbeat, and when I felt it racing with mine as we made love, I felt your love."

"It doesn't matter," she said, twisting away from him. "It doesn't matter what I feel for you or what you feel for me. I had my chance at happiness. I married my soul mate. He walks with me in spirit every day. I've already dishonored his memory enough by making love with you."

For the first time since he'd arrived she saw a flash of something in his eyes—a kindling of a fire that had nothing to do with love or desire. "What do you think? There's a quota on soul mates and you've met yours so you don't get another one?"

He reached out as if to grab her once again, but she sidestepped him, feeling as if she'd shatter into a million pieces if he touched her one more time. "Savannah, the moment I met you, the moment I got a chance to talk to you, I felt a connection like I'd never felt before. And every moment I've spent with you has only confirmed to me that we're soul mates. We were destined to meet, to share our lives together. I want to marry you. I want you to have my children, to share my dreams."

Each of his words was like a knife through her heart. A torturous emotional conflict raged inside her. On the one hand she yearned to fall into his arms, to take a chance on what he offered.

But she didn't have to take a chance on Jimmy's love. It had been a constant presence in her life since she'd been a young girl. Jimmy would love her forever and always.

Jimmy had adored her. He'd spent his life with her happiness as his only real goal. Didn't she owe him more?

Didn't she owe him a heart full of memories, a heart so filled with him that there was no room for any other man?

She looked at the array of photographs on the end table next to the sofa, her gaze locking on her favorite, the one of Jimmy in his parka.

"He's gone, Savannah." Before she realized he'd moved, Riley was in front of her. He once again grabbed her by the shoulders and forced her to look into his eyes.

"Jimmy is gone and he's never coming back." Riley's eyes burned into hers with fierce intensity. "He's your past, Savannah. Let it go…let him go and let me be your future."

She wasn't sure why, but anger coursed through her at his words, a rich anger that half blinded her. How dare he tell her to forget the man who had been the love of her life. How dare he tell her to let go of the man she had pledged her love, her life to.

She jerked away from him. "You're one to talk about letting go of the past, Riley. You've kept your parents' house like a shrine, waiting for people to just walk back in after a two-year absence."

He reeled backward as if she'd physically struck him, and shame washed over her. She hadn't meant what she'd said, but he'd made her so angry. "Riley…I'm sorry, that wasn't fair." She could barely see him through her tears, and this time it was she who took a step toward him.

He held up a hand to stop her, his jaw clenched tight. "No, you're right. But there's a difference between me clinging to the past and you clinging to the past." He reached out and grabbed her favorite photo of Jimmy off the table.

"The difference is my mother's body has never been found. I never got the luxury of a funeral, of saying goodbye. Your husband's body was found. He's buried in the Cherokee Corners Cemetery." His voice was hard and she knew she'd made him angry. "I don't know if my mother is ever coming back. But you know Jimmy never is. That's the difference."

"Riley...I'm sorry," she repeated.

"Is this what you want for your future?" He held the photo out before him. "A photograph to keep you warm at night, memories for companionship? You love me, Savannah. I know you do, but you're a coward. You'd rather hold on tight to a dead man than face the possibilities with me. You're afraid to take a chance on loving again...on living again."

He reached out to place the photo back on the table, but somehow the photo slipped off the edge and, as if in slow motion, it fell to the floor where the glass shattered into a hundred pieces.

He looked at her, obviously horrified. "Savannah..."

"Just go, Riley," she exclaimed. "Just get out of here. There's nothing here for you."

For a long moment he gazed at her, and in his gaze she saw all his love for her, all the dreams he would have shared with her, all the desire that would have been hers. Then he turned away and stalked out of the house.

She stood like a statue, tears coursing down her cheeks as she played and replayed their conversation in her mind. He loved her. He wanted to build a life with her. He'd wanted her to have his children.

Children. She and Jimmy had talked about having babies, but the time had never seemed right. She'd thought her desire for babies had died with Jimmy, but the moment Riley had mentioned her having his babies a well of want had opened inside her.

On leaden legs she moved to where the picture had crashed, and bent down to pick up the pieces of glass. Thankfully the photo wasn't damaged, but the frame had been destroyed.

He wouldn't be back, she thought as she swept the last of the glass into a dustpan. There would be no more evening phone calls, no more messages left on her machine. She would no longer enjoy his smile, his laughter, his kisses. He was gone and she knew in her heart he wouldn't be back.

She plucked the photo of Jimmy from the damaged frame and held it to her. This was her past…and this was her future. What she didn't know was if the sobs that now choked her were for Jimmy…or Riley…or for herself.

As Savannah wept, her mother explored the room where she was held captive, fighting the fear that had taken hold of her ever since total consciousness had claimed her.

She'd begun to keep track of time by when the slot in the door would open and a tray of food would be handed to her. No words were ever spoken despite her pleading, begging for the person on the other side of the door to let her go, talk to her, explain why she was here.

In the mornings she got a cheese omelet, toast and coffee. Noontime brought a chicken or turkey sandwich, a small salad and a soda…what she often ate for lunch at home. Dinner was usually a broiled chicken breast, some kind of vegetables and the bean bread that was traditionally Cherokee and one of her favorite foods.

She wondered if it was a fellow Cherokee who held her? She was clear enough in the mind to recognize it wasn't a mythical Raven Mocker holding her. But if it was another of her people, then why?

She'd marked four days since she'd become conscious of time and had no idea how many days before that she'd been here. What was she being held for?

When she wasn't exploring the room, trying to find some way out or at least to summon help, she thought of her family. She tried not to think of Thomas, for the pain of thinking of him was too great to bear.

Instead she focused on her children. She worried about Clay, knew that her absence would be deeply felt by him because they'd had a tiff right before she'd been kidnapped.

It all seemed so silly now. She'd wanted him to take part in one of the ceremonies at the Cherokee Cultural Center, but as usual he'd refused.

Her son had always been somewhat of an enigma to her. Something had happened to him when he'd been a teenager that had made him turn his back on his Cherokee heritage. She'd watched him transform from a carefree, loving young man into an angry loner who seemed to find pleasure only in his work.

Thankfully, after Breanna had been left by the man who had married her, gotten her pregnant, then left her, she'd finally found love with Adam. With the kind, strong Adam by her side, Rita knew Breanna would be fine.

Savannah was another worry. When she'd lost her husband, Jimmy, a little over a year before, she'd lost not only the sparkle in her eyes, the smile on her lips, but her interest in living, as well. Oh, she went through the motions, going to work, visiting with her siblings, but there was a darkness in her heart, a barrier around her that Rita and nobody else seemed able to penetrate.

"Keep them safe," Rita whispered aloud. "And, please, make me strong enough to survive whatever lies ahead."

CHAPTER FOURTEEN

It had been two days since he'd left Savannah's apartment, and still the ache in Riley's heart hadn't eased one little bit.

He alternated between being incredibly angry with her and wanting to rush back over to her place and try again. But pride kept him from going over or calling her. She'd told him there was nothing for him there, had never said that she loved him, and he'd be a fool to pursue it any further.

She was bound to her dead husband, and there was apparently nothing that would break that bond. Riley had given her all that he had to give, but it hadn't been enough. Jimmy Tallfeather must have been one hell of a man.

He reared back in his chair and looked out the window, where storm clouds threatened. All day long dark turbulent clouds had chased each other across the sky, promising that before the day was done there would be a storm.

So far they'd been lucky, and the rain had held off for

the workday. That was important because they'd begun digging a new lot to prepare it for the foundation work. If they were really lucky, the dark clouds would blow over completely without shedding a drop of rain and therefore not stopping the work on the job site.

Business was booming, but Riley hadn't felt any kind of excitement about it since the day he'd brought Savannah to Riley Estates. On that day he'd dreamed of sharing all this with her. He would never suggest she quit her job as a cop, but he saw visions of evenings together with her sharing the events of her days and him sharing his.

He'd envisioned her helping him plan new ways to serve families in the community he was creating, had dreamed of going to sleep each night with her in his arms after making love to her.

Dreams and fantasies, wishes and hopes, that's all they had been. But, damn it, he'd wanted them to be real. He'd wanted it all with her.

Irritated by his continuous thoughts of Savannah, he got up out of his chair and went to the window, where he could see a cloud of dust rising from the earthwork being done on a distant lot.

She'd been right about one thing: he had been clinging to the past where his parents' place was concerned. He'd fooled himself into believing that after all this time, one day his mother would just reappear and pick up the life that had been left behind.

It was time to stop fooling himself. Even if she did come back, she wouldn't be the same woman she had once been. Whatever she'd been through, whatever had happened would have transformed her forever.

The house he'd kept exactly as it had been when she'd been there was nothing more than an empty shell filled with items that had served their life span. For him, it was time to let go.

With this decision in mind, he picked up the phone and dialed the number of a friend in real estate sales who had also been a friend of his parents. "Janet," he greeted her as she answered her phone. "It's Riley."

"Don't tell me…you've finally broken down and decided I can handle your homes in the Riley Estates."

He laughed. She'd been at him since the first home had gone up, wanting an exclusive to sell his homes. "Not a chance. Why should I split my hard-earned money with you?"

"I keep telling you, honey, you let the buyers pay my commission."

"Not interested," Riley replied.

"All right, I won't push anymore." She released a long, practiced sigh. "So, what's up? What can I do for you?"

For a moment the words stuck in his throat. Letting go was easy in thought, more difficult in actuality. It was a little bit frightening, and more than a little bit sad.

"Riley? You still there?" Janet asked.

"I'm here." He drew a deep breath. "I was wondering if you'd handle the sale of my parents' house."

There was a long moment of silence, then she finally spoke. "Honey, are you sure?"

"Don't you think it's time?" he countered.

"It's past time," she said softly. "I loved her, too, Riley, but it's been a long time. It serves no purpose for that house to stay like it has been."

"It will take me a couple of weeks to pack things up and get them into storage someplace."

"Take whatever time you need. Call me when you're ready, and we'll sit down and figure out a selling price."

"Thanks, Janet. I appreciate it."

"No problem, and Riley…it's the right thing to do."

He hung up and once again left his chair and moved back to the window, feeling an odd sense of relief now that he'd made the decision to let go. If his mother, by some miracle, ever returned, she knew where Riley lived. She'd know how to find him.

Now, if there was just a way he could wave a wand and help Savannah to let go. But he couldn't. He didn't have a magic wand in his possession.

Maybe she just didn't love him enough. Maybe it would be another man who would reawaken her to life, to love. Maybe eventually she'd find a man who would convince her to put her deceased husband in the past and face a new future. He just couldn't imagine that man not being him.

He frowned as he saw his foreman's truck roaring toward the trailer. There was still an hour of work time left. This could only be trouble. If the foreman was threatening for the sixth time to quit, Riley would let him. He was tired of the old man's temperament.

Leslie Heaton, the burly older man who'd been in the construction business for years, climbed out of his truck and moved faster than Riley had ever seen him toward the trailer. Riley instantly went on alert.

"Boss." Leslie yelled the moment he entered the trailer.

"What's wrong?" Riley faced the foreman, whose usual ruddy complexion was pale as a summer night moon.

"We'd just started 'dozing on lot fifty-four and we turned up something." If it was possible, Leslie's face grew more pale. "We need to call the cops. There's a body out there, boss."

Riley made the call to the Cherokee Corners Police Department, then stood on the front porch of the trailer to wait for their arrival. In the calm before the storm he knew was about to occur, he tried to keep his mind blank.

He had no idea if the body found was that of a man or a woman, had no reason to believe that it had anything at all to do with him personally. But there was a ball of dread in his stomach that only grew bigger as streaks of lightning flashed across the sky followed by an explosive clap of thunder.

"All I know for certain is that Sam McClane was a ladies' man and Greg Maxwell apparently had a good and stable marriage. Sam's wife has a solid alibi for the night of his murder. She was at a fund-raiser for our mayor at the time of his murder." Savannah slumped into the chair opposite Glen Cleberg's desk as she finished giving what little report she had on the murders.

"This isn't good enough, Savannah. We've got to get these solved. It's the mayor who's busting my butt about the fact that we have two heinous unsolved murders in a town where murder has been rare."

"I know, I know, but what do you want me to do, Glen?" she said irritably.

"I want you to solve these cases."

"Yeah, well I wouldn't mind doing the same," she snapped. She ruffled a hand through her hair and drew a deep breath to calm herself. She'd felt as if every nerve in her body was on edge since her last encounter with Riley.

"No witnesses have come forward. I've chased down every lead that has come in. I'm still waiting for some of the forensic reports to come back, but I can only do what I can do."

"Well, try to do better," Glen said, and she knew these final words were a dismissal.

She left his office and flung herself into her desk chair, fighting against anger and frustration, depression and grief.

The things Riley had said to her when he'd left the other night had been playing in her head, causing her near sleepless nights. When she did sleep she dreamed of Riley and Jimmy, and in the dreams Jimmy was nearly transparent and when he tried to wrap his arms around her all she felt was chilled and empty.

Was it time to give up her grief? The thought was so frightening. Her grief had become a warm and familiar friend and to live without it meant opening herself up to other human emotions.

"Heard you got your butt chewed by the chief."

She looked up to see Jason Sheller standing in front of her desk, his usual smirk crossing his handsome face. "Somebody must have exaggerated, my butt is just fine, thank you very much."

He raised a dark eyebrow. "That's the understatement of the day. Your butt is more than fine."

"Go away, Jason," she exclaimed.

Instead, he sat in the chair opposite her desk. "I was just wondering what kind of progress you're making on the murders? Got any suspects?" He wiggled in the chair, his gaze not quite meeting hers.

"Why do you care? You don't work homicide."

"Just curious, that's all. So, got any suspects?"

Savannah sighed, realizing the best way to get rid of him was to give him what he wanted. "Initially, Greg Maxwell's wife was at the top of my suspect list in his murder, then Sam McClane wound up dead. I can't tie her to Sam and we're pretty sure the same perp killed both men, so

Virginia is off the list for now and nobody else has taken her place."

"Bummer," he said. "Sounds like you've hit a dead end." To her relief he got up. "Keep me posted, would you? Maxwell was a friend of mine." He wandered back toward the break room, and Savannah sighed once again.

Odd, she hadn't known that Jason even knew the Maxwells. She sighed. Murder cases, a missing mother, a grieving, angry father...and Riley. She felt as if her head might explode from all the chaos inside.

Thomas's transition from the hospital to the house had not been a smooth one. Twice today Uncle Sammy had called her to tell her that Thomas was out of control, throwing things and cursing, then weeping inconsolably.

Savannah had told him to call the doctor and see if there was anything he could do. But she knew there was nothing anyone could do other than find her mother safe and sound and return her to the man who loved her with all his heart. Nothing would be right in Thomas's life until the day Rita was returned to him.

And nothing would be right in her life ever. Riley had been her single chance for moving on, but he'd been right. She was a coward, afraid to face an uncertain future with him when she could cling to the memory and the thought of what might have been with Jimmy.

"You're my woman, Silver Star," Jimmy had said to her so often. "You're my woman forever and always." But neither of them had known that forever and always would only last two years.

The phone rang, and for a moment she hesitated to pick it up. What if it was Riley? She quickly dismissed the very idea. He hadn't called since the night he'd left, and the absence of his nightly phone calls had only increased her sense of loneliness, of emptiness in what she called her life.

She grabbed up the phone. "Officer Tallfeather."

"Savannah, it's me."

"Hi, Bree." She relaxed a bit as she heard her sister's familiar voice. "How's my favorite sister?"

Breanna laughed, sounding oddly happy. "I believe I'm your only sister."

"Then, how is my favorite niece?"

"A handful," Breanna replied, but Savannah could hear the smile in her sister's voice. "She's particularly excited today."

"Why? What's going on today?"

"She's just learned she's going to be a big sister."

It took a moment for Breanna's words to sink in, then Savannah gasped in surprise. "Oh, Bree! You're pregnant?"

"I am." She laughed with happiness. "You're the first person I've told…I mean beside Adam and Maggie. I figured this family needed a little good news."

"That's great news. I'm so happy for you. Tell Maggie I know she's going to be a terrific big sister."

"I will. I've got to run now. Even though I'm only eight weeks along, Adam seems to think we need to go out today and buy a few things."

"Go and have fun. We'll talk later." The two sisters hung up.

Savannah was thrilled for Bree. She'd been so lucky in meeting Adam, who had moved into the little rental house next to her Victorian home. Love had bloomed, marriage had followed and now a baby was on the way.

Yes, Savannah was positively thrilled for her sister but

she couldn't seem to control the tears that seeped from her eyes and ran down her cheeks.

Lucky, lucky Breanna. Her house would be filled with children and love and laughter. There would be no children for Savannah. No laughter, no love would fill her small apartment.

"Hey, have you heard?" Jason came toward her desk, a cup of coffee in his hand.

"Heard what?"

"You know that guy you've been seeing…that builder from Sycamore Ridge?"

"Riley Frazier. What about him?" Even his name on her lips made a pain shoot through her. She stood and grabbed her purse, deciding she was ready to call it a day.

"I just heard from one of the guys in the break room that apparently they were digging a foundation out at his place and found a body."

"A body?" Horror swept through her and it was suddenly difficult to draw a breath.

"Yeah, guess his business will be shut down for a few days. But the real stinker of it is, the body has been identified as his mother." He jumped back in surprise as she shoved past him.

Blindly she pushed past him and headed for the station house door. Pain like she'd never known before raked through her.

Riley. Poor Riley. His mother was dead. She was dead… dead. The words reverberated around and around in her head as she ran for her car.

She had to get out of here…she had to go.

The hope she'd entertained that her own mother would be found alive and well crashed and burned with the news that Riley's mother was dead…had probably been dead since the day she'd gone missing.

But Savannah's pain went beyond that knowledge. Her pain was too enormous to figure out its source, it was a combination of shattered hopes and broken lives and unfulfilled dreams. It was the stark, raving pain of the living.

She got into her car and began to drive, not knowing, not caring where she was going, just knowing the need to try to outrun her pain.

A nightmare. Riley felt as if he'd been plunged back into his deepest, darkest nightmare. He'd thought he'd prepared himself for the knowledge that his mother was probably dead, but he knew now there was no way to prepare oneself for such a thing.

It hadn't taken long to make the identification. Joanna Frazier still wore the distinctive wedding ring her husband had bought for her so many years before. Around her neck was a locket, with a picture of Riley inside.

The police had brought him the ring and locket and in the first instant of seeing the two pieces of jewelry, that last vestige of hope he'd maintained had shattered. He'd clutched the last of his hope in his hand and had known the pain of deep bereavement.

Both his parents were gone now. He was alone…utterly alone in the world. From that moment the evening had been a study in sheer torture.

Yellow crime-scene tape took on a garish aura as the ominous clouds overhead grew darker. Workers stood in small groups, waiting for the police to talk to them.

Riley had already been grilled for several hours as the

murder of his father was revisited and new questions were asked about his mother.

The County Medical Examiner had already left after determining that his mother had been killed by blunt-force trauma to her head.

The bulldozer operator had indicated that the body had been uncovered with the first scraping of earth. It had been a relatively shallow grave.

"At least you finally know," Lillian had told him when the news had come that it was his mother they had found. "At least you finally have some closure." She'd hugged him tight, and he'd welcomed the warmth of her hug.

Yes, he now had closure. For that he was grateful. The unknowing had always been difficult, and deep in his heart, in a place he'd never really wanted to acknowledge, he'd always known she was probably gone.

He waited until the last of his workers had been dismissed, and only then did he leave the trailer and head for home.

It was while he was driving home that his thoughts turned to Savannah. A sudden fear gripped him. Had she heard? Did she know that his mother had been found dead?

He'd known for some time that somehow in her mind she'd tied the two women together—his mother and hers, both missing, but hope not lost.

If she'd heard that his mother had been found dead, then what state of mind would she be in? No matter what had happened between the two of them, no matter that she couldn't love him enough to have any kind of future with him. He loved her enough to be scared.

She hadn't promised him. When he'd asked her to promise that she'd never again go to the bridge, never again allow the pain of life to drive her over the edge, she'd refused to promise him that.

He had to find her. He had to make certain she was all right. He wasn't sure why, but as he headed toward Cherokee Corners, a terrible sense of dread accompanied him.

CHAPTER FIFTEEN

He drove fast despite the slash of lightning that rent the blackened sky and the crashes of thunder that shook his car.

He, more than anyone, knew how fragile Savannah was and he feared that the news about his mother's death would drive her straight over the edge. He didn't fear for her sanity. He feared for her very life.

She wouldn't promise me. She refused to promise me. Over and over again these words played and replayed in his head, haunting him, scaring him.

Deep in his heart he knew that the driving need to see that she was okay was compounded by his own need to hold her, to help ease the pain he felt at knowing his mother was truly and really gone.

By some miracle the rain continued to hold off. It was as if the heavens knew that enough tears would be shed tonight so the clouds' weeping wasn't necessary.

He drove by her parents' place on the way into town, but her car wasn't there. When he reached Cherokee Corners the first place he went was her apartment. But her car wasn't in its usual place in the parking lot. The next place he checked was the police station.

Despite the fact that he didn't see her vehicle, he parked and went inside. Maybe she was out chasing some lead and hadn't heard the news about his mother. He hoped that was the case. If she had to hear the news, he thought it would be better if she heard it from him.

He was greeted in the police station by a handsome officer who introduced himself as Jason Sheller. "Yeah, she was here, but she flew out of here like a bat out of hell a couple of hours ago," he informed Riley.

"Do you know where she was going?" Riley asked, a sense of urgency filling his soul.

Jason shook his head. "Don't have a clue. But, hey, sorry to hear about your mother."

So, the news had made the rounds here in Cherokee Corners already. "Thanks," he said distractedly. "Did Savannah know…about my mother?"

"Yeah, it was the last thing I told her before she flew out of here." Jason offered him a sly grin. "I figured she was on her way to console you. I know you two have a thing going on."

The words irritated Riley, seeming to diminish what he felt for Savannah. "That *thing* is called love and I need to find her."

"Can't help you there," Jason said with a shrug.

Riley didn't waste any more time. He left the police station knowing there was one other place she could possibly be, and the thought of her there chilled him to the bone.

The storm outside seemed to have intensified, the sky

electric and noisy as Riley got back into his car. Fear slashed through him as lightning lacerated the black night.

If she had lost all hope of finding her mother alive, had she also lost the last of her will to live? Was she finally ready to make that leap into the river to join her husband in the spirit world?

"No." The single word ripped from his throat.

His heart pounded as loudly in his ears as the thunder boomed overhead. Even if Savannah didn't love him, he didn't want her to join her Jimmy.

He wanted her alive and well and even if it wasn't with him, he wanted her to find love and happiness once again with another man.

He didn't want the authorities dragging the river for her body. He stepped on the gas, frantic, as sweat beaded up on his forehead. He had to get to that bridge and he hoped, he prayed she wasn't there…that it wasn't too late.

His heart tumbled to the depths of hell as he approached the bridge and saw her car parked nearby. "God…no," he whispered as he parked his car and plunged out.

He stared up at the structure, but found it impossible to see clearly in the darkness. He got back into his car and reached into the glove box for a flashlight.

"Please God," he prayed as he once again left the car. The grass and underbrush between the road and the base of the bridge was overgrown, thick with tangles and thorny bushes. He clicked on the flashlight to aid him as he made his way to the old wooden structure.

As he hurried through the brush, he alternated between shining the light on the ground just ahead of him and upward toward the bridge, but the light wasn't strong enough to allow him to see anything, anyone that the bridge support might harbor.

When a flash of lightning occurred, he quickly looked upward, but before he could focus, the light was gone, replaced by a thunderous roar that sounded like God's fury.

He had no capacity for any thought except for her. Savannah filled his every pore, she raced in his heart. The need to save her from herself usurped any other desire, superceded anything he'd ever wanted in his life.

He reached the bottom of the bridge and once again shone the light upward. "Savannah!" Her name ripped from his throat, but was swallowed by a booming clap of thunder.

"Savannah!" he yelled again, the anguished cry coming from the very depths of him.

He focused his light first on one area of the bridge, then on another, and a sob escaped him as he finally saw her, crouched in the underbelly of the structure, sitting on a support beam just over the river below.

Looking around frantically, he saw the way he suspected she'd climbed up, a crisscross of beams that created a kind of ladder.

Laying the flashlight on the ground with the beam pointed in that direction, he grabbed the first beam and began to ascend.

"Savannah," he yelled once again as he got closer. In the flash of lightning he saw her turn her head toward him, shock momentarily shining on her features.

"Riley...get down," she said.

In another flash of light he saw that her face was shiny with tears. He didn't get down. Instead he went higher. "Not without you," he replied.

Thunder rattled the earth, and Riley clung to the wood, for a moment afraid that they'd both be shaken off into the river below.

"Please, Savannah, please come down with me. Just because my mother was found dead doesn't mean there isn't still hope for yours. Don't do this. You can't do this. Even if you don't love me, don't do this to your family, don't do this to yourself. You have people who love you, who need you in their lives."

For a moment he thought it had begun to rain, for his face was wet. Then he realized it was tears...tears for her, for her pain, for the anguish that would drive her to be here now.

"Riley, get down before you fall," she exclaimed, and he heard fear in her voice.

He held out a hand toward her even though he wasn't close enough to touch her yet. "I told you, I'm not leaving without you."

Lightning flashed once again, and their gazes met. In hers was an expression he couldn't read, but it didn't appear to be the expression of a woman on the verge of suicide.

A sob released itself from him again as she scooted toward him. Closer...closer...closer she came, then her hand was in his.

Together they descended the bridge support and it was only when they reached the firmness of the ground beneath them that he pulled her tight against his chest.

He held her so tight it was impossible for her to speak, impossible for her to do anything else but desperately cling to him.

When he finally released her, he framed her face with his hands. "There's life after tragedy, Savannah. No matter how desperate you feel right now, no matter how bleak things seem at the moment, it passes. Even if you don't love me, even if you don't want to build a life with me, at least believe me when I tell you that things will get better."

"I do believe you," she replied softly. She paused a moment as thunder roared, then continued in the stillness that followed. "Oh, Riley. I didn't go up there to jump off the bridge. I went up there to say goodbye…goodbye to the past…goodbye to Jimmy."

"Goodbye?" he echoed in surprise.

She nodded and took a step back from him. "I'm so sorry about your mother." Tears filled her eyes. "I'm so sorry for your loss. It was when I heard the news that I realized everything in my life had changed."

"What do you mean?"

Lightning flashed, and she waited for the responding blast of thunder before speaking once again. "Riley, when I heard about your mother, the only thing I wanted…I needed to do was be with you. I wanted to be the one who grieved with you, who held you if you cried. I wanted to be the one to help pick up the pieces, and I knew then how deeply, how completely I love you."

He started to move toward her, but she held up a hand to stop him. She needed to talk, to get out all the emotions that had assailed her over the past couple of hours. "At first I thought it was just the shock of finding out about your mother. My first reaction was to run here…to be with Jimmy."

She turned and looked at the river, which reflected the turbulence of the sky overhead. "I've always found a certain amount of peace here. I'd climb up there and talk to Jimmy, see his face reflected in the waters below. But this time there was no peace for me and when I looked in the water, all I saw was you."

She turned back to look at him. "I knew then that it was

time to say goodbye." Her words caused pain to swell in her heart, but she knew there would always be a certain amount of pain when she thought of the man who had once been her husband.

"Jimmy was a wonderful man with a beautiful heart, but he wouldn't have wanted me to close off my heart because he was no longer here. He would have wanted me to go on, to find happiness. I'm ready, Riley. I'm ready to take that chance on you…if you'll still have me."

"Still have you?" In one long stride he had her wrapped in his arms once again. "Savannah, when I thought of this earth without you in it, my heart went dead inside. Even if I couldn't have you in my life, I needed to know that you were okay, that you'd eventually find love and happiness."

"I want that with you, Riley. I think you're right, there isn't a quota on soul mates. I've been lucky, Jimmy was my first soul mate…but you, you're my second and hopefully my last."

She could speak no more, for his mouth covered hers in a kiss that absolutely took her breath away. Filled with love and desire, the kiss confirmed what she knew in her heart. It was time to move on with this man that fate had brought her way.

At that moment, the skies opened up and rain began to pelt them. With a squeal, Savannah jumped away from him, but he grabbed her by the hand and pulled her toward his car. "Come on," he said. "I'll bring you back to your car later. I'm not letting you out of my sight for a second."

Laughing with an abandon she hadn't felt in over a year, she raced with him to his car through the pouring rain. She felt so light, so filled with possibility, with happiness.

When they reached his truck and were in the dry interior, she turned to him, realizing that her epiphany of where her happiness lay had come at a tremendous cost... the discovery of his mother's body.

"Riley, I'm so sorry about your mother."

Although his eyes darkened, he nodded. "It's all right. I've known in my heart for a long time that she wasn't coming back, that she was probably dead." He reached across and took her hand. "But you can't lose hope about your mother. According to the medical examiner, my mom had been dead for no longer than four or five months."

"Four or five months?" Savannah was grateful for the warmth of his hand around hers. "But, Riley, she'd been missing for almost two years."

"That's my point, honey. If the person who killed my father and took my mother is also responsible for what happened to your father and mother, then whoever had my mother kept her alive for over a year. You have to hang on to that fact. My mother was alive for about sixteen months after she disappeared."

He reached out and pulled her into his arms, and she came willingly, knowing that even though he'd just suffered a tremendous loss, his thought was to ease her pain.

"It doesn't make sense, does it?" she asked. "That your mother was alive for all that time and yet we don't know where she was, what she was doing."

His arm tightened around her. "No, it doesn't make sense. But I'm certain of one thing. If she'd been able to, she would have been home. The only thing that makes sense to me is that she was being held somewhere...a prisoner."

A chill walked up Savannah's spine as she thought of her own mother. Was that the answer? Had she been taken captive on the night Thomas had been hit over the head? It had been nineteen days since that night. How many days did they have before she was found like Riley's mother, in a shallow grave?

She shook as another chill possessed her.

"Let's get out of here," he said. "We need to get you someplace dry. We'll come back tomorrow to get your car." He started the engine of his truck, but before he pulled away from the bridge, he turned back to look at her.

"Someway or another you'll get through all this, Savannah. I'll make sure you do. I'll be your strength."

She shook her head. "I don't need you to be my strength, Riley. Alyssa once told me I'm one of the strongest people she knows. At the time, I didn't believe her, but as I sat up there telling Jimmy goodbye, I realized that I am strong. But that doesn't mean I don't need you to love me."

"I do. I love you, Savannah Tallfeather."

"And I love you, Riley Frazier," she said.

Again his lips sought hers in a kiss that spoke of her future. Despite the fact that her mother was missing, that she had two unsolved murders on her plate, in spite of the fact that she would always hold sweet memories of the man she had lost to the waters of the Cherokee River, she felt a happiness that had no boundaries.

It was the happiness of a future filled with a man who would share her dreams, a man who would give her passion and love in return for her own, a man who was the builder of dreams—the man who would be her husband, her life.

"Take me home, Riley. Take me to my house. I want you in my bed."

His eyes shone bright from the truck's interior lights. "At this moment, I feel as if I'm the luckiest man on earth," he said softly. "I can't believe fate brought you to me,

I can't believe that after all these years, finally fate has brought me my soul mate."

Savannah snuggled against his side as he put the truck in drive and pulled away from the bridge. Goodbye, Jimmy, she thought. There will always be a place in my heart for you and what we shared, but now there's a new place opened in my heart, a space to allow in new love, new life…Riley.

* * * * *

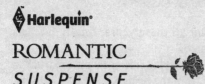

Harlequin®

ROMANTIC
SUSPENSE

CARLA CASSIDY

Rancher Under Cover

American surgeon Caitlin O'Donahue nearly lost her life
during volunteer work in the sultry jungles of El Salvador.
She escapes to her childhood ranch to discover her father in
hiding. Now the place that was once safe seems dangerous.
And the only man she can trust is a stranger—a sexy rancher
with his own agenda and deep-set secrets.

Look for the next installment of

THE
KELLEY
LEGACY

**Family. Lies.
Full exposure.**

Available in October wherever books are sold!

www.Harlequin.com

RS27746CC

Harlequin® Romantic Suspense presents the latest book in the scorching new **KELLEY LEGACY** *miniseries from best-loved series author Carla Cassidy.*

Scandal is the name of the game as the Kelley family fights to preserve their legacy, their hearts…and their lives.

Read on for an excerpt from
RANCHER UNDER COVER

Available October 2011.

"**W**ould you like a drink?" Caitlin asked as she walked to the minibar in the corner of the room. She felt as if she needed to chug a beer or two for courage.

"No, thanks. I'm not much of a drinking man," he replied.

She raised an eyebrow and looked at him curiously as she poured herself a glass of wine. "A ranch hand who doesn't enjoy a drink? I think maybe that's a first."

He smiled easily. "There was a six-month period in my life when I drank too much. I pulled myself out of the bottom of a bottle a little over seven years ago and I've never looked back."

"That's admirable, to know you have a problem and then fix it."

Those broad shoulders of his moved up and down in an easy shrug. "I don't know how admirable it was, all I knew at the time was that I had a choice to make between living and dying, and I decided living was definitely more appealing."

She wanted to ask him what had happened preceding that six-month period that had plunged him into the bottom of the bottle, but she didn't want to know too much about him. Personal information might produce a false sense of intimacy that she didn't need, didn't want in her life.

"Please, sit down," she said, and gestured him to the table. She had never felt so on edge, so awkward in her life.

"After you," he replied.

She was aware of his gaze intensely focused on her as she rounded the table and sat in the chair, and she wanted to tell him to stop looking at her as if she were a delectable dessert he intended to savor later.

Watch Caitlin and Rhett's sensual saga unfold amidst the shocking, ripped-from-the-headlines drama of the KELLEY LEGACY *miniseries in*

RANCHER UNDER COVER

Available October 2011 only from Harlequin® Romantic Suspense, wherever books are sold.

REQUEST YOUR FREE BOOKS!
2 FREE NOVELS PLUS 2 FREE GIFTS!

INTRIGUE
BREATHTAKING ROMANTIC SUSPENSE

YES! Please send me 2 FREE Harlequin Intrigue® novels and my 2 FREE gifts (gifts are worth about $10). After receiving them, if I don't wish to receive any more books, I can return the shipping statement marked "cancel." If I don't cancel, I will receive 6 brand-new novels every month and be billed just $4.49 per book in the U.S. or $5.24 per book in Canada. That's a saving of at least 14% off the cover price! It's quite a bargain! Shipping and handling is just 50¢ per book in the U.S. and 75¢ per book in Canada.* I understand that accepting the 2 free books and gifts places me under no obligation to buy anything. I can always return a shipment and cancel at any time. Even if I never buy another book, the two free books and gifts are mine to keep forever.

182/382 HDN FEQ2

Name _____ (PLEASE PRINT)

Address _____ Apt. #

City _____ State/Prov. _____ Zip/Postal Code

Signature (if under 18, a parent or guardian must sign)

Mail to the Reader Service:
IN U.S.A.: P.O. Box 1867, Buffalo, NY 14240-1867
IN CANADA: P.O. Box 609, Fort Erie, Ontario L2A 5X3

Not valid for current subscribers to Harlequin Intrigue books.

**Are you a subscriber to Harlequin Intrigue books
and want to receive the larger-print edition?
Call 1-800-873-8635 or visit www.ReaderService.com.**

* Terms and prices subject to change without notice. Prices do not include applicable taxes. Sales tax applicable in N.Y. Canadian residents will be charged applicable taxes. Offer not valid in Quebec. This offer is limited to one order per household. All orders subject to credit approval. Credit or debit balances in a customer's account(s) may be offset by any other outstanding balance owed by or to the customer. Please allow 4 to 6 weeks for delivery. Offer available while quantities last.

Your Privacy—The Reader Service is committed to protecting your privacy. Our Privacy Policy is available online at www.ReaderService.com or upon request from the Reader Service.

We make a portion of our mailing list available to reputable third parties that offer products we believe may interest you. If you prefer that we not exchange your name with third parties, or if you wish to clarify or modify your communication preferences, please visit us at www.ReaderService.com/consumerchoice or write to us at Reader Service Preference Service, P.O. Box 9062, Buffalo, NY 14269. Include your complete name and address.

HIIIB